With love, to my wife
on mother's day.

New York,   John
May 9-1937

I read this Book Feb 10, 1967
Living with my dear husband
I'm still very happy in Newark.
I liked this book and found it
very informative.
                Mary

COPYRIGHT 1927
BY ALFRED·A·KNOPF·INC

NEW EDITION JUNE, 1935

THIS EDITION IS BASED ON THE GERMAN EDITION
EDITED BY ERICH BOEHME AND PUBLISHED
BY THE INSEL-VERLAG, LEIPZIG

MANUFACTURED IN THE UNITED STATES
OF AMERICA

PREFACE

IN August, 1923, I saw in the Kremlin a group of men and boys in smocks at work restoring icons. I paused and watched them at their patient labors. Inch by inch, they were removing the oil paintings by which the original pictures had been overlaid. Gilt, varnish, and bright colors gradually came away beneath the workman's hand; and as each fragment disappeared, scraps of the original painting came clearly into view. Finally, in the course of weeks and months, the lost icon was restored.

We passed into the great cathedral, known as the Uspensky. With the same incredible, unyielding patience, the vast interior was being scraped. Two great columns were already done. Against a gorgeous background of modern decorations, they stood forth in Greek simplicity. Colors, never mixed with oils, were still fresh and luminous. Angels which were half men, half gods, seemed to soar imponderably. I stood in awe before them.

"How long will this work take," I asked my cicerone. "Twenty years," he answered carelessly.

Such patience was inspiring. I thought of my own labors and

the biography which had brought me to Russia. Although possibly less deeply, the real figure of my subject, Catherine the Great, had been likewise overlaid by much gilt and varnish. The romantic colors of the nineteenth century had disguised the early portrait. Voltaire's airy classic, Semiramis of the North, had become the shameless mistress of three hundred lovers; a feminine Blue-beard, who had murdered her own husband. The woman and the Empress were lost beneath the legends. Catherine the Great had to be restored.

Hitherto biographers lacked data on her childhood. Bilbassov's monumental work, Brueckner's and Walishevsky's, contained but meager information about her early years. Her life began for all historians when she arrived in Russia. She was responsible for that. The Memoir which she wrote for publication and which Alexander Herzen eventually published set the original example. It left her childhood blank. When Grimm wished to go to Stettin and explore her childhood home, she discouraged him. "What do you wish to do there?" she wrote peevishly. Presumably Grimm never went.

Yet Catherine once told the story in detail herself. It was in a paper addressed to Countess Bruce and was supposed to have been lost. Like all of the memoirs that she wrote, even the longest, it was fragmentary. On her death these various papers were found in a single package addressed to her son Paul. They were read by a few, laboriously copied and quietly shown to trusted

PREFACE

individuals. During the reigns of Paul and Alexander this surreptitious circulation went on without impediment. But when Nicholas I, the grandson whom the Empress had neglected and who had been taught to hate her, came to the Russian throne, the memoirs disappeared. The Secret Police traced the existing copies and destroyed them. The implacable Nicholas then sealed and locked the originals in the state archives and no one dared to open them until the end of his long reign.

It was not until Nicholas was safely in his tomb that Herzen dared to publish the memoir in his possession. A solitary copy had escaped the Czar's police and been smuggled out of Russia. It was published simultaneously in England, France, and Germany.

Although disowned officially, this document was rightly viewed as Catherine's own confessions. For fifty years it was regarded as her one and only Memoir. The rest of her reminiscences had passed into oblivion. Brueckner said that the Bruce document had been lost. Bilbassov, more cautious, said that nothing was known about it. Finally, in 1907, the lost Memoirs were published. They appeared as the twelfth volume of Catherine's works, brought out by the Russian Academy of Sciences. The event passed almost unnoticed.

A German edition, translated and annotated by Dr. Erich Boehme, formed the exception to this. Dr. Boehme was able to restore the intimate passages which had been omitted by the Russian editors. With the exception of the well-known Herzen Memoir, which the German work included, I have followed the arrangement and the notes of Dr. Boehme. His text forms the basis of the present English version. The eight documents included are given here for the first time in English.

Catherine once told her *souffre-douleur*, Grimn, that she had written no memoirs. In a sense this was true. She never wrote a complete autobiography. All her reminiscences were very fragmentary. Like most *parvenus*, she ignored her early years. The story of her life in Russia was never carried through or beyond the death of Peter and her accession to the throne. The murder of her husband was a subject on which she kept unbroken silence to the end.

Her life in Russia as a Grand Duchess was her favorite theme. The history of those years is told repeatedly and not always in exactly the same way. Discrepancies between the different versions are pointed out by Boehme. Not all of them are lapses of memory. Catherine adapts herself to her audience. Nothing is more characteristic than her attitude toward Bruemmer in the sketch addressed to Williams, and her picture of the Prussian in all the other papers. Catherine was by nature a good deal of an actress. This does not however vitiate her Memoirs. Her personal confessions are strikingly sincere.

The longest of her Memoirs, Catherine wrote in French. The first six sections of this volume were written in that language;

PREFACE

the last two were in Russian. The Empress was a linguist and interested in philology; but, like Frederick the Great, she had no taste for German. Russian she admired exceedingly and French was still the language of the educated classes. Catherine and her mother corresponded in it. Her father, however, wrote in ponderous, unwieldy German. The extracts from his letters, which appear in Boehme's footnotes, refuse to take the form of English sentences. The translation merely tries to give the sense of his vague, well-meaning passages.

Catherine's own literary style leaves much to be desired. The Empress wrote fluently, vigorously, and often carelessly. She repeated words and phrases and spent little time revising. Still her Memoirs, as Kornilovich points out, are not mere reminiscences but a literary effort. She plans effects and tells the truth with an air of writing fiction. The figure of the author moves through the story in the manner of a heroine. The Grand Duchess in her teens is a touching character. Her struggle with the Empress and her political intrigues are presented like a drama. There is almost no attempt in these memoirs to justify herself, and only slightly more in the Herzen document. She saw the Russian world and the part she played in it from the standpoint of an artist. Catherine the Great did not condescend to argue.

K. A.

December 11, 1926.

CONTENTS

PART 1: DEDICATED TO COUNTESS BRUCE   3

PART 2: DEDICATED TO BARON TCHERKASOV   91

PART 3: CONTINUATION OF PART TWO   167

PART 4: TO SIR CHARLES HANBURY WILLIAMS   221

PART 5: WRITTEN DURING PETER'S REIGN   257

PART 6: WRITTEN AFTER PETER'S DEATH   263

PART 7: AN EXPLANATION   283

PART 8: A DOCUMENT FROM HER LAST YEARS   299

APPENDIX   311

INDEX   331

ILLUSTRATIONS

CATHERINE THE GREAT — Frontispiece

PRINCESS JOHANNA ELISABETH OF HOLSTEIN-GOTTORP — 20
From a painting by Pesne

CATHERINE THE GREAT AS THE PRINCESS OF ZERBST — 50
From a painting by Pesne
Courtesy of the Staatliche Bildstelle of Prussia

EMPRESS ELISABETH — 102
From a painting by Ericsen

GRAND DUKE PETER FEODOROVICH — 168
From a painting by Grooth

CATHERINE THE GREAT — 274
From a painting by Ericsen

CATHERINE THE GREAT — 300
Painted by Ericsen for Baron Dimsdale

CATHERINE THE GREAT — 306
From a painting by Roslin

PART ONE

BEGUN APRIL 21, 1771

Dedicated to my friend,

COUNTESS
BRUCE BORN RUMYANTSOV

to whom I can speak freely

without fear of consequences

justly. I felt this without being perfectly clear in my mind about it.[3]

When I was almost four years old Madeleine Cardel married a lawyer by the name of Colhard, and I passed into the hands of her younger sister Elisabeth. The latter, I can freely say, was a pattern of virtue and cleverness. She had nobility of soul, cultivation of mind, and goodness of heart. She was patient, gentle, cheerful, just, consistent; in short, I could only wish that all children could have someone like her.

At Madame Colhard's wedding I drank too much at the table and refused to go to bed without her. I yelled so that I had to be carried out and put to bed in my parents' room.

At first Babet Cardel did not please me at all; she did not pet me and flatter me like her sister. By gifts and bribes of candy and sweets, which incidentally ruined my teeth, the latter had taught me to read after a fashion, although I could not spell. Babet Cardel, who was not so fond of false appearances as her sister, put me back at work on my A, B, C's, and made me practice my spelling until she thought I no longer needed it.

I had lessons in penmanship [4] and dancing. The writing teacher had me trace with ink the letters which he had drawn with a pencil, and the dancing teacher taught me to walk and execute steps on a table. But I think that was only money thrown away for I did not really learn to write and dance until much later. Such premature teaching usually leads to nothing.

When I was three years old, my parents took me with them to Hamburg for a stay with my grandmother.[5] The only experience of the journey that I now remember was a visit to the German opera. I saw there an actress, who was dressed in blue velvet embroidered with gold. She had a white handkerchief in her hand and when I saw that she was drying her eyes with it I began to weep and bawled so honestly that I had to be sent home. This scene impressed itself so deeply on my memory that I still remember it.[6]

On my return to Stettin, I nearly killed myself in the following manner. I was playing in my mother's room which contained a cupboard full of toys and dolls to which I had the key. One day I managed so cleverly that the cupboard toppled over and buried me underneath, so that my mother thought I must be crushed to pieces. She sprang up and ran to me; but it fortunately chanced that the cupboard doors stood open and I lay safe and sound beneath, having received no harm except the shock. Another time I almost put my eye out with the shears, but the point only injured the lid.

I remember that in the year 1733 I wrote a letter to my mother who was absent on a journey. I also recall having seen King Frederick William that same year in Brunswick. I was led into the room in which he was staying. After I had made a deep curtsy, I am told that I went up to my mother, who was sitting beside her aunt, the Dowager Duchess of Brunswick,[7] and said to her, "Why does the king wear such a short coat? He is certainly rich enough to have a longer one." He asked what I had said and they had to tell him. It is said that he laughed but did not enjoy it very much.[8]

In the year 1734 my mother was delivered of a second son, Friedrich August. The elder was a cripple and only lived to be thirteen.[9] He died of spotted fever. It was not until after his death that they learned the cause of an illness which had compelled him to walk always with crutches and for which remedies had been constantly given him in vain and the most famous physicians of Germany consulted. They advised that he be sent to the baths at Baden, Teplitz, and Karlsbad; but he came home each time as lame as when he had gone away and his leg became smaller in proportion as he grew. After his death his body was dissected and it was found that his hip was dislocated and must have been so from his infancy. It was recalled that at the age of a year and a half he had had so hot a fever that they thought it was inflammatory fever, and that afterwards he could not walk. Clearly we must suppose that the women to whose care he had been entrusted had let him fall and thereby suffer a dislocation of the hip which neither they nor the others had noticed in time to use the proper remedies.

In the year 1736 my mother was delivered of a second daughter, who died several weeks later.[10]

Up to the age of seven I was never really sick. But I had frequently on the head and hands, an eruption which is common among children, which the Russians call *Zolotucha*,[11] and which it is so dangerous to cure. In my case also no remedy was employed against it. When the breaking out appeared on my head, my hair was shorn, the scalp was powdered, and I was obliged to wear a cap. If it appeared on my hands, they were put into gloves which were not removed until the scales fell off. At the age of seven I took a severe cough. It was the custom to have us kneel each night and morning to say our morning and evening prayer. One evening as I knelt and prayed I was obliged to cough so violently that the effort made me fall on my left side and the stabs of pain almost took my breath away. Someone rushed to me and I was carried to my bed, which I kept for three weeks. I lay always on my left side and coughed, had stitches, and a very high fever. A proper physician was not in the neighborhood; they gave me remedies but God knows of what they were composed. At last after a long period of suffering I was able to get up, and when I was dressed it was seen that I had almost taken on the form of a Z. My right shoulder was higher than my left, my back-bone formed a zig-zag, and my left side was hollow. My women, and those of my mother whom the former asked for advice, decided that my parents' attention should be called to it. The first step taken in the matter was to impose the strictest silence on everybody concerning my condition. My parents were very unhappy that one of their children should be lame and the other hunch-backed. At last, when several experts had been questioned in the greatest secrecy, it was decided to seek out a skilful person who knew how to heal dislocations. They searched in vain, for they had a horror of calling in the only person who had skill at it because he was the hang-man of the place. This uncertainty lasted for some time, but at last it was decided to fetch him secretly in any case. Only Babet Cardel and a maid were entrusted with the secret. The man examined me and then gave orders that every morning as I lay in bed a maiden, still fasting, should rub my shoulder, then my spine with her spittle.[12] Then he made a kind of jacket which I never laid aside by day or night except to change my linen. Every other day he came in the early morning to examine me again. Besides this he had me wear a large black ribbon which passed around my neck, went from the right shoulder around the right arm, and was fastened in the back. In short, I do not know whether it was that I had no tendency to grow crooked or whether these means accomplished it, but at any rate after a year and a half of this treatment there was hope that my health would be restored. I did not lay aside the uncomfortable jacket until I was ten or eleven years of age.

When I was seven years old, all dolls and other playthings were taken from me and I was told that I was a big girl now and they were no longer suitable for me. I had never liked dolls but nevertheless I liked to play. My hands, my handkerchief, anything that I found, served me as a plaything. In this way I continued as formerly, and apparently they took the toys away only as a matter of good form, for they quietly let me go my own way. Very early my good memory was noticed, in consequence of which I was constantly tormented with learning by heart. They called it memory training but I believe it was a weakening rather.[13] At first it was Bible verses, then especially prepared pieces, or even fables from La Fontaine which I had to learn by heart and recite. If I had forgotten anything, I was scolded, but I believe it was not humanly possible to retain all that I was required to memorize, nor do I consider it worth the trouble. I still possess a German

Bible in which all the passages that I had to know by heart are underlined with red ink.

I had a master who taught me religion and instructed me in history and geography.[14] French and German I learned from actual use. One day I asked this reverend gentleman, for my teacher was a pastor, which of the Christian Churches was the oldest. He mentioned the Greek Church and said that in his opinion it corresponded most nearly to the faith of the apostles. From this time on I felt a great respect for the Greek Church and always wished very much to inform myself about its teaching and its rituals. And now I am the head of this Church!

I remember several disputes with my teacher for which I was almost given the rod. The first arose from my contention that it was unjust that Titus, Marcus Aurelius, and all the great men of antiquity, who were nevertheless virtuous, should be damned because they had not known salvation. I argued stubbornly and hotly and held fast to my conviction in opposition to the clergyman, who based his argument upon scriptural passages while I allowed only justice to prevail. Finally he took refuge in the means of persuasion employed by Saint Nicholas; that is, he complained to Babet Cardel and expressed his wish that the rod should convince me. But Babet Cardel was not empowered to do this; she merely said in a gentle way that a child should not be positive toward a reverend pastor and that I should be subservient to his opinion. The second dispute revolved about the subject: what went before our world. He told me "Chaos," and I wanted to know what chaos was. Nothing that he said satisfied me, and finally we both grew angry and Babet Cardel was summoned to our aid. I had the third quarrel with the Herr Pastor about circumcision; he would not however explain the subject to me. This time Babet bade me to be silent. Properly speaking I only gave way to her. She laughed shrewdly and with the greatest friendliness offered me reasons which I could not oppose. I must admit that I have retained it as life-long characteristic, only to listen

1 : DEDICATED TO COUNTESS BRUCE

to reasoning and friendliness. To every resistance I have always opposed a resistance.

The reverend gentleman had made me almost melancholy, he told me so much about the last judgment and how hard it was to be saved. At one time during the autumn I used to go into the window corner every day at twilight to have a good cry. At first no one noticed my tears but then Babet saw them and wanted to know the cause. It was hard for me to confess to her, but finally I admitted the reason and she was sensible enough to forbid the pastor to frighten me in the future with such terrors.[15]

I was instructed in all kinds of feminine occupations but I did not bother about anything but reading. I would have liked to write and also to draw but I was taught almost no drawing at all because there was no teacher. Babet had a special means of driving me to work and of making me do what she liked. She liked to read and when my lessons were at an end and I had satisfied her, she read to me; if not, she read only to herself. Hence it was very sorrowful for me when she did not do me the honor of admitting me to her reading.[16] Babet taught me singing.[17] She had a beautiful voice, liked to sing, and was musical. After seven years of useless pains she declared that I had neither voice nor aptitude for music and in both respects she was correct. Never have I heard anyone praise my voice. The only exception was a lute-maker by the name of Belogradsky, who assured me and declared also to others, that my voice was a perfect contralto. We often had to laugh about it! I must admit that music was for my ear seldom more than noise.[18] I once encountered an Italian musician, who undertook to teach me in two hours to sing an aria. I made the attempt but nothing came of it. The peculiar part is that I can read the notes, and if I step up behind one of the players midway in a concert, I can point to the place where he is playing.

My mother, Johanna Elisabeth von Holstein-Gottorp had been married in the year 1727[19] at the age of fifteen years to my father, Christian August von Anhalt-Zerbst. He was at that time forty-two years old. Apparently they lived quite excellently together in spite of this great diversity of age and although their inclinations were quite different. Thus for example my father was very economical; my mother, on the other hand, very extravagant and open-handed. My mother was extraordinarily fond of amusement and society; my father preferred retirement. She was cheerful and wilful; he, earnest and austere. But in one respect they were exactly alike; both of them enjoyed the greatest popularity, had a firm religious foundation, and esteemed justice highly, especially my father. I have never known a man more honorable in principle as in deed. My mother was regarded as wiser and more witty than my father; but he was a man of upright character and sterling worth with wide information. He liked to read, as did my mother, but what she knew was very superficial. Her sprightliness and beauty had brought her a wide reputation; besides she understood the ways of the fashionable world better than my father.

My mother had been brought up by her godmother and relative, the Duchess Elisabeth Sophie Marie of Brunswick-Lueneburg. The latter had also married her and outfitted her as a bride. My mother spent several months every year with the Duchess who lived at Grauenhof [20] in Brunswick, on account of which she was generally known in Germany as the Duchess of Grauenhof. She lived to be over eighty years old, and died in the year 1767 or 1768.[21] After my eighth year my mother was accustomed to take me with her on all of her journeys, and especially on her visits to this Duchess. There I met and came to know the widowed Princess of Prussia,[22] sister of Karl, the Duke, and his consort,[23] the sister of great King Frederick of Prussia. The other sisters of the Duke whom I knew were Queen Elisabeth Christine of Prussia, already married at that time, Princess Antoinette,[24] later married to the Duke of Saxe-Coburg; Princess Charlotte, who died as Abbess of Gandersheim;[25] Princess Therese, after

1 : DEDICATED TO COUNTESS BRUCE

her sister Abbess of the same cloister; and Princess Juliane Marie, later Queen of Denmark.[26] Of the Princes, their brothers, I knew Prince Ludwig, who was the guardian of the Stadtholder of Holland,[27] Prince Ferdinand, who made a great name for himself as commander of the army of the allies; Prince Albert and Prince Franz,[28] both of whom fell in the war. I was, so to speak, educated with the youngest of them; the elder ones I merely knew, as I was still a child and they were already grown up.

In Brunswick I learned to know the famous grandmother[29] of Duke Karl, who had so many princes as grandchildren. She was descended from the house of Oettingen and was still, at the age of more than seventy years, a very beautiful woman. Of her three daughters, one[30] was married to Emperor Karl VI, the second[31] to the son of Peter the Great, and the third[32] to Duke Albert of Brunswick; consequently Maria Theresa, the Roman Empress, Peter II, Emperor of Russia, Queen Elisabeth Christine of Prussia, and Queen Juliane Marie of Denmark, were her grandchildren. Her great-grandsons and great-granddaughters will provide Europe with monarchs: the Austrian princesses on one side, the princes on the other side, and third the Prince of Prussia.

I knew also the Brunswick-Bevern line. There was a Princess Marianna,[33] my intimate friend, who promised to be very beautiful. My mother was very fond of her and prophesied crowns for her. But she died unmarried. One day there came to Brunswick with the Prince Bishop of Corvey a monk from the house of Mengden who was accustomed to prophesy the future from the lines of the face. He heard how my mother praised the Princess and what she prophesied for her, and he said he saw not a single crown in the features of the Princess but over my forehead there were three at least. Subsequent events have confirmed this prediction of his.[34]

The court of Brunswick had at that time a truly royal splendor. This was due to the many stately buildings with their equipment, the courtly manner of life, the many people of all sorts who belonged to the court, and the great croud of strangers who were always present, as well as the splendor and magnificence of all the arrangements of life. Balls, operas, banquets, concerts, hunting parties, carriage drives followed one after the other, day after day. This I witnessed in Brunswick for at least three or four months during all these years, from my eighth to my fifteenth birthday. The Prussian court was not nearly so formally regulated and did not make the same impression of magnificence, as did that of the Duke of Brunswick.

On the way from Stettin to Brunswick or on the return journey, my mother stopped over in Zerbst or Berlin, especially if my father was staying at either of these places. I remember that at the age of eight I visited for the first time with my mother the late Queen,[35] mother of King Frederick the Great. The King, her husband, was still living at the time. Her four children, the eleven-year-old Prince Heinrich, the seven-year-old Prince Ferdinand, Princess Ulrica, later Queen of Sweden, and Princess Amalie, both of marriageable age,[36] were with her; the King was absent. It was during this meeting that my friendship with Prince Henry of Prussia grew out of our play, at least I know of no earlier time to name. We have frequently agreed with each other that its origin goes back to this first meeting in childhood.[37]

My mother would have preferred a residence in Berlin to anywhere else. My father thought otherwise; also his duties took him now to Zerbst, his home, now to Stettin, where he was Commandant, and later Governor. In the house of my father there lived a man by the name of Bolhagen, who had been an assistant of his, then an adviser, and had finally become his confidential friend. My father did almost nothing without at least consulting him. My mother did not think so much of him, and since he was very thrifty and they were therefore not always of the same opinion, she often found the old subordinate much too refractory, and in excited outbursts she frequently reproached him because he did not like her. I do not know how much there was in it, I was still too young to judge of it, but the people in the house were of the opinion that there was too much bad temper on the one side and that zealousness on the other side often went too far. I only know for certain that this Herr Bolhagen, who was very old and feeble, used to live on the ground-floor, that from there he came every evening at five o'clock to the third floor where we lived, and that he spent at least an hour and a half in my rooms and my brothers' telling to us what he had seen on his journeys, combining it always with moral lessons. He spoke well and intelligently and devoted himself zealously to our education. I have never discovered anything that I heard from him to be otherwise than honest.

The first stirring of ambition that I ever felt was stimulated by Herr Bolhagen. In the year 1736 he read in my room a newspaper notice concerning the marriage of the Princess Augusta of Saxe-Gotha, my cousin in the second degree, with the Prince of Wales,[38] son of King George II of England. Apropos of this he said to Mademoiselle Cardel, "Do you know, this Princess is by no means as carefully educated as ours and notwithstanding she is now destined to become Queen of England. Who knows what ours may yet become?" He then began to preach to me about wisdom, Christian virtue, and strict morality, in order that I might be worthy to wear a crown should I ever be awarded one. This crown never again went out of my head and afterwards gave me a great deal to do.

I do not know whether I was really ugly as a child; but I remember very well that I was often told that I was and that for this reason I ought to strive for inward virtues and intelligence. Up to the age of fourteen or fifteen, I was firmly convinced of my ugliness and for that reason actually strove for inward excellence and was not so much concerned with my outward appearance. I have seen a portrait of myself, painted when I was ten years old, and that is certainly very ugly. If it really resembled me, then they told me nothing false.[39]

My mother often drove from Zerbst to the Abbey of Quedlinburg. The Abbess was her aunt [40] and an elder sister of my mother was Provost there. These two Holstein Princesses, who remained unmarried and had to live in one and the same house, quarreled incessantly and often did not see each other for several years. My mother often attempted to mediate between them and on several occasions she was even successful.

The Princess Provost Hedwig Sophie Augusta was a great friend of dogs and loved especially the so-called pugs. As a child I was once astonished to find in her room, which measured at most four arshins [41] square, sixteen pugs. Many of the curs had young, which also lived in the room where my aunt usually spent her time. They slept and ate there and befouled the place. A girl was employed to clean them and the task kept her in motion the whole day. There lived in the same room besides a large number of parrots; the fragrance which prevailed can be imagined. When the Princess drove out, she had always at least one parrot and half a dozen dogs in her carriage, and the latter accompanied her even to church. Never have I seen anyone who loved animals as much as she did; she was busy with them the whole day through and scarcely stirred herself except for them. Consequently she had grown very stout, which looked very ugly with her short stature and all the more disfigured her. The Princess might have had her attractive qualities perhaps, if she had only taken a little pains. She wrote German and French in the most beautiful hand that I have ever seen.

I had another aunt, the sister of my father, who was the exact opposite of the one described above. She was more than fifty,[42] very tall and lean, so that at eleven years I had a larger waist than she, but she was very proud of her slender figure. At six o'clock she rose and laced herself carefully upon rising and did not take her stays off until she went to bed. She used to insist that she had once been very beautiful, but that an accident which had happened to her had spoiled her good looks. When she was ten years old, her powder-mantle had caught fire, and the lower part of her face had been badly injured so that the chin and lower half of the cheeks were shrivelled up and the shrunken skin really looked horrible. She was good and kind but very stubborn, when she wanted anything. She had made serious demands on each and all of the German princes who had passed under her survey, and were it not for their lack of willingness, she might have been well married. She made wonderful embroidery and was devoted to birds. Owing to her kind heart, she was interested chiefly in those which had suffered some kind of misfortune. I have seen in her room a thrush which had only one foot; a lark with a broken wing; a one-eyed goldfinch; a hen whose head had been half-way hacked to pieces by the cock; a cock whose tail-feathers had been torn out by the cat; a one-sided, crippled nightingale; a parrot that could not use his feet and for that reason lay on his belly; and many other birds of every sort which ran and flew about her room. I was a very lively and rather wilful child and I remember that I once severely offended this princess, for which she never forgave me. I was, namely, left alone in her room for a few minutes and the thought occurred to me to open a window. Naturally, half of the menagerie flew forth! I closed the window quickly and ran away. When my aunt came back to her room, she found only her little cripples present. She could imagine how this had happened and her room was barred to me in the future.

My liveliness at that time was very great. I was always put to bed early, and when my women and Mademoiselle Cardel thought I was asleep, they went into another room to carry on their fine conversation until they felt a longing for their beds. I pretended to be asleep so that they would go, and when I was alone seated myself astride of my pillow and galloped in my bed until my strength forsook me. I remember that many a time I made such a noise in my bed that the women came hurrying in to see what was going on. They found me lying quietly and pretending that I was asleep. They never caught me and never knew that in my bed I played at being a postilion on my pillow.[43]

I liked very much to stay in a country palace of my father's in Anhalt, which belonged to his *apanage*. It was called Dornburg and was not only beautifully situated but was fitted out inwardly and outwardly as prettily as possible. When school hours were over, Babet Cardel went walking with me but I also exercised in another way of which Babet knew nothing. She was with me the whole day and even slept in my room, which she only left for reasons of necessity; for this purpose she had to pass through a little corridor. Before she returned, I ran up and down the four flights of the long stone stairway and resumed my place again. Babet always arrived afterwards and found me where she had left me. She was to be sure rather stout but still agile and brisk for her weight. I was as light as a feather.

In the year 1739, if I remember correctly, Duke Karl Friedrich of Holstein died.[44] He was the head of my mother's house and by his mother [45] a nephew of King Charles XII of Sweden. He had well-founded claims to the crown of Sweden. His wife was the eldest daughter of Peter the Great,[46] who in the year 1728 left behind her a son [47] who was entitled to make claims on the imperial Russian crown. Prince Adolf Friedrich of Holstein-Gottorp, the elder brother of my mother, at that time Bishop of Luebeck, was the natural guardian of this heir to the crowns of both great northern empires. For this reason my mother wished to visit her family in this particular year. But before I give an account of the journey, I will just mention that in May of this year, King Frederick William of Prussia also died.[48] Never, I believe, did a people show more joy than did his subjects at the news of his death. On the streets the passers-by embraced and congratulated each other on the death of the King, to whom they attached all kinds of nicknames; he was in short abhorred

1 : DEDICATED TO COUNTESS BRUCE   17

and hated by great and small. He was severe, rough, close-fisted, and hot-tempered; although he undoubtedly had great qualities as a king, there was nothing likable either in his public or his private life.

His son, the Crown Prince, who succeeded him and to whom his contemporaries already gave the name of Frederick the Great, was beloved and respected, and there was great joy over his accession to the throne.

My mother, who knew that the Berlin court would put on mourning, had a robe made for herself, another for Fraeulein von Khayn, and another for me. She tried to induce the ladies of Stettin to do the same, but they refused and that created a discord between all the ladies of the city and my mother, who wore her robe on one or two Sundays and then did not put it on again. Some time later, after my father had accepted the allegiance of Pomerania in the name of the King of Prussia, my mother made a journey to Berlin, and in the course of the conversation there was asked about the story of the court dress. She denied the fact. I was present and wondered greatly at this; it was the first time that I had heard anyone deny the existence of a fact. I thought to myself, how is it possible that my mother has forgotten something which happened so recently? I was near to reminding her of it; but I restrained myself, which was certainly my good fortune.

At the beginning of summer my mother went to Hamburg [49] to visit her mother Albertine Friedrike of Baden-Durlach, widow of the Bishop of Luebeck, Christian August of Holstein-Gottorp. There a part of her family was united, namely, her sister, Princess Anna, and her brothers, the Princes August and George Ludwig; and she took me with her. Never had I so much liberty and freedom as then. I did what I liked, I ran about from morning till night in every corner of the house and was welcome everywhere. Mademoiselle Babet had not accompanied us and literally no one bothered about me. I enjoyed myself with the attendants of my grandmother and those of my aunt; only my own did I fear. She was certainly a sulky, unaccountable, whimsical person; she knew well how to pull my hair while combing it if, on the evening before, I had not had the honor of pleasing her.

After a short sojourn in Hamburg, where every day there was some new amusement, my grandmother went with her children to Eutin, the residence of the Prince Bishop of Luebeck, the administrator of Holstein. The Prince had brought thither from Kiel his ward, Duke Karl Peter Ulrich, at that time eleven years old. It was there that I saw the Duke, who later became my husband, for the first time. He seemed then well brought up and wide-awake, although his liking for drink and his dislike of everything in any way uncomfortable were already noticeable.[50] He was friendly with my mother, but me he could not endure; he was jealous of the freedom that I enjoyed while he was surrounded by tutors and every step that he took was regulated and counted. I did not trouble much about him, for I was very busy; twice a day between meals I made milk-soup with the women of my grandmother, and then ate it up. At the table I was very moderate until dessert, when *confiture* and fruits finished my meal. Because I was well-behaved, nobody ever noticed my way of life and I was careful not to speak of it.

From Eutin my grandmother and my mother returned to Hamburg. My mother then went on to Brunswick and from there, by way of Zerbst, to Berlin and Stettin. The death of the King had made many changes in the Berlin court; people there still thought only of amusement. A host of strangers came from all directions and the first carnival was very brilliant.

On the return journey to Stettin that year my mother had a peculiar adventure. It was a December day towards five o'clock in the afternoon. There prevailed so fierce a snow-storm that the postilion lost the way. He then proposed to my mother that he should unharness the horses and go with them to seek a guide in some village or other near by. My mother agreed and he un-

1 : DEDICATED TO COUNTESS BRUCE

hitched his horses and left us behind. In our traveling coach was my mother, then myself, Fraeulein Khayn, and a chambermaid; besides these, my mother told the two lackeys to get in because she was afraid that they might freeze. Finally at daybreak the postilion came back with guides, but it took endless trouble to free the carriage from the snow in which it was buried. The winter of 1740 was very severe; people compared it with the winter of 1709, the worst within the memory of man.

During this year's sojourn in Brunswick I had a peculiar experience. I slept in the same very small room with Fraeulein von Khayn, the companion of my mother. My bed stood against the wall, hers at a little distance from mine, and only a narrow passage separated our two beds; another passage remained free between the windows and the bed of Fraeulein von Khayn. On a table between the windows stood a water pitcher, a silver basin, and a night light. The only door of the room was at the foot of the beds and it was locked. Toward midnight I was suddenly awakened by someone getting into my bed beside me; I opened my eyes and saw that it was Fraeulein von Khayn. I asked her why she wished to come into my bed. She said to me, "For God's sake, let me be and go to sleep quietly." I wanted to know what had caused her to leave her bed to sleep with me, for I saw that she was trembling from fright and almost speechless. When I pressed her, she said at last, "Do you not see then, what is going on in the room and what there is on the table?" and she drew the cover over her face. Whereupon I sat up in bed on my knees and reached over her to open the curtain and see what was there. But I heard and saw literally nothing at all; the door was closed; candle, basin, and silver pitcher were on the table. I told her what I saw and she became somewhat quieter. A few moments later she arose to shove the bolt on the door, but it was already locked. I went to sleep again, and the next morning she looked wretched and quite distraught. I wished to know why and what she thought she had seen in the night; but she merely replied that she could not say. I knew that she believed in ghosts and apparitions and that she often insisted that she had seen visions. She used to say that she was a Sunday child, and those who were born on the other days of the week were not as clear-sighted as she. I related the experience to my mother, who was already accustomed to the tales of Fraeulein von Khayn. Many a time however she had frightened my mother and made her uneasy. I have often wondered that this adventure did not make me fearful.

In October of this year, Empress Anna of Russia died and was followed soon afterwards by the Roman Emperor, Charles VI.[51] The death of the latter had staggering consequences for a part of Germany, but it did not disturb the Berlin Carnival which I was now enjoying. I was at that time eleven years old and rather tall for my age.[52] It was in the year 1741 I believe that Prince August Wilhelm of Prussia married Princess Louise of Brunswick-Lueneburg.[53] I took part in this wedding at which Duke Charles Eugene of Wuerttemberg and his two brothers were present.[54] The Duke was a year older than I and his brothers were still little boys. Prince Henry of Prussia singled me out on this occasion; that is, at every ball we danced a minuet or a *contredanse* together.[55] One day I heard Duchess Philippine Charlotte of Brunswick, the sister of the Prince, whisper something to my mother about her brother's interest in me; thus I began to notice for the first time that attentions were being paid me. In my innocence I had not thought of that. Besides I did not think myself attractive and bestowed little care on my clothes, for I had been taught to have a horror of coquetry. I did not even understand what it was and only knew the word.

At the beginning of the year 1742 in Stettin my father had a stroke of paralysis on the left side. At this time the first Silesian War broke out, and I remember that he was still in bed when they brought to Stettin a great number of Austrian officers who had been taken prisoners in the middle of the winter at Glogau

PRINCESS JOHANNA ELISABETH OF
HOLSTEIN-GOTTORP

From a painting by Pesne

1 : DEDICATED TO COUNTESS BRUCE

in Silesia by the troops of the Prussian King. When he was better he was ordered to leave Stettin and with his regiment to occupy an observation camp near Brandenburg. My mother accompanied him to the camp and then went to Dornburg. There I played at teaching penmanship to my brothers; I wrote at that time a very beautiful hand.

Since the day I left Stettin I have never again seen my birthplace.[56] But before I leave it, I must tell the following history. I lived in the third story of the castle in the wing on the left as you enter the court; my room lay next to the church against a secret stairway of stone.[57] Very often in the evening and during the night the organ was heard playing in the church without anyone knowing how it happened; inquiries were even ordered to discover it. The circumstance filled all the inhabitants of the castle with terror. For my part I believe it was the servants of my father, among whom there must have been people who were capable of such a joke.

During the summer my mother made another journey to the camp where I saw old Prince Leopold of Anhalt-Dessau, who was in command, and the Princess his wife, an apothecary's daughter,[58] and his two daughters, Princess Wilhelmine and Princess Henriette.

My mother became pregnant this year. My grandmother came with her daughter, Princess Anna of Holstein, to visit her in Dornburg which is only two miles from Zerbst. It happened that Prince Wilhelm of Saxe-Gotha, nephew of the reigning Duke, was staying there with the reigning Prince of Anhalt-Zerbst. The Prince, who was lame, sat at church beside me. Be it that my singing pleased him, although it has never charmed anyone else, or that there was some other cause: in any case, it was maintained that he wished to marry me but that my father turned him away. Thereupon he proposed to my father that he should give him the hand of my thirty-six-year-old aunt, Princess Anna of Holstein. My father referred him to my grandmother and my aunt.

The marriage was arranged and the betrothal took place at Zerbst.

A few weeks later my eldest brother died at the age of twelve.[59] My mother was inconsolable and the presence of the whole family was necessary to help her bear this sorrow. My grandmother then departed and my mother went to Berlin, where she gave birth to a daughter [60] who died in the year 1745. While she still lay in childbed, my father received information that his cousin, the reigning Prince Johann August of Anhalt-Zerbst,[61] was dying. My father betook himself thither and after his death, in his own name and in the name of his elder brother Prince Johann Ludwig who lived in Jever, took possession of the principality of Anhalt-Zerbst. For the house of Anhalt the rule of primogeniture did not prevail; all the Princes of an Anhalt branch have a right to a division, and they have divided so often that almost nothing is left to divide. For this reason the younger sons recognize in general the eldest as the reigning prince and satisfy themselves with an *apanage*. But since my father had children and his elder brother was unmarried, they reigned together.

When my mother was restored in health, she followed my father to Zerbst in order to establish herself there. Living therefore in one house were Prince Johann Ludwig, my father, my mother, my aunt (the sister of my father), the widow of Prince Johann August from the house of Wuerttemberg-Weiltingen,[62] my brother Friedrich August, who has accomplished so many peculiar acts of heroism in the world, and my new-born sister Elisabeth.

It was said that the harmony of the family was not always very great. In particular, my aunt was accused of sowing discord between the two brothers, who had the best intentions to dwell peacefully together, and possessed all the qualities necessary for that. But however it was, there was nothing to be noticed outwardly.

In the year 1743, my mother received from Dornburg the information that her brother, Prince Adolf Friedrich, had been chosen Crown Prince of Sweden in place of his ward, Duke Karl Peter Ulrich. The latter had renounced the crown of Sweden, adopted the Greek faith, and received the name of Peter, and had been denominated, with the title Grand Duke, heir of All the Russias and successor of Empress Elisabeth. Both pieces of news caused great joy in the household of my parents for more than one reason. Formerly they had often argued jestingly about the husband to whom I should be given, and whenever the name of the young Duke of Holstein was mentioned, my mother said, "Not to him; he needs a wife who can support his rights and claims by the prestige and power of her family; hence my daughter is not suitable for him." And to tell the truth, they had hitherto agreed on no one; there were always buts and ifs. In fact, it was not pressing, for I was still very young. After these unexpected changes, however, it was no longer said that I was not suitable for the Grand Duke; they kept silent and smiled. That put something in my head and in my secret thoughts I decided upon him, becauses of all the matches that had been proposed this was the most brilliant.

My parents, as well as my uncle and my aunt, brother and sister of my father, made this year a journey through the dominion of Jever, which belonged to the house of Zerbst [63] and on which the daughters had hereditary claims. My brother and I accompanied them. The last Prince of East Friesland,[64] who had been married to a Princess of Brandenburg-Bayreuth,[65] came from his castle Aurich to Jever to visit us; likewise the Countess of Bentinck, daughter of the Count of Altenburg, a natural son of the last Count of Oldenburg.[66] This lady had made a great sensation in the world. I think if she had been a man she would have distinguished herself, but as a woman she was a little too independent of what the world might say. She had the figure of an androgyne; she was ugly but possessed wit and cultivation.

My father went with the whole family to Aurich to visit the Prince of East Friesland, whose castle was beautiful and whose court was very large. The Princess, who had no children, devoted herself with painstaking care to the education of a little Countess Solms, who was about eleven years old and already beautiful as an angel.

After a short sojourn in Jever, where I lived in a sort of tower occupied by Countess Marie,[67] who was mistress of the whole surrounding country, and had only one room, we went on to Varel to the mother of the Countess of Bentinck, widow of the Count of Altenburg [68] who was descended from the house of Hessen-Homburg. Frau von Bentinck came to meet us on horseback. I had never seen women riding and was enraptured with it. She rode like a riding-master. On my arrival in Varel, I made friends with her; that displeased my mother and still more my father. It was true we had begun quite oddly. Frau von Bentinck had scarcely changed her clothes when she went upstairs. I had been present at her toilette and did not leave her. She put no restraint upon herself, showed herself a moment in the chamber of her mother which was also mine, and we began immediately to dance a *Steiermaerker* in the ante-chamber. This drew everyone to the door to look at us and I received a severe scolding for my behaviour. In spite of that I went the next day under pretext of a visit again to Frau von Bentinck, whom I thought fascinating. And how could she seem otherwise? I was aged fourteen! she rode, danced, when she was in the mood, sang, laughed, skipped like a child, although she was at the time fully thirty years old.[69] She was already living apart from her husband. I saw in her room a very beautiful three-year-old child and asked who it was. She said laughing that it was the brother of Fräulein Donop who lived with her; but to other acquaintances she said without formality that the child belonged to her and that she had it by her page.[70] She sometimes put her hat on the child and said, "See, how much it looks like me!" I witnessed this also, and as I saw no harm in it, I urged her to send the child up to her mother with her bonnet. She replied, "My mother does not like the child."

But I insisted and she had it carried up with us as we went. When the old lady saw the child from a distance, she made a sign that they should take it away.

In one of the apartments was a portrait of Count Bentinck, who must have been a very handsome man. The Countess looked at it and said, "If he had not been my husband, I should have loved him madly."

After dinner I returned to the room of the Countess, who had promised to let me ride in the afternoon. The only difficulty was to obtain permission from my father, without which I would not have dared to do it. The Countess undertook the negotiations and obtained permission by her insistence. She placed me on the horse and I made several rounds in the court-yard. From that day forward this exercise was my chief passion for a long time. Whenever I saw my horses I would leave all in the lurch for them.

My parents soon left Varel and returned to Jever. This was partly I believe to wrench me from the claws of this woman. She stimulated too much my natural vivacity which was already sufficiently developed and needed to be restrained, for at the age of fourteen years one is not receptive to prudent or wise considertions.

From Jever my father, his brother, the Prince, his sister, and my brother went back home. My mother went to Hamburg [71] and I accompanied her thither to visit my grandmother, who had staying with her, her son, the Prince Bishop of Luebeck, as well as his brothers, Prince August and Prince Georg Ludwig and his sister, Princess Anna, with her husband Prince Wilhelm of Saxe-Gotha. They were expecting the official embassy of the Swedish States which was to fetch the Prince Bishop who had been elected successor to the throne of Sweden; or, more rightly stated, the terms of the peace concluded between Sweden and Russia had denominated him Crown Prince of Sweden. The ambassadors arrived immediately after us with a numerous retinue. Among them were Senators Loewen and Wrangel; the secretary of the embassy was Count Borck; among the Swedes, who accompanied them, I remember only Count Versen, Ungern-Sternberg, Gyllenborg and Horn, and Baron Ribbing. The Crown Prince departed with them after he had said farewell to his family, whom he never saw again.

In Hamburg at that time was Baron Korff, a Courlander in the Russian service; he had married a Countess Skravronsky. My grandmother had my portrait painted by the famous Denner [72] and General Korff had a copy made which he took to Russia. A year before Count Sievers, at that time Groom of the Bed-Chamber to Empress Elisabeth, had brought the ribbon of the Order of St. Andrew to the King of Prussia. One morning before he had presented it to the King, he showed it to my mother, who happened to be there just then, and asked to see me. My mother had me come, with my hair half dressed as it was. Apparently my ugliness had grown less, for Messieurs Sievers and Korff seemed to be satisfied with my appearance. Both of them took away my portrait, and people whispered to each other that it was at the order of the Empress. That did not displease me, but an incident intervened that came near wrecking all these ambitious plans.

My uncle, Prince George Ludwig, who had left the Saxon service for the royal Prussian two or three years before, came as often as he could to the house of my mother. She was delighted with his frequent visits and used to say with appreciation that none of her brothers and sisters showed a more cordial attitude toward her. When my mother went out, or when she had visitors or wrote, which she very often did, he came to my room. He was ten years older than I and had a very cheerful disposition, which I also had. I thought no harm of it and liked him very much; he did all kind of things for me. Babet Cardel was the first to protest against the frequent visits of my uncle. When we were in Berlin she found that he held me back in my lessons. To be sure, he

1 : DEDICATED TO COUNTESS BRUCE

scarcely ever left my room. But he soon took his departure and the affair rested there.

When we were all assembled in Hamburg, with Babet absent, as she had remained with my sister, the visits of my uncle became ever more frequent. I regarded it as a well-meant friendship and we were almost inseparable. From Hamburg we journeyed to Brunswick and on the way my uncle said to me: "I shall be in a difficult position there; I can scarcely talk with you as freely as I have been accustomed to." I replied, "And why?" "For the reason," said he, "that it would lead to gossip which we must avoid." To this I said again, "But why then?" He gave me no answer and in Brunswick he really changed his behaviour quite noticeably; he saw me less frequently and talked less with me. He became reflective, distrait, but instead he drew me aside in the evening to the window in my mother's room and complained of his fate and the restraint from which he suffered. One day the remark escaped him that his greatest sorrow was that he was my uncle. Up to that time I had always comforted him as well as I could and most innocently, without knowing the cause of his grief, and I was in the highest degree astonished at this speech. I asked him then what I had done, whether I had perhaps made him angry with me. He replied, "Not in the least, but the trouble is that I am too fond of you." I thanked him sincerely for his friendship, but he now grew angry and said rudely, "You are a child with whom one cannot talk anyhow." I wished to excuse myself and begged him to tell me the cause of his trouble, of which I understood nothing, and was very urgent with him. "Very well," said he; "have you enough friendship for me to comfort me in my way?" I assured him that I had and that he need not doubt it. "Then promise to marry me." It struck me like a bolt of lightning out of a clear sky; I had not thought of anything of the kind. My friendship was pure and I loved him as the brother of my mother, to whom I was accustomed and who had shown me many kindnesses. Love I did not in the least understand and had never suspected it in him. He saw that I was taken aback, and was silent. But I said, "You are jesting; you are my uncle; my parents would not wish it." "And you also not," he answered. My mother called me and for this evening the matter ended there.

From now on, however, he never turned his eyes away from me, and his eagerness increased. I, on the contrary, felt more restrained than formerly with him. At the first convenient opportunity, he returned to the subject and spoke without reserve of his passionate love for me. At that time he was very good-looking and had beautiful eyes. He was familiar with my disposition, I was accustomed to him; and so it came about that I liked him and I did not avoid him. He carried it so far that I consented to marry him, provided that my parents put no hindrance in our way. Later I arrived at the conclusion that my mother knew all this. It was impossible that she had failed to notice his advances and if she had not been in agreement with him she would certainly not have suffered his frequent visits. This idea occurred to me many years later; at the time, it did not enter my head.

After gaining my consent, my uncle gave himself up to the full strength of his passion, which was vehement. He lay in wait for opportunities to kiss me, he knew how to bring them about; but except for a few tender embraces, all that passed was most innocent. In the meantime he remained meditative and *distrait*; he would sit beside me without saying a word; I tried to wake him up but he only sighed and groaned. I did not understand this behaviour. He was a timid lover, quite shut up in himself; he ate and drank nothing, lost his sleep, and above all his natural cheerfulness. I did not know what to do with him. Before he left Brunswick, he made me promise not to forget him. He could not endure that anyone should mention the name of Heinrich of Prussia because he believed that the latter had a liking for me. I have never really known how much there was in it.

My uncle left Brunswick, and we directed our journey toward Zerbst. This winter my mother did not wish to go to Berlin.

On January 1st, 1744, we were sitting at dinner, when a large package of letters was handed to my father. He tore the outside cover off and gave to my mother several letters intended for her. I was sitting next to her and recognized the handwriting of the Lord Marshal of the Duke of Holstein, now the Russian Grand Duke. He was a Swedish nobleman by the name of Bruemmer.[73] My mother had written to him several times since 1739 and he had replied to her. She opened the letter and I saw the words: "With the Princess, Your eldest daughter." I took warning from this and guessed the rest, and it proved that I had guessed right. At the command of Empress Elisabeth he invited my mother to come to Russia under the pretext of thanking Her Majesty for all the gracious favors which she had bestowed upon my mother's family. My grandmother in fact received from her a pension of ten thousand rubles; the Prince Bishop, my mother's brother, had been made by her the Swedish Crown Prince; and my mother had received, after the birth of my sister Elisabeth whose godmother the Monarch was,[74] the portrait of the Empress set in diamonds. When we left the table, my parents locked themselves in, and there was a great running about within the house. This one and that one was called in but not a word was said to me. Three days passed like this.

Since our last journey to Hamburg my mother had taken much more pains with me than formerly. That had also brought me nearer to her. Two reasons had helped to bring this about. The first was that the Count Henning Adolf Gyllenborg mentioned above had been a daily visitor at the house of my grandmother and had had the opportunity of knowing my mother and me well. He saw that my mother took very little notice of me and one day said to her: "Madame, you do not know the child; I assure you, she has more mind and character than you give her credit for. I beg you therefore to pay more attention to the maiden than formerly. Your daughter deserves it in every respect." Count Gyllenborg always strove to improve my mind with fine principles and the noblest rules of life which one could possibly give to young people. I welcomed it all most ardently and profited by it. The second reason which affected my mother's feelings toward me was the liking of my uncle which had strongly bound me to her soul. She now saw me in her future sister-in-law. I know not and have never known whether she had in any way entered into an engagement with him; but I believed I might assume that, for I know she wished to dissuade my father from the Russian journey and it was I that finally induced them both to make up their minds to it.

It happened thus. After three days I went one morning to my mother's room and told her that the letter which she had received at New Year had set the whole house into an uproar. She asked me what was being said about it. I replied that various things were being said, but for my part I thought I already knew what it contained. She wished to hear what I knew about it; and I said it was an invitation from the Russian Empress to come to Russia and that above all I should accompany her. She then wanted to know whence I had this knowledge. I said, "I have a presentiment of something of the kind"; and as we had shortly before spoken of a person who claimed that he could guess everything from points and figures, I said that I understood the art of this man also. She began to laugh and said, "Very good, young lady; if you are so wise, perhaps you can guess the rest of this political letter of twelve pages." I replied that I would work on it; and in the afternoon I brought her a slip of paper on which I had written the words:

> "The omens say
> Peter III will be your husband."

My mother read that and seemed somewhat surprised. I seized the opportunity and told her that if they had really made such a proposition from Russia, we should not turn them aside; for in the end it would be a great piece of good fortune for me. She said that we ran many dangers when we considered how ill-regulated conditions were there. I replied that the good God would take care of the conditions if such was His Will; that I had the courage to risk everything and the voice of my heart told me that all would go well. She could not suppress the question: "But what will my brother George say?" (This was the first time that she had referred to it.) I grew red and answered: "He can only wish my happiness and good fortune." She was silent and went to speak with my father, who wished to decline the whole business and the journey as well. He wished to speak with me, or rather my mother asked him to do so. I explained to him that since the question concerned me, he should allow me to call attention to the fact that the journey obligated us to nothing. Once we had arrived there my mother and I would see whether it was advisable to return home or not. At last I persuaded him to give his consent to the journey. He gave me written instructions for my conduct [75] and we departed for Berlin with him.[76]

Before our departure I had a little scene with Mademoiselle Cardel, the first that had ever occurred between us, and the last as well, for we never saw each other again. I was very fond of Mademoiselle Cardel and had no secrets from her, except my uncle's love, which I took care to conceal, as a matter of course. My parents had admonished me to preserve the strictest silence about the Russian journey. Babet noticed that I left my room oftener than usual to go to my mother, and questioned me about the journey and about the letter which had arrived at the table. I replied that I could not tell her anything about it. There upon she said to me, "if you love me, you must tell me what you know about it; or have you been forbidden to speak of it?" I responded, "Dear friend, do you think it would be nice of me to tell something which had been forbidden?" Babet was silent and pouted a little;

but I said nothing and saw that she was angry. I was sorry about it, but on this occasion my principles were stronger than my friendship.

A year before I had given her a proof of friendship which had touched her very much. She had fever and ague in Dornburg. My mother forbade me to visit Babet during the attacks of fever because she feared I might contract it from the bad air. In spite of this prohibition I ran to her as often as I could escape and gave her every imaginable proof of affection. I remember that I prepared her tea one day when her chambermaid was out; another time I gave her her medicine; in short, I performed all the little services which were in my power.

When the day of my departure came I took leave of Babet; we both wept and I continued to repeat to her that we were only going to Berlin.

In Berlin my mother did not think it appropriate for me to show myself at court or otherwise in public; but it turned out differently. The King of Prussia, through whose hands had passed all the letters for my mother from Russia, knew quite definitely the reason for my parents' journey to Berlin.[77] The case was namely this: At that time there were two parties at the Russian court, that of Count Bestushev, who wished to marry the Grand Duke to a Saxon Princess, daughter of August II, King of Poland, who later married the Kurfuerst of Bavaria.[78] The other was the so-called French party, to which Bruemmer, the Lord Marshal of the Grand Duke, belonged, furthermore Count Lestocq, General Rumyantsov, and several others, all friends of the French Ambassador, Marquis de la Chétardie. The latter would have preferred to give in marriage to Russia a daughter of the French King, but his friends did not dare to expose themselves by such a proposition. The Empress would hear nothing of the kind. Count Bestushev also, who had great influence with her at that time, advised against it. He had little liking for France. They therefore chose the middle way, and proposed me to Empress

1 : DEDICATED TO COUNTESS BRUCE

Elisabeth. The Ambassador of the King of Prussia [79] and his master also were taken into their confidence. Apparently out of consideration for Count Bestushev, in order that he might not think that it was done with the express intention of working against him (which was however really the case), they circulated the rumor that I had been sent for without the knowledge of Monsieur de la Chétardie (who was the soul of the affair) in order to prevent the marriage of one of the French Princesses to the Grand Duke. In truth he had only allowed them to consider me after he had lost all hope of succeeding with one of the daughters of the King his master.

When the King of Prussia, who knew exactly whither the journey tended, learned that I had arrived in Berlin, he wished by all means to see me. My mother reported that I was ill. Two days later he had her invited to dine with the Queen his consort, and personally requested her to bring me along. My mother promised to do so, but on the appointed day she went alone to court. When the King saw her, he asked her how I was. She replied that I was sick. He answered that he knew very well it was not true. Then she said that I was not dressed, to which he replied that he would wait with the dinner until the next day for me. Finally my mother said I had no court dress. He ordered that one of his sister's should send me one. My mother then saw that no excuse would be accepted and sent me word to dress and come to the castle.

So I had to attire myself and was ready at three o'clock in the afternoon. At last I arrived at the castle; the King received me in the anteroom of the Queen. He drew me into conversation and accompanied me to the apartments of the Queen. I was shy and embarrassed. Finally we seated ourselves at the table, which we did not leave until very late.

As we rose, Prince Ferdinand of Brunswick, brother of the Queen, whom I knew very well and had known for a long time, and who at that time moved not a step from the King of Prussia, approached me and said: "This evening at the masquerade in the

Opera House, Madame, you will be at the table of the King." I replied that it would be a great pleasure for me. On our arrival at home I told my mother about the invitation of the Prince of Brunswick, and she said, "That is strange, for I am invited to the table of the Queen."

My father had been given one of the tables at which he was to do the honors, so that I sat alone at the table of the King. My mother drove first to the Princess of Prussia and together with her to the masquerade.

I walked about the whole evening with the elderly Countess Henkel, who was the lady-in-waiting to the Princess of Prussia, and when I told her that I was to sit at the table of the King, she led me to the hall in which supper would be eaten. Scarcely had I entered when the Prince of Brunswick met me and took my hand. He conducted me to the end of the table, and as the other couples also came along he pushed his way so skilfully toward the front that he seated me at last beside the King. When I saw that he was my neighbor I wished to withdraw, but he told me to remain, and during the whole evening he talked continually with me and said many polite things.[80] I withdrew as well as I could from the affair; nevertheless I reproached the Prince of Brunswick seriously because he had seated me next to the King, but he turned it aside jestingly.

At last the dinner ended and we departed from Berlin presumably for Stettin.[81] Near Stettin my father took a tender leave of me. It was the last time I ever saw him and I wept bitterly.[82]

My mother travelled through Prussia and Courland under the name of a Countess,—the name I have forgotten.[83] The escort was but small; it was composed of Fraeulein von Khayn, her maid of honor, Herr von Lattorf, her chamberlain, a couple of servants, and a cook. In Courland I saw the terrible comet which appeared in the year 1744. I have never seen a larger one and one would have thought it was very near the earth.[84]

When we arrived at Mitau,[85] Monsieur Vojejkov, now Governor

General of Kiev, had himself announced to my mother. He was at that time Colonel and commanded the Russian troops in Courland. My mother received him as a Countess, but he was apparently instructed by the Russian Court and inquired whether she wished to be announced in Riga under this name or another. My mother replied that if he had orders to put this question to her, she would inform him that her name after crossing the boundary of Courland would be another. With this information he retired and sent a message to Riga.

The next day he accompanied us to Riga; awaiting us there were the court equipages, Chamberlain Semyon Kyrillovich Narishkin, now Chief Master of the Hunt, Monsieur Ovtsyn, at that time Lieutenant of the Guard; kitchen, servants, and equipages of the Court. The Magistrate of Riga appeared for our reception, a salute was fired, and we drove in the state coaches of the city across the Dwina. As we left the carriage Monsieur Narishkin, on behalf of the Empress, presented to my mother and myself mantles and collars made of sable skins.[86]

The next day Marshal Lascy paid us a visit; with him were the persons of highest rank in the city, among others General Vasili Feodorovich Saltikov, who was here because he was entrusted with guarding, in Castle Duenemuende, Prince Anton Ulrich of Brunswick and his consort Princess Anna of Mecklenburg with their children and household. Empress Elisabeth had determined at the beginning of her reign to send them back to their own country, and that would have been the best thing that she could have done. When they got as far as Riga, however, the Empress ordered that the journey be postponed until further orders. This new command came several days after we had arrived at Riga, and instead of sending the unfortunate family out of the country, they were brought back and sent to Ranenburg, a city which the famous Prince Menshikov had had built on the other side of Moscow. Little Prince Ivan, Julia Mengden (the confidante of the Princess), and Herr Heimberg (the favorite of the Prince) were there separated from the Prince and Princess, who after a short stay in Ranenburg were taken to Cholmogory.

After we had received in Riga all the ladies and gentlemen of importance, we departed for St. Petersburg in sleighs.[87] I was very awkward at getting into these sleighs, in which one must lie down. Monsieur Narishkin, who accompanied us and whom I had already known very well in Hamburg, said to me, in order to teach me to climb in the sleigh: "Sprawl your legs; you must sprawl your legs." This expression, which I had never heard used, made me laugh so much on the way that I could not think of it without breaking forth anew into laughter.

We went through Dorpat,[88] where all the traces of the bombardment of the city during its conquest by Peter I were visible. We stayed there in a house which had belonged to Prince Menshikov, and journeyed from there onward to Narva,[89] and then to Petersburg, where we were greeted on our arrival[90] toward midday with the thunder of cannon and immediately conducted to the Winter Palace. There, drawn up on the stairs to meet us, were all who had not yet followed the court to Moscow, at the head of whom was Lieutenant General Prince Vasili Nikitich Repnin, whom the Empress had left in St. Petersburg as Chief in command. In the vestibule we were met by the four ladies-in-waiting who had been commanded by the Empress to accompany us on the journey; namely, Mademoiselle Mengden, the sister of Julia, later married to Count Lestocq, Mademoiselle Karr, the future consort of Prince Peter Golitsyn, Mademoiselle Saltikov, later the spouse of Prince Matvei Gagarin, who was Major of the Guard, and Princess Repnin, who was later married to Peter Petrovich Narishkin.

When we were in our apartments, the whole city was introduced to my mother and me; then Narishkin invited those whom he considered worthy to dine. Of those present I remember now, except Prince Repnin, only Senator Prince Yussupov and Count Michael Petrovich Bestushev (brother of the Vice-Chancellor

1 : DEDICATED TO COUNTESS BRUCE 37

Alexei Bestushev; he had been Chief Marshal of the Court, went at that time as Ambassador I believe to Sweden which was a sort of banishment and people whispered to each other that his brother's stock at court was low), General Loubras, Captain of Marines Poliansky, and Korsakov, the four ladies-in-waiting; and many others whom I have forgotten.

After dinner Monsieur Narishkin orderd that the elephants which Tahmasp-Kuli-Khan (also known as Shah Nadir) had presented to the Empress should be brought for our entertainment. There were fourteen of them in Petersburg, which performed all sorts of tricks in the court-yard. Then Monsieur Narishkin proposed to us that we should take a drive. It was in the Carnival Week, called in Russian *maslenitza*. We went to have a look at the city and also at the slides which are for the purpose of coasting in great open sleighs with runners.[91]

We returned to the palace where we found all the ladies assembled (Countess Bestushev, the wife of the Vice-Chancellor had visited us in the morning because she was leaving for Riga; she made the impression of a rather crazy and extraordinary woman, which she was). We sat down to play cards; then came the Marquis de la Chétardie, an old acquaintance of my mother, who had remained in St. Petersburg. He advised my mother to hasten, in order to arrive in Moscow on the 10th of February, the birthday of the Grand Duke. My mother begged Monsieur Narishkin, to hasten our departure; and we set forth in fact two days afterwards.

On this first day I formed a closer acquaintance with the ladies Karr and Saltikov, and they proposed that I should arrange my hair the next day as they wore theirs. At the court and in the city they were imitated, but we did not know that the Empress disliked this fashion which had been invented by the Princess Anna of Brunswick. One could really imagine nothing uglier. The hair was left unpowdered and uncurled, it was combed flat and covered the temples but left the ears free. Over the ears was a stiff little lock, from which a few hairs were drawn down as a beaucatcher to the middle of the cheek, where it was fastened to the dimple with a little glue. Then a very broad ribbon was folded once around the head about a finger and a half's breadth above the forehead; this ribbon ended above the ears in knots, from which the ends hung down upon the neck. In the knots on both sides flowers stuck up stiffly four fingers or more in height; smaller flowers likewise were fastened in the loops and hung down with the beau-catchers to the middle of the cheek; besides a quantity of ribbon, of the self-same piece, was allowed to hang down to the neck and waist, and at least twenty archins of ribbon were used for this comical head-dress. Four long locks formed the chignon.

After our departure from Petersburg,[92] the sleigh in which my mother and I were travelling struck in turning against a house, whereupon an iron hook fell out of the conveyance upon my mother's neck and shoulder. She insisted that she was severely hurt; but outwardly there was nothing to be seen, not even a blue spot.[93] This incident delayed the journey several hours.

We travelled day and night and at the end of the third day we found ourselves in Vsesviatskoye. The Empress had sent Chamberlain Sievers to meet us and bring greetings to my mother. He told Monsieur Narishkin that Her Majesty desired us to cross Moscow in the night. I say, should cross Moscow, because the Imperial Palace was at the end of the city on the other side of the Yautsa. On the same spot stands another now, for that one was burned down in 1753. It was necessary to go all the way through Moscow to reach it. We waited therefore until five or six o'clock in the evening for our departure, and while we waited we all dressed as well as we could. I remember that I wore a close-fitting gown without hoop-skirts, of rose-colored moiré and silver. As we left here, Herr Schriever, whom my mother had known in Berlin as Secretary of the Legation and who had accompanied Sievers, threw a paper into the sleigh which she read with great intensity. But it was really interesting, for it contained character descriptions of all the most important people at the court, including those who were to form our household; likewise the degree of favor in which the different favorites stood.

Toward seven or eight o'clock in the evening on the 9th of February, 1744, we arrived at the Annenhof Palace,[94] which the court occupied at the time. This palace was burned down in 1753, as I said above; it was rebuilt in six weeks and was burned down again in 1771 when the pest was raging in the city.[95]

We were met on the great staircase by the Prince of Hessen-Homburg, at that time Adjutant-General of the Empress, Field Marshal, Lieutenant-Colonel of the Ismailovsky Guards and Lieutenant-Captain of the Body Guard, who stood at the head of the entire court. He gave his hand to my mother and led us to the apartments designed for us. A few moments later the Grand Duke arrived with his household and towards ten o'clock came Count Lestocq who informed my mother that the Empress sent congratulations on her arrival and begged Her Highness to come to her apartments. The Grand Duke gave his hand to my mother and the Prince of Hessen took mine. As we went through the ante-chamber, the ladies and gentlemen of the court were presented to us. After we had passed through all the apartments, we were led into the audience chamber of the Empress.

On the threshold of the state bed-chamber, the Empress came to meet us. I must say that one could not behold her for the first time without being astonished at her majestical appearance. She was tall and, though very stout, it was not offensive, and her movements showed no lack of freedom. Her head also was very beautiful. On this occasion she wore an enormous hoop-skirt, as she liked to do when she appeared in state costume, which incidentally she only donned when she showed herself in public.

Her dress was of shining silver taffeta trimmed with gold lace; she wore on her head a black feather which stood upright on one side; and many diamonds glittered in a head-dress of her own hair.

My mother greeted her and thanked her for the numerous

marks of favor which she had shown her family. Then the Empress entered her bedroom and bade us likewise enter. There were chairs about but neither she nor consequently anybody else sat down.[96]

After about half an hour's conversation she dismissed us, saying that she presumed we were probably fatigued by the journey. While she spoke with my mother, the Grand Duke conversed with me. He escorted us back to our apartments, where he supped with us, his household; and a number of other persons whom I no longer remember. I sat at the left of the Grand Duke and on my left sat the Lord Steward of the Empress, Count Muennich, brother of the Marshal of that name who since the beginning of the reign of Empress Elisabeth had been banished to Siberia. (I remember my neighbor at dinner this day because I wondered at his odd way of speaking, very slowly and always with his eyes closed. For the rest he was a very cultivated and upright man, although a little pedantic. He was the laughing-stock at court because of the peculiar habit he had of reading his wife's letters aloud to everybody; he began with the Empress and left off with the pages when he found no other listener.) During supper the Empress came to the door of the apartment to look on incognito while we ate. After the meal, everyone retired.

The next day, which was February 10th, and Friday of the first week of Lent, was also the birthday of the Grand Duke. It was a day of show and pomp; towards eleven o'clock in the morning we were requested to come to the apartments of the Empress. We went thither; in all the ante-chambers, through which we had to pass to reach the state bed-chamber of the Empress, many people were assembled. We met there Madame Vorontsov and Madame Tchoglokov, both relatives of Empress Catherine I.

A few moments later the Empress came out of her dressing-room in state toilet; she wore a brown dress embroidered in silver and was entirely, that is, her head, neck, and bodice were covered with jewels. She was followed by the Grand Master of the Hunt

1 : DEDICATED TO COUNTESS BRUCE 41

Alexei Gregorievich Razumovsky. He was one of the handsomest men that I have ever seen in my life; he carried on a golden plate the insignia of the Order of St. Catherine. I stood somewhat nearer to the door than my mother; the Empress hung the Order of St. Catherine on me and then did my mother the same honor, after which she kissed us both. Countess Vorontsov fastened the star on my mother and Madame Tchoglokov fastened it on me.[97] The Empress proceeded to mass through her small rooms and we remained in the audience chamber. After mass we were invited to repair to the apartment of the Grand Duke; a few moments after we had entered the Empress also appeared. She told us that she was preparing for communion and would go to confession on that same day and on the following day would partake of the Holy Supper. After she had retired, we dined with the Grand Duke and most of his court.

I forgot to say that on the way from the apartments of the Empress to those of the Grand Duke, we made the acquaintance of the Princess of Hessen-Homburg, born Princess Troubetsky, as well as all the ladies of the court and of society in the city.

The next day we were allowed to go into the royal chapel to be present when the Empress took communion.

On Sunday evening the Empress held court and there was a concert.

The early days of our stay in Moscow were taken up with visits which had to be received and paid. In the evening the Grand Duke came to us to play cards; the foreign embassadors and many members of the court made their appearance also. The Empress came once or twice. Later she went with a selected retinue to the Troitsa Monastery[98] and came to take leave of us. On this day she wore a long-sleeved dress of black velvet with all the Russian Orders, that is, the Order of St. Andrew as a scarf, the Order of St. Alexander around her neck, and the Order of St. Catherine at her left side.

On the tenth day after our arrival in Moscow[99] we were to dine with the Grand Duke. I dressed myself; when I was ready I was overcome by a severe chill. I told my mother, who did not believe much in effeminacy and thought it was nothing of importance. But the chill increased so much that she was finally the first to advise me to go to bed. I undressed myself, went to bed and to sleep, and lost consciousness so completely that I remember practically nothing of what took place during the twenty-seven days of this awful illness. The court physician Boerhaave, nephew of the great Boerhaave, was called and from the fever and the pains which I felt on my right side recognized at once a clear case of pleuritis. But he could not persuade my mother to let him bleed me. When she saw that I had a high fever, she thought I was going to have the small-pox which I had never had. So nothing was done for me, except a few warm bandages which were laid upon my side, from Tuesday to Saturday.

Boerhaave had in the meantime written to Count Lestocq about the situation, and when the latter told the Empress, she returned from the Troitsa Monastery on Saturday evening [100] at seven o'clock and came straight from her carriage to my room, followed by Count Lestocq, Count Razumovsky, and Werre, the surgeon of the latter. She seated herself at the head of my bed and held me in her arms while they bled me. At this moment I came to myself a little and saw how everybody around me was occupied; I noticed also that my mother was in deep trouble. But I relapsed at once into unconsciousness. After the bleeding the Empress sent me a pair of earrings and a diamond brooch worth 25,000 rubles. I was bled sixteen times before the abscess broke. Finally on Palm Sunday I vomited it out.[101] The physicians Sanchez and Boerhaave never left me, and next to God I have to thank them for the preservation of my life.[102]

I remember that the Empress, the Grand Duke, and following their example the entire court paid a thousand different attentions on this occasion to my mother and to me as well; although there were people, at their head the Vice-Chancellor Bestushev,

1 : DEDICATED TO COUNTESS BRUCE

who were already trying to degrade my mother in the eyes of the Empress. This was easy, for the latter was inclined by nature to be jealous of all women whom she had not been on her guard against. The objection which my mother had made to the bleeding and which sprang only from her great concern, was interpreted as a lack of affection for me. In order to find out what was behind this and under the pretext of taking greater care, the Empress ordered Countess Rumyantsov to remain with us.

When I was bled, Lestocq bolted the doors, and they bled me doubly four times in forty-eight hours. My mother was very sensitive and could not see this without suffering. When she wished to enter at these times, she was told that the Empress bade her remain in her room. Naturally that offended her and she imagined that everybody was conspiring to separate her from her daughter.

Added to this were the lamentations and the chatter of the gossips, which only made things worse. For example, during my convalescence, around Easter, my mother could not find materials to her taste; perhaps, also, a piece of cloth which belonged to me just happened to please her. So she asked me for it in the presence of Countess Rumyantsov. Owing to my weakened condition, I was not yet in possession of my five senses, and I showed perhaps an inclination to keep it for myself, because it came from my uncle, the brother of my father. But finally I gave it up to my mother. The story was reported to the Empress, and she sent me two wonderful pieces of the same color and was angry with my mother, who was alleged to have thoughtlessly brought pain to one lying almost at the point of death. My mother for her part noticed that they wished to offend her and became ill-humored.

When I was well again I found great changes everywhere. Where only festivals, amusements, and comfort had formerly been talked about, now strife and wrangling, partisanship and enmity formed the whole conversation.

Since our arrival, Monsieur Betsky, at that time Lord of the

Bed-Chamber to the Grand Duke, and Prince Alexander Troubetsky, his Groom, had been assigned to us for permanent service. Monsieur Narishkin had besides retained his post, and one of the Grooms of the Empress with two of her ladies-in-waiting were on duty in turn. Little by little, my mother took into her confidence Monsieur Betsky, who signified for her an alliance with the Prince and Princess of Hessen-Homburg. He was natural brother of the Princess, being the illegitimate son of old Marshal Troubetsky by a Swedish lady during the time of his imprisonment in Sweden under Charles XII after the battle of Narva. This alliance displeased many, among them, Count Lestocq, and the Lord Marshal of the Grand Duke, Bruemmer, who had brought my mother to Russia; but most of all Countess Rumyantsov, who often tried to slander my mother to the Empress.

The quarrel was disseminated everywhere by Count Bestushev, in accordance with the dreadful maxim that one must divide to rule.[103] He succeeded in arousing everybody; never was there less harmony in the city and at the court than during the time when he was minister. Finally he was the victim of his own intrigues, which usually happens to people who rely upon intrigue rather than honesty and sincerity of action.

During my illness the Grand Duke had shown me every attention.[104] When I was better he kept it up. He seemed to like me; but I can neither say that I liked him nor that I disliked him.[105] I only knew how to obey, and my mother had to marry me; I believe in truth however that the Russian crown meant more to me than he.

I was sixteen years old at the time. Before he had the small-pox, he was quite handsome, but was very small and child-like. He used to talk to me about his playthings and toy soldiers with which he busied himself early and late. To be polite and agreeable, I listened to him, but I often yawned without exactly knowing why. But I did not go away and leave him and he thought that he ought to talk to me; as he spoke only of things that gave him pleasure,

1 : DEDICATED TO COUNTESS BRUCE

he was well entertained when he talked with me a long time. Many people looked on this as a genuine attraction, especially those who desired my marriage. But we never used between us the language of tenderness; it was surely not my business to bring it into use, my modesty would not have allowed that even if I had felt so inclined, and my natural pride was sufficient to prevent my taking the first steps. But it did not at all occur to him, which, frankly speaking, did not prepossess me in his favor. For no matter how well brought up a maiden may be, she always likes to hear the words of flattery and tenderness, especially from one to whom she may listen without blushing.

After my illness I made my first public appearance on April 21, 1744, my birthday; [106] I was fifteen years old.

After this day, the Empress and the Grand Duke wished to have Bishop Simon Todorsky of Plescau visit me and speak with me about the dogmas of the Greek Church. The Grand Duke thought he would convince me, of what I had been firmly convinced since my first entrance in the empire,—that the heavenly could not be separated from the earthly crown. I listened humbly to the Bishop of Plescau without contradicting him. I had besides been instructed in the Lutheran religion by a Churchman by the name of Wagner, a clergyman in my father's regiment, who had often told me that every Christian up to the day of his first communion might choose the religion that seemed the most convincing to him. I had not yet been to communion, and so I found that the Bishop was right in every respect. He caused my faith to grow no less, strengthened me in dogma, and had no trouble in converting me. He often asked me whether I had an objection to make or doubts to utter; but my answer was always brief and satisfactory to him, because my decision stood firm.[107]

In the springtime of this year, the Empress, who had not stood on the best footing with my mother for some time, went again to the Troitsa Monastery, whither the Grand Duke, my mother, and I followed her. The Archimandrite of the Cloister was at that time in high favor with the Empress; together with the Bishops of Moscow and Petersburg, he accompanied her everywhere, even to plays and masquerades, unmasked, naturally.

When we arrived in Troitsa, Count Lestocq came into my mother's room; he looked alarmed and said to her: "Madame, you may prepare for your departure and pack your things." My mother asked him what this speech signified. He replied that the Empress was violently angry with her; Marquis de la Chétardie had been arrested and expelled from Moscow. In his papers had been found a charge against my mother; she had heinously insulted the Empress. My mother begged him to assist her to an interview with the Empress in order that she might at least discover before her departure of what she was accused and of what she was guilty. This explanation took place; the Empress and my mother remained for a long time alone, and after this conversation they both reappeared bright red. My mother wept and thought she had mollified the Empress. But the latter did not forget so easily and she never again had any liking for my mother. There were as a matter of fact too many people and circumstances which served to set them at variance.

All that I could gather from the different reports I heard on the subject is limited, properly speaking, to what I may say here. Before Elisabeth ascended the throne as Empress, Marquis de la Chétardie, Ambassador of the French Court in Russia, had closely allied himself, partly out of hatred for the regent,[108] but also out of liking and self-interest, to the former Princess Elisabeth. He visited her often, lingered long with her, and only Count Lestocq, her personal physician, was present at their conversations. I know that from Madame Tchoglokov, who was at the time lady-in-waiting to the Princess. Marquis de la Chétardie, the intimate friend of Lestocq, knew of the revolution which was under way and which was to raise Princess Elisabeth to the throne; he even loaned money to Lestocq, which was later returned to him. But Lestocq concealed from him the hour and

1 : DEDICATED TO COUNTESS BRUCE

the day, because Marquis de la Chétardie had presumed to say that, on the day when Princess Elisabeth ascended the throne, he would have the Swedes attack the Russian Army, which was suspected of devotion to the Regent, in order, as he said, to make it easier to seize the throne, which was not thought to be so simple as it afterwards turned out to be. In this he doubtless followed his instructions; he sowed unrest and endeavored to weaken the power of Russia by inciting the enemies of the country to attack the army, which, so to speak, covered the capital, at the moment when he expected the outbreak of a civil war. But God disposed otherwise! Lestocq was clever enough to conceal a part of his plans from Marquis de la Chétardie. As the Ambassador had already been recalled, he departed, laden with gifts, a few days after the Empress's accession.

The French Court then sent him back to Russia in a private capacity, but he had credentials in his pocket as Ambassador and Minister of the second rank and they could be shown if he found it useful and to the purpose. During his absence things had greatly changed. The Empress had perceived that the interests of the Empire were not the same as those which the Princess had had at heart for some time. So Monsieur de la Chétardie found that the doors which had formerly been open to him were closed. He took offense at this and wrote to his court without moderating his language or sparing anybody. He had fancied that he held the Empress and her affairs in the hollow of his hand and he had deceived himself! His style was bitter and biting. In the same tone he had talked with my mother, as an old acquaintance; she had laughed, and in her turn had contributed a good deal to the laughter; had probably entrusted all kinds of things to him with which she had reason to be dissatisfied. Thus conversations had taken place between them which among decent people are not allowed to go any further. Monsieur de la Chétardie used them for dispatches to his court; Vice-Chancellor Bestushev had his letters intercepted and deciphered, and then laid all before the Empress. Monsieur de la Chétardie was arrested and banished from the country,[109] and the Empress fell into a terrible rage with my mother. Count Bestushev was the only one who had any satisfaction from all this; in this way he succeeded more and more in mixing up the cards.

But the party which was interested in my marriage, brought things tolerably into order again, and when the court returned to Moscow,[110] began to further my conversion and betrothal.[111] For the first ceremony, June 28th was fixed as the date; for the second, June 29th.

The Bishop of Plescau had written my confession and translated it into German. I learned it by heart in Russian, like a parrot, for I had acquired only a few popular expressions although since my arrival, that is since February, I had been instructed in the language of the country by Adadurov, at present the Senator.[112] The Bishop of Plescau, with whom I rehearsed my confession of faith, had the Ukrainian pronunciation; Adadurov pronounced the language as is customary in Russia.

So I gave both gentlemen the opportunity to correct me, because each wished that I should use his style of pronunciation. When I saw that they were in disagreement with each other, I mentioned it to the Grand Duke, who advised me to follow Adadurov; "for," he said, "the Ukrainian pronunciation will make the people laugh." He told me to recite my confession, and I did it, first with the Ukrainian accent and then with the Russian. The Grand Duke advised me to choose the latter, which I did, against the wish of the Bishop of Plescau who insisted that he was right.

For the last three days before June 28th, the Bishop imposed a fast on me. When I arose early on the morning of the 28th, the Empress sent for me and desired that I should let myself be dressed in her apartments. No one knew who would fill the place of godmother to me. The Empress could not do it, because she had performed this once for the Grand Duke and according to the rule of the Greek Church two people could not marry who had had

1 : DEDICATED TO COUNTESS BRUCE   49

the same god-parent. Everybody aimed to be my god-mother. The Princess of Hessen desired it very much, the Princess Tcherkassky, widow of the Grand Chancellor, wished it still more, and various others whom I can not enumerate. Madame Ismailov, the favorite of the Empress, told me herself that on the morning of this day she had made so bold as to ask Her Majesty whether she had forgotten that a god-mother was necessary and to remind Her Majesty that she could not perform this office. The Empress had replied that all would be provided in its time and place. She told me also that all the ladies of rank wished to be considered for this office.

When I was dressed I went to confession, and as soon as it was time to go to Church the Empress came herself to fetch me. She had had a dress made for me like her own, crimson and silver,[113] and in a great procession we passed through all the apartments, in which a vast number of people had taken up their positions, and then into the Church. At the door I had to kneel upon a cushion. The Empress then commanded that the ceremony wait a little; she passed through the church and withdrew to her apartments. A quarter of an hour later she returned, leading by the hand the Abbess of the Novodeviche Cloister, who was at least eighty years old and in the odor of great sanctity. She was to be my god-mother, and now the ceremony began. It was said that I made my confession of faith in the best manner, that I spoke loudly and clearly and well and correctly. When I came to the end, I saw that many of those present were in tears, among them the Empress. I preserved my self-control and was praised for it.[114] After the mass the Empress came for me and took me to communion.[115] When we had left the Church and were again in the apartment of the Empress, she presented me with a necklace and a decoration of diamonds.[116]

On the same evening the entire court moved from the Annenhof Palace to the Kremlin.[117] The next morning the Empress sent me her portrait as well as that of the Grand Duke in a bracelet

50 CATHERINE THE GREAT : MEMOIRS

set with diamonds; the Grand Duke sent me a watch and a gorgeous fan.[118] When I was dressed, my mother led me to the Empress where we found the Grand Duke waiting. Her Imperial Majesty left her apartments with a great train and went on foot to the Cathedral where I was betrothed to the Grand Duke by the Bishop of Novgorod, who had received my confession the day before.

In the church, immediately after the betrothal, I received the rank of "Grand Duchess" with the title of "Imperial Highness." [119] When Prince Nikita Yuryevich Troubetsky, at that time Procurator General of the Senate, received the order from the Empress to have the Senate draw up the ukase for the title which according to old custom she had given me, he asked whether the word *naslednitza*, which means the right of succession to the throne, should be added. The Empress said no. But he tried all his life to acquire credit with my mother and me for having asked this question. His family knows that also, but with the exception of this question, he has never done anything in the matter, or dared to do anything, and I have always regarded it as nothing more than what it was, namely, the action of a courtier.

Following this day I had precedence over my mother; I must say however that I avoided the opportunities as well as I could.[120] My hand was now kissed also. Many did the same with my mother, but many omitted the ceremony also, as for example Grand Chancellor Bestushev. My mother regarded that as ill-will on his part and it helped to make the quarrel worse between them.

On July 17, 1744, the Empress celebrated in Moscow the first anniversary of the peace with Sweden.[121] For this purpose she went to the Kremlin, and after attending a solemn Te Deum in the Cathedrals repaired to the Granovitaya Palata, the ancient audience chamber, where she distributed commissions and distinctions in great numbers. I mention here those which I remember; there were many others which I have forgotten. Marshal Lascy received a dagger with diamonds; Vice-Chancellor Count

CATHERINE THE GREAT AS THE PRINCESS OF ZERBST

From a painting by Pesne

Courtesy of the Staatliche Bildstelle of Prussia

Bestushev was made Grand Chancellor; Vorontsov, Groom of the Bed-Chamber, was made Vice-Chancellor and Count; the Grooms, Hendrikov, Skravonsky, Tchoglokov, were made Gentlemen of the Bed-Chamber; Countess Rumyantsov and Madame Narishkin became ladies-of-honor; Princess Kantemir, daughter of the Princess of Hessen, maid-of-honor; Messieurs Bruemmer, Lestocq, and Rumyantsov received the title of Count, the first two from the Roman Emperor Charles VII, the latter from the Empress.

My court was formed and the following persons were assigned to it: Prince Alexander Michailovich Golitsin, now Field Marshal, became my Chamberlain together with Count Yefimovsky and the younger Count Hendrikov; as Groom of the Bed-Chamber, I was given Count Zachary Gregorievich Tshernishov, now General in Command and Vice-President of the War College; Monsieur Villebois, afterwards Master of Ordnance in the Artillery, and Count Andrei Bestushev, the son of the Grand Chancellor.[122]

After the peace festival had been carried on with balls, masquerades, fire-works, illuminations, operas and comedies, for at least eight days, the Empress departed for Kiev. The Grand Duke, my mother, and I had set out a few days before her.[123]

During this journey serious dissensions arose in our retinue, the following in particular. The Grand Duke was supposed to occupy a carriage with his Lord Marshal, Count Bruemmer, the Lord High Chamberlain Bergholz, and his Grand Master of the Hunt, Herr Brehdal, that is to say, the gentlemen who were entrusted with his education. I rode with my mother, Countess Rumyantsov, and Fraeulein von Khayn, the lady-in-waiting of my mother. The Grand Duke, who found it tedious in the carriage with the pedagogues, wished to ride with my mother and me, and he summoned as a fourth companion one of the gentlemen of his retinue. Usually it was Prince Golitsin or Count Tshernishov, my gentlemen-in-waiting, who were fully as lively and exuberant as we. My mother in turn found it tiresome to be left alone with three children on such a lengthy journey. In order to make it right for everyone, therefore, she had boards and pillows laid in the carriage in which our beds were placed, so that eight or ten people could sit in it. When this vehicle was finished, we refused to leave it again, and besides my mother, the Grand Duke, and myself, only those persons who knew how to entertain us and amuse us were allowed in it. From morning until evening, we did naught but laugh and play and carry on absurdly.

Countess Rumyantsov, Herren Bruemmer and Bergholz and Fraeulein von Khayn were never admitted, which offended them very much. They criticised, condemned, and scolded at everything we did. The party of four rode together in one carriage and, while we amused ourselves light-heartedly, they gave themselves up to ill-humor and bitterness at our cost. In our carriage we knew that, but we only turned it into ridicule.

We went through the cities of Serpuchov, Tula, Sevsk, reached Ukrainia, passed Gluchov, Baturin, Neshin, and finally arrived at Kozelets,[124] where Count Razumovsky had had a large house built.[125]

Here we waited three weeks for the Empress. At every station were eight hundred horses; the Empress camped most of the time, she also went on foot and often hunted. Finally, on August 15th, she arrived in Kozelets. Here the time was spent with music and dancing. Card-playing was also indulged in, and for stakes so high that often as much as forty or fifty thousand rubles rolled on the various card tables.

After we had spent some time in Kozelets, we set out for Kiev. The Empress had driven on ahead; we overtook her encamped on the hither bank of the Dnieper. The view from here of the city of Kiev on the other side is wonderful. On the 29th of August, 1744, the Empress crossed the bridge over the Dnieper with us and entered Kiev. Here, as in all the cities we had touched since leaving Moscow, the clergy of the city came to meet us. As soon

1 : DEDICATED TO COUNTESS BRUCE

as the Church banners came in sight, we left the carriages and made our entrance into the city on foot behind the cross.

The Empress went to the Petshersky Monastery and the Church in which the miracle-working portrait of the Holy Virgin said to have been painted by St. Luke is found. In my whole life nothing ever made such an impression on me as the gorgeous splendor of this church, in which all the sacred pictures are covered with gold, silver, and jewels. The church itself is spacious and in the Gothic style, which gives a more imposing look to churches than is now given them, when so much light and such large windows leave nothing to distinguish them from ball-rooms and summer-houses.

On the following day the festival of the Order of St. Alexander Nevsky was celebrated by a high mass, at which contrary to custom we had to appear in court dress, although the Empress had directed us in Moscow to take no state costume with us.

In Kiev we met Count Flemming, who had been sent by the King of Poland to present his greetings to the Empress on her arrival at the border of the Kingdom.

On September 5th, the name-day of the Empress, a grand festival was held in Kiev. All the other days were spent in visiting churches and cloisters, or else in taking trips whereby the Empress turned in one direction, and the Grand Duke, my mother and myself in the other. The Empress did not wish either myself or the Grand Duke to visit the caves; she thought the air was damp and bad.

Towards the end of our sojourn in Kiev the Empress went with us to visit a monastery in which a comedy was to be played. The performance began at about seven o'clock in the evening. We had to go through the church in order to reach the theater. The comedy really consisted of several. There was prologues, ballets, a comedy in which Marcus Aurelius had his favorite hanged, a battle scene in which Cossacks beat the Poles, a fish haul on the Dnieper, and choruses without number. The Empress held out until almost two o'clock in the morning; then she sent to ask whether it would end soon. The answer came that only one half had been given, but if Her Majesty so ordered, they would stop at once. She sent word that they should make an end. They then obtained permission to set off some fire-works in the theater, which was built in the open and opposite which the Empress sat with the entire court beneath a tent-cover; behind them stood the carriages. The Empress gave her consent to the fire-works, but what happened? The first rockets that were thrown flew directly into the tent and on it and behind it; the horses shied; the people in the tent did not know which way to turn. The confusion was great and might easily have led to dangerous consequences; so the fatal fire-works were stopped and the audience departed somewhat frightened, although I heard nothing about anybody's being hurt.

A few days later [126] the Empress and the entire court left again for Moscow. On the way we met Madame Leontyev, the daughter of Countess Rumyantsov, and her husband. We constrained them to enter our carriage. But that did not at all reconcile her mother; on the contrary it angered her still more as the daughter herself admitted.

When we reached Kozelets again, we made a short stop. Here my mother had an excited passage with the Grand Duke, which had no consequences for the moment but still left its traces. It happened thus. My mother was sitting in her room and writing when he entered. Beside her on a chair stood her jewel-case, in which she was accustomed to keep everything that was important, even letters. He was at that time very lively, and as he romped about the room, he struck against the little case (my mother had asked him not to touch it) and threw it to the ground. My mother thought for an instant he had done it intentionally. He wished at first to beg her pardon, but when he saw that his excuses were not accepted, he also became angry. I entered the room just as the scene was at its height, and he turned to me to prove his

1 : DEDICATED TO COUNTESS BRUCE

innocence. I saw myself between two fires, and as I did not wish to fall out with either, I kept silent. But my silence affronted them both. A little more and I should also have been scolded. My mother sulked with me; the Grand Duke I knew how to reconcile. When my mother had gone, he told me what had happened and so naturally indeed I could not doubt the truth of the facts. I knew how easily excited my mother was and that her first impulses were always very violent. But there continued to exist between the Grand Duke and my mother an inward strain, which since that time has steadily increased.

When we were again in Moscow,[127] the entertainments for the fall and winter were continued: operas, comedies, and masquerades.

At this time the Empress thought it suitable to give me three ladies-in-waiting and her ladies ceased to serve me. She selected for this purpose the two Princesses Gagarin, Princess Nastasia, who died as the betrothed of Prince Golitsin, the present Field Marshal, and Princess Darya, who became his wife, as well as Mademoiselle Kosheliov, whom a little misfortune subsequently befell.

At that time I liked so much to dance that, under the pretence of taking ballet lessons from Landé, the usual dancing teacher for society and the court, I danced in the morning from seven until nine. At four o'clock in the afternoon Landé came again and under the pretext of a test I danced until six o'clock again. Then I dressed for the masquerade, where I danced again through a part of the night.

In those days there was a sort of masquerade at court every Tuesday, which was indeed not to everyone's taste, but it pleased me and my fifteen years very much. The Empress had decreed that at these masquerades, to which only those persons had access who had been selected by her, all the men had to be dressed as women and all the women as men. I must say there could have been nothing more ugly and at the same time more laughable than most of the men so disguised, and nothing more miserable than the women in men's clothing. The Empress alone, who was best suited to men's clothing, looked really well; thus costumed, she was in fact very beautiful.[128] As a rule, the men were in a churlish humor at these masquerades, and the women were in constant danger of being knocked over by some frightful Colossus, for the men moved about most clumsily in their *gigantic* hoop-skirts. One was being constantly struck against, for however cleverly one managed, one was always getting between them again, for custom required that the ladies should approach the hoop-skirts.

At one of these balls I once saw a very funny sight. The very tall Monsieur Sievers, in those days Chamberlain, wearing a hoop-skirt which the Empress had given him, was dancing a polonaise with me. Countess Hendrikov, who was dancing behind me, was over-thrown by the hoop-skirt of Monsieur Sievers as he gave me his hand in turning. In falling she struck me in such a way that I fell beneath the hoop-skirt of Monsieur Sievers which had sprung upright beside me. Monsieur Sievers entangled himself in his long skirts, which were in great disorder, and all three of us lay on the ground with me entirely covered by his skirt. I was dying of laughter and trying to get up; but they had to come and lift us up because the three of us were so tangled in Monsieur Sievers' clothing that no one could rise without causing the other two to fall.

We noticed at these masquerades that the old Countess Rumyanstov was holding frequent conversations with the Empress and that the latter was very cool to my mother. Not much was needed for us to guess that Madame Rumyantsov was egging her on and trying to imbue her with the grudge which she had nursed since the Ukrainian journey against the inmates of the carriage, as I have related. The reason she had not begun earlier with this was that she had urgently devoted herself to gambling which had lasted up till now. She was often the last one to leave

1 : DEDICATED TO COUNTESS BRUCE

the table. Card-playing had now ceased and her bad humor had no longer any restraint.

As I was quite without suspicion, I attached myself more closely to the second daughter of Countess Rumyantsov, the present Countess Bruce, who was two years older than I.[129] At my request she often slept in my room and even in my bed and then the whole night went in romping, dancing, and absurdities; sometimes we only went to bed toward morning, we carried on such terrible pranks. Her mother knew this but she nevertheless did not spare me with her gossip and backbiting. The desire to make herself indispensable ruled her in spite of all.[130]

One day in the theater Count Lestocq came to our box, just after we had seen him talking very vivaciously and excitedly to the Empress in her box. He told us that the Empress was very much provoked because my mother and I were reported to have debts. She said since my betrothal she had set aside for my support the sum of 30,000 rubles; she had herself as a Princess never had so much, and yet I had made debts already. She had said all this, he told us, with great bitterness and seemed to be very angry. I excused myself as well as I could, and told him that I had received for the first six months not more than 15,000 rubles and that my debts would be paid at the end of the year. But he uttered all the reproaches with which the Empress apparently had charged him. I had at the time debts amounting to twelve to thirteen thousand rubles, not more.

The truth was that I would probably have had no debts if I had not been constantly making presents to my mother, Countess Rumyantsov, the Grand Duke, and many others.[131] I was so open-handed at the time that I was ashamed to withhold anything from anybody who liked it. The Empress disapproved of these gifts and she was not in the wrong. I could have gotten on very well without them. But I had begun with the habit and did not give it up again until my accession to the throne. Yet I became gradually more reserved, as circumstances permitted.

These presents had their basis in a natural generosity and in contempt for riches, which I have never otherwise regarded than as a means of obtaining the things which give one pleasure.

When I felt that I had gained a firm foothold in Russia, I came to the following conclusion or rather made the following resolution, which I have never lost sight of for one moment:

(1) to please the Grand Duke.
(2) to please the Empress.
(3) to please the Nation.[132]

I would have gladly fulfilled all three points, and if I was not successful, the reason was that the matter was not of such a nature or that Providence had not so decreed it. For in truth I neglected nothing in order to achieve it; obligingness, humility, respect, the effort to please, the effort to do good, sincere affection,—everything was employed on my part from the year 1744 to 1761. I confess that when I gave up hope with regard to the first point, I redoubled my efforts and strove all the more eagerly to fulfill the other two. More than once I have been successful in regard to the second; in the third, success was granted me in the fullest sense without any limitation at any time whatever. So I ventured to believe that I had reasonably carried out my purpose. What I have yet to say will throw still more light on what I have already said. Incidentally this intention originated in my head when I was fifteen years of age without any suggestion from anyone else in that direction. I could say at the most it followed from my education. But if I may openly express my opinion, I regard it as the child of my spirit and ascribe it to myself alone. I have never lost sight of it, and all that I have done in general is connected with it, and my whole life was a struggle for the means of achieving this.

In the Fall the Grand Duke fell ill of the measles, which greatly alarmed the Empress and all the rest of us. It is true that after this illness he grew considerably, but his mind remained very childish. He was contented with training his valets, lackeys, dwarfs, and attendants in his room (I also had my rank and grade, I believe). He had them exercise and drill, but as far as possible this went on without the knowledge of his tutors. They really neglected him sorely on one hand, and dealt with him on the other harshly and clumsily, and left him a great deal to the servants, especially when they could not manage to get the better of him. Whether it was due to his bad training or his innate tendencies, at any rate it is a fact that his desires and passions could not be controlled. I shall often have occasion to speak of this and I will add here that I was at the time the confidante of his childishness. In the end it was not my business to improve him; so I let him talk and do as he liked.

In December, 1744, the Court was ordered to prepare to go to Petersburg. The Grand Duke, my mother, and I travelled in advance.[133] When we arrived in the village Chotilovo, which was about half way, the Grand Duke fell ill. Two days before he had felt unwell, and they had ascribed it to an attack of indigestion. We remained twenty-four hours at this place.

The next day about noon I entered the Grand Duke's room with my mother and approached his bed. The physicians took my mother to one side; a moment later she called me, led me from the room, had the horses harnessed, and set forth with me. I begged her to tell me what this sudden departure meant, and then she told me that the Grand Duke had the small-pox. I had not yet had it. She took me away and left Countess Rumyantsov and Fraeulein von Khayn with the Grand Duke to take care of him until the Empress, who had overtaken and passed us and to whom a courier had been sent to Petersburg, should make other provisions.

During the night following our departure from Chotilovo, we met the Empress coming with great haste from the direction of Petersburg on her way to the Grand Duke. She ordered her great sleigh to stop beside us on the highway and asked my mother about the Grand Duke's condition. My mother gave her information and a moment later the Empress drove onward towards Chotilovo and we onward towards St. Petersburg.[134] The Empress remained with the Grand Duke during his entire illness and only returned when he did six weeks later.

When my mother arrived in Petersburg[135] and saw that the Empress had given orders that she should occupy apartments separate from mine, she fancied this was done to keep her away from me. I do not think, however, that this was the intention; but it was to provide her as well as me with as convenient a residence as possible. For on nearer examination nothing lay between her quarters and mine except a dining-room. To be sure in Moscow she had occupied the same suite of rooms with me and I had slept next to her, while here my rooms were quite separate from hers. This division of the rooms annoyed and troubled my mother.

Gradually the rest of the court arrived from Petersburg; the foreign ambassadors also, among them Count Henning Adolf Gyllenborg, whom we had known in Hamburg and who had come to Moscow as envoy of the Swedish Court to announce to the Russian Court the marriage of the Crown Prince of Sweden with Princess Louise Ulrica of Prussia. They all visited us every day in the morning as well as in the evening.

In those days the ladies had no other occupation than dress, and their extravagance went so far that they changed their costume at least twice a day. The Empress herself loved adornment and changed her dress several times a day. Naturally everyone else followed her example. Card-playing and dressing filled up the day. Since I tried on principle to please the people with whom I had to live, I adopted their habits and customs. I wished to be a Russian in order to be liked by the Russians. Besides I was fifteen years old and no one at that age dislikes adornment.

Count Gyllenborg saw how blindly I fell in with everything at Court, and because he had thought more highly of me in Hamburg, he confessed to me one day that he wondered at the change which he remarked in me. "How comes it," said he, "that your character, which was strong and competent in Hamburg, permits itself to grow effeminate at this court which is ruled by luxury and pleasure? You only think of dress. Remember your nature and your talents. Your gifts were granted you in order that you might accomplish great things and you condescend to this childishness! I would like to wager that you have not had a book in your hand since you came to Russia!" He had guessed right, but in Germany also I had read scarcely more than I was obliged to.

I asked him then what he would advise me to read. He named three books: first, "Plutarch's Lives of Famous Men"; second, the "Life of Cicero"; third, "The Causes of the Greatness and Decline of the Roman Republic" by Montesquieu.

I promised him to read them and really ordered that the books be sought for. I found the "Life of Cicero" in German [136] and read a few pages of it. Then they brought me "The Causes of the Greatness and Decline of the Roman Republic." [137] I began the book and fell into a dream; I could not read it continuously, it made me yawn. I thought, "That may be a very good book"; but I threw it down and returned to my dressing-table. Plutarch's "Lives of Famous Men" I could not succeed in getting; not until two years later did I read it.[138]

I had another conversation with Count Gyllenborg, who apparently saw very well that my mind had not yet succumbed to the frivolous environment. I proposed to him that I should draft in writing a portrait of my mind and character, for I insisted that he did not know them. He accepted my proposal and in the course of the next day I wrote a dissertation, entitled: "Attempt at a portrayal of the character of a fifteen-year-old philosopher." For it pleased Count Gyllenborg to call me this. I found the composition again in the year 1757 [139] and must confess that I was amazed to see how well I knew already at the age of fifteen the most secret corners of my soul. I decided that the work had been carefully thought out and in the year 1757 I had not a word to add. In thirteen years I had discovered nothing new in myself, nothing which at the age of fifteen I had not already known.[140] The paper which, to my great regret, has been burned in the meantime, I gave to Count Gyllenborg. He kept it several days and then gave it back to me with an accompanying letter, in which he pointed out the dangers to which my character exposed me. I gave him back his letter and after a long conversation this remark escaped him: "What a pity that you will marry!" I wanted to know what he meant by that but he did not care to tell me.

I must add that in all our conversations, which usually took place in my mother's room, he took the greatest pains to strengthen in my mind the ideas of virtue, morality, and diplomacy. I confess also that the oftener he spoke to me in this tone, the more confidence I had in him. I called him, "My friend, who tells me the truth." I have preserved toward him throughout my life feelings of friendship and gratitude.[141] Certainly I am indebted to him for strengthening my character and calling my attention to a thousand dangers to which I was exposed in a court where the way of thinking was so base and corrupt.

When I was left alone with my mother in Petersburg during the absence of the Empress, I showed her all the marks of respect and attention that I could. She had made close friends with the Prince and Princess of Hessen, their daughter, Princess Kantemir, and Monsieur Betsky. I knew very well that this close friendship was displeasing to the Empress, and although I was polite to them in every way, I held somewhat aloof from the great intimacy. My mother did not take that very well. She saw in this more diplomacy than confidence in her. Consequently she did not let the slightest thing pass by in me and regarded all I did for her merely as my duty. When she fancied I was wanting in the smallest trifle, she ascribed it to forgetfulness of duty. My relation to her became more difficult from day to day, all the more as she was very often in a bad humor and her mood could be seen by those about us. I must say I took pains to prove my devotion in every conceivable way; and I got on well with everybody without anyone's noticing anything in me and without saying to anyone that that was my intention, although I acted thus from principle.

In February the Empress and the Grand Duke arrived from Chotilovo.[142] I was shocked when I saw him, he was so disfigured ... that he could not be recognized. He had grown
... was still just as childish as

... suddenly decided to give
... ly one of them understood
... whom I had brought with
... in the Russian language.
..., and in the evening when
... e. Blind-man's-buff was the

... from Araya, the leader of
... is to say, when Araya came
... m. In the evening the cover
... s; that is, we laid the mat-
... laid on the mattresses the
... rmed a slide on which we

... nent in my apartment when
... I liked very much, because
... d, a particular office. Maria
... st, had the key to my jewels;
... ught with me, was to have
... Balk, my laces; the elder
... r, my ribbons; one of the
... other, the paint, pins, and
patches. ... with the care of my ward-

Artifacts

The Sefer Torah

The Five Books of Moses Written on parchment scroll fixed on two wooden rollers. Wrapped in an embroidered mantle and adorned with figured silver ornaments.

robe were to take charge of the furniture of my room. Countess Rumyantsov ran and told this to the Empress; I was criticised and orders came that everything was to remain in the hands of Fraeulein Schenk. Why, I do not know.

In the spring of the year 1745 the preparations began for the celebration of my wedding. With the greatest reluctance I heard them name the date, and it gave me no pleasure to hear it spoken of.

In the first week of Lent, while I was preparing for confession and communion, I met with a very exciting experience. About ten o'clock one morning I went to my mother and found her on the floor in the middle of her room stretched out on a mattress and unconscious. Her women ran about excitedly and Count Lestocq stood close by, apparently much disturbed. I screamed as I entered and asked what had happened. Only with the greatest trouble could I discover that she had wished to be bled as a precautionary measure. The physician had not succeeded with the arms; he then wished to try on her foot and went about it awkwardly with both feet. My mother, who had a great fear anyway of being bled, fell into a faint and they had to work with her some time to bring her back to consciousness. I sent in all directions for physicians and surgeons, but consciousness returned to her and they only arrived afterwards.

When my mother was again herself, she ordered me to go to my room. From her tone and her expression I knew that she was angry with me. I wept greatly and obeyed only when she had repeated her command. I turned to Fraeulein von Khayn to learn the cause of my mother's anger which I tried in vain to guess. Fraeulein von Khayn said: "I know nothing about it, with me also she has been angry for some time." I begged her to tell me frankly anything that concerned me; she promised and continued: "Her circle talks her into believing something against everybody; her relations displease the Empress; I wanted to tell her the truth but I do not dare to try it again; she will not listen to anything from me." I continued to be as attentively concerned with my mother as I was able to be and she seemed to take a more forgiving attitude toward me. Yet she refused to set her foot across my threshold again and only talked with me about indifferent subjects. Naturally both of these things attracted attention.

We saw the Empress very little although, as in Moscow, we all repaired to her ante-chamber at six o'clock in the evening. Except on Sundays and holidays, however, she never made an appearance outside of her apartments. Mostly she slept at this hour, or it was said that she slept. At night she stayed awake with her intimates. She often supped at two o'clock at night, went to bed after sunrise, dined at five or six o'clock in the evening, and slept for an hour or two after dinner.

On the other hand, the Grand Duke and I were required to lead the most regular lives conceivable: we dined punctually at twelve, supped at six and at ten everything was over. The Grand Duke visited me in my room often in the evening, but it did not matter much to him whether he came or not. He preferred to play by himself with his dolls, although he was already seventeen years old. I was sixteen, so he was one year and three months older than I.

One day I had been talking for some time in the Empress's apartment with Count Peter Shuvalov, whose wife stood in high favor with the Empress. When my mother returned with me to her apartment, she reproached me vehemently for this conversation because she said that I gave my favor to her sworn enemies. I tried to justify myself; I could say upon my oath that I had known nothing about her enmity with Count Shuvalov. In general I knew nothing about the quarrels and all the rest that was going on.

When the weather was fine, we moved over to the Summer Palace. Here the visits of the Grand Duke became even less frequent. I must say his lack of attention and his coldness, on the eve of our wedding so to speak, did not exactly enlist me in his favor. And the nearer the time came, the less could I avoid seeing that my marriage might be very unhappy. But I had too much pride and too much self-respect to make complaints or to let the world even guess that I thought myself unloved. I regarded myself too highly to believe that I could be despised. The Grand Duke also had rather a free way of associating with the Empress's ladies-in-waiting, but I was on my guard against speaking of it and nobody even suspected my innermost feelings. I tried to distract myself by romping with my maidens in my room.

When it began to grow warm, the Court went to Peterhof; there I strolled about the livelong day in the gardens. One evening after supper I took my maids and my ladies-in-waiting and went walking until one o'clock in the morning. When we returned Fraeulein Schenk, who had stayed at home, reported that my mother had meanwhile come to my room to look for me. I wished to go to her at once but they told me she was already in bed and was asleep. The next day when I was up and she was awake, I went to her; I found her extremely angry with me because I had gone walking so late. She reproached me as never before and as I really did not deserve. I begged her to listen to me at least, but in her excitement she could see nothing but the most terrible things of which I was incapable. I swore by all that was sacred to me that I had gone to her to tell her that I wished to take a stroll; but since I did not find her (she had driven out to the country to have supper with the Prince of Hessen) I had taken all my women and had gone walking in the garden. There was not a single man with us, not even a servant. This was all literally true. I begged her to ask everybody who had been present; she would see that I had not lied by a single syllable. Nevertheless my mother's anger was so great that she did not even permit me to kiss her hand, which in her whole life she never refused me but this once.

The next day I told the whole story to the Grand Duke, who saw nothing wrong in the affair. There was in fact nothing in it. But perhaps only the lateness of the hour displeased my mother. It may also be that as she knew the Empress was very lenient in her humors toward herself but more than strict toward others, she feared perhaps that such tricks might harm me in her opinion.

Around St. Peter's the whole Court returned to the city from Peterhof. As nearly as I can remember, it was on the night before the feast day that I hit upon the notion of having all my ladies-in-waiting and chambermaids sleep in my room. For this purpose, I had the beds for myself and the whole company made on the floor and in this way we spent the night. Before we went to sleep there was a great argument among us about the difference between the sexes. I believe that most of us were still entirely innocent; as far as I was concerned I can swear that in spite of my sixteen years I still had no idea wherein the difference consisted. I did still more; I promised my maidens to ask my mother about it the next day. They listened to that and at last we went to sleep. The next day I really asked my mother some questions, for which I was scolded.

Soon afterwards I had another idea. I had had my hair cut short in front because I wished to wear it curled with irons and had demanded that my band of maidens should do the same. Many of them tried to offer a resistance; others wept and said that they would look like birds with a topknot; but finally I accomplished it that they all wore a frizzled bang.

When the preparations for my wedding were almost completed, the date was fixed for the 21st of August in the year 1745. The Empress desired that the Grand Duke and I should go to confession and communion before the ceremony on one of the fast days of this mouth. We went therefore on the fifteenth of August with the Empress to take communion in the Cathedral of the Virgin of Kazan. A few days later we accompanied the Empress on foot to the Alexander Nevsky Cloister where the whole Court supped after the evening mass.

The nearer my wedding day approached, the sadder I became, and often I felt obliged to weep without exactly knowing why. Although I concealed my tears as well as I could, my women who were always near naturally could not fail to notice them and took pains to cheer me up.

On the day before the 21st of August, we moved from the Summer Palace to the Winter Palace. Up to that time I had occupied, in the garden of the Summer Palace, the stone building on the Fontanka behind the pavilion of Peter the Great.

My mother came to my room in the evening where we held a long and very friendly conversation. She preached to me a great deal about my future duties; we wept together a little and then parted very tenderly.[143]

On the festive day I arose at six o'clock in the morning;[144] at eight o'clock the Empress had me come to her apartments where I was to be dressed. I found a costume laid out in her state bedchamber and her palace ladies were already assembled. They began to dress my hair; my servant Timofei Yevreinov was curling my front hair with irons when the Empress entered. I rose to kiss her hand. Scarcely had she kissed me when she began to scold my attendant and forbade him to dress my hair with a frizzled bang. She wished to have my hair quite smooth because she believed the jewels would not stay on my head with this style of head-dress. Then she went out. But my servant was obstinate and would not give up his curling irons. He persuaded Countess Rumyantsov, who liked the frizzled hair and could not endure to have it so smooth, to present the case in favor of my *toupet* to the Empress. The Countess went back and forth two or three times between the Empress and the attendant, while I waited peacefully for what was to happen; finally the Empress, somewhat provoked, sent word that he should do what seemed best to him.

When my hair was dressed, the Empress put the grand ducal crown upon my head and then allowed me to put on as many of her jewels and my own as I wished. She withdrew and the ladies of the palace completed my costume in the presence of my mother. My dress was of silver glacé with silver embroidery at all the seams and astonishingly heavy.[145]

About mid-day the Grand Duke entered the adjoining room. Towards three o'clock the Empress accompanied the Grand Duke and myself in her state coach [146] to the Church of the Holy Virgin of Kazan where the Bishop of Novgorod performed the marriage ceremony. The Prince Bishop of Lueback held the wedding crown over the head of the Grand Duke and the Grand Master of the Hunt Count Alexei Razumovsky held it over mine. At my coronation later he also carried the crown.

During the sermon which preceded the consecration of our marriage, Countess Avdotya Ivanovna Tshernishov (the mother of Count Peter, Count Zachary, and Count Ivan), who stood behind us with the other ladies of the Court, approached the Grand Duke and said something in his ear. I heard him say to her: "Get you gone! Such nonsense!" He then turned to me and said that she had advised him not to turn his head while he stood before the priest, for whichever of us first did this must be the first to die and she did not wish that he should be the one. I did not think this was a very friendly compliment for a wedding day, but I gave no sign. She however saw that he had repeated to me her good advice. She grew red and made reproaches to him which he also repeated to me.

We then returned to the Winter Palace where towards six o'clock we sat down to a banquet in the gallery.[147] For this purpose a canopy had been raised. Under this sat the Empress with the Grand Duke on her right and with me on her left. One step lower and next to the Grand Duke sat my mother and next to me opposite to my mother was the place of my uncle, the Prince Bishop of Luebeck who was then in Petersburg.

After we had risen from the table the Empress retired to her apartment in order to give time for clearing away the table and arranging the gallery for the ball. When I rose from the table I feared a headache in consequence of the weight of the crown and the jewels, and I begged Countess Rumyantsov to remove the crown for a moment. I did not think that that would make any difficulties. But the Countess said she did not dare do that; she feared some evil omen might be attached to it. But when she saw that I was suffering she let herself be persuaded to speak with the Empress about it, who after some hesitation gave her consent. At last the crown was taken off until all was ready for the ball; then it was put on again. At this ball only polonaises were danced and it lasted altogether not more than an hour.

After that the Empress escorted the Grand Duke and me to our apartment, the ladies undressed me and conducted me to bed between nine and ten o'clock. I begged the Princess of Hessen to stay with me a little while but she would not consent.

They were all gone. I remained alone more than two hours not knowing what I ought to do. Should I get up again? Should I stay in bed? I knew nothing. At last my new waiting-woman, Madame Kruse, came in and reported with great merriment that the Grand Duke was waiting on his supper which was about to be brought up to him. After His Imperial Highness had supped well, he came to bed,[148] and when he had lain down he began to talk about how it would amuse his servant to see us both in bed. He then fell asleep and slept very comfortably until the next morning. The folds of fine linen on which I was lying were extremely uncomfortable in the summer weather and consequently I slept very badly, all the more as the daylight when morning came disturbed me greatly. For the bed had no curtains, although it was otherwise very handsomely fitted out in red velvet with silver embroidery. The next morning Madame Kruse tried to question the young married couple. But her hopes proved deceptive. In this state matters remained during the following nine years without the least alteration.

1 : DEDICATED TO COUNTESS BRUCE

NOTES

[1] On Monday, in the house at No. 1, Grosse Dom Strasse, to which a memorial tablet is affixed at present.—Prince Christian August writes from Stettin to the reigning Prince at Zerbst, May 2, 1729, that "this morning at half past two o'clock" his wife was delivered of a Princess-daughter, and that she is to be baptized the "day after tomorrow," and that she is to receive the name of Sophie Auguste Friedrike; she was called Fike (Figgy) by the family.— As governor of the city, Prince Christian August later took up his residence in the castle, (cf. p. 21).—Catherine writes from Peterhof to Grimm, June 29, 1776: "What do you want to do in Stettin? You will not find anyone there still living, at most perhaps Monsieur Laurent, an old weak-head, who was only a simpleton in his youth. But if you can not withstand the itch, know then that I was born (German) 'in Greifenheim's house in Marien-Kirchhof,' that I lived and was educated in the wing of the castle to the left as you enter the great court-yard, where I occupied three arched rooms situated next to the church and forming the corner. The bell-tower adjoined my sleeping room. Here Mademoiselle Cardel instilled wisdom in me, and here Monsieur Wagner administered his examinations. Here also I ran two or three times a day the length of the whole wing in order to visit my mother who occupied the other end. But I see nothing interesting in all this, unless you think the place is well adapted for the making of tolerable Empresses. In that case you should propose to the King of Prussia that he found there a training school of this kind."—At that time the house belonged to Herr v. Aschersleben, as No. 791, and lay in the district of the Marien Kirche, the church which was afterwards burned down. Catherine's erroneous mention of the owner may be explained as a confusion with the designation of a quarter of the city.

[2] Wilhelm Christian Friedrich, born November 17, 1730.

[3] Catherine to Grimm, from Peterhof, July 1, 1779: ". . . Never would anyone more than he have deserved a b . . . o . . . t . . . e . . . , can you guess what? Mamma often gave me one, when she was in a bad humor, scarcely with reason."

[4] Catherine to Grimm from St. Petersburg, January 30, 1776: ". . . Monsieur Laurent taught me to scribble French, but the ashes of the worthy Pastor Wagner would turn over in his grave if he knew that anyone besides himself had the reputation of having taught me to write German. . . . Monsieur Laurent was a foreigner, who spoke German like a Spanish cow."—Concerning Monsieur Laurent cf. also Note 1 above, and p. 75, Note 43.

[5] Duchess Albertine Friedrike von Holstein-Gottorp, born Princess of Baden-Durlach.

[6] The account of this visit to the theater differs very much from that given in Part IV, which was written at an earlier date (p. 221). Catherine probably did not have Part IV at hand when she wrote these lines. Cf. also p. 72, Note 12, and p. 252, Note 18.

[7] Duchess Elisabeth Sophie Marie, widow of Duke August Wilhelm of Brunswick-Wolfenbuettel, who died in 1731.

[8] According to Part IV, this meeting took place in Stettin. In the earlier account the little four-year-old Princess is not yet malicious enough to allude so pointedly to the well-known avarice of the king.

[9] Wilhelm Christian was born November 17, 1730, and died August 27, 1742; hence he was not yet twelve years old.

[10] Augusta Christine Charlotte lived from November 12 to November 24, 1736.

[11] Scrofula.

[12] According to Part IV, it was a woman who gave this advice.

[13] Catherine to Grimm, July 1, 1779, from Peterhof: "(German) My God, what nature does not do, learning cannot accomplish; but learning often chokes out mother wit."

[14] Catherine to Grimm, December 11, 1781: ". . . Whatever I know or think I know, I teach to Monsieur Alexander. Recently he brought the conversation around to the shape of the world, so that I had to have the globe fetched from the library of the Hermitage. When he had that he began to travel around the sphere as if mad, and I believe that after half an hour, if I mistake not, he knew fully as much about it as the blessed Herr Wagner was able to cram into me in several years."—Monsieur Alexander is Catherine's grandson, Grand Duke Alexander Pavlovich (Czar Alexander I), born 1777.

[15] Catherine to Grimm, from Czarskoe-Selo, May 16, 1778: ". . . By no means do I cherish any grudge against Herr Wagner, but I am convinced in my innermost soul that he was a block-head and that Mademoiselle Cardel, on the other hand, was a clever girl."—Of this Wagner she speaks in other letters to Grimm, thus January 2, 1779: (German) "Yes, there are many things, and among them the sacred *inquisition*, which sully the eighteenth *seculum*, but what can be done? The world is like that; it is not worth much; as the departed Pastor Wagner used to say, on account of 'original sin.' "—February 2, 1780: "My good friend, you will be hearing one of these days that a certain declaration has been given out (the declaration of armed neutrality of 1780); you will call this volcanic, but it is not possible to do otherwise, (German) for the Germans hate nothing so much as having people try to take any advantage of them. Herr Wagner also did not like this."—April 15, 1785: "Herr Wagner never said 'the lambkin'; he said 'the lamb,' and I believe he had nothing in common with Dr. Faust."—February 15, 1794: "You tell me that evils for which there is no remedy can only be accepted with quiet and submission. You learned that from your father; the late Herr Wagner, of ancient memory, used to say exactly the same thing."—But Babet is mentioned June 1, 1779, and November 1, 1785: "Mademoiselle Cardel of glorious memory."—Cf. also the following foot-note and p. 75, Note 43, and page 45.

[16] Memories of Mlle. Cardel are very numerous in Catherine's letters to Grimm. Thus on November 19, 1778: "Do you know, Mademoiselle Cardel made me mistrustful toward all physicians and toward medicine in general; she was always very much in favor of having me read the comedies of Molière." February 27, 1775: "I regard this as a courtesy from you, Monsieur!

1 : DEDICATED TO COUNTESS BRUCE   73

You see, I am not forgetting the word 'Monsieur' to-day. Mademoiselle would doubtless have scolded me for an omission of this kind, for the departed used to say repeatedly, the word 'Monsieur' would not break anybody's jaw-bone. I think she must have acquired this expression from some comedy or other. Besides her other knowledge, she had all possible comedies and tragedies at her fingers' ends, and Mademoiselle Cardel was for that reason extremely entertaining."—September 20, 1775: "You shall not be called 'Monsieur' again if you do not wish it. That is very convenient for me, and Mademoiselle Cardel is dead."—November 30, 1778, and April 11, 1779: "She used to call me a 'left-handed spirit' (esprit gauche)."—December 21, 1774: "Mademoiselle Cardel and Herr Wagner had to deal with an *esprit gauche,* who turned upside down everything that was said to her. Herr Wagner wished 'examinations' of quite another kind and the *esprit gauche* said to herself: to be something in this world, one must have the necessary qualities for this something; let us search our little soul seriously to see if we have them. If not, then we will develop them."—August 23, 1779: "Ah, Herr Wagner and Mademoiselle Cardel, what all did you not preach to the *esprit gauche?*"—July 8, 1781: "I believe that Mlle. Cardel and Herr Wagner belonged to a by-gone period or to the 17th century; they preached (German) 'the best' to me so strongly that the *esprit gauche* set forth (German) 'to seek the best wherever it was to be found.'—October 16, 1779: "Usually I do not succumb to the first temptations to which apparently Mlle. Cardel and Herr Wagner gave me a strong resistance."—Catherine calls herself on June 30, 1775, "the pupil of Mademoiselle Cardel" and on November 29, 1775, "half Mademoiselle Cardel's, half Herr Wagner's pupil." Cf. the preceding note and p. 75, note 43.

17 In her letters Catherine also mentions a music teacher. To Grimm from Czarskoe Selo, May 16, 1778: "About the poor devil Roellig I have never yet told you, because you know what success his lessons had. He always brought a creature with him who roared bass; he had him sing in my room; I listened to him and said to myself: 'He roars like an ox.' But Herr Roellig was beside himself with delight whenever this deep voice was in action."—To the same from Czarskoe Selo, April 16, 1779: "As for the rest, I have not progressed any farther in music than formerly. The only tones which I really recognize are the barking of nine dogs, which have in turn the honor of being in my room and each one of which I recognize from afar by his voice and his organ; also the music of Galuppi. To that of Paisiello I listen and am amazed at the tones which he combines but I scarcely recognize them. Yet the song delighted me, something which neither Herr Roellig nor the man who roared bass next to him was able to do."

18 Catherine writes to Voltaire May 20/31, 1771: "I have never in my life known how to make verses or music."—To Grimm, December 22, 1777: "By the way, do you know that Paisiello's opera was entrancing? I forgot to tell you about it. I was all ear for this opera, in spite of the natural insensibility of my ear-drum for music."—Masson remarks in his Memoirs (1800): "Catherine liked neither verses nor music and often said so. She could not even stand the orchestra between acts and as a rule had the music interrupted."

19 In a letter of November 23, 1727, the Prince informs Emperor Peter II that

he was married on November 8th at the country-seat of Vecheln in Brunswick-Wolfenbuettel and that "he had increased the number of nobles in the world on Nov. 29, 1690"; thus he was not forty-two but only thirty-seven years old.

[20] The palace built as a residence by Duke August Wilhelm at Grauenhof was burned down in 1830.

[21] She died April 3, 1767, almost eighty-four years old (born Sept. 12, 1683).

[22] Luise Amalie Philippine, wife of Prince August Wilhelm, who died in 1758.

[23] Duchesse Philippine Charlotte.—Prince Henry of Prussia writes August 15, 1774, from Rheinsberg, to Catherine: "I have had the good fortune to talk about your kindness to my sister, the Duchess of Brunswick, who has been with me about two weeks. She knew you, Madame, at the age when the mind begins to develop, and recalls with lively interest to the last insignificant detail those early years which promised all that your great genius was to unfold in the time to come."—To this Catherine replied from Czarskoe Selo, August 22: "I have every reason to preserve a lively recollection of the Duchess of Brunswick, of whom Your Royal Highness speaks. The details of my frequent sojourns at her court still rise vividly before me, and among other things I recall how at the age of eight or nine I vowed eternal gratitude to her because by her intervention I was spared a well-deserved punishment which my departed mother wished to bestow upon me."

[24] Sophie Antonie, married (1749) Ernst Friedrich of Saxe-Coburg-Saalfeld.

[25] This must be an error. Of the two unmarried sisters of Duke Carl, the one, Therese Natalie, was Abbess of Gandersheim after 1766, but the other, Christine Caroline Louise, died in 1766 as Dean of the Chapter-House of Quedlinburg.

[26] As consort of King Frederick V.

[27] Ludwig Ernst was guardian of Wilhelm V from 1759 to 1766.

[28] This refers to Prince Albert, who fell at Soor in 1745, and Prince Friedrich Franz, who fell at Hochkirch in 1758.

[29] Christine Luise, daughter of Prince Albert Ernst of Oettingen, wife of Duke Ludwig Rudolf, who died in 1735.

[30] Elisabeth Christine.

[31] Charlotte Christine Sophie, who married Czarevich Alexei Petrovich.

[32] Antoinette Amalie, who married Duke Ferdinand Albrecht II of Brunswick-Bevern.

[33] Marie Anna, daughter of Ernst Ferdinand of Brunswick-Bevern.

[34] "In the year 1742 I was in Brunswick with my mother on a visit to the widowed Duchess, who had brought my mother up; the Duchess as well as my mother were of the house of Holstein. It chances that the Catholic Bishop of Corvey and several of his canons were there, among whom there was one from the house of Mengden. He occupied himself with prophecy and palmistry. My mother asked him whether the Princess Marianna of Bevern, with whom I was very friendly and whom we all loved for her beauty of face and character, would not for all her excellences be one day awarded a crown. He would say nothing about her and finally he said to my mother, 'I see crowns, at least three, on the head of your daughter.' My mother took it for a jest but he told her she should not doubt it at all and led her away to the window. Later she told me in the greatest amazement that he had said strange things

1 : DEDICATED TO COUNTESS BRUCE 75

to her which she had even forbidden him to speak of. She told me at the time that the prophecies of Mengden had been fulfilled, but more than that I could not learn from her. The gardener Lambertus at Oranienbaum also prophesied that I would reign and attain a very great age, more than eighty years.—Long before the Empress Elisabeth ascended the throne, he had told her that she would rule." (From a fragment of notes in Catherine's own handwriting printed in 1858.)

35 Sophie Dorothea of Hanover, who died 1757.

36 Princess Louisa Ulrica, later consort of King Adolf Friedrich of Sweden, was (1737) seventeen; Princess Amalie, only fourteen years old. The latter remained unmarried and became Abbess of Quedlinburg.

37 Prince Henry twice sojourned at Catherine's court, in 1770–71 and in 1776, and also corresponded with her. Cf. p. 74, Note 23.

38 Frederick Louis, Prince of Wales, married Princess Augusta in April, 1736. It was not decreed that she should become Queen, for her husband died in 1751, and her son George III succeeded George II on the throne in 1760.

39 Cf. note on the Princess's appearance p. 76, Note 52.

40 Duchess Maria Elisabeth of Holstein.

41 Arshin: twenty-eight inches.

42 Princess Sophie Christiane von Zerbst, Canoness of Gandersheim, was fifty-eight years old when Princess Sophie was eleven.

43 We find the following information about the life of the Princess Sophie in Stettin in letters to Grimm: From St. Petersburg, Jan. 20, 1776: "You think that Monsieur Laurent was a Lutheran, but he was a Calvanistic schoolmaster who could not read the Table-talk of Luther. These Table-talks were the delight of an old great-aunt of my mother's, and she used to quote them on all occasions. But the 'esprit gauche' saw it all quite differently from the way in which it was preached to her. That happened every day to Mademoiselle Cardel and Herr Wagner. One can not always know what children are thinking; children are hard to understand and especially when careful training has accustomed them to be obedient and experience has made them cautious in conversations with their teachers. Will you not draw from that, if you please, the fine maxim that one should not scold children too much but should make them trustful, so that they will not conceal their stupidities from us. To be sure, it is much easier for the schoolmasters to develop the spirit of a ruler than to govern their classes in this way."— From St. Petersburg, Feb. 2, 1778: "Furthermore, apropos . . . of the city which was my cradle, I remember in that connection that Mademoiselle Cardel was often visited, especially on Sundays, by Monsieur de Mauclerc, preacher of the gospel in the royal chapel. This Monsieur de Mauclerc was a son-in-law of the historian Rapin Thoiras, of whose history of England he was, I believe, the editor. He was the friend and adviser of Mademoiselle Cardel. The son of Rapin Thoiras, the brother-in-law of Mauclerc, was a privy counsellor at the same place, and they were all intimate friends of Mademoiselle Cardel and took an interest in her pupil. So far as Wagner was concerned, he had nothing in common with these arch-heretics, who did not understand his language nor he theirs."

76   CATHERINE THE GREAT : MEMOIRS

44 Duke Karl Friedrich died June 18, 1739.
45 Hedwig Sophie, sister of Charles XII.
46 Anna Petrovna.
47 Prince Karl Peter Ulrich (Emperor Peter III).
48 King Frederick William did not die until May 31, 1740.
49 Catherine to Frau von Bielcke on Jan. 20, 1767, from St. Petersburg: ". . . About the 10th of February, by our style, I start for Moscow. I shall arrive there after a four days' journey. My mother, to be sure, used to take as long to go from Stettin to Hamburg; but here the distances do not count."
50 Cf. this description of the 70's with what Catherine wrote about the first meeting with her future husband in the 50's (p. 223) and in the 90's: "At the time of this family gathering I heard it said that the young Duke had a leaning toward drink and that his people had trouble in preventing him from getting drunk at the table; that he was scornful and hot-tempered and did not like his people, especially Bruemmer; that for the rest he had a certain liveliness but was frail and sickly looking. In truth his color was pale, he looked thin and seemed to have a delicate constitution. His people wished the boy to appear grown-up and he was therefore tormented and subjected to continuous pressure, which was bound to make him insincere from his outward to his inward character."
51 Emperor Charles died on the 20th of October in the year 1740, Empress Anna not until the 28th (Old Style, the 17th).
52 A lady of rank, who often saw the young Princess, portrays her as follows: "Her manners were always extremely good from infancy on; she was unusually well-developed and tall for her years. The cast of her features, without being beautiful, was very pleasing, and this impression was increased by the particular graciousness and friendliness which she always showed. Her education was conducted entirely by her mother who kept a tight rein and did not overlook the slightest expression of pride, to which she had a tendency. On the contrary she required her from earliest childhood on to kiss the skirt of the grand ladies who came to visit the Princess."
53 The marriage of Prince August Wilhelm with Princess Louise Amalie took place on January 6, 1742.
54 Ludwig Eugene and Friedrich Eugene.
55 October 7, 1766, Frau von Bielcke wrote from Hamburg to the Empress: "I beg Your Majesty's gracious permission to relate that I had the honor of seeing Prince Henry [of Prussia] about two years ago. He deigned to visit me and to chat with me about two hours. He spoke of Your Majesty with such a lively admiration, with so much interest, that I could not refrain from thinking that if he had had the good fortune to be united with the charming Princess Sophie, he would not have been guilty of the terrible things which darken his reputation to-day. But Pope declares 'whatever is, is right.' "—To this Catherine replied, November 9, 1766: "The conversation which, as you report, you had with Prince Henry, and the interest which he has for his old acquaintance, naturally give me pleasure. It is not the first time that I have heard it spoken of, but I find, as well as Pope,

1 : DEDICATED TO COUNTESS BRUCE

that many things which are, are right. I do not regret therefore that the *contredanses* had no consequences."

56 Still in Stettin Princess Sophie wrote on the 20th of March, 1742, to the Countess Ulrica von Mellin: "I will not fail to send you my portrait, since you do me the honor to ask for it, and I beg you, Madame, to accept it, as a token of my friendship, and I beg you at the same time to preserve yours for me. I commend myself to your regard and remain, Madame, your true friend and servant, Sophie Auguste Friedrike."—Forty-seven years later the Countess reminded Empress Catherine of this promise and received with a miniature portrait a letter dated March 31, 1789. ". . . It is true that the many interruptions I have had since caused me to lose sight of this obligation. But the matter is not so regarding my memory of you: this has never left my heart and I have often recalled the pleasant moments spent in your society."

57 Catherine to Grimm, June 29, 1779: "I lived and received my education in the wing of the castle to the left as you enter from the great court-yard, where I occupied three vaulted rooms next to the church which formed the corner. The bell-tower adjoined my bedroom." Cf. p. 71, Note 1.

58 Anna Louisa, born Foese.

59 August 27, 1742.

60 Elisabeth, born in Berlin, December 17, 1742.

61 Died November 7, 1742.

62 Hedwig Friedrike, daughter of Duke Friedrich Ferdinand of Wuerttemberg-Weiltingen.

63 After 1667. Jever fell to Catherine II in 1793.

64 Karl Edzard, the last of the house of Greetsyl.

65 Sophie Wilhelmine.

66 Countess Charlotte Sophie was not the daughter but the granddaughter of Count Anton of Aldenburg, a legitimate son of Count Anton Guenther of Oldenburg.

67 Not a Countess but a "Froichen" (Fraeulein) Marie von Jever.

68 Count Anton Posthumus von Aldenburg, died in 1738.

69 She was twenty-eight years old.

70 In fact Court Marshal von Donop of Saxe-Meiningen passed as the natural son of the Countess.

71 Two Hamburg recollections of Catherine's. June 10, 1765, to Frau von Bielcke in Hamburg: "I was very frivolous at the time when you knew me; now after twenty-two years I remember with great pleasure my old acquaintances"; to which Frau von Bielcke replied July 30 (August 9): "There was already recognizable twenty-two years ago in the charm and gaiety appropriate to your years at the time, in your vivacity and amiability of spirit, the germ of all the talents and qualities which now inspire the admiration of all Europe."—To the same, August 26, 1766, "I have not yet seen the Countess Wachtmeister who, twenty-two years ago in Hamburg, used to scold me, when I did not curl my hair."

72 Balthasar Denner had already painted many members of the ducal family of Holstein.—Stehlin remarks in his memoirs: "(1743) Arrival of Prince

August of Holstein. His Highness brought with him for Her Majesty a portrait of the Princess of Zerbst, painted in Berlin by the artist Pesne."

73 This letter of Bruemmer's from St. Petersburg, December 17, 1743 (New Style), reads: "At the explicit and especial command of Her Imperial Majesty, I have to inform you, Madame, that the sublime Empress desires Your Highness, accompanied by the Princess, Your eldest daughter, to come to our country as soon as possible and repair without loss of time to the place where our Imperial Court may then be found. Your Highness is too intelligent not to understand the true meaning of the great impatience of Her Majesty to see you soon here, as well as the Princess, Your daughter, of whom report has told so much that is lovely. There are cases in which the voice of the world is in fact no other than the voice of God. At the same time our incomparable Monarch has expressly charged me to inform Your Highness that His Highness, the Prince, your husband, shall under no circumstances take part in the journey. Her Majesty has very important reasons for wishing it so."—On December 21 (New Style) Bruemmer wrote a second letter, in which he said, "I take the liberty of most humbly begging Your Highness get your journey under way as quickly as possible, without losing any time. You know, Madame, that one must strike while the iron is hot and there are fortunate moments which one may not allow to pass without the risk of losing them forever."

74 This portrait had been presented October 15, 1742, by Schriever, Counsellor of the Legation.

75 "Pro memoria, given my consort to accompany her." This document is in the archives at Zerbst, so the Princess must have brought it back with her from Russia. It deals with a possible change of religion, which should by all means come about without violence to conscience, and gives all sorts of general regulations.

76 Jan. 10, 1744. Evidence of the impression which the Princess made upon her environment at the time of her departure is given by Thiébault in his Memoirs. The Baroness von Printzen said to him: "Under my eyes she was born, grew up, and was educated; I was a witness of her school years and her progress; I helped her with her packing before she left for Russia. I enjoyed her confidence to such a degree that I can assume that I knew her better than anybody else. But I would never have believed that the fame would be awarded her which she has achieved. In her youth I noticed in her only a serious, calculating, cold intelligence, which was as far removed from anything distinguished or brilliant as it was from error, caprice, and frivolity. In short, I regarded her as an average maiden and you can imagine therefore my astonishment when I heard of her unusual destiny."

77 A few hours after Bruemmer's letter (cf. p. 29) there arrived a letter from King Frederick from Berlin, December 30, which said: "The high respect which I have for you, Madame, and for all that concerns you, compels me to tell you what in truth is involved in this journey. And the confidence which I have in your estimable qualities leads me to hope that you will handle rightly what I have to tell you about a matter whose success depends upon the greatest secrecy. In this confidence, therefore, Madame, I

will no longer withhold from you the fact that, on account of the regard which I entertain for you and for the Princess, your amiable daughter, I desired to secure for her an unusually good fortune, and the thought came to me whether there might not be a possibility of seeing her united with her cousin, the present Russian Grand Duke, . . . I beg you to rest assured that I will not cease to endeavor to be useful in the matter in question. . . ." Before the Princess's answer to this letter had reached Berlin, a second letter (Jan. 6th) came, in which the King writes: "According to all that I have heard from Petersburg in the meantime, the business in question is so far advanced that we can hope it will be ripe for words, assuming that the secret is well guarded for the present and that you can make the decision to hasten as much as possible your departure for Moscow in order not to lose these favorable moments."

[78] Maria Anna, who married Kurfuerst Maximilian Josef of Bavaria.

[79] Axel Baron von Mardefeldt.

[80] On October 1, 1780, Catherine says in a letter to King Frederick that to her constant regret she "had only been able to see and hear him talk at an age which was capable of respect but not of understanding."

[81] January 16.

[82] The family separated in Schwedt. The Princess and her escort arrived in Stargard January 18, in Koeslin January 20, went by way of Schlawe, Stolp, Dantzig on January 24 to Marienwerder, to Koenigsberg January 27, where she remained until the 29th.

[83] The Princess travelled under the name of the Countess of Rheinbeck.

[84] The comet Chéseaux was visible in December, 1743, and in the first months of 1744.

[85] February 5, 1744. On January 31st, they left Memel; on February 1st, the Princess wrote from Libau to her father: "I had in the last days a little trouble with the stomach, but it has had no further consequences. I was partly myself to blame, because I have consumed all the beer that I could hunt up on the way. Dear Mamma has put an end to that and I am well again."

[86] Narrative of the Princess: "Towards ten o'clock in the morning I started. At mid-day I met Chamberlain Narishkin, whom Her Imperial Majesty had placed at the head of an escort of honor, which she honored me by sending. He handed me letters and extended greetings from Her Majesty, which heaped honors and favors upon me. . . . A quarter of a mile from the city I was received by Vice-Governor Dolgorukov. . . . We drove upon the ice across the Dwina. As the carriage in which I drove was just leaving the great bridge, the first salvo was fired from the cannons on the fortresses. . . . I found here (in my apartment) . . . two gorgeous sable skins lined with gold brocade, for my daughter and myself, two collars of the same fur and a rug of another kind, but also a very beautiful fur, to cover us in the sleigh."

[87] Jan. 29 (Feb. 9). From Riga the Princess wrote, Feb. 8, to her consort: "So far as my daughter and myself are concerned, the former is so healthy and cheerful that I must wonder at it; I am somewhat more fatigued."

88 January 30 (February 10).

89 Narrative of the Princess: "The streets through which we had to pass were illuminated, but we did not see all the beautiful sights because we arrived very late."

90 Friday, February 3d (14). St. Petersburg Vedomosti, No. 11, 1744: "St. Petersburg, February 6. Last Friday Her Highness, the Princess of Anhalt-Zerbst with Her Highness, the Princess, her daughter, arrived here and was received in the Winter Palace by the high official persons of both sexes remaining here, while the cannon thundered from the Fortress and the Admiralty. The following day and yesterday Her Highness deigned to take a drive in the city and this morning to set forth upon the journey to Moscow."

91 From Petersburg the Princess writes to her consort: "Figgy endures the fatigue better than I, yet we are both well, praise God, may He guide and direct us further."—To Frederick II she writes: "Add to that the strain of the season, the journey, and the change of air. Really I need an iron constitution to keep up my resistance. My daughter is more fortunate. Her youth supports her health and like the young soldiers who scorn danger because they do not know about it, she delights in the splendors by which she is surrounded."

92 February 6, 1744. Cf. Note 90 above.

93 The narrative of the Princess says: "The blow which the sleigh received loosened a thick iron stake which held the cover and served to open it when one wished to sit in the air; this stake drew with it one from the middle which held a curtain that kept out the sun. Both struck me directly on the head. . . . I thought that I was wounded, but I was not. The blow had not struck with full force on account of the fur; otherwise without a doubt my head, neck, and arms, would have been crushed to pieces."

94 Cf. p. 229. "in the Golovin Palace."

95 This does not sound as if these lines were written in the year 1771 as the dedication says.

96 The Princess writes: "While we were still busy with laying off our furs and caps, silently into the room came the Grand Duke, whom I instantly recognized, however, followed by the Prince of Homburg and several others of the court. His Highness embraced us in the warmest manner and said that the last hour had been so unbearable to him that he would have liked to harness himself to our sleigh to hasten our progress. After a few moments Her Imperial Majesty sent word to the Grand Duke that he should bring us to her, the sooner the better. We hastened therefore to her august presence; it is impossible to describe how all those who were present looked at these Germans from head to foot. Her Imperial Highness came several paces to meet us in her first ante-chamber; she scarcely gave me time to take off my gloves, and embraced me, I must say, with tenderness. After I had kissed her hand, I said (in French): "I have come to lay at Your Majesty's feet feelings of the deepest gratitude for the benefactions which Your bounty has heaped upon my house and of which new instances are given me at every step I take in the realms of Your Majesty. I have no other merits

1 : DEDICATED TO COUNTESS BRUCE   81

except the deep appreciation which enables me to dare to beg Your Majesty for the honor of your protection for myself, my family, and my children, whom Your Majesty has graciously permitted to accompany me to your court." Her Imperial Majesty replied: (in French): "All that I have done is but little in comparison with what I would like to do for my family, my blood is not more dear to me than yours; my intentions will always be the same and my friendship must give value to my deeds on your behalf." After these words I presented my daughter, whom Her Imperial Majesty embraced in the same manner. Her Imperial Majesty then bade me enter her state chamber and had a fauteuil moved up and compelled us to be seated. The conversation grew so animated at this time that it was forgotten. Meanwhile Her Majesty retired for several moments, I thought to give a few commands, but afterwards learned that she was so moved by my resemblance to my departed brother that she could not restrain her tears and it was for that reason that she withdrew; after a short stay she came out of her cabinet again."

[97] The Princess writes: "The following day, the birthday of the Grand Duke was celebrated in state; the court was very numerous, so that when we were fetched by the Prince of Homburg to Her Imperial Majesty we could scarcely pass through. We were led to Her Majesty's apartment, and when she had entered the state bed-chamber she had the two Lords of the Bed-Chamber *du jour* bring the Order of St. Catherine, which with a very gracious compliment she presented, throwing it over me first together with the star and afterwards my daughter. The ladies von Vorontsov and Tchoglokov assisted us to hang it on and fasten it. . . . Her Majesty then took us with her to the Grand Duke and presented us to him, saying that she hoped these new knights of the Catherine Order would not be displeasing to her dear son. The latter showed that he was delighted, for, as the Empress told me, he had wished to request the order for us but he had not dared."

[98] March 3, 1744.

[99] This does not tally; the Princess fell ill March 6, cf. Note 101 following. On the 29th of February, she writes to her father: "Dear Papa, I am very well, thank God. . . ."

[100] Friday, March 9 (Journal of the Quartermasters of the Court, 1744.)

[101] This would have been March 17, for Easter fell on March 25. In the newspaper report however the 19th is expressly mentioned as the day of the crisis.

[102] St. Petersburg Vedomosti, 1744: "From Moscow, March 15. On the 6th of this month Her Royal Highness, the young Princess of Anhalt-Zerbst, fell ill with rheumatic fever. Although every possible precaution was taken by both of the Court Physicians, Sanchez and Boerhaave, under the supervision of the first Physician in ordinary to Her Imperial Majesty, Privy Counsellor von Lestocq, there followed several days after the fever a dangerous rheumatism with difficult breathing, to relieve which the doctors took the more tireless pains and care, all the more as Her Imperial Majesty deigned to be alarmed and to sympathize with the condition of Her Serene Highness,

the said Princess, who in the worst moments of her illness showed an admirable character. By the constant use of the best remedies and frequent blood-letting, the greatest danger of her illness passed over, with God's help, so that Her Imperial Majesty and the whole court were no little rejoiced at the hope regained for the restoration of her health. When Her Serene Highness was bled the first time, Her Imperial Majesty deigned to present her with a diamond brooch and ear-rings worth 50—60,000 rubles, and His Imperial Highness the Grand Duke gave her a watch and chain richly set with diamonds." "Moscow, March 22. Her Imperial Highness deigned to drive to the palace every evening to visit the bed-side of Her Serene Highness, the Princess of Anhalt-Zerbst. Although Her Serene Highness was somewhat better from the 13th to the 19th, it was still necessary to alternate between hope and fear because of the constant changes which are usual in such a sickness up to the 19th, which was the most dangerous day; and when with God's help and through the constant use of remedies on the said day, in fact, one hour before the end of the fourteenth day, Her Highness suddenly vomited forth much phlegm, there was inexpressible joy at court at this evidence that the greatest danger was past and renewed hope for the recovery of the Princess."—Dispatch of the Austrian resident Count Hohenholz to Count Uhlfeld from "Mosco," March 23, 1744, (New Style): "The ladies and gentlemen here are in good health except the bride destined for the Grand Duke, namely, the Princess of Zerbst. As I hear, this Princess has lain for several days dangerously ill of a fever not unlike inflammatory fever, and a very bad pleurisy. They have already bled her for the fourteenth time, without at all relieving the violent and continuous pains in her side; the court is in great anxiety about it."—From "Mosco," April 9: "The young Princess of Zerbst who is ill is but recently out of danger; but since the sickness was an *ulcus* on the lungs and had reached the stage of suppuration, there seems notwithstanding to be a question whether she can be radically cured."—Concerning the gift the Princess wrote: "The wound was bound up with a diamond brooch and ear-rings with *breloques* worth about twenty thousand rubles from the Empress, and by a watch set with rubies and diamonds which must have cost at least three or four thousand rubles from the Grand Duke"; of the illness she says that the physicians ascribed it "to the inflamation of the blood induced by the fatigue of the wearisome journey."

[103] But on August 4, 1756, Grand Duchess Catherine Alexeievna had written to Sir Charles Williams: "To rule one must divide."

[104] The Princess writes to her husband: "The Grand Duke has been desperate as long as the young person was sick."

[105] The Princess had already written February 18/29, 1744, to her husband: ". . . Our daughter makes a very good impression here; the monarch loves her tenderly, and the successor is fond of her. The thing is done!" Marquis de la Chétardie writes February 23 (Mar. 5) to Hamburg: ". . . Her Imperial Majesty has as much good-will and affection for the said Princess, as the Grand Duke has for her, which says not a little."

[106] Journal of the Court Quartermasters: "April 21, 1744, Saturday. Her

1 : DEDICATED TO COUNTESS BRUCE 83

Imperial Majesty held a banquet in the Golovin Palace to celebrate the birthday of her Highness, the Princess of Zerbst.

[107] Princess Sophie writes to her father May 3, 1744: "As I find almost no difference between the Greek and the Lutheran religion, I have decided (after an examination of the gracious instructions of Your Highness), to change my religion, and I will send you at the first opportunity my confession of faith; I flatter myself with the hope that Your Highness will be satisfied with it." In his answer from Zerbst, June 5th, the Prince writes: ". . . I give you then herewith my paternal blessing and consent, with the admonition that you put your faith and trust in no one but the threefold God and in His Word, and that you test yourself well by my Instructions, and strive with diligence to reflect on what will bring eternal happiness."

[108] Princess Anna Leopoldovna of Brunswick, mother of Emperor Ivan VI.

[109] June 6, 1744.

[110] June 13, 1744.

[111] The Empress had asked Prince Christian August on May 1st for his consent to his daughter's change of religion and her marriage to the Grand Duke. The Prince answered the Empress from Zerbst, June 5th: ". . . The extreme grace and favor with which Your Imperial Majesty has chosen my daughter and your devoted servant, Princess Sophie Auguste Friedrike, is an act of Providence, for which, besides thanking my God and Your Imperial Majesty, I remain most constantly and humbly beholden; at your gracious command however and with the most fervent joy I give most respectfully herewith, though to Your Imperial Majesty and His Imperial Highness, the Grand Duke, my paternal blessing and consent to the marriage with Grand Duke's Imperial Highness." To the Grand Duke he wrote on the same day: "My paternal blessing and consent I have already most obediently and unreservedly declared to Her Imperial Majesty and hereby also to Your Imperial Highness." The Grand Duke manifested great joy over this letter, as the Princess reports: ". . . I did not believe that, since he scarcely needed to have any doubt of your consent, the actual arrival of the same and your letter would move him so . . . Your letter was embraced a thousand times, and if all the good and kind wishes of your new son-in-law are fulfilled, you will be happy for time and eternity."

[112] Soon after the arrival of the Princess in Moscow there appeared in the St. Petersburg Vedomosti this notice: "The young Princess shows great interest in learning the Russian language and deigns to spend several hours daily in the study of it."

[113] In her account of the ceremony, Princess Johanna Elisabeth describes the appearance of her daughter as follows: "Her Imperial Majesty had made for her a dress *adrienne* which was in all respects like the one which she herself wore on this day, of red *gros de tour,* trimmed at all the seams with a pattern of silver lace. On her head she wore a white ribbon without any other ornament; her hair was unpowdered; she wore no jewels except the large ear-rings and the brooch which Her Imperial Majesty had presented to her during her illness. She was a little pale; the elegant costume enhanced her customary paleness, and I can say I thought her beautiful."

[114] The Princess reports: ". . . My daughter spoke all the articles with a clear, firm voice, and with a pronunciation at which all those present wondered, and did not omit a single word. I was already so much moved that she had scarcely spoken the first word when I burst into tears. Her Majesty had covered her face from the gaze of everybody. All those present prayed with us, the old people sobbed, the young people who were present had tears in their eyes. . . . She spoke and answered all the articles of the creed with self-possession and firmness. Her deportment from the moment she entered the church and for the continuation of the entire ceremony was so full of nobility and dignity that I should have admired her, had she not been to me that which she is."—The Prussian Ambassador reported: "Everybody present shed streams of tears. But the young Princess did not shed a single one during the ceremony and conducted herself like a true heroine. She also spoke the Russian language with great correctness; in short, she has won the admiration of the Monarch, of her future consort, and of the entire nation." Dispatch of June 29, 1744.—The St. Petersburg Vedomosti 1744, No. 55, p. 438, wrote: "It is impossible to describe the dignity and fervor which the illustrious Princess displayed during the impressive performance, so that Her Imperial Majesty herself and the greater part of the noble persons present could not refrain from tears of joy."

[115] On this day Princess Sophie received the name of Catherine Alexeievna.

[116] Narrative of the Princess: "She presented her with a clasp of diamonds and a necklace valued at 150,000 rubles."—The St. Petersburg Vedomosti 1744, No. 55, speaks of a "clasp and folding icon set with diamonds, which were worth several 100,000 rubles."

[117] Narrative of the Princess: "For this whole day I still had precedence over my daughter. . . . Scarcely had we accomplished this [undressed ourselves] when Her Imperial Majesty appeared. The gracious monarch came to inform herself how her children felt after the fatigue of the day. She gave me the ring which my daughter was to exchange with the Grand Duke. These rings are tiny marvels in every respect. Together they may easily have cost 50,000 ducats."

[118] Narrative of the Princess: "Privy Counsellor Lestocq brought my daughter as a present from the Empress her portrait and that of the Grand Duke set in a diamond bracelet."—According to the Princess's account the Grand Duke did not send his gifts in the morning but presented them in person after the ceremony: "After we had rested a little, the Grand Duke came to us. He brought my daughter a watch set with large diamonds valued at 15,000 rubles and a fan set with diamonds in exquisite taste."

[119] On July 1st/12th the Princess writes her husband: "By the present Courier I have at last to inform you that, after our beloved daughter on last Thursday, the 9th of this month, had made her public confession of faith and had acquitted herself to the complete satisfaction of Her Imperial Majesty, she was betrothed to the Grand Duke on the day after, that is the day before yesterday, in the great Cathedral of the Kremlin here with the blessing of the Arch-Bishop and with the exchange of rings by Imperial Majesty Herself; and was immediately declared to have the title of Grand

1 : DEDICATED TO COUNTESS BRUCE

Duchess of All the Russias and Imperial Highness in public prayers as well as in the ukases issued for the purpose."

[120] Narrative of the Princess: "We were informed that Her Highness awaited us, and went to her. The Grand Duke gave me his hand; my daughter followed alone. When we had entered Her Majesty's presence I yielded for the first time precedence to my daughter."—The Princess writes July 10/21 to her husband: "Catherine Alexeievna, whose first steps toward great fortune have already been reported to you, lays at your feet her childlike obedience, which her good disposition will certainly never allow her to forget. She adapts herself precociously to her new position, but as often as she must pass in front of me, she can not refrain from blushing."

[121] The peace of Åbo, 1743. The peace celebration however did not begin on the 17th but the 15th of July.

[122] The Princess writes of this: "What displeases me is that there are none but young people; we kept hoping that your acquaintance Narishkin would be named among them or would be Lord Chamberlain, but nothing came of it; perhaps as no one has been named as yet, he may still be added.

[123] St. Petersburg Vedomosti 1744: "Moscow, July 26. On the afternoon of this day Their Imperial Highnesses, the Grand Duke and the Grand Duchess, as well as Her Highness the Princess of Anhalt-Zerbst, accompanied by several gentlemen of their court and a small train set forth from here on their journey to Kiev . . . and Her Imperial Majesty has the intention to set forth to-morrow evening or the morning of the day after for the same place and to cover one hundred versts of the distance on foot."

[124] August 2, 1744.—This refers to Kozelets (Gubernia Tchernogov, formerly Kiev) not Kozelsk (Gubernia Kaluga) as Catherine erroneously says, also in the Herzen memoirs.

[125] "A right imperial house, well furnished and well divided," writes the Princess.

[126] September 8, 1744.

[127] St. Petersburg Vedomosti 1744: "Moscow, September 24. Their Imperial Highnesses, the Grand Duke and the Grand Duchess, returned from Kiev safe and sound and in a welcome state of health on the afternoon of the 20th of this month."

[128] The Princess writes once to her husband that she has seen the Empress "dressed as a Cavalier; anything more beautiful nature has not formed; I could not turn eye away from her."

[129] Catherine to Grimm, April 14, 1785: "This family Rumyantsov has suffered a heavy loss in the person of Countess Bruce, who died last week in Moscow. Those who knew her well will miss her grievously, for she was very amiable."

[130] These remarks about Countess Rumyantsov and the style of reference to Countess Bruce (born October 7, 1729, hence almost the same age as Catherine) leads to the conclusion that the latter never saw the documents really dedicated to her, and that Catherine in writing these lines no longer had the dedication in mind.

[131] A letter from the Grand Duchess to her father of July 5/16, 1744, says:

"I learned with great pleasure that Your Highness has sent my brother to Homburg; and as I remember that the expenses for that must be very great I take the liberty of begging Your Highness to leave him there as long as may be necessary for his complete recovery; I promise to pay the necessary costs."

[132] In her inscription for her grave-stone, written in her own hand, Catherine says: "Here lies Catherine the Second. . . . At the age of fourteen she made the threefold resolution, to please her husband, Elisabeth, and the Nation. She neglected nothing to succeed in this." Cf. p. 326.

[133] St. Petersburg Vedomosti, 1744: "Moscow, December 17. At eleven o'clock this morning, Her Imperial Majesty, our most Gracious Sovereign deigned to depart amid the thunder of cannon, from the residence city on her way to St. Petersburg, for which their Imperial Highnesses, the Grand Duke and the Grand Duchess in the company of the illustrious Princess of Anhalt-Zerbst set forth last Saturday, that is, on the 15th of this month."—The Princess writes: "Her Imperial Majesty most graciously decided, for the sake of taking better care of the health of the Grand Duke and the Grand Duchess than the condition of the quarters here permit, to have us go away from Moscow two days before she left, on December 26th, at nine o'clock in the morning after we had breakfasted. The august Empress was present when we entered the sleighs, in spite of the snow on which they stood, and as the furs and rugs with which the Grand Duchess was covered did not seem to her sufficient she took a very beautiful ermine which she wore and wrapped her up in it."

[134] Journal of the Court Quartermasters, 1744: "December 23. At three o'clock in the afternoon Her Imperial Majesty deigned to leave the Winter Palace and set forth from St. Petersburg, and on the 25th at two o'clock in the night she deigned to arrive in Chotilovo." The Princess writes: "I hoped to conceal from her under various pretexts the reason for our departure, but she was not to be persuaded and was so deeply troubled that I was obliged to pity her. We discussed it at length; she wished herself to act as nurse, she would not be considered, until finally I had to be in earnest and convince her that by some means, good or bad, I should take her away. We sent an officer in advance with news of our approach; we found Her Imperial Majesty no longer here but met her on the way. We met the august Empress in the night; she opened her sleigh and spoke with us. However much she tried to restrain herself, her grief was expressed in her countenance and the tears sprang forth. . . . Meantime the Grand Duchess has not suffered from the shock or the great speed of the journey, but is still very well."

[135] St. Petersburg Vedomosti, 1744: "St. Petersburg, December 27. Her Imperial Highness, the Grand Duchess, with Her Serene Highness, the Princess of Anhalt-Zerbst, arrived here last Monday evening from Moscow in a welcome state of good health."

[136] A book list of Catherine's from a later date names as No. 2, "History of Cicero by Middleton." This refers to Conyers Middleton, Life of Cicero, London, 1741, 2 vol. A French translation was made by Abbé Prevost, Histoire de Cicéron, Paris, 1743; a German translation by Th. Jak. Dusch ap-

1 : DEDICATED TO COUNTESS BRUCE 87

peared under the title "Roemische Geschichte unter der Lebenszeit des M. Tullius Cicero" in Altona and Luebeck, but not until 1757–59.

[137] Ch. Montesquieu, Considérations sur les causes de la grandeur des Romains et leur décadence. Amsterdam, 1734.

[138] Without doubt in the famous translation of Amyot: Les Vies des hommes illustres comparées l'une avec l'autre by Plutarque de Chaeronée translatées premièrement de grec en francois par Jasques Amyot lors abbé de Bellozane. Paris, 1559, 6 vol.

[139] In the year 1758.

[140] Later, in 1791 Catherine drew another portrait of herself. Cf. p. 325. Letter to Sénac de Meilhan.

[141] Catherine to Count Gyllenborg, 1766: "The letter which your son brought me from you gave me much happiness, all the more as I thought I recognized in it the same friendly attitude of which you gave me so many proofs more than twenty years ago. Rest assured that I well know the value of the interest you show in all that concerns me. . . . I know that I owe you thanks in more than one respect, and if I have had a certain amount of success you have had a share in it, for you encouraged in me the desire to accomplish great things."—To Williams, September 28, 1756: "I forgot to tell you that this Henning Gyllenborg is altogether my man, and I am delighted to know that he is with the King. . . ."

[142] Journal of the Court Quartermasters: "On January 27, 1745, that is, on Sunday afternoon in the 9th hour, they deigned to arrive at the Winter Palace in St. Petersburg."

[143] Along with the manuscript of Part III, have been preserved some short chronological notes of Catherine's, partly written with a pencil, which she probably followed in working out her Memoirs. This entry is among them: "1745. Bath before the wedding, the Empress comes to see me."—In the account of the Princess we read that on the 20th of August: "According to the commands of Her Imperial Majesty we made inquiries about the following days. The Grand Duchess was ordered to go to the bath forthwith and then to sup alone."

[144] Narrative of the Princess: "I had to be ready first and it was half-past six o'clock. I sent to enquire if the Grand Duchess had arisen. She had just got up."

[145] Narrative of the Princess: "When the Grand Duchess was seated at her dressing-table, all the ladies of the Court received permission to enter. Her hair was dressed by her women and her hair-dresser. Her Imperial Majesty only arranged here and there a few small ornaments. The color of her hair is pure black, but with a sheen, which enhances her youthful appearance, and to the charm of the brunette she adds the delicacy of the blonde. She herself put the small imperial crown upon her head. She wore no powder; her dress, or more properly speaking, her robe, was of the most magnificent silver glacé that I have ever seen, cut low and trimmed with tinsel. This lovely decoration and the magnificent jewels with which she was covered, gave her I must say an enchanting appearance. They had put on a very little paint and her

88   CATHERINE THE GREAT : MEMOIRS

color was never lovelier than on this day."—To her husband the Princess writes of the wedding: "The procession was delayed until ten o'clock and was imperial; the carriages passed along until finally Her Imperial Majesty ascended to the church at eleven o'clock. The arrival lasted until one o'clock and the ceremony until four o'clock. After our return to the imperial palace we dined in state after a little delay; after dinner there was dancing and the bridal pair were escorted to their apartment towards one o'clock after midnight and therewith closed the first day."

[146] Dispatch of the English Ambassador August 24th, 1745: "The procession was the grandest that has ever been in this country and surpassed everything that I have ever seen."—The French resident d'Alion writes to Minister d'Argonson on the same day: "One could scarcely behold anything more splendid and more stately."

[147] Journal of the Court Quartermasters 1745: "August 21. In the afternoon at the beginning of the 7th hour Her Imperial Majesty and Their Imperial Highnesses deigned to arrive in the gallery to dine. The dinner ended in the middle of the 9th hour and in the 10th hour the ball began in the gallery and lasted until the middle of the 11th hour; in the third quarter of this hour it ended."

[148] The words from here to the end are suppressed in the edition of the [Russian] Academy.

PART TWO

CONTINUED IN THE YEAR 1791

To

BARON TCHERKASOV

from whom I must elicit at least

one shout of laughter daily, or

to discourse

with whom from morning until evening

I make a point of duty

because both amusements are

the same to him

and I like to give pleasure **to**

my friends.

On the day after the wedding we received general congratulations in the Winter Palace and then drove to the Summer Palace to dine with the Empress. In the morning she had sent me a cushion with a wonderful decoration of emeralds and another trimmed with sapphires to the Grand Duke that he might present it to me. In the evening there was a ball in the Winter Palace.[1] Two days later the Empress came to dine with us in the Winter Palace.

The wedding festivities lasted ten days. Among other things there was a masquerade with quadrilles in dominos of different colors, each consisting of twelve couples. The first quadrille was that of the Grand Duke in rose and silver; the second, in white and gold, was mine; the third, that of my mother, was in pale-blue and silver; the fourth, in yellow and silver, was that of my uncle, the Prince Bishop of Luebeck.[2] On entering the ball-room we found it was arranged that the different sets should not mingle with each other but that each should dance in the particular position indicated in the hall. It was very difficult for mine to obey this command, for when the ball was about to begin there was not a single gentleman present capable of dancing. They were all people from sixty to ninety years of age at whose head was Marshal Lascy, my partner. This unpleasant business brought me near to weeping. But fortunately I encountered the Court Steward, to whom I presented the matter so successfully that he procured an order countermanding the provision that the sets should not mingle with each other.

Never in my life have I seen a more woful and stupid amusement than were these quadrilles. In one enormous hall only forty-eight couples were dancing, and among whom were numerous lame, gouty, and decrepit figures; all the rest were spectators in ordinary dress and did not dare to mingle with the quadrille dancers. The Empress however considered it so lovely that she had it repeated all over again. After the ball the quadrille dancers supped. But I almost had tears in my eyes.

During the festivities the Empress sent word to Countess Rumyantsov, who had remained with me ever since my illness, that she might return to her husband. Both great and small at Court rejoiced at this.

When the celebration came to an end, they began to talk about my mother's departure. After my marriage I felt most comfortable when I remained with her. I sought all the more eagerly opportunities to do this as my own home could scarcely be considered pleasant.[3] The Grand Duke's head was full of childish tricks; surrounded by his servants, in whom alone he took any interest, he occupied himself constantly with playing at soldiers. In my rooms I was no longer allowed to romp with my maidens; Madame Kruse knew how to intimidate them mortally; she almost forbade them to speak with me.

I should certainly have loved my young husband if he had only wished to be amiable or could have been so. But in the early days of our marriage I came to a bad conclusion about him. I said to myself: "If you love this man you will be the most unhappy creature on God's earth; your innermost being will demand response. But the man scarcely takes any notice of you. He scarcely talks of anything but dolls and he comes near to paying more attention to every other woman than he does to you. You are too proud to complain about it; so take care, please, regarding any tenderness toward this gentleman. Think of yourself first, Madame." This first impression, made on a heart as soft as wax, remained with me; and this idea never again went out of my mind.

But naturally I was on my guard against letting any word escape me about my firm resolve, which was never to love anyone devotedly who would not reward me with an unlimited response. But as my heart was constructed, it would have belonged wholly and completely to a husband who loved me and from whom I had no cause to fear all the mortifications which were allotted to me from mine. I have always regarded jealousy, doubt, mistrust and all that proceeds from them as the greatest misfortune and I have always been convinced it is in the husband's power to have his wife love him if she is good-hearted and amiably disposed. Kindness and good manners on the husband's part will always win her heart.[4]

When I could not seek out my mother, to whom, by the way, the Grand Duke only went reluctantly, I sat down with a book in my room. The first that fell into my hands was "Tiran le Blanc":[5] I was delighted with the Princess who had so fine skin that when she drank the red wine could be seen flowing down her throat. My mother often came to spend the evening with me and in those days I would have given a great deal to leave the country with her.

I forgot to say that, the Empress, on September 5th, her name day, left for Gostilitsy, an estate belonging to Count Razumovsky;[6] she sent the Grand Duke, my mother and myself to Czarskoe Selo. We spent several days here, not without a good deal of bustle and dissension; the young wished to dance and spring and carry on all kinds of childishness; their elders did not think that this was right. My mother managed so that she never left her room at all; I divided my time between her and the noisy ones.

At this time my mother gave me to understand by her conversation that she had known about the attachment of her brother, Prince George Ludwig, to me; but as she only lightly touched upon it, it was rather that I guessed it than that she told me.

When we returned home from the little journey, the departure of my mother was more definitely spoken of. The Empress sent her 60,000 rubles to pay her debts; but it developed that my mother owed 70,000 rubles more than the Empress had sent. To help my mother out of this embarrassment, I assumed the obligations she had incurred in Russia. This laid the foundation of the debts which I incurred during the life-time of the Empress, which at her death had swollen to the vast sum of 657,000 rubles, and which I only paid off after my accession to the throne in quarterly installments. I have often grieved because it was impossible for me to pay them with an income of 30,000 rubles and because in the last days of the blessed Empress I was in the sorry state of having no more credit,—not even enough to order a dress made at Christmas. On that day the Empress died, which I could not foresee. My only anchor of safety was my diamonds, whose value was much more than this sum; but I did not dare to sell them or to pawn them.

But it would be anticipating should I speak further of this here. I will resume, then, the interrupted thread.

My mother took her departure, laden with presents, as was her whole retinue.[7] The Grand Duke and I escorted her as far as Krasnoe Selo. I wept very much and in order not to make me any sadder my mother went away without taking leave of me.

Several days preceding her departure she had had a long conversation with the Empress; heaven knows what they had to say to each other. I have never discovered anything more about it than that access to her dressing-room was granted to me by the Empress; that is, towards twelve o'clock in the morning and at five or six in the evening I might tarry there as long as I wished in the company of her women, for Her Majesty did not always make her appearance. Nevertheless, this permission was a certain mark of favor, although it did not last long as we shall see in the sequel.

We returned to Petersburg. When I entered my apartment I remarked the absence of Maria Petrovna Shukov, to whom I was especially attached. I asked where she was. The other women, whose downcast eyes and troubled air caught my attention, reported that her mother had suddenly fallen ill and had had her daughter summoned while she was at dinner with her companions. For this evening I attached no further significance to the matter. The next day I inquired again for her and was told that she had not slept in the house. This struck me as peculiar, for my women had tears in their eyes. I made it possible to question Mademoiselle Balk (who later married the poet Sumarokov) privately. She implored me not to betray her, which I promised. She then told me that, while they were sitting at the table, a Sergeant of the Guard and a Courier of the Cabinet had entered the room and informed Mademoiselle Shukov that her mother was ill and she must go to her. Turning pale, she rose; and while she entered the carriage with one of the messengers, the other ordered her maid to pack her mistress's belongings. It was whispered that she had been banished and they had been forbidden to speak to me about it. No one knew the reason but they suspected it was because I liked her and paid her particular attention. I was much astonished and troubled by all this; that I should see a person made unhappy merely for the reason that I liked her gave me great sorrow. But the departure of my mother, which had made me very sad, afforded a cover for the concealment of this second trouble. I talked about it to no one, because I feared to make Mademoiselle Balk unhappy. But I confided in the Grand Duke, who was sorry for the maiden because she was more sprightly and more clever than the others.

The next day with the Empress we moved from the Summer Palace to the Winter Palace.[8] Scarcely had we reached the state bedchamber of the monarch than she began to say the worst things imaginable about Mademoiselle Shukov. She insisted that the latter had been entangled in a couple of affairs and that my mother had urgently begged Her Majesty in her last conversation to remove the maiden from my household because I had formed a youthful attachment for her and the maiden was unworthy of my liking. I answered not a word; I was too astonished and troubled. Her Imperial Majesty spoke with so much anger and resentment that she turned quite red with excitement while her eyes flashed. In the first place I did not know whether Mademoiselle Shukov's conduct was good or bad; she had been given to me and had been there scarcely six months. In the second place, it was true that I had singled her out and showed her marks of favor, but without any extravagance or outspoken attachment, because she was cheerful and less stupid than the others and really very innocent. In the third place, I thought it peculiar that my mother should have asked the Empress to remove the girl. For she had never said a word to me about my interest in her, although she always scolded me unsparingly and frankly when she thought that I deserved it. Had my mother spoken to me about it I should certainly have paid attention, simply because I was accustomed to obey her.

I have never yet discovered whether my mother really made this request of Her Imperial Majesty. I thought I might well doubt it because I do not know what could have induced my mother to grieve me so publicly or abuse me to the Empress when, with a word, she could have settled the whole matter. On the other hand, I must admit that my mother was very cold to the girl; but that could be explained by the fact that she could not speak with her for the latter understood only Russian. It may seem strange to many that I doubted the words of the Empress. To that I can only reply that experience has taught me to accept with caution whatever the sovereign said in anger. However that may be, they could have handled the matter otherwise and much better if their purpose was to keep my harmless interest in the maiden within bounds.

Subsequent experiences have convinced me that really the only offense of the maiden was my attachment to her and her supposed devotion to me. Later years have confirmed this assumption. All those who were merely suspected of the same thing during the following eighteen years were sent on a commission or removed, and their number is not small. I shall have occasion to speak of this in those special years.

A few weeks later Count Zachary Tchernishov was removed and sent to Regensburg as Ambassador. His mother had recommended his removal to the Empress, for she had said to her: "I am anxious lest he fall in love with the Grand Duchess. He watches her constantly, and when I see that I tremble with fear of the follies he might commit."

For the fall and winter of this year it was arranged that two masked balls should take place every week, one at the Court and the other at the grand houses of the city in turn.[9] People pretended to be well entertained by them, but at bottom everyone was dreadfully bored by these balls, which were stiff in spite of the masquerading and so little frequented that the ball-rooms at Court looked empty while the houses in the city were too small to hold the few guests who did appear. One should not compare the city of that time with the Petersburg of to-day. The only stone houses were on the Millionaya, the Lugovaya, and the English Quay. These were a sort of curtain behind which were concealed the most unpleasant wooden barracks that can be imagined. In fact the only house with damask hangings was that of the Princess of Hessen; all the others had white-washed walls or wretched hangings of paper or painted linen.[10]

This winter on the day before the birthday of the Empress I had a bad tooth-ache. Nevertheless I dressed myself to bear my congratulations to Her Majesty as custom required. In the apartments of Her Majesty I encountered Captain Korsakov-Voin of the Marines, an entertaining man whom the sovereign valued highly. I complained to him of my tooth-ache and he declared that he would cure me in a moment.

He fetched a large iron nail and requested me to scratch the gum where it pained me until the blood came. I did it and he took his nail and went away. As a matter of fact the pain disappeared over-night and this tooth has never hurt me since that time.

We lived, as far as it went, quite well, I and the Grand Duke. He liked to see a few gentlemen or ladies at supper in the evening. On Sylvster Eve also we amused ourselves in this way in his chambers. At midnight my waiting woman Madame Kruse appeared and requested us in the name of the Empress to go to bed because the Empress thought it wrong to stay up so late on the eve of such a solemn festival. At the hint the whole company withdrew without a word of opposition. Still it struck us as peculiar because we knew the irregular hours which were kept by our precious aunt. It was more a matter of bad humor than of reason and of principle.

I cannot say whether the carnival balls or our living conditions were to blame but at the end of the winter, or, to put it better, at the beginning of the year 1746 the Grand Duke fell ill with inflammatory fever. In any case he contracted the fever. At the balls he danced a great deal and used to come home covered with perspiration. Our rooms were situated very strangely; between his room and mine was a large vestibule with an enormous staircase. He slept in my room but dressed and undressed in his own.

While I am on the subject of the Grand Duke's residence, I must describe one peculiarity the sense of which has never been quite clear to me but which the Empress most strictly enforced. The Grand Duke had three rooms; in the one next to the vestibule stood the bed of the Lord High Chamberlain and Assistant-Governor Bergholz, who slept there; the second room was empty; but in the third was the bed of Lord Marshal Bruemmer, the Grand Duke's Governor. The two gentlemen went to bed when the Grand Duke left to sleep in my apartment. In the course of the day Herr von Bruemmer never came to the Grand Duke, but Herr von Bergholz spent his time in the first ante-chamber in which he slept.

Herr von Bruemmer's influence was declining at the time.[11] One day he took me aside and told me he would certainly be dismissed if I did not support him. I asked him how he would advise me to go to work in order to succeed. He said he saw no other method than that I should be less timid in my attitude toward the Empress and should pay more frequent visits to the room to which I had access. I replied that that would have no purpose because the Empress almost never appeared when I was there. As far as my timidity was concerned it was difficult to lay it aside in my relations with a Princess whose disposition was so hard to fathom, who communicated only with a few people, and with whom you always ran the risk in conversation that she would seize upon some word or other that displeased her as an excuse to fall upon you and to scold you. I often witnessed how the Grand Duke fared in conversation with her. For this reason I cultivated the greatest reserve in her presence and carefully considered every word before I uttered it. He spoke to me two or three times again to the same effect but I considered that what he wished was wholly excluded. I am to-day still firmly convinced that I should have probably drawn down upon myself the wrath of the Empress (to which she was already all too much inclined) and that I should not have succeeded in sending upward again the fallen stock of Herr von Bruemmer. As for the rest, the Grand Duke hated him with his whole heart; so this would only have become a new cause for coldness between us two. Already he did not like it because I conversed with Bruemmer on too many occasions. Some time later Herr von Bruemmer and Herr von Bergholz asked for their leave and received it.[12]

About this time I found a Sergeant of the Guards, by the name of Travin, who agreed to go to Moscow and marry Mademoiselle Shukov. But when the Empress heard of it, she sent an order that the young couple should be transferred to Kizliar. Why I never understood; it must again have been a case of mere ill-humor.

The sickness of the Grand Duke lasted about two months; he was bled several times and caused the Empress much uneasiness. My natural sensibility led me to sympathize with his condition, but I was timid and reserved toward him and the Empress. Both of them seemed inclined to pounce upon me and I feared to expose myself with them. On the other hand my resolution not to be a burden often did me harm because it was frequently the reason why I stood aside when I thought that might be the case. With a little more daring and less sensibility I should have got on better. But my natural desire to please often led me to yield my place when without that I might have held it very well.

During the sickness of the Grand Duke, the Empress received news of the death of Princess Anna of Brunswick, who died in Kolmogory of a severe fever following her last confinement.[13] The Empress wept a great deal on the receipt of this news and ordered that the body should be brought to Petersburg for a solemn burial. Along about the second or third week of Lent the corpse arrived and was interred in the Alexander Nevsky Cathedral. The Empress took part in the ceremony and I accompanied her in her carriage;[14] she wept a great deal during the entire ceremony. Princess Anna was buried in the Church between her grandmother, Czarina Prascovia Feodorovna and her mother, the Duchess of Mecklenburg.[15]

During this fast the Empress sent me word by Sievers that she would like it very much if I would observe it. I replied that Her Majesty had anticipated me; I had already had the intention to ask for her permission to do so. Sievers reported that this had pleased Her Majesty very much.

In the place of Herren von Bruemmer and Bergholz, Prince Vasili Nikitich Repnin was assigned to the Grand Duke in the year 1746. The Empress's choice was displeasing neither to the Grand Duke nor to me. Prince Repnin was a man of the finest, noblest character.[16] Both of us, the Grand Duke and myself, took pains to win his liking and he, in his turn, took pains to testify his good will in every way. He began to introduce more carefully selected and more cultivated society about the Grand Duke and to remove him from the company of lackeys.

I must relate here an occurrence of this winter which will perhaps contribute to an understanding of the characters. The apartments of the Grand Duke to which I have referred were adjacent to a room in which the Empress had installed a mechanical table (in Russia called a "Hermitage"). Here she often ate with her intimates and confidants, who were often waiting-women, choristers, and even lackeys. The Grand Duke had taken it into his head to see what went on in this room and he bored holes in the door between this room and his own. But it was not enough for him to peep through the holes alone; he desired that his whole household should enjoy the view with him. I called his attention to the fact that this might have unpleasant consequences; I did it once to please him but refused to enter into it a second time. He laughed at me and called Madame Kruse in the bargain. She saw Count Razumovsky dining with the Empress in his dressing-gown.

That was Friday. On Sunday morning after mass the Empress entered my apartment and scolded the Grand Duke frightfully about the holes he had made in the door. She said outright all that her rage suggested and held no insults back. To me she said nothing at all, but Madame Kruse whispered in my ear that the Empress knew I had advised against boring the holes in the door and took it kindly of me.

At the beginning of spring we moved from the Winter Palace to the Summer Palace. The Grand Duke now began to take lessons in violin playing, at first from the musician Wilde and later from another by the name of Pierri. He was very enthusiastic about music and often gave concerts in his chambers. He had a good ear but did not know a note; in spite of that he played throughout his life in all the concerts that were given merely by virtue of his good ear. He took great credit for his music; at bottom however he understood only the first elements. The musicians knew this perfectly but they let him talk and do as he liked because they derived their profit from it.

One Saturday, May 24th, during a concert of the Grand Duke's, I retired for a moment to my chamber, and as it was very hot I decided to open my door, which led into the great hall of the Summer Palace to the right of the throne. It was just being decorated and was full of work people. The Empress was in Czarskoe Selo but was expected home that evening. I saw at a distance an attendant of the Grand Duke by the name of Andrei Tchernishov, for whom he had a great partiality because of his good looks. I called him and spoke with him four or five minutes, during which I stood on my side of the open door and he stood in the hall. When I turned around, I saw standing behind me the Chamberlain, Count Devier, whom the Grand Duke had sent to fetch me to listen to an aria. Count Devier confessed to me several years later that he had been ordered by the Empress to spy upon our footsteps and to keep a watchful eye on everything that Andrei Tchernishov did. I closed the door, followed Count Devier, and the evening passed away.

The next day, Sunday, we went to church. As I came out of mass my attendant Timofei Yevreinov handed me a note from Andrei Tchernishov saying that he and two cousins of his, who were lackeys at the Court, had just been ordered to set out for Orenburg as Lieutenants.[17] Yevreinov added: "He does not dare to enter the apartment of the Grand Duke again; but in case the Grand Duke and yourself wish to see him, he is in the vestibule between your apartments and the audience chamber of the Grand Duke."

I ran to the Grand Duke and together we went through the vestibule, where we found him dissolved in tears. The Grand Duke was greatly troubled because Tchernishov was banished, and I also. He seemed to have great loyalty for both of us, especially for me. We took an affectionate leave of him and all three of us wept.

This incident caused the Grand Duke and myself to make some troubled observations in the course of the day; within less than a year the second person whom we liked had been banished. All of

EMPRESS ELISABETH
From a painting by Ericsen

our servants were upset. Besides this I felt not at all well. Under the pretext of taking an afternoon nap, which was then quite customary at the Court, I went to bed and wept bitterly.

A few hours later I rose to dress myself for Court. Madame Kruse appeared and announced that Grand Chancellor Bestushev and Madame Tchoglokov, lady-in-waiting and kinswoman of the Empress, wished to speak to me.[18] This visit greatly surprised me. I bade them enter. The Count informed me that the Empress had appointed the lady to be my governess. Forthwith I began to weep exceedingly. I knew that Madame Tchoglokov was considered the most malicious and peevish woman at court. I then told them that the commands of Her Imperial Majesty were absolute law for me, and dismissed them.

I requested Madame Tchoglokov to excuse me to Her Majesty; because of a severe headache, from which I had suffered several days and for which I was to be bled the next day, I was not able this evening to have the honor of paying my respects at court. Madame Tchoglokov went to the Empress and returned after a time to let me know that there would be no court this evening. Besides this she brought as an introduction the pleasant compliment that the Empress had charged her to tell me I was very stubborn (vy deskaty ochen upriamy!). I desired Madame Tchoglokov to tell me why I was accused of stubbornness by Her Imperial Majesty. She replied she had delivered the message which she had been charged to deliver; she did not know the reason and she was not in a position to put questions to Her Majesty. Fresh cause for tears from me!

I strained my memory to discover why it was that I was stubborn. It seemed to me that I had always obeyed most promptly. I did not see the Grand Duke the whole day; he did not come to me and in the state in which I was I also did not go to him. Throughout my life I have known how to conceal my tears, and that from pride. I have never liked to let myself be pitied. Could I have brought myself to reveal the sad state in which I found myself, I might have lessened it somewhat; but my heart was too proud to ask for sympathy, no matter from whom.

The next morning I was bled. Scarcely was my arm bound when the Empress came into my room; the others withdrew and we remained alone. The Empress began by saying my mother had assured her that I was marrying the Grand Duke for love; but she had evidently deceived her and she knew very well that I loved another. She scolded me roundly, angry and excited, without however mentioning the name of him whom I was supposed to love. I was so startled at this unexpected insult that I could not find a word with which to respond. I burst into tears and conceived a horrible fear of the Empress; I saw the moment coming when she would beat me, at least I apprehended it. I knew that in her anger she beat her ladies, her household, often even the gentlemen. I could not escape by flight for I stood with my back against a door and she was exactly in front of me. Madame Kruse who was always very zealous when it came to making trouble had run to fetch the Grand Duke from his bed, that he might be a witness of the scene. He came in his dressing-gown; but Madame Kruse erred in her calculations, for as soon as the Empress saw him, she moderated her tone and talked with him affectionately about indifferent subjects. She spoke no more to me, did not look at me again, and after a short conversation withdrew to her apartments. The Grand Duke retired to his. It seemed to me that he was put out with me.

I remained in my room, not daring to open my heart to a living soul, and felt at the same time as if a sharp knife had been turned within me. Meanwhile I dried my tears and dressed for dinner. When I had finished, I threw myself, worn out as I was, in all my clothes upon a sofa and took up a book. When I had been reading a little while I saw the Grand Duke come into my room; he walked straight over to the window. I rose, went to him, and asked him what was the matter and whether he was angry with me. He became embarrassed and said after a short silence: "I wish that you had for me the same love as for Tchernishov." "But there are three. Which of them am I supposed to love? And from whom have you heard this?" He said: "Betray me not and tell it to no one. Madame Kruse told me that you loved Peter Tchernishov." When I heard this, I was very glad and said to him: "This is a frightful scandal; I have almost never in my life spoken to this lackey. They could better have suspected me of having a partiality for your favorite, Andrei Tchernishov. You know yourself that you are always sending him to me. I have seen him every time I came to your apartment, and have talked with him there; we have both, as you know, always had our jokes with him." The Grand Duke then said: "I confess to you quite frankly, it was hard for me to believe it. What hurt me in the matter was that you had not confided in me if you had a liking for some one other than myself." That struck me as very strange; nevertheless I thanked him for the cordial way in which he spoke with me and it seemed to me that I had allayed his suspicion. I swore to him that I had never thought of Peter Tchernishov, and that I could boldly swear, for it was the truth.

I do not know to this day how they had figured out that he was suspicious, when the elder could have been considered with so much greater probability. For I really liked him, and the Grand Duke himself had given the occasion for it by his preference. He talked only of him, saw only him; in short, he was really the favorite of us both. It was an extremely innocent, youthful attachment, but nevertheless it was one! This Tchernishov was also a very handsome youth; his cousin could not be compared with him. One of the good qualities which we both valued in Andrei Tchernishov was that he could make Madame Kruse drunk when he wanted to; he provided us thereby with the opportunity to dance about to our hearts' content and romp without being scolded for it.

Another person often rid me of Madame Kruse, namely, my purveyor, the merchant Schriever, who very often invited her at my wish to dinner or to supper.

I have every reason to assume that they took much trouble at the time to separate the Grand Duke and myself. For one day shortly afterwards Count Devier told me outright of the Grand Duke's interest in Mademoiselle Karr, lady-in-waiting to the Empress, which he pretended to have noticed. Then again he confided to me the trouble which my husband took for the sake of Madmoiselle Tatishtchev.

Again, a few days later, Madame Tchoglokov announced to me that the Empress would release me in the future from coming to her dressing-room, to which my mother had procured me access. If I had anything to impart to Her Majesty, I was to address the Empress through her in the future. I answered there was nothing I had more at heart of course than to obey always the wishes and commands of Her Imperial Majesty. At bottom I made nothing of sitting around in this room between the chambermaids of the Empress. It bored me and I went there as seldom as was at all permissible.

Several days afterwards the Empress informed us that she was going to Reval and that we were to accompany her. In fact she departed and we also. There were four of us in the carriage, namely, the Grand Duke, myself, my uncle the Prince Bishop of Luebeck, and Madame Tchoglokov. Prince Repnin, his wife, and several gentlemen of the Court, formed our retinue. That of the Empress was however very large.

This journey was extremely disagreeable owing to the terrible heat which prevailed, as well as the slow progress and bad quarters; and then because the hours for departure, arrival, and mealtimes were in no way regulated. The Empress required the posthouses for herself; for sleeping and dressing, rooms were often given us in which bread was baked. From the stoves therefore unbearable heat streamed forth. Or we were supposed to occupy tents, but they always came too late. Never in my life have I had to endure such hardships and discomforts as on this journey in the train of the Empress.

Moreover gloom and boredom reigned in our carriage, thanks to the ill humor of Madame Tchoglokov, who took offense at everything, grew angry at everything, and looked on the dark side of everything. Whatever she said concluded with the words: "I will make a report to the Empress." I accommodated myself to this and simply slept through the entire journey. The Grand Duke endured the state of things much less patiently; he was provoked because, when he wished to play all kinds of little games in the carriage, Madame Tchoglokov said it was not proper. In reality she ran to the Empress with it and made a terrible crime of it. I do not know what answer the Empress gave, but after her arrival in Reval I heard that she had said in her circle of intimates that Madame Tchoglokov had filled her ears with all kinds of laments and childishness; she had complained among other things that we wanted to play little games. But it rested entirely with Her Majesty to employ sensible people instead of such malicious ones.

Finally, we arrived in Reval. All Esthonia was afoot. The entrance of the Empress in Catherinental took place with great pomp between two and three o'clock in the morning [19] during a fearful rain-storm and in such darkness that nothing in general could be seen. We were all in grand attire but as far as I know no one saw us, for the wind blew out the torches and as soon as we left the carriages, we retired to our apartments. I lived upstairs on the left of the great hall entrance.

From the day of our arrival, cards were played for high stakes; the favorites of the Empress, Count Razumovsky and Countess Shuvalov, could not get along without this. Besides, cards were indispensable at a court where the art of conversation was not known, where hatred was mutual and sincere, where slander was wit, and where the slightest serious word was a crime and *lèse majesté*. Dark intrigue was looked upon as worldly wisdom. Of art and science not a word was spoken, for all were wholly ignorant. One could wager that half of the company could scarcely read, and I am not so sure that a third of them had any skill at writing.

Madame Tchoglokov never missed a single game of cards, and when she lost her ill humor grew. There was something else which influenced her also in this direction; her husband, whom she madly loved, was absent. The Empress had sent him to Vienna to announce the Grand Duke's marriage with me to the Court.[20] But the beloved husband returned while we were in Reval. Although he was so much adored, he was not in the least lovable. He was the most puffed-up, most conceited man in the world; he thought himself unusually handsome and clever. He was a silly coxcomb, arrogant and spiteful, and to say the least, quite as malicious as his wife, which was not a little.

During our sojourn in Reval there was a quarrel between the Tchoglokovs and Prince Repnin. The latter was friendly with Madame Shuvalov; the former had been chosen by Count Bestushev apparently because he could not find anyone who was more spiteful. Prince Repnin arranged it so that Madame Shuvalov could speak to me at cards of the unbearable peevishness of Madame Tchoglokov, at whose expense she liked to laugh as she did with every other person whom she happened to speak of in the course of the day. Madame Shuvalov took a great deal of trouble on this journey to shake the confidence of the Empress in the Tchoglokovs; but she did not succeed in displacing them. They had gained a firm foothold and were well protected; they allowed themselves to be guided solely by the advice of Count Bestushev. Yet the Order of the White Eagle, which Monsieur Tchoglokov had brought from Dresden in his pocket without the Empress's permission, had come near to arousing her anger when she heard of it. But Count Bestushev and Madame Tchoglokov smoothed everything over and Tchoglokov received permission to wear the order in Reval.

A few days after our arrival in the Esthonian capital, the Ambassador of the Vienna Court, Herr Bretlach, arrived there. He came to sign, with Count Bestushev, the famous treaty of 1746 between his own and the Russian Court; ten years later (in 1756) this treaty, badly understood and falsely interpreted during the incompetent ministry of Vorontsov and owing to the intrigues of the Courts of Vienna, France, and Saxony, made of Russia, which was only an ally according to the treaty, a party to the war. It was in fact the country which attacked the King of Prussia with all its forces, although it had no difference with him and not a single occasion for war. It was not even officially declared, either from neglect or because they had nothing to write into a declaration of war. It was nevertheless bitterly and stubbornly carried on for six long years. Herr Bretlach, full of triumph over his accomplished task, much fêted and very proud, followed us to Rogerwyk,[21] where every evening regularly, when their political business was finished, he got drunk with Count Bestushev.

The Empress intended to go as far as Riga. The royal equipages had been sent on to the border city and all was being made ready for departure when she suddenly changed her plans and said that she would attend the manœuvres of the fleet and then return to Petersburg. No one knew whence came this sudden change. Yet a secret cause was suspected and dark motives which could not be spoken of. I only discovered the secret two years after I ascended the throne. Early one morning as, according to my custom, I was rummaging in an old chest full of dusty papers half eaten up by rats, I found a long communication in German from a fanatical and crazy Lutheran pastor, who implored the Empress in God's name and commanded her in that of the Holy Trinity, not to go to Riga, where, according to his statement, someone lay in wait to murder her. The madman sent this letter to the Empress at Reval, who became seriously frightened at it and so excited that she returned to Petersburg. The pastor was put into the fortress where he was recognized as a mad fanatic. That was all.

From Rogerwyk, we returned then to Reval, instead of going on to Riga. On the way, the Empress went on a hunt at which her horse reared and she ran the risk of having a serious fall; but we escaped with no more than the shock. The Grand Duke accompanied her upon this hunt. He hunted frequently with Count Razumovsky, who was at that time Grand Master of the Hunt and the favorite of the Empress. I was never invited on these trips, although it was well known that I passionately loved to ride.

So I remained at home and the time hung heavy on my hands, or else I stayed with Madame Tchoglokov, whose talk was all unpleasant chatter. Whether owing to my way of life or to an inward tendency, in any case I suffered from attacks of hypochondria, which often made me weep. I know not whether, in spite of all the pains I took to conceal my tears, they were observed by Madame Tchoglokov or my women; in any case, they summoned Dr. Boerhaave, who was greatly esteemed by the Empress. He advised that I should be bled. I agreed to this and to my great astonishment Madame Tchoglokov proposed a walk in the gardens of Catherinenthal and handed me 3,000 rubles as a present from the Empress. As one can easily imagine, I did not reject either, and really I felt better.

I was very thin at the time and after the severe illness I had passed through in Moscow, Boerhaave feared for seven years that I might become tubercular. It is astonishing that I did not, for I lived a life for eighteen years from which ten others would have gone crazy and twenty in my place would have died of melancholy.

Some time later we returned to Petersburg in the same uncomfortable fashion in which we had come. Arriving at Narva, we did not wish to remain in the city but to spend the night outside in tents. The Empress had driven onward in advance. It had rained the whole night and the water stood six inches high on the spot where the tents were stretched. Whether it was the fault of the damp or only the strain of the journey, or perhaps both, in any case I rose with a sore throat and fever, and a bad headache, and we continued on our journey. I arrived in Petersburg [22] sick, but a few days of rest put me again in order.

Several days later the Court went to Peterhof, where [23] the Grand Duke again trained his gentlemen and lackeys and established, half secretly and half openly, a watch under his windows. We lived in the lower story. The palace was still as Peter the Great had built it. After a few days, the Grand Duke asked the Empress, who was going to Gostilitsy, if we might go to Oranienbaum, which belonged to him, during the absence of Her Majesty. She gave her permission, and now all grew military there.[24] He and his attendants spent the whole day on guard or in other military exercises, while I sat alone with Monsieur and Madame Tchoglokov, Prince and Princess Repnin, and three ladies of the court. This life became unbearable. My only amusement was to play feather-ball with my ladies-in-waiting, while Monsieur and Madame Tchoglokov grumbled in one corner and Prince and Princess Repnin yawned in the other. At last I became reconciled to it; I went hunting all day long with a gun across my shoulder or else I remained in my room and read a book, any one that came to hand. In those days I read romances only; they merely excited my phantasy, which I did not need at all. I was already lively enough and this liveliness was increased by the horrible life I had to lead. I was constantly left to myself and suspicion surrounded me on all sides. No amusement, no conversation, no creature's interest, kindness, or attention helped to alleviate this tedium for me.

We left Oranienbaum and went to Peterhof; [25] there the Empress sent us a message that we should prepare ourselves for communion. That was very peculiar; neither of us took it twice a year and we had taken it at Easter. I did not long remain in doubt whence came this sudden eagerness to send us to confession. When the moment was there, my father confessor, the Bishop of Plescau, asked me whether I had kissed one of the Tchernishovs. I replied to him, "No, my father." "How is that?" he responded; "the Empress has been told that you gave a kiss to Tchernishov?" "That is a slander, my father. It is not true." My sincerity allowed no doubt of what I said, and there escaped from him the words: "What wicked people!" He admonished me to be on my guard and in the future never to give occasion for such a suspicion. Apparently he went to the Empress to report to her what had been said between us. I heard no more from it.

While we were in Peterhof, Count Michael Vorontsov and his wife came home from abroad. He found that his influence had enormously declined. Among other things, he was criticised because the King of Prussia had paid his expenses in his country. But Count Vorontsov was Vice-Chancellor of Russia and could accept courtesies and attentions from foreign courts.

During this whole year I suffered constantly from headache and sleeplessness. Madame Kruse brought me every evening when I was in bed, presumably as a remedy, a glass of Hungarian wine, which I was supposed to swallow regularly for several days in succession. I declined this so-called remedy for sleeplessness and Madame Kruse drank it in my stead to my good health. On arriving once more in the city, I complained about my sufferings to Dr. Boerhaave. He was a very intelligent man; he knew the kind of life I was obliged to lead and my relation to my husband as well as to my environment. He bade me to show him my head some morning before my hair was dressed and felt my skull thoroughly. At last he decided that, although I was seventeen years old, my head still had the formation of a six-year-old child, and that I must take great care and never allow the upper part of my head to get cold. In short, my skull bones had never yet closed up. He said the bones would not close until the age of twenty-five or twenty-six, and that that was the cause of my headaches. I followed his advice and in truth I only lost the perceptible cavity between the skull bones when I was twenty-five or twenty-six years old, as he had prophesied.

After our return to the city, we did not stay long in the Summer

Palace, but moved to the rooms in the Winter Palace which Empress Anna had occupied. The rooms of the Duke of Courland were assigned to Prince Repnin and the Tchoglokovs. As they were so close together, they began to play hazard, which people in those days were quite wild about. The courtiers played with them to be obliging. Madame Tchoglokov liked to win and grew angry when she lost. Cards estranged her from everybody and once she was at odds with anyone she lost no opportunity to harm. Since she had the ear of the Empress, she told her the most terrible things about those whom she disliked. In reality she hated everyone at the outset; she and her husband were all bitterness. Cards gave her the opportunity this winter to inflict harm on many people, and gradually she succeeded in causing the removal of all persons not agreeable to her.

This particular winter was rather entertaining. I was less bored than formerly. My uncle, the Prince Bishop of Luebeck, was nearly always in the Grand Duke's apartments, to which besides a number of young people came who did nothing but romp and play about. Often the Grand Duke and the whole company came to my private rooms and Heaven knows what all that we did there. The most unconstrained members of this circle in those days were Count Peter Devier, Alexander Villebois, Prince Alexander Golitsin, Prince Alexander Troubetsky, Sergei Saltikov, Prince Peter Repnin (a nephew of the Prince who had been assigned to the service of the Grand Duke; he was only an officer of the guard but was admitted, thanks to the protection of his uncle), and many others, of whom the eldest was not yet thirty years old. Blindman's buff was very popular, and we often danced the whole evening; or there was a concert which was always followed by a supper. This even attracted members of the great court.

One fine day this winter, the Empress suddenly had a fancy to order all the ladies of the court to have their heads shaved. The ladies wept but all of them obeyed. The Empress sent them black perukes, badly made, which they were to wear until their hair grew out again. The ladies of the city were instructed not to appear at court without these perukes. They had to wear them over their own hair and looked much worse than the ladies of the court. The hair underneath pushed the perukes upward, while with the ladies of the court the wigs at least were better fitted to their heads. Since the Empress like all the rest had been shaved, which was of course the reason why the ladies had to submit to the operation, I assumed that my turn would come next. But Madame Tchoglokov, who had suffered patiently, announced that the Empress would exempt me because my hair had only just grown out again. For my hair had all fallen out after my sickness at Moscow and my head was at that time as smooth as my hand. I had the most beautiful hair imaginable now; it had natural waves and so it was not curled with irons. As her reason for this benevolent idea, the Empress said that once on a holiday she had not been able to remove the powder from her hair when she wished to appear unpowdered; she had therefore had her hair dyed black and the color would not come out again. I do not know what there was in this story, but everybody knew that Her Majesty was blonde and that she always dyed her hair, eyebrows, and even her eyelashes.

In December the Empress invited us to accompany her on a pilgrimage to Tishvin, where a miracle-working portrait of the Virgin was to be seen. When the day of our departure came, we waited long in the morning for the start. We were informed that the journey had been postponed until afternoon; towards evening we heard that it had been given up for the time being. Everyone was curious to know the reason; inquiry finally brought out the fact that Count Razumovsky was ill of the gout.

About this time Prince Alexander Golitsin, then our Chamberlain and at present Field Marshal, sued for the hand of my eldest lady-in-waiting Princess Anastasia Gagarin, who had lain ill of inflammatory fever for some time. He had just received permission for the marriage from Her Majesty, when the Princess became so much worse that they were obliged to give her the sacrament. Two days later she died. I mourned for her a great deal; she had been amiable and very pretty. The Empress now appointed her elder sister, Princess Anna Gagarin, in her place. She wished to be present at the removal of the body to the Nevsky Cloister; she therefore came to my apartments and from the door she watched the funeral train go down. The Carnival led us to forget the event, and Prince Golitsin consoled himself by marrying Princess Darya, the sister of the deceased.

Every afternoon at six o'clock we had to repair to the great gallery of Her Majesty's apartments, supposedly to pay her our respects there. But we almost never saw her and as a rule we did not meet her courtiers. The ladies came regularly and we spent an hour or two playing cards with them. This sitting in state was the most tedious business conceivable. Twice a week a French comedy was played; now and then but seldom there were masquerades. Still this winter was one of the best in all the eighteen years that I spent this way.

After New Year's the journey to Tishvin took place. We travelled by way of Schluesselburg and Ladoga. The Empress had ordered that all the ladies should wear sable caps on the journey, like those now worn by middle-class women in the provincial towns. Mine was lost, I know not how, on the way, and Tchoglokov procured for me another from a merchant's wife. Arriving at Tishvin, we went with Her Majesty into the cloister where the picture was to be seen. But in truth neither the Empress nor anyone else could see it; it was so black that from neither near nor far could you recognize anything on the board on which it was supposed to be painted. The Empress related reverently at table that the Swedes had once besieged the cloister, but fire had come from heaven and driven them away. They had even abandoned their tableware and the silver platters of the Swedish general were still in the cloister. But they were not shown to us.

We saw a Bishop in the cloister who had lived there in banishment since the days of Empress Anna. I believe that he continued to remain there.

After our return the Empress ordered us to move into the apartments in which she had previously lived, because she had had a wooden wing built against hers, which extended from the corner of the Winter Palace to the moats of the Admiralty. I think they were in a hurry to move us out of our apartments because the cheerful atmosphere which prevailed there displeased the Tchoglokovs, who called everything that was not tedious improper. They were to occupy a low wing beneath my windows which had hitherto served as a kitchen.

Only Prince Repnin stayed in his room. They wished to remove him gradually from us; this intention existed and soon became noticeable. His greatest crime was that he approved of our cheerfulness and encouraged us in it. Count Bestushev and the Tchoglokovs disliked that and knew how to sway the Empress to be of their mind. Although she was disposed by nature to be cheerful, they goaded her passions at every opportunity and especially her jealousy, which could always be successfully aroused.

When we had moved into our apartments of the previous year, new outlooks were opened up. In the first place Madame Tchoglokov gave me to understand that my ladies were no longer to have access to my private apartments,—they seldom came anyhow; that furthermore no gentlemen were to visit me,—but they never came of course without the Grand Duke. But since she had no authority over him, everything remained with him as before. I received this command in the name of the Empress with resignation, but almost with tears in my eyes.[26]

During Lent this year, 1747, the Empress went to Gostilitsy; we had orders to accompany her but Prince Repnin remained in the city. We had dances there and made merry somewhat because the Empress wished it to be so.

After our return to the city, I was informed of the death of my father.[27] I wept a great deal and grieved so profoundly that I fell ill. They allowed a few days for my tears; they bled me and the Empress came to see me. When I was better Madame Tchoglokov came and said: the Empress desired her to command me to cease my weeping; my father had been no king and the loss was not so great. I answered her: "It is true that my father was no king, but he was after all my father; I may then assume it is no crime to mourn for him." She said all kinds of unpleasant things to me; I was silent and allowed her to talk, but I could never forget that. I assume that Madame Tchoglokov probably repeated about what the Empress had said but from stupidity perhaps not in the right context. To the credit of Her Majesty I refuse to believe that the woman reported accurately what she had been told to say; for it does not show a kind heart exactly! This harshness quite perplexed me and I must confess that I cannot think of it to-day without rebellion in my heart. The mourning which I was to wear for my father was reduced to six weeks; and it was to be only black silk. I let them all talk and do as they liked and obeyed silently.

I learned this winter from my servant, Timofei Yevreinov, that Andrei Tchernishov, whom we believed to be on his way to Orenburg or already arrived there and from whom we had had news from Moscow, had been taken before the Secret Chancellory. This Secret Chancellory was at that time the fright and terror of all Russia. This was brought to light in the most accidental way imaginable, which was as follows: A secretary of this Chancellory by the name of Nabokov was riding with his friend, a secretary of the magistrate, on the back of a sleigh in which their wives were returning from mass. He said to his friend, who had invited him to dinner: "I have no time; I must go with my Chief Count Alexander Shuvalov to Rubatshia Sloboda (a country place where the Empress had a castle); there is game there for us." The friend, a relative of my servant, told him this story and they were curious to find out what kind of game this was; so it seems they undertook an excursion thither to visit the manager. While they were there a soldier came into the room to set a gold watch which my servant recognized as belonging to Andrei Tchernishov. A prayer-book also fell into his hands which he recognized and in which he read the name of his former comrade. This discovery made him very uncomfortable. They had been intimate friends; he was dying of fear lest the other by a thoughtless word should draw him into his situation. Beyond all he begged me in God's name to say nothing of this discovery to the Grand Duke, for the latter was very indiscreet. I promised to be silent and kept my word.

I passed as so trustworthy at the time, not only among my people but also in wider circles, that everyone told me frankly what he thought, nor did anyone ever have cause to regret that he had been open with me. Such communicativeness towards me had no bad consequences.

To this habit of mine I owed the confidence and respect of many and I learned thereby a great deal which was useful for me to know. As if before my eyes many characters have unfolded, which I should never otherwise have become acquainted with.

Some time later, when the Empress had gone to the country,—which she frequently did,—it occurred to me one evening after dinner to propose to Madame Tchoglokov, from boredom, that we take a stroll through the new apartments of the Empress, which we had not yet seen. Madame Tchoglokov replied in Russian, "As you will, Kak izvolish." I took this rather ambiguous reply as a tacit consent, and in fact the Grand Duke, she and I made the round of the apartments. We had often been in the old apartments formerly, so I saw nothing wrong in going to inspect the new ones. When the Empress returned, Madame Tchoglokov came to me in her name with a severe reprimand. She told me that the Empress was very angry because I had been so impertinent and bold as to look at her apartments; it showed a lack of respect to cross her threshold without her permission. She used many other similar expressions, no excuses were accepted, and the matter ended in my weeping bitterly. It was now especially to be noticed that the Grand Duke deserted me when I was scolded, and often scolded me on his part in order to make himself agreeable.

Soon afterwards Prince Repnin was removed from the household of the Grand Duke and the Empress made Monsieur Tchoglokov his successor. It was a thunderclap for us. This Tchoglokov, stupid, proud, malicious, puffed-up, secretive, silent, who never wore a friendly look, was an object of terror to everyone, even to Madame Kruse. And yet her sister was first lady-in-waiting and favorite of the Empress, and she had the powerful protection of Lord Marshal Sievers, who with his wife, a daughter of Madame Kruse, was among the intimates of Her Majesty. So even the well-protected Madame Kruse trembled when she heard of this most disagreeable appointment. From this one can judge what kind of man it was that they had given to us. I suppose he had been chosen by Count Bestushev because he could not find anyone more spiteful. In the first days of his activity we were told that three or four pages, whom the Grand Duke liked, had been arrested and led off to the fortress. New cause for terror! Monsieur Tchoglokov forbade the gentlemen to enter the apartments of the Grand Duke, and thus compelled him to sit alone with one or two servants; and if it was observed that he showed greater favor to one than to the others, he was at once banished or sent to the fortress.

In the meantime, the Empress began to speed the departure of the Prince Bishop of Luebeck. She bestowed gifts upon him and his retinue and dismissed him to rule over the Grand Duke's possessions in Germany, as Lieutenant-Governor.[28] A short time previously Count Bestushev, in order to injure the Crown Prince of Sweden (who governed Holstein during the minority of the Grand Duke and was a brother of the Prince-Bishop of Luebeck), had sought a dispensation from the Court of Vienna, the purpose of which was to declare the Grand Duke of age before the time established by the laws of Germany or Holstein. As soon as the dispensation arrived, the declaration of the Grand Duke's majority took place,[29] and he was obliged to dismiss all of his Holsteiners, even those quite unimportant, like Brehdal and Ducker. The Grand Duke regretted most painfully, the loss of his personal groom, Kramer, an orderly, quiet man devoted to him from his birth, who was very sensible and gave him good advice. This dismissal cost the Grand Duke bitter tears. Another one of his attendants was shut up in the fortress.

Thus the Grand Duke was separated from everyone who was even suspected of loyalty to him, and since he no longer had anyone to whom he could pour out his heart, he turned to me. He often came to my room. He knew, or rather he felt, that I was the only person to whom he could speak without having every insignificant word interpreted as a crime. I understood his situation and was sorry for him. I took pains therefore to give him every comfort that depended on me. Often I was bored by the length of his visits; they also fatigued me, for he never sat down and I had to walk up and down the room with him. He walked fast and took long strides and it was not always easy for me to keep up with him and listen in the bargain to his detailed accounts of military matters. He loved to talk of these things and when he had once begun, he could never finish with them. I avoided as well as I could allowing him to see the boredom and fatigue which often overcame me, for I knew that his only amusement now was to bore me in this way without being aware of it.

I liked to read and he read too. But what did he read? Stories of street bandits or romances that were not to my taste. Indeed there were seldom two people so mentally unlike as we. We had no tastes in common; our ways of thinking and looking at things were so different that we should never have come to an understanding on a single point if I had not mostly given in in order not to offend him.

Yet there were moments when he listened to me; but that was always when something troubled him. I must say that this was often the case for in the botton of his heart he was fearful and his head was weak. He had intuition but no judgment. He was very secretive when he thought it necessary, but extremely indiscreet at the same time. This went so far that when he had promised not to speak of a thing, you could be sure that by a gesture, a look, by his attitude or in some other way, he would indirectly betray it. I think these indiscretions and similar thoughtless actions were the reason why they treated all those who served him as I have described. At least I know of nothing else, for I have not seen their hearings, although of course I would only need to take them from the Archives.

Count Bestushev did not think much of Herr Pechlin Vater, the Grand Duke's Privy Counsellor for Holstein. In his hands the Grand Duke had to lay the affairs of Holstein. He was given a certain Herr Bremse, the meanest fellow and the craftiest scoundrel that ever lived.

Thus I had come almost to the Spring of 1747. I must still place in this period the command of the Empress which forbade me to write to my mother otherwise than through the College of Foreign Affairs. It was so: when I received a letter,—it had obviously always been opened,—I had to send it to the College of Foreign Affairs, where these letters were answered, and I could not even suggest what should be written.[30] This decree hurt me very much, as one can well believe; but my mother was much more disturbed by it.

I cannot conceal another adventure which seemed very peculiar to me. While I was in mourning for my father, I met one afternoon, when we had gone as usual to the gallery, the Chief Master of Ceremonies, Count Santi. I addressed myself to him. I was accustomed to draw everyone into conversation, and talked with him a few moments about indifferent subjects. Two days later Madame Tchoglokov came from the Empress with a message that Her Majesty considered it very improper of me to complain because the foreign envoys and ambassadors had not expressed their sympathy to me on the death of my father, as I had done in conversation with Count Santi. I replied to Madame Tchoglokov that I had never thought of such a thing even remotely and if Count Santi had reported that he had lied. But I could swear by Heaven that I had not only not said it but had not even thought it and had not hinted anything of the kind to Count Santi; and that was the absolute truth. Madame Tchoglokov repeated once more that my father had not been a king; I replied to her that I already knew that without her telling me again. She promised to report to the Empress what I had said and informed me then that the Empress would question Count Santi once more and if he had lied she would have him punished. The next day she brought me a paper in which Santi admitted that he might have failed to understand me. But that was out of the question, for in our conversation there had been no reference to ambassadors nor anything of the kind. Count Vorontsov delivered to me later the excuses of Count Santi; he insisted that Count Bestushev had induced him to say something which had never come into his mind. I do not know how matters really stood; in any case this business of the falsehood was very strange.

With the arrival of Spring, we moved to the Summer Palace. I continued to attach great importance to retaining the liking and trust of the Grand Duke. When he was not with me I went into his room with my book and read there while he scraped his violin.

Madame Kruse had gradually grown more obliging since the appointment of Madame Tchoglokov, whose insolence she bore only with an effort. She considered herself of much more importance because she had brought up Madame Tchoglokov. To be sure, this did not speak very well for the educational talents of Madame Kruse. I think, however, she was only good as a duenna; and that is, in the last analysis, the same office as that of Cerberus, who according to the legend is the dog of Vulcan and has nothing else to do but bark all the time. During this summer Madame Kruse's friendship went so far that she procured for the Grand Duke as many children's toys as ever he wanted. He loved this kind of thing quite madly. But he could not venture to play with them in his room without exposing himself to Monsieur Tchoglokov's questions; for he came frequently into his room and would not have failed to question him narrowly as to how and from whom he had received them without his permission. That would have had unpleasant consequences for Madame Kruse, and so the Grand Duke could only play with his dolls in bed. When he had supped for the night, he undressed himself, came into my room and went to bed. I was obliged to do the same in order that my maids might withdraw and the doors could be closed. Then Madame Kruse, who slept next to my room, brought him so many dolls and playthings that the whole bed was covered with them. I let them do as they liked, although I was often scolded because I did not show sufficient interest in this wonderful occupation, which lasted from ten o'clock until midnight or even until one o'clock.

By the terror which they inspired the Tchoglokovs had accomplished a peculiar result. Everybody was united against them because every one feared them on his own account. Every one detested them, only a few stood by them, and still less did people do what they commanded, although they always spoke in the name of the Empress.

When we removed to the Summer Palace, Count Peter Devier and Count Alexander Villebois were removed; the former was Brigadier, the latter Colonel in the army. I think the reason for their removal was simply that the Grand Duke and I talked more with them than with the others; and that they were accused of loyalty to the Grand Duke and myself. This was regarded as a horrible crime and was never forgiven.

It was at this time that the Swedish Ambassador, Monsieur Wolfenstierna, came up to Petersburg. He was really the handsomest man whom one could imagine; everybody and especially the women, though quite innocently, were enthusiastic about his appearance. When I heard them praise him at the table, I did the same; of this again they made a crime. It is my opinion however that one should not scold young ladies for such lightly spoken words. That is the surest way of fixing their attention on someone and putting silly thoughts into their heads, when unnecessary importance is attached to such careless remarks. It is very dangerous to develop feelings that are still unformed, the germ of which however every person brings into the world with him.

From the Summer Palace we went to Peterhof. The Grand Duke no longer dared to drill his people; in Peterhof he amused himself by giving me a military polish. Thanks to his pains, I can shoulder arms to-day as well as the best-drilled grenadier. For hours at a time I had to stand guard with a musket on my shoulder at the door of the room which lay between his room and mine.

When he permitted me to leave my post, I read. My partiality for romances disappeared; accidentally the letters of Madame Sévigné fell into my hands and gave me much pleasure. After I had devoured them, I read the works of Voltaire and never again got loose from them. When I had finished with this reading I looked for something similar, but since I could find nothing like it, I read in the meantime whatever fell into my hands.[31]

At that time it could have been said of me that I was never without a book and never without sorrow, but also never without amusement. My disposition, cheerful by nature, did not in the meantime suffer under these circumstances; the hope of the prospect, if not of a heavenly, at least of an earthly crown, kept my spirit and my courage firm.

The festival of St. Peter was celebrated at Peterhof. The ball took place in the little castle of Monplaisir which Peter I had built and it was planned that we should eat in the open at the fountain of the little park of Monplaisir. The tables had been

2 : DEDICATED TO BARON TCHERKASOV

set up and covered when a heavy rain disturbed the feast. Tables and dishes were then carried into the two low galleries of Monplaisir and we ate there. The table-cloths and napkins were all wet through; the sauce and the meat were swimming in rain water.

Almost the same thing had happened the year before in Reval, when the Empress was staying there. She had had a large table set up in the park of Catherinental at which the entire nobility of Esthonia was to have the honor of dining with Her Majesty and all her Court; towards the end of the meal a mighty downpour put out the candles and drove us from the table.

From Peterhof we went to Oranienbaum. This palace was at that time in a fair state of decay. Nevertheless we lived there. The Empress came with us on horseback, and the Ambassadors of Vienna and England. The former was the same Herr Bretlach of whom I have already spoken; and the second, Lord Hyndford, whom the other with the help of Count Bestushev had made into a complete drunkard. Otherwise he was a very intelligent man, as the English usually are, although they are all strange people. He was a Scotchman.

When Her Majesty had supped at Oranienbaum, she went back to Peterhof for the night. The two Ambassadors and Count Bestushev remained at Oranienbaum over-night, dined the next day with us and in the afternoon drove to the city.

We stayed at Oranienbaum about ten days. The Grand Duke was occupied a great deal with his dogs and I roamed through wood and valley with a rifle. I had my musket carried hither and thither by the pages who accompanied me. One of my pages was Ivan Ivanovich Shuvalov. I noticed that he always sat in the anteroom with a book in his hand and because I also liked to read he attracted my attention. I talked with him while hunting several times; the young man seemed to me to have sense and industry. Therefore I encouraged him in his likings, which were also mine, and prophesied more than once that he would make his way if he went on striving to increase his knowledge. He often complained that his relatives neglected him. He was eighteen at the time, very good looking, eager to serve, very attentive, and seemed to have a gentle disposition. I took an interest in him and praised him before his relatives, all of whom stood in high favor with the Empress. By this I won his gratitude, for he felt that I wished him well, and his relatives began to treat him more attentively. Furthermore, he was very poor. A long time afterwards, when he had made his fortune, which happened very swiftly, he took it kindly of me that I had first noticed him and he flattered me by saying and having others say that I had been the first onward spur of his career.

After Oranienbaum he began to pay court to Princess Anna Gagarin, whom I liked very much at the time. The following year his attachment increased so that he wished to marry her. He threw himself at the feet of his relatives to implore their consent but they would hear nothing of it. I do not exactly know why, for this match would have been good fortune for him at the time. Princess Gagarin was not only an intelligent lady, but she also possessed more than a thousand peasants. It was probably the great difference in age which aroused their opposition. For he might have been about eighteen years at the time and she was at least ten years older.[32] Yet I never learned the exact grounds of their refusal.

From Oranienbaum we returned to Peterhof. Here the Grand Duke had the idea of playing in my room one evening a long uproarious game of blind-man's buff with my maids and his servants. Madame Tchoglokov came and saw the fine performance and put an end to our noisy though innocent amusement; she scolded us all and threatened the participants with the wrath of the Empress. Madame Kruse received her share as well as the rest. She tried to convince her that there was no occasion to threaten us with the wrath of Her Majesty. The whole company waited breathless to see who would win the field; Madame Kruse succumbed and was threatened with dismissal like all the rest, who generally preferred to go to bed very much dejected.

It can truly be said that the chief amusement of Madame Tchoglokov was to be able to scold everyone and utter abusive words. This habit was twice as strong when she was pregnant, and after her confinement she always began anew again. From 1746 until the death of her husband, who died in the year 1754, I never saw her except when she was either pregnant or lying in childbed.

When we were again in the Summer Palace in the city, the Grand Duke and Madame Kruse began to play with dolls again on my bed. One evening when they were quite absorbed in their play, we heard someone knocking on the door of my bed-chamber which had a double lock. Madame Kruse asked who was there and heard the awe-inspiring voice of Madame Tchoglokov bidding her to open. She trembled with fear lest the playthings which were scattered all over the bed might be discovered, and made a great leap from the door to the bed; but the Grand Duke and I had meanwhile hidden all the toys that we could under the bed cover. Madame Kruse quickly brought the rest to safety and went to open the door. Madame Tchoglokov entered, and naturally began to scold because she had had to wait and wanted to know why. Madame Kruse, who was always armed and ready when it came to lying, said that she had to go to her room for the key. Then Madame Tchoglokov asked why we were lying in bed without sleeping. She received a curt reply; the Grand Duke said simply, because he did not want to. Madame Tchoglokov asked a few more questions of the kind and then vanished without discovering anything on which to vent her ill humor and without mentioning the cause of her sudden appearance. But it looked very much as if she had got wind of the playthings and wished to surprise Madame Kruse in the act. The latter did not let herself be put upon; she knew what it was about.

A few days later a palace functionary, a good friend of Madame

Kruse's, whose dishes were much liked by the Grand Duke, was suddenly dismissed. We were both much troubled about it.

At the beginning of winter we were ordered to move into the Winter Palace. The Grand Duke and I, who in obedience to necessity had become inseparable, made a little plan about how we should spend the winter; our secret conference decided that we should remain chiefly in a little cabinet of my apartment which had a lovely view. Previously our icons had hung there. Half of the pictures, which covered the four walls, were to be banished to the store-room in order to make room for a sofa which had previously stood in my dressing-room. The other two walls were not touched and remained covered with icons. Here then, the Grand Duke would scrape his violin or gaze out of the window, but I would read my book or occupy myself with needle-work.

Against this plan with its total innocence, we thought no kind of objection would be made. I therefore ordered my attendant Timofei Yevreinov to arrange my room in the Winter Palace in correspondence with it. It is not clear to me why he reported my orders to Madame Tchoglokov; for I am certain, had he remained silent, the matter would have gone through without opposition. But whether he did not dare to touch the furniture in my room without her knowledge or whether it was only from talkativeness, in any case she learned from him about our plans. She came to me in my room and declared that the Empress forbade me to change the sofa and remove the pictures (which, incidentally, I had hung there the preceding winter without the knowledge of the Empress) and that the arrangement I had planned was as stupid as it was insolent. I made answer that I was astonished that she bothered Her Majesty about the removal of a sofa and that I thought it was not worth while to report such trifles to her.

On this occasion I answered Madame Tchoglokov without making any circumstances about it, quite contrary to my usual habit of bowing and remaining silent, and the exchange of words between us grew rather lively. I believed that I had right upon my side, but Madame Tchoglokov thought she had the power and in spite of all that I could bring forward and say I was obliged to obey.

I do not know whether the Empress was angry with me on this occasion. In any case it seemed as if she was never in a good humor with me, for she seldom did me the honor to address a word to me. Besides, although we both lived under the same roof, and our apartments in the Winter Palace as in the Summer Palace were adjacent to each other, we did not see her for months at a time and often even longer. We did not dare to enter her apartments without being requested to do so, and that almost never happened.

We were often scolded in the name of the Empress for little things which one really would not have expected to make her angry. For this purpose she sent not only the Tchoglokovs but often dispatched a maid or a lackey or some person of that sort to say not only the most disagreeable things imaginable but outright rudeness which often amounted to improperly abusive language.

But in truth no one could have managed more skilfully than I did to omit no act of obedience and respect owing to Her Majesty. The Grand Duke was not quite so easy to handle, yet he was still obedient at that time; to be sure he only came to terms unwillingly and grudgingly. I shall have further occasion to speak of this.

His childishness and indiscretion had already harmed him and robbed him of the respect of the best-disposed people. Once I dared to speak quite openly to him about it; but he took it ill and declared that he wished to hear no more sermons from me; the sermons of the others bored him already quite enough. It may be that I had not begun in the right way to say such serious truths to him. Besides he was always being urged not to let himself be governed by his wife, and that made him suspicious even towards the reasonable things that I might say to him. For this reason he only followed my advice when the sternest necessity compelled him and when things went badly with him. Furthermore, I must admit that owing to the great difference between our characters the advice or suggestions that I was able to give to him did not correspond either to his insight or his character and were never therefore to his taste. I do not think they would have dared to treat me as they treated him, had I been in his place. In the first place, I should have endeavored not to let things come to such a point and further I should certainly have answered with more consistency and firmness than he did.

The wedding of Count Lestocq and Mademoiselle Marie Mengden, lady-in-waiting of the Empress, fell in the autumn of this year.[33] At the behest of Her Majesty I took the bride in my carriage to the Lutheran Church, where the ceremony was held, and from there back to the palace. It had been the same two years before at Count Sievers' wedding.

In general the wedding ceremonies of the ladies-in-waiting were held in carnival time, and many a carnival passed without any amusement other than these weddings, which on account of the attendant ceremonies were not only very tedious but also very fatiguing. They lasted for two successive days until far into the night. Besides this they were so expensive for the young couple that they often swallowed up the dower of the young wife and the newly married pair began their married life with debts.

Several days after his wedding Count Lestocq gave a great supper to the Empress and the entire court. The Grand Duke and I were among the guests.

At that time Madame Tchoglokov married her sister Maria Semionovna Hendrikov to an officer of the guard by the name of Safonov, a handsome man. The Empress made him a Groom of the Bed-Chamber. He was as stupid as his bride was simple. Instead of bringing such a creature into court (she was a lady-in-waiting to the Empress), in every other country the family would have combined to hide them in some secret corner.

This wedding gave rise to a terrible story over which court and city made merry for some time. Scarcely were the two of them married than the young wife complained to her sister of bad treatment on the part of her husband. She insisted that when her husband went to bed with her, he tied her to the bed post, and beat her and abused her. Madame Tchoglokov went to the Empress and complained. The Empress summoned Monsieur Safonov, gave him a scolding, heaped abuse upon him, boxed his ears, and finally sent him to the fortress, where he remained for a long time. His wife was left pregnant and Madame Tchoglokov took charge of her. Some years later the simple-minded person insisted on having her husband back; he was restored to her and they were allowed to breed a race which did not bely the father and mother. How far the woman carried her stupidity the following fine story shows: She was quite astonished at the skill of the mid-wife who, as she said, had prophesied that she would bring either a girl or a boy into the world. She could not understand whence the mid-wife had this knowledge.

This winter I adorned myself a good deal. Princess Gagarin often told me, furtively so that Madame Tchoglokov would not hear (it was, by the way, an unpardonable crime to praise me before her), that I was noticeably growing prettier; it was no doubt my age, for I was eighteen years old at the time. Now and then I encountered flatterers who told me the same. Gradually, I came to believe it and stood before my mirror more often than before.

I had a little Calmuck boy who handled the curling irons very well. Often I employed him twice during the day, when the occasion demanded it. I was tall and had a fine figure, except that it was a little lacking in fullness. I was rather meager. I liked to go unpowdered and had really beautiful brown hair, very thick and beautifully grown. Yet the fashion of going unpowdered was on the decline and so this winter I often powdered. Madame Lestocq told me some time after her marriage that the Swedish Ambassador, Monsieur Wolfenstierna, thought me very beautiful.

I took that in no wise ill of him; only it made me somewhat embarrassed in my attitude when I approached him to draw him into conversation. I do not know whether this was modesty or coquetry,—at all events the embarrassment was there.

Soon after this came the marriage of my chamberlain, Prince Alexander Golitsin, with Princess Darya Gagarin, my lady-in-waiting. There were several marriages this winter and one or two masquerades. The young people of the Corps of Cadets, which was then under the direction of Prince Boris Yussupov, performed a comedy which the Empress had them play once or twice at the Court Theater. "Zaire" was given, and Melissino played "Orosman." He had very beautiful eyes; but the whole company pronounced the French very badly. Osterwaldt played the rôle of Lusignan.

On Twelfth Night, that is January 6th, 1748, I rose in the morning with a bad sore throat, a heavy head, and indisposition in my whole body. Nevertheless I dressed to go to mass and take part in the procession which went to the Neva for the dedication of the waters. But the Empress, although all the preparations had been made for it, did not take part in the procession, as she had always done on other occasions, and she also excused the Grand Duke and myself.[34]

When I went back to my room, I was obliged to lie down, because I took a fever and had already had a high temperature the whole night. When I awoke, Madame Kruse came to my bed; she looked into my face and uttered a loud cry; she said I surely had the small-pox. I had a deadly fear of it; I looked at my hands and my breast and saw that they were thickly covered with small red pimples. The physician Boerhaave was summoned; Count Lestocq, the personal physician of the Empress, came, and they all thought I had the small-pox. My surgeon Guyon said however that it was still very doubtful; it might be some other breaking out, like the measles or what is called in German "rote friesel" and in Russian I believe "lapucha." It turned out that he was the only one who was not in error and I escaped with nothing but the fright.

They took me from my bed into a warmer and more comfortable room, for there was a strong draft in the alcove of my bed-room which was only separated from the vestibule by a thin board wall. Every winter that I slept there I suffered constantly from colds. I must say that Madame Tchoglokov, although it was shortly before her confinement, bestowed the best care imaginable upon me in this sickness. She scarcely left my room, avoided all unpleasant conversation and showed herself in general much milder. Sometimes, though still seldom, she condescended to small favors. I wondered very much at it and the reason, which I shall explain later, remained unknown to me for a long time.

Towards the end of the carnival I left the sick-bed and intended to go to communion during the first weeks of Lent. We, the Grand Duke and I, had been preparing ourselves for several days when Madame Tchoglokov told us with great friendliness that the Empress said we might postpone it until the last week. I replied that, according to the rules of the Church, it was not permissible for me at that time of the month. Madame Tchoglokov replied that she had already made this objection to Her Majesty, but the Empress wished that we should take communion together with her. So I yielded to the wish of the Empress and we gave up our devotional exercises.

Monsier Tchoglokov was obliged by the express command of the Empress to sleep in the ante-chamber of the Grand Duke; he came thither when the Grand Duke went to bed and rose when he was told that the latter was awake. To this day I do not understand the meaning of the rule; it could not have been for the sake of watching the main door of an empty room which had another entrance and that an unguarded one.

Madame Tchoglokov was very fond of one of my ladies, Mademoiselle Kosheliov. She was a great stupid damsel, very ungainly in everything she did, but a perfect blonde, the only thing that could be said in praise of her. The maiden was always with her and Madame Tchoglokov, who was not especially brilliant herself, often laughed at Mademoiselle Kosheliov's stupidity and awkwardness. Since her husband, in consequence of the arrangement above mentioned, slept at home but seldom and then secretly, Madame Tchoglokov had the maiden either sleep with her or in a small bed next to her own. She had rather narrow quarters, as everyone at court had then. Monsieur Tchoglokov came down in his dressing-gown and had nowhere to go except into the chamber of his wife. He found her almost always in bed with Mademoiselle Kosheliov or lying next to her. But opportunity makes the thief and so he took a liking for the stupid thing, which is not to be wondered at, for he had no more sense than she. His wife, who loved him madly, suspected nothing.

My illness came just right for this pair of lovers. Monsieur Tchoglokov was able to convince his wife that it was her duty to nurse me during my sickness; and in order that she might not turn her back on me in a bad humor and possibly come home to grumble, he managed to make her feel more reconciled to me. During Lent, however, Princess Gagarin, the companion of Mademoiselle Kosheliov, noticed Monsieur Tchoglokov's interest in her. The better to conceal it, he arranged that his wife should invite the Princess also to her room. She was a clever girl and soon discovered what was going on. She said nothing about it except to me. I was on my guard not to betray the secret, which incidentally had as its effect that things went better with me than before. Tchoglokov treated many a one with more consideration now; his attention was taken up in another quarter and he was therefore less spiteful than usual.

Towards the end of the fifth week of Lent I requested through Madame Tchoglokov the Empress's permission to go to communion in the sixth week, as I should be prevented in the seventh. The Empress sent me word that she was in the same situation and would take communion with me in the sixth week. The Grand Duke postponed it for himself until the seventh.

In the meantime Madame Tchoglokov was confined. On Friday I went to confession and then went to bed but in the night the expected came to pass. As I knew the Empress was awake, I sent one of my maidens whose sister belonged to the household of Her Majesty, to inform her of what had befallen me. I feared that over and above all I should be scolded because I had erred in my reckoning. But the Empress directed that I should plead illness and stay at home that day. I stayed in bed and complained of pains in my side. So my communion was for the second time postponed, that is, until the last week.

On Wednesday of this week after the evening meal, I had a severe chill, a heavy head, and pains in my whole body, and I was obliged to lie down. In the night I had such a high fever that the maiden whom I had called said that when she opened the curtains the air had struck her as if from an overheated oven. My condition remained unchanged until Easter Sunday; then I rose, and they gave me the sacrament in my bed-chamber. I went to the door, conducted by two chambermaids, and could scarcely hold myself erect. The fever was still the same. My weakness increased in consequence of insufficient nourishment; for in the previous week I had fasted and had only mushrooms in my stomach. After I had received communion I went back to my bed.

The next morning, Easter Sunday, they brought me some bouillon. When I had swallowed it, I rose to have my bed made up and had them take me to the window. I thought that I was feeling a little better and called Madame Kruse. She looked into my face and called my attention to the fact that I was again quite covered with pimples. The physicians and surgeons were summoned. This time they all decided it was the small-pox. I alone would not believe it, because in January they had been mistaken. I was taken again to the room where I had lain the first time, and in reality they saw after twenty-four hours that it was the measles; but so severe that in some places the spots were as large as a ruble and my whole body from head to foot was covered with them. On this occasion I observed that the illness is contagious. I was very fond of a little Calmuck girl, about ten or twelve years old; the child did not stir from the head of my bed and in fact caught the sickness from me.

During this Easter-time Count Lestocq, who was still the Empress's physician, came to see me. He took advantage of a moment when no one could hear him to say: "The Swedish Ambassador sympathizes greatly with you in your illness; he commissioned me to tell you that." As I knew that he was always jesting, I answered in the same tone: "Say to him that I am very much obliged for his sympathy." There was some point in the matter but to this day I do not know what it was. Princess Gagarin also spoke to me about the Swedish Ambassador and his devotion, and that was doubtless the reason why I regarded him more closely than the others; but that was all.

The Ambassador played for high stakes; during the Carnival he won considerable sums from Count Razumovsky and the other gentlemen at court. Everyone up to the Empress wished to play with him, for he was regarded as a skilful and agreeable player.

On the 21st of April (Old Style), 1748, that is, the day on which I entered my twentieth year, I was still feeling rather weak. It seemed strange to me I had grown so old; it did not seem so very long since I was still a child and was treated as such. On this day I did not go out because of my great weakness; also the spots from the measles were still to be seen. It was probably at the advice of the physicians that the Empress had me and the Grand Duke come to Czarskoe Selo at the beginning of May.[35] I had a severe cough left over from the measles. The palace was then under construction, but it was the work of Penelope;[36] what they built one day they tore down the next. The palace was six times torn down and built anew from the ground up to the roof. The bills are still in existence for the 1,600,000 rubles and more which it cost. Besides this the Empress put a great deal of money out of her own pocket into the building, and there are no reckonings for that.

We remained in Czarskoe Selo eleven days. At first the Empress allowed her gentlemen to dine and sup with us in our downstairs apartment, whenever she ate alone, which was almost daily. This was very pleasant for us but the Grand Duke spoiled it all by his reckless behavior. From association with servants and lack of good society, he had acquired the habit of vulgar, common speech, which when employed even jestingly was received in well-bred company as a coarse insult, especially by small-minded people who attach more weight to the words than to the sense. One day General Buturlin dined with us and made the Grand Duke laugh a great deal. In the gayest of humors the latter doubled over his chair in salvos of laughter and let himself go so far that he cried out in Russian: "Oh, this son of a bitch will kill me with laughing; o, etot sukin syn menia umorit so smechu segodni!" I was sitting next to him and I felt that this expression would not pass without being discussed and criticised, and the blush of shame rose to my cheek on his account. Buturlin was silent; there were several gentlemen from the great court at our table, three-fourths of whom had, to be sure, heard nothing, because they sat too far away. But Buturlin reported the incident to the Empress, and she forbade her gentlemen to visit the Grand Duke again and sent word to the latter that no one else should come to him because he did not know how to receive company.

Buturlin never forgot the words, and shortly before his death, which occurred in the year 1767, he said once to me: "Do you remember the business at Czarskoe Selo, when the Grand Duke, as he then was, called me 'a son of a bitch' at a public dinner?" One can see from this what consequences a stupid, carelessly uttered word can have. It can never be made good again. And yet it was really nothing more than the rashness of a young man who let himself be carried away by his hilarious humor, who was compelled by circumstances to keep bad company, with which he was locked up by his precious aunt and her factotums. In reality one should have pitied the young man rather than have carried a grudge against him!

During the eleven days that we spent in Czarskoe Selo I went bird-hunting twice a day in a cabriolet. The sojourn in the country and the spring weather did me good.

We then returned to the city, and towards the end of May the Empress commanded us to follow her to Gostilitsy, the country place of Count Razumovsky.[37] We had already been there during Lent and the little wooden house where the coasting begins had pleased us very much. Count Razumovsky thought he was doing us a favor to lodge us in this little house, which had fine air and a beautiful view. We too were very happy about it. The upper story which we occupied had besides the stairway chamber a small salon and three rooms; we slept in one, Madame Kruse in the other, and the third was the Grand Duke's dressing-room. The Tchoglokovs and the rest of our court lived downstairs, partly in the house itself and partly round about in tents.

Herr Bretlach, Ambassador of the Court of Vienna, took his departure at that time.[38] In order to show him respect and partly too because the country place lay somewhat on his way, the Empress permitted him to come thither. For his reception she ordered all the ladies to wear short pink skirts over hoop-skirts, over that, full skirts, still shorter, of white taffeta; with this white hats, lined with pink taffeta, which were turned up on both sides and half-way covered the eyes. We looked quite mad in this mummery, but in the end it was all only to obey.

We walked, played, and supped until six o'clock in the morning of the 25th of May, when Herr Bretlach took leave and we went very tired to bed. I was sleeping quite soundly when Tchoglokov's voice awakened me at eight o'clock in the morning. He had broken the lock on the glass door of our sleeping-room and ordered us to get up as quickly as possible because the foundations of the house were giving away. The Grand Duke made one leap from the bed to the door. I inquired of Tchoglokov first what that meant for I did not understand whether there was danger or not. He requested me again to get up as quickly as possible; he would not leave the house without me. I bade him withdraw in order that I might rise; he did so and I dressed rather quickly. I drew on my stockings, a petticoat and a skirt, and went to wake Madame Kruse, who lay in another chamber in deep slumber and whom nobody had remembered. Then I waited until she had got up and put something around her, seized a small fur and said: "Forward! Let us go now." Scarcely had I uttered these words and set my foot across the threshold of Madame Kruse's chamber, when we heard a noise as if a man-of-war were let loose from the staple. Madame Kruse cried: "An earthquake!" We wished to hasten but we had taken only three or four steps when the floor beneath our feet rose and fell like waves in a great storm, so that all three of us, Madame Kruse, myself, and a chambermaid who had joined us, fell flat on the heaving boards and were severely hurt.

In the meantime a Sergeant of the Preobrashensky Regiment by the name of Levashov, who had come up to rescue me, came through the door of the room opposite the spot where we lay on the floor. He held fast to the door with one hand so that he would not fall, and the floor became a little quieter. He came to me and took me in his arms; he was in fact a great strong man. By chance my glance fell upon the two stoves which rose half-way up the wall and formed a very sharp corner. Fortunately no stones were loosed, for they would then have fallen together and we should certainly have been crushed or at least severely hurt. I could still see through a window which opened on the precipice that at least half an arshin [39] of the slide was above us. The day before the house had been about that height; this represented then the approximate distance which we had travelled with the house, which had sunk half an arshin if not more. Levashov wished to descend the stairs with me but they fell in before us. Several servants now climbed by hook or crook over the ruins and bore me forth, passing me from arm to arm across the wreck, until they brought me at last into safety.

The Grand Duke and Tchoglokov were there. The latter thought me lost, seemed at all events to be more disturbed on account of the reproaches which he might meet because he had not brought me out with him than by the misfortune which had overtaken me. His wife, much frightened, was with him; also Mademoiselle Kosheliov, half dead. The Grand Duke spoke not a word; he regarded the drama which went on before his eyes without showing in any way what kind of impression it had made on him. He was very pale and seemed to be not yet quite awake.

From outside you saw nothing of the house. No wooden house could have slipped more neatly from its foundations than had ours. It was wholly unhurt; a little hill had arrested its descent and that was perhaps the reason why it did not fall toward the opposite side. Four rows of stones (called *plita*) had come into view on one side beneath the house and lay scattered on the grass.

But terrible was what we saw coming out of the house. The first thing that struck my eye was a woman whom they brought out with blood streaming down her face. I wished to hasten thither to see who it was but Tchoglokov held me back by the arm. He said I might be crushed; one could not be sure but that the house might not yet fall in. At last I heard that it was the Princess Anna Gagarin, severely wounded; her nose was slit open and the skull was broken in several places. They sent at once for a priest, who gave her absolution on the grass, and then turned her over to the hands of the surgeon. The number of wounded and killed was large. Sixteen persons, who were employed on the slide, partly workers, partly peasants, had perished in the cellar. In the

2 : DEDICATED TO BARON TCHERKASOV

kitchen the hearth had fallen on three persons who lay beside it; one was killed, the other two were wounded; they died soon afterwards. Mademoiselle Kosheliov's maid was injured in the head by the same stove which had fallen on the Princess Gagarin. Besides this all the stoves in the lower story had fallen in and many persons had received less serious wounds and injuries.

The misfortune might have been much greater had not a remarkable accident arranged that Sergeant Levashov, who brought me out, had come over from Oranienbaum, where he was engaged on the buildings. He was sitting by the sentry waiting for Tchoglokov to awaken when he heard a strange cracking in the house where all lay in the deepest slumber. He questioned the sentry. The man told him that this peculiar cracking had been going on all night. Levashov suspected evil; he went to waken Tchoglokov and communicate his fear. Tchoglokov had just time enough to get up, when the house began to totter.

While we were still looking at the sad picture, Tchoglokov was summoned to the Empress, who was staying in the house of Count Razumovsky several hundred paces from our little house. Tchoglokov hastened thither and left us with the wounded on the grass.

Soon the Empress sent for us also. When I entered her presence, I did what I thought was the best thing possible in asking Her Majesty to grant a favor to Sergeant Levashov who had borne me from the house. But she looked askance at me and said not a word. Immediately afterwards she asked me if I was very much frightened. I said, "Yes, very much." That displeased her still more and Madame Tchoglokov obtained with difficulty permission to have me bled. They were angry with me the whole day; I will die upon the spot if I knew why. It must have been because I did not notice that they wished to look upon the whole occurrence as a mere bagatelle. But the shock which all had received was so great that one could not regard the event with calmness.

Our host, Count Razumovsky, was in despair. In the first moment, he seized his pistol and wished to take his life. He wept again and again in the course of the day, and at dinner he drank from a large glass, while the cannon thundered, to the downfall of the host and the welfare of the imperial family. The Empress burst into tears and all those present were staggered. He emptied his glass and everyone sprang up from the table; it was impossible to pledge him or empty the glass. The misfortune had gone to everybody's head.

The Empress could not conceal her distress over the condition of her favorite. She had him closely watched; before all she was afraid that he would get intoxicated for he was naturally inclined to that and in his cups was vicious. He was often unmanageable and raving. This man, at other times so gentle, was one of the most powerful when intoxicated. They were afraid that he would do violence to himself and bled him in the course of the day, whereupon he became quieter.

In the afternoon I lay down but the slightest noise made me tremble and start up out of my sleep, so severely had the shock of the morning affected my nerves. Several months after the accident I was still in the same condition. When I rose from my bed towards six o'clock in the evening, I noticed that I had a quantity of blue spots on different parts of my body; among others an especially large one in the hollow of the right side which was also painful, not to speak of my arms and legs which felt as if they had been beaten.

Madame Kruse and Mademoiselle Sytin, the maid, who had hastened to our assistance and had fallen with us, were just the same. I have, by the way, never known a more perverse maiden than the last mentioned and I believe that many a one in the lunatic asylum is not half so mad as she. Prince Semyon Meshtshersky married her soon afterwards. She fancied she had done me a great service when she came to me that time and asked for her reward at the time of her marriage. That was not exactly mad; she was right in the long run. Instead of placing herself in safety outside of the house, like the others, she had come to me and in recognition of this I gave her a good dowry. Her chief madness consisted in imagining that she resembled me and could imitate me; she insisted that everyone took her for me when they saw her at the window or met her on the street. But that was not possible, for her style of hair-dressing alone distinguished her from all others. She was always comically made up, painted herself besides, and was as lean as a skeleton, so that even I, who was at that time anything but stout, could pass for portly in comparison with her. Besides there was no resemblance in our faces and just as little in our figures.

On May 26th, we left Gostilitsy early in the morning to return to the city. On account of her injuries, which were rather dangerous, Princess Gagarin was very carefully transported. Her condition sincerely troubled me for I was very fond of her. I saw her on the way and although she had been forbidden to speak on account of her wounds, she found an opportunity to tell me that the Empress had sent several servants of Count Razumovsky to the fortress because of the accident with the house.

When we were again in the city,[40] we heard that they had traced the accident to the fact that the house was built in the autumn of 1747 on half-frozen earth and that the foundation had been laid at the same time. The architect had set up six or eight posts in the vestibule to support the house and had expressly forbidden anyone to touch them before he returned from Ukrainia whither he had been sent. The posts made a bad impression and disfigured the vestibule. When the Court came to Gostilitsy during Lent, the steward of Count Razumovsky (who was incidentally a nobleman and a relative of Vice-Chancellor Bestushev) was so thoughtless as to have the poles removed. As it was winter and the ground was frozen, it had no consequences for the moment. But when the ground thawed in May, the house met with the fate I have described. Yet it may be assumed that the architect also was not free from blame, for I have heard that he built two wooden stables, one in Gostilitsy and one in Ukrainia, both of which suffered the same fate.

According to the proverb, every misfortune serves some purpose. The ruin of the house caused such alarm that all the palace buildings which had not been improved for a long time were investigated a few months later, among others Peterhof and Oranienbaum. I shall have further occasion to speak of this.

In June of this year, Chevalier de Sacromoso of the Maltese Order came to Petersburg and was received with high honors. He found an opportunity to tell me that he had various commissions for me from my mother which he had written on a small roll of paper and which at the first court day he would slip into my hand as he kissed it. I told him I should die of fear lest someone should notice it, for I was closely watched. He answered: "Leave that to me and fear nothing." My heart stood still when I thought of the note which he would give me. At last the terrible Sunday came, and I saw that, after Chevalier de Sacromoso had kissed the Grand Duke's hand and while he was making his bow before him, he put his hand into his coat pocket. He brought forth a small paper roll as long as the breadth of two fingers and allowed it to slide into my hand as he kissed it, in the presence of the Grand Duke, the Tchoglokovs, and many others. I must say to this day I do not know why they did not see it. My heart was beating as if it would burst; I took the tiny roll and in order not to drop it I stuck it into the glove of my right hand which I carried in my left. I would not have dared to put my right hand in my pocket from deadly fear that someone might notice I had put something in it. Sacromoso certainly played a daring game, no matter how innocent that matter was. They would at least have driven him from the country with insults and disgrace if he had aroused any suspicion and they would have locked me up and guarded me more strictly than ever.

When I found myself alone in my room I read in secret what was written on the dangerous bit of paper. It informed me that my mother was in deadly anxiety because I no longer wrote to her, and she wanted to know the reason why; she also wished to know whether she could have Courland for my brother. Then she wished to hear particulars about me.

A few days later during the weekly concert in the Grand Duke's apartment, I approached the orchestra. A musician, Gaspari, who played bass, said to me without turning his head: "Monsieur de Sacromoso charged me to give you his respects and begs you to let me have your answer during the next concert." I replied: "Very well," and went away.

I was in great embarrassment to know how I should obtain paper, pen, and ink. For I did not dare to keep writing materials in my room; they would have asked me why I needed it. I did not like to arouse suspicion; what was I to do then? I was always reading some book or other, and in pretty nearly every book there is at least one sheet of white paper. So I tore a white page out of my book. In order to obtain a pen, I had a collection of silver and gold trinkets brought to me under the pretex of selecting presents for my people,—for which they were always greedy and which they were therefore handy in providing for me, and I bought a silver pen, a so-called endless pen, in which an ink-holder is fixed. Now I had everything except ink. In order to procure that I addressed myself quite openly to my attendant, who filled my pen with ink.

When I had collected all that was needful, I set about writing my dispatch. It was not long; I wrote as concisely as possible what I thought I should reply to the questions of my mother; I told her that I was forbidden to write; Courland was not for my brother because it had been decided that they could get along without a Duke of Courland. As far as I was concerned I was fairly satisfied and happy.

At the next concert I went up behind Gaspari and slipped the note into his pocket. But Sacromoso wrote to me again through the same channel and demanded more detailed information for my mother. So I wrote another letter and sent it to him. A few days afterwards he took his departure.

On St. Peter's day, I had lain down in the afternoon on the sofa in my room and had gone to sleep. The Grand Duke came in and since it was in those days a great crime in his eyes to sleep in the afternoon or get up late in the morning—he could not abide either—he scolded me thoroughly and I burst into tears. The only reason that I know why he could not endure it was that this usage had introduced in the court and in society habits of idleness, sloth, and laziness. Although the Grand Duke did not follow it, he none the less spent his whole day in idleness.

I dressed and went to the ball. When the Empress appeared she came up to me and asked why my eyes were red. My eyes had not seemed red to me; otherwise I should not have gone out. I tried to smile and assured her it was an accident; but she said in a very kindly tone it could not be so and begged me to tell her why I had wept in the afternoon. But I feared that the Grand Duke would regard this as if I had complained of him to his aunt. She reassured me on this point, however, because she comprehended my embarrassment. She anticipated me by asking me to tell her what had happened; the Grand Duke should know nothing about it. So I told her the circumstance; whereupon she shook her head and said the Grand Duke was stubborn and peevish. My frankness pleased her and she treated me better than usual the entire evening. Some one or other of my people, I know not whom, must have told her of my quarrel with the Grand Duke and she had wished to bring out the truth.

We went to Peterhof and from there to Oranienbaum.[41] Tchoglokov had the roofs and the floors of the palace tested. It had been built and occupied by the famous Prince Menshikov, and after his banishment it had served as a Marine Hospital, until the Empress presented it to the Grand Duke. I believe the palace had never been improved since it was built. It was discovered that the beams were so decayed that they would not have lasted a single month without giving way.

So we dwelt this summer in the lower wings and on the left of the court and ate in a tent which was set up in the middle of the court.

I arose every day at three o'clock in the morning in order to go hunting before the heat of the day and every afternoon when the weather was fine I went hunting. When I had followed this way of life for several days and just at the time of the greatest heat, I felt so wretched that I feared inflammatory fever. I complained to my surgeon Guyon; he wanted to know how I spent my time and I informed him. He thought my condition came from the fact that I did not sleep enough; I should not rise so early. I followed his advice and was better.

It was rather strange that while in the city I was so strictly watched, in the country I enjoyed the greatest freedom imaginable. When I left the house, as for example on these morning excursions for which I arose at the first dawn of day, I had only one hunter with me, and often, though not always, one servant. The reason for that was solely the laziness of my guardians. It was easy to get the better of them, if they only feared making some kind of effort. Walking was especially hard on them, for they preferred to sit always in one place, particularly Tchoglokov, who in spite of his youthful years, was very fat and clumsy in body and in spirit.

Besides this, since his flirtation with Mademoiselle Kosheliov had begun, he had a great deal to do at home. His wife too could not walk; she was always pregnant and always concerned about her olive skin. All the others took more pleasure in sleeping than in following the calling of an Argus. And so I went about alone.

We returned to Peterhof [42] and were quartered in the upper rooms of the castle which Peter I had built. It still existed at that time, but they had begun to build on both sides of it the two enormous structures of stone which now seem to crush the little house. The Tchoglokovs, several ladies-in-waiting, and the rest of our retinue dwelt below our apartments in the same building. Only Madame Kruse, as duenna, was housed upstairs next to my bed-chamber.

The Empress with her retinue occupied the rooms of the new and the old Monplaisir; the former had just been built. When the Grand Duke was tired of scraping his violin, we played two-handed *l'hombre* to relieve the tediousness of the afternoon. I did not take much pleasure in it, because I had only to choose between losing or being scolded. We played high; I played better than he and more prudently. Often I had to lose to avoid the abuse which always followed when I won.

One afternoon as we were passing the time in this way and I had already been scolded a great deal, I went at last from the Grand Duke's apartments into mine to get my breath. There I found Madame Kruse skipping and dancing in the most joyful excitement. I asked her the reason for her great joy. She took me by the arm, led me into a room where we were alone, and told me she had noticed since yesterday that Madame Tchoglokov was constantly going back and forth to Monplaisir and that vice-versa people from there were continuously going back and forth to the Tchoglokovs'. She had grown curious and had likewise gone over, under the pretext of visiting her sister, who as first lady-in-waiting and favorite of the Empress lived next to the apartments of Her Majesty in Monplaisir. There she had heard that the dismissal of the Tchoglokovs from our household was being talked about. The Empress was beside herself with anger at Monsieur Tchoglokov; she had learned that Mademoiselle Kosheliov was with child and by him. She had sent for his wife and told her all. The wife was, to be sure, furious with her husband whom she had hitherto loved madly and who had now betrayed her; but when the Empress gave her the choice between separating from her husband or leaving the court with him, she was so magnanimous as to plead for him and move heaven and earth to appease the wrath of Her Majesty. Out of consideration for her numerous family, she did not wish to separate from him, and she insisted that the whole affair concerned herself and no one else. She had even tried to deny all to the Empress. But on the day before, while we were at court with the Tchoglokovs, the Empress had sent Madame Izmailov, her favorite, to Mademoiselle Kosheliov, who for several days had represented herself as ill and whose rotundity we all noticed, in order to induce her to confess her condition. After much conversation and many tears, the latter had confessed; thereupon the Empress had called Madame Tchoglokov back again and had reprimanded her properly for trying to deceive her. The latter had replied, she had herself been deceived, which was of course a fact. At this the Empress called her a simple-minded fool and a stupid idiot. In short Her Majesty's anger with the Tchoglokovs was so great that the court counted on their banishment at any moment. With the Tchoglokovs naturally everything was topsy-turvy; the wife felt herself seriously injured and spared him nothing. She was by nature choleric and excitable and when she once began, she did not soon stop again; and one might say that it gave her the greatest pleasure to say disagreeable things, once she had struck that tone. Monsieur Tchoglokov, it was said, had gone so far as to fall on his knees before his wife; she had declared that she would forgive him, but he need not expect that she would love him as ardently as formerly. Only out of consideration for her large family did she remain with him.[43] On the whole Madame Tchoglokov conducted herself throughout the whole affair sensibly and firmly and showed withal a certain magnanimity of which no one up to that time had thought her capable.

Madame Kruse begged me for Heaven's sake to preserve the greatest silence about what she had told me. For if they found out that she had informed me of all that, she was lost. She bade me urgently to say nothing to the Grand Duke. Everyone repeated this request on all occasions when confiding anything to me. I promised all that she asked and begged her to let me know the end of the story, whose final catastrophe, as we all hoped, would be the removal of the Tchoglokovs, which we both alike ardently desired. This wish we shared, furthermore, with everyone who had anything to do with these malicious people. She promised me to visit her sister as often as she could without rousing suspicion and she kept her word. I was entranced at the prospect of getting rid of the Tchoglokovs.

Because I knew that it would delight the Grand Duke also, I went to him and told him, without mentioning Madame Kruse's name, how matters stood, adding however that if he let out the least thing about it, he might thereby prevent the dismissal of the Tchoglokovs. He promised me to be cautious.

Besides our way of living at Peterhof gave me fair security that his first joyous excitement would pass before the opportunity to babble could be offered.

Meanwhile we received orders to return to the city. It was indeed time, for our apartments threatened to fall in. If one passed through my dressing-room, the whole floor rocked; and by its small convulsions we could see that the beams were either too thin or else rotten. As I was still anxious because of the accident in Gostilitsy and the condition of the floor and roofs in Oranienbaum, I sent for Count Fermor, who was then in charge of the buildings and told him of the matter. He promised me to have everything investigated. This was done and it developed that the beams were in the same condition as in Oranienbaum.

Yet the real reason for leaving the place was not the bad condition of the palace; this only served as an excuse. Our departure was resolved on in order to remove Mademoiselle Kosheliov from court without noise and sensation. The Empress had commanded her to return to the city with her aunt, the wife of the Lord Marshal Shepeliov (through her husband also an aunt of Madame Shuvalov,[44] the favorite of the Empress.)

2 : DEDICATED TO BARON TCHERKASOV

Madame Shuvalov scorned these relatives, who were all simple-minded people of the lowest origin, for Madame Shepeliov and her sister,[45] Mademoiselle Kosheliov's mother, were of Finnish descent. After the conquest of Finland they had come to the court and there they had done washing for the children of Peter the Great; then they had swept the rooms, and had gradually risen to be chambermaids. Monsieur Shepeliov, at that time Denchik of Peter the Great, had married one of them and Kosheliov, a groom of Empress Catherine's, had married the other. The men made their fortune in consequence of their long service in the reign of the Empress, to whose relatives they had been assigned by Emperor Peter the Great. During his life-time these relatives lived in Czarskoe Selo, which they never left, so that nobody ever saw them. When the Czar died, it caused great amazement that Empress Catherine had a couple of brothers and a couple of sisters of whose existence nothing had been known up to that time.

They were not the kind of people whom one could show in the fine world, for they were all drunkards and block-heads, and one could notice in every way their low origin.[46]

The reader will excuse these slight digressions; I shall perhaps make them often when they contribute some interesting anecdote or my memory recalls something of the kind.

On the way from Peterhof to Petersburg, we met our riding horses. The Grand Duke and I mounted ours; Monsieur and Madame Tchoglokov remained in the carriage. They were not in the best of humors. So we felt less constrained with the attendants who accompanied us, and on the way all spoke quite openly of Mademoiselle Kosheliov's adventure and the critical situation of the Tchoglokovs. Peter Saltikov and his brother Sergei were with us. They talked like the others, but no one, not even his brother, knew that Peter Saltikov, who, though a chamberlain, was bantered by the entire court because of his stupidity, would report all that he heard to the Tchoglokovs. Madame Tchoglokov rebuked every one the next day for this talk. No one doubted then that Peter Saltikov was the betrayer and his brother rebuked him; his parents did the same. Again he went to the Tchoglokovs and told all; and I think it was this and the endeavors of their protector, Count Bestushev, to raise their fallen stock, that induced the Empress to leave them in their posts undisturbed. The whole thing gradually sank into forgetfulness in spite of the sensation that it caused at the time.

Madame Kruse was the first one to discover that the influence of the Tchoglokovs was not as much reduced as we had thought. Her many trips at Peterhof from the upper palace to Monplaisir during the excitement of that time had not escaped Madame Tchoglokov. Besides this they were not on a good footing with each other and already there had been more than one passage between them. Madame Kruse wished to show me one day how to cut Dutch linen in order to make chemises. Madame Tchoglokov came in, found this improper, and told her the next day in the name of the Empress she had to leave the court. She retired to the home of her son-in-law, Lord Marshal Sievers. I regretted her removal, for her attitude toward me had greatly improved. The Grand Duke missed her still more; the playthings with which she always provided him had made her very valuable to him.

A few days afterwards Madame Tchoglokov brought me in the name of the Empress Madame Vladyslav, called also Prascovia Nikitichna. She was the mother-in-law of the chief secretary of Count Bestushev and wholly devoted to him. She was however a woman of spirit and good manners, and knew how to enlist people on her behalf. This woman pleased me from the very beginning. By somebody or other, I no longer know by whom, I had been advised to be very cautious with her, because she was said to be as insincere as she was fascinating and entertaining. I took warning; I observed her and treated her with prudence. From the first day she neglected nothing to set herself right with me. With the Grand Duke, she wished to do the same, but he had a great prejudice against her. Her greatest fault for him was that she was a Russian, and the second, that she displaced Madame Kruse, who came from Holstein.

He was passionately fond of the little corner of the earth where he had been born. He constantly occupied himself with it. At the age of twelve or thirteen years, he had left his native land; his phantasy grew heated whenever he spoke of it, and since nobody in his household, beginning with myself, had been in this country so marvellous by his accounts, he told us daily stories about it which almost put us to sleep but which we were supposed to believe. He grew angry when he saw that he was not believed.[47]

The connection between human vices and virtues is one of the most peculiar things imaginable. Who would have thought that the love of the Grand Duke for this corner of the world would gradually make him into one of the worst liars that ever was on earth? I saw it with my own eyes imperceptibly increasing, though not without fighting steadily and with all my strength against the disgraceful, harmful tendency, as I call on God and all those who may know about it to witness. But nothing could restrain him; on the contrary, the older he grew the more he became angry and enraged by opposition which only made him the more stubborn. Finally his blindness went so far that he was self-convinced that the lies which he invented and spread abroad were incontrovertible truths. Besides his quite excellent memory assisted him in lying. Whatever he had once related, he would tell again with the same accompanying circumstances which he had brought out the first time, with possibly the difference that by repetition his accounts were extended and ornamented with new particulars not before included.

One of the facts which contributed the most to degrade Madame Vladislav in his eyes was her piety,—something which he never forgave. Also she had a little lamp before the icons in her room, which he could not endure although it was in keeping with the practice of our church, for which however His Imperial Highness had no sympathy. On the contrary he fancied that he held fast to the Lutheran religion in which he was brought up. But at bottom he adhered to nothing at all, and he had no conception of the doctrines or the moral teachings of the Christian religion. In reality I have never seen a more completely atheistic person than himself, who nevertheless trembled before God and the devil and still oftener despised them both, according to the occasion and his humor of the moment.

On St. Alexander's day, I took it into my head to put on a white dress which was trimmed with wide Spanish lace of gold. In this costume I appeared at court without suspecting what consequences it would have. When I was in my room again, the Empress sent me word through Madame Tchoglokov that I should take off my dress; it was not suitable for me to wear on this day a dress that resembled the costume of an order. I begged the Empress to pardon me and said to Madame Tchoglokov that it had never once occurred to me that my dress was like the garments of the knights. Madame Tchoglokov said I was right and advised me to put on another for the afternoon, which I did. In fact my dress, with the exception of being white in color, had nothing in common with the uniform of the order, which is also white and trimmed with silver lace, with the jacket, lining, and facing in fiery red. I wore the ribbon of the Order of St. Catherine. Perhaps the Empress had found my dress more beautiful than hers, and that was the real reason why she commanded me to take it off. My precious aunt was much given to such petty jealousies, not only in relation to me but to all the other ladies also. She had an eye especially on all those who were younger than herself. She carried this jealousy so far that one day, before the assembled court, she called Madame Narishkin, wife of the Grand Master of the Hunt, whose beauty, splendid figure, distinguished bearing, and exquisite taste in dress had become an annoyance to her, and in the presence of the whole company cut from her head with a pair of scissors a charming ribbon decoration which she wore on that day. Another time she cut from the foreheads of two of her court ladies half of their frizzled locks, under the pretext that she did not like this style of hair-dressing. I refer to young Countess Yefimovsky, who later married Count Ivan Tchernishov, and Princess Repnin, subsequently the wife of Monsieur Narishkin. The young ladies insisted that Her Majesty had cut off a little skin with the hair.

In the autumn of this year, when we were again in the Winter Palace, there came from France a Madame Launoy, who had once belonged to the household of the Empress and her sister Anna. She had followed the latter to Holstein and from there had gone to her fatherland. In the first days the Empress seemed much occupied with this woman and she believed herself really on the way to becoming the favorite of the Empress. Her Majesty showed her to everybody, obviously favored her, and devoted herself a great deal to her.

In the evenings the Empress assembled the entire court in her private rooms and there they played cards and gambled. Once as I entered the apartments of Her Majesty [48] I approached Count Lestocq and addressed him, but he said: "Keep away from me!" I thought that he was jesting; he often said to me: "Charlotte, hold yourself up straight!" by this playfully referring to the way I was treated. I was about to answer him with this expression, but he said, "I am not jesting; keep away from me!" That hurt me and I said: "So you flee me also!" He replied: "I tell you to leave me alone!" A little disturbed by his looks and words, I left him. Two days later my servant said as he dressed my hair, "Yesterday Count Lestocq was arrested and it is said that he was taken to the fortress." [49] The mere name of this place brought terror to everyone at the time. He begged me not to let it be seen that I was informed of this fact. I kept my promise but was very much disturbed about the matter for Count Lestocq had always given me his friendship and confidence. I knew Count Bestushev's enmity towards him and regarded this as the source of everything disagreeable which was done to me; knew also that he stimulated the uncordial attitude of the Empress towards me.

I went to church and on the way I met Vice-Chancellor Vorontsov, who was then the intimate friend of Lestocq and the bitter opponent of Count Bestushev; his influence had suffered under him and had greatly fallen. As I gave him my hand to kiss, I said cautiously, "What will come of it?" He shrugged his shoulders and shook his head without giving me an answer. In the evening at court I learned that Count Bestushev, General Stephan Apraxin, and Count Alexander Shuvalov had been appointed commissioners to give Lestocq a hearing. The affair lasted until our departure for Moscow, which was fixed for the middle of December, and not a trace of it came through. A few days after our departure we heard that the Empress had presented the house of Count Lestocq to General Apraxin and from that concluded that the affair must be ended. It was even whispered that in spite of all the investigations nothing against him had been brought to light. Nevertheless he had been banished and all his property had been confiscated.[50] The Empress was not strong enough to do justice to an innocent man; she would have feared his resentment, and for that reason no one, guilty or innocent, came out of the fortress during her reign, without at least being banished.

At the beginning of this winter, my servant Yevreinov dug out again his old friend Andrei Tchernishov. Along with the Grand Duke's pages, of whom I spoke at the beginning of the year 1747, he had been held in the so-called Smolny Dvor, an old barrack of Her Majesty from the time when she was still a Princess. I say barrack because it was a wretched little wooden house on the spot where the young ladies' seminary now stands. I had a Finnish maiden [51] who swept the room and made the bed. This girl was betrothed to a relative of Yevreinov and in order to be able to marry him she accepted our religion and received the name of

Catherine Petrovna; I had been her god-mother. Her sister served the Empress in a similar capacity.

Her betrothed dwelt in the house of Countess Bruce opposite the palace. On St. Andrew's day, Tchernishov made his guards and comrades drunk, took an *izhvoshtchik* and drove to the residence of the fiancé of Catherine Petrovna; the three had planned the affair several days before. The maiden went thither and brought me a long letter from him, in which he told me of his adventures during the last two years. She could only speak freely with me when I sat on my night-stool. I stuck the letter between my garter and my leg, and when they were going to pull off my stocking, I put it the moment before in my sleeve. I did not dare to leave it in my pocket for fear some one might search it. I read the letter when all were asleep, answered it, and sent him money and other trifles which he perhaps might need. He wrote me several times again and I answered him through the same channel. This all went on without the knowledge of Timofei Yevreinov who would have scolded us severely if he had known it. But I learned to attach a high value to Catherine Petrovna because of her way of acting. We took the most careful pains to conceal all that we knew.

The girl was gay and lively, and since Madame Vladislav scolded less than Madame Kruse my people at least breathed a little more freely. The girl had a natural tendency to all kinds of apishness. Among other things she could imitate wonderfully the walk of Madame Tchoglokov when she was in the family way. For this purpose she tied a great cushion underneath her skirt in front and made all of us laugh when she waddled through the room.

All went well until the end of the year when we set out for Moscow. I will save this journey for Part Three.

NOTES

[1] Journal of the Court Quartermasters, 1745: "August 22. At 10 o'clock in the morning the gentlemen of the Court and the foreign ambassadors as-

158 CATHERINE THE GREAT : MEMOIRS

sembled in the apartments of His Imperial Highness and extended their congratulations to His Imperial Highness. At 12 o'clock noon Their Imperial Highnesses deigned to proceed by carriage from the Summer Palace to the Winter Palace, where Her Imperial Majesty condescended to receive them.— Her Imperial Majesty deigned to leave the new Summer Palace and arrive at the Winter Palace at the beginning of the 9th hour. After the arrival of Her Imperial Majesty the ball began."

[2] Journal of the Court Quartermasters, 1745: "On the 26th of August in the 7th hour the ball was opened with four quadrilles in masks, each consisting of 16 couples, altogether of 136 persons."—Narrative of the Princess: "On the 26th towards evening we returned to the Winter Palace. There was a ball in dominos, that is, in four quadrilles, each of 16 couples, the leaders of which were the Grand Duke, the Grand Duchess, my brother, and myself . . . Her Imperial Majesty and all those who did not take part were in customary dress. . . . The same quadrilles assembled again on the 27th with their leaders in the Summer Palace."

[3] The Princess writes to her husband: "The Grand Duchess commends herself to you but has no time to write, as she is still so newly married that she and her husband can scarcely force themselves to be apart from each other for a quarter of an hour."

[4] Catherine writes, January 20, 1767, to Frau von Bielcke: "Nothing is so bad as to have a child for a husband. I know what that means and I am one of those women who believe that it is always the man's fault if he is not loved. I would have gladly cared for mine if it had been possible and if he had been so good as to desire it."

[5] This is the great knight-errant of the Catalans, whose travels were described by Mossen Johanot Martorell in "Tirant lo Blanch, Valencia, 1490." A French imitation of this book was written by Count A. Cl. de Caylus: Histoire du vaillant chevalier Tiran le Blanc. Londres (Paris, about 1737).

[6] Journal of the Court Quartermasters, 1745: "September 8. Her Imperial Majesty deigned to go from Gostilitsy by way of Ropsha to Peterhof; . . . on the 9th of September from Peterhof to Czarskoe Selo, . . . on the 10th of September . . . to St. Petersburg."

[7] Journal of the Court Quartermasters, 1745: "September 28. At the conclusion of dinner in the third hour of the afternoon Her Highness, the Princess of Anhalt-Zerbst, deigned to leave the Summer Palace and set forth on her journey. At the same time Their Imperial Highnesses travelled to Krasnoe Selo as her escort. . . . His Highness, Prince August, accompanied her as far as Koskovo."—Bustushev-Ryumin writes to Count Vorontsov, October 6, 1745, from St. Petersburg: "On the 28th of last month, in the afternoon, Her Highness, the Princess of Zerbst, set forth on her journey from here. Their Imperial Highnesses accompanied her to Krasnoe Selo and Prince August to Koskovo. Her Imperial Majesty deigned to present her, before her departure, with fifty thousand rubles in cash and two chests filled with Chinese objects and damask; to the Groom Latorff she gave five thousand rubles and a sable skin and to Fraeulein Khayn, four thousand rubles and a diamond brooch."— The Princess writes to her husband: "Our farewell was very touching; it was

almost impossible to take leave of Her Imperial Majesty and this great monarch on her side did me the honor to be deeply moved, so that the courtiers present were also deeply affected by it. Innumerable times, farewell was said and finally this most gracious ruler, with tears and expressions of tenderness and kindness, accompanied me to the stairway."—But a dispatch of the English Ambassador Hyndford dated October 1st, 1745, reads: "When she said farewell, she fell at the Empress's feet and begged her with a burst of tears to forgive her if she had in any way offended Her Majesty. The Empress told her that it was too late to think of that now, and that if she had always been so humble it would have been better for her."

[8] Journal of the Court Quartermasters, 1745: "September 30. In the middle of the 2nd hour of the afternoon Her Imperial Majesty and Their Imperial Highness deigned to betake themselves from the new Summer Palace to the old Winter Palace and take up their residence in the latter. As they arrived in the Winter Palace, a salute was fired."

[9] Journal of the Court Quartermasters 1745: "September 15. Court Quartermaster Nesterov was charged to announce that Her Imperial Majesty had deigned to appoint that, from now on throughout the winter, on the week days specified there shall take place at the Court of Her Imperial Majesty the following: Sunday—Court; Monday—Intermedien; Tuesdays—Court Masquerade; Thursdays—French Comedy."—Count Bestushev-Ryumin writes to Count Vorontsov, January 23, 1746, from St. Petersburg: "We have at present carnival, and masked festivities . . . have begun in such a way that they are held on specified days in the houses of the first and second rank, at which our Most Gracious Autocrat and Ruler with the Most High Imperial family and the Court deign to appear. Also the Generals and the nobles are invited so that from three to four hundred masks are assembled."

[10] Among Catherine's letters to Grimm in her own handwriting, a page was found (behind the letter of Dec. 7, 1779, Jan. 2, 1780) with a *Chanson* which ridicules the wooden houses:

> Jean bâtit une maison
> Qui n'a ni rime ni raison;
> L'hiver on y gèle tout roide,
> L'été ne la rend point froide;
> Il y oublia l'escalier,
> Puis le bâtit en espalier.

[11] Dispatch of the English Ambassador Hyndford, April 12th, 1746: "Count Bruemmer's fall approaches. The Grand Duke has advised him to ask for his dismissal; if he does not do that he will be driven forth with insults. . . ." A dispatch of the French Ambassador d'Alion said, as early as December 10, 1745, ". . . He has great trouble to maintain his position."

[12] Bruemmer was dismissed May 21, 1746.—Count Bestushev-Ryumin writes to Count Vorontsov from Petersburg, June 17, 1746: ". . . His Imperial Highness has offered them as a reward for their services an important post in Holstein. . . . but instead of accepting this high favor with gratitude, they requested their discharge from the service of His Imperial Highness, where-

upon, with the august consent of Her Imperial Majesty, leave was granted them the following day . . . and they will, it is hoped, presently depart from here."—Stehlin remarks in his Memoirs: "The Grand Duke dismissed his former Lord Marshal Count Bruemmer and his Lord High Chamberlain Bergholz and offered them a post in Holstein. But they did not trust him and declined it. They received through Grand Master of the Hunt Count Razumovsky a yearly pension from the Empress, the first gentlemen 3,000 rubles and the second 2,000 rubles, and chose Wismar as their residence, where Count Bruemmer died within a few years." According to Buesching's account (1789) Bergholz erected a tombstone in St. Mary's Church at Wismar to Bruemmer "who died there in 1752 in needy circumstances."

[13] Count Bestushev-Ryumin to Count Vorontsov, from St. Petersburg, March 14, 1746: "The news has lately arrived that Princess Anna is dead."—She had died March 7th, after the birth of a son (Alexei Antonovich) February 27th.

[14] Journal of the Court Quartermasters, 1746: "March 21. Toward the end of the 10th hour Her Imperial Majesty and Her Imperial Highness the Grand Duchess deigned to repair to the Alexander Nevsky Cathedral to attend the burial of the Princess Anna. His Imperial Highness the Grand Duke was not well."

[15] A note in Catherine's handwriting preserved in the state archives: "Anecdote: The Czarina Prascovia Feodorovna, consort of Czar Ivan Alexeivich, was descended from the house of Saltikov. She had three daughters: The oldest, Catherine, was married to the Duke of Mecklenburg; the second, Anna, married the Duke of Courland and later became Empress; the third, Prascovia, died unmarried. The Czarina was morose and *difficile* in character; her daughters were badly brought up and were always at odds with each other and their mother. Toward the end of her life, the latter had the whim to curse all of her daughters. When she lay dying, Peter the Great begged her to take back the curse; when he could not achieve that, he cast himself upon his knees and implored her to forgive them. Only in favor of the Duchess of Courland did she allow herself to soften; the other two and their houses she cursed to all eternity. The youngest had no descendants except an illegitimate daughter who remained entirely unknown. But from the eldest sprang the unfortunate family of Princess Anna of Brunswick, whose son was dethroned and came to an unhappy end in the Schluesselburg. The four other children, namely, Catherine, Alexei, Peter, and Elisabeth, are still in Kolmogory with their father, Prince Anton Ulrich of Brunswick. I write this October 18, 1772. Prince Ivan was weak minded. I saw him in the year 1762; besides this, he stuttered. One of his brothers limps, the other is hunchbacked; one daughter has melancholia, and the other has temporary attacks of insanity. One can therefore say that the Czarina's curse on this unhappy family has been fulfilled. All that I have here related is authentic fact, for I have it from eye-witnesses.—Empress Elisabeth had the story from her father Peter the Great; Countess Vorontsov had it from Empresses Catherine I and Elisabeth, and from her husband Count Vorontsov; Countess Rumyantsov knew about it as fact which was known to every one at the time; the Tchernishovs and Buturlins knew about it, the latter being contemporaries of these events."

[16] Dispatch of the French resident d'Alion, May 28, 1746: "Prince Repnin is one of the most amiable Russians that I know and one of the best intellects in the country."
[17] The Tchernishovs were banished May 23, 1746.
[18] Madame Tchoglokov's appointment as Governess took place May 26, 1746.
[19] Journal of the Court Quartermasters, 1746: "July 9. Her Imperial Majesty and Their Imperial Highnesses deigned to arrive at the beginning of the first hour after midnight in the Palace of Catherinental."
[20] Count Bestushev-Ryumin to Count Vorontsov, from St. Petersburg, January 29th, 1746: "Her Imperial Majesty has lately deigned to charge Nikolai Naumovich Tchoglokov with a mission to the Roman Emperor, to congratulate him on the attainment of this high dignity; but he will not depart before the confinement of his wife, that is, in the middle of March." On March 14: "Maria Semyonovna (Tchoglokov) and also the wife of Stepan Feodorovich (Apraxin) have recently given birth to little daughters. And Nikolai Naumovich leaves here soon for Vienna."
[21] The Baltic seaport of to-day.
[22] Journal of the Court Quartermasters, 1746: "July 30. Their Imperial Highnesses deigned to arrive on the 30th in St. Petersburg."
[23] Journal of the Court Quartermasters, 1746: "August 7. Her Imperial Majesty deigned to arrive from Czarskoe Selo at Peterhof in the 8th hour of the evening."
[24] Stehlin's Memoirs: "1746. The Court of the Grand Duke spent the summer at Oranienbaum. There the military mania showed itself for the first time in His Highness."
[25] Journal of the Court Quartermasters, 1746: "August 6. Their Imperial Highnesses deigned to arrive at Peterhof frm Ornienbaum."
[26] Catherine to Frau von Bielcke, August 21, 1766: "From my fifteenth to my thirty-third year I never really had any opportunity to converse with women; I was allowed to have only maids about me. If I wished to speak with anyone I had to go into another room in which were only men. So it is partly due to habit, partly to my taste which was thus developed, that I really only understand how to carry on a conversation with the latter."
[27] Prince Christian August died March 16, 1747.
[28] Count Bestushev-Ryumin to Count Vorontsov, from Petersburg, November 13, 1745: "Also I have the honor to report to Your Excellency that yesterday, with the most gracious permission of Her Imperial Majesty, His Highness, Prince August, was appointed by His Imperial Highness, the Grand Duke, Lieutenant-Governor of Holstein."
[29] The declaration of majority took place June 17, 1745.
[30] The Instructions composed by Count Bestushev-Ryumin May 10, 1746, for persons attached to the service of the Grand Duchess contain the following: "To avoid the suspicion of useless and secret correspondence, Her Imperial Highness can always order the College of Foreign Affairs to compose any letters that are necessary and to bring them to her for her signature."
[31] Catherine to Voltaire, 1763: "I can assure you that since 1746 I have been under great obligations to you. Previous to this I had only read romances but

162 CATHERINE THE GREAT : MEMOIRS

accidentally your works fell into my hands and since then I have never ceased to read them; and I have wished for no other books which were not equally well written and from which I did not derive the same profit."—In a book list which Catherine drew up later No. 1 reads: "Voltaire's Works, without omitting from them the least trifle, for they teach one to exclude the dull kind, and one finds everything in them except dullness, the worst of all."—In her letters to Grimm Catherine admits repeatedly the influence of Voltaire; thus she writes October 1st, 1778: "He is my teacher, or, better said, his works have formed my mind and spirit." On October 17th she orders several hundred copies of his works: ". . . I desire that they shall be a pattern, shall be studied, shall be learned by heart." To compare anyone with Voltaire is with her the highest praise; after reading M. A. von Thuemmel's "Wilhelmine" and Th. F. Nicolais's "Sebaldus Nothanker," she writes, June 23, 1781: "I have this Spring read German books which pleased me very much. . . . Oh, how well German is written in spite of all the critics of German Literature. Confound it, the Germans have learned to use their language like Voltaire, and I believe, Heaven help us, he has taught them to write." And on July 8th, 1781: ". . . and all this is not only enough to make you die of laughing but with a gracefulness which in such trifles I have hitherto found only in Voltaire. If I find many German books like this I shall provide myself with a German library, with the permission of His Prussian Majesty, who has abused German literature so much."

[32] He was born in 1727; she, in 1716.

[33] November 11, 1747.

[34] Journal of the Court Quartermasters, 1784: "January 6. Her Imperial Majesty was pleased on this day not leave her private apartments."

[35] Journal of the Court Quartermasters, 1748: "On the 9th of May, in the morning, Their Imperial Highnesses were pleased to drive to Czarskoe Selo."

[36] Sic.

[37] Journal of the Court Quartermasters, 1748: "Their Imperial Highnesses deigned to drive from St. Petersburg to Gostilitsy."

[38] Journal of the Court Quartermasters, 1748: "May 19. After mass followed the farewell audience of the Ambassador of His Imperial Roman Majesty, Herr Bretlach."

[39] Arshin: Twenty-eight inches.

[40] Journal of the Court Quartermasters, 1748: "May 27. Her Imperial Majesty and Their Imperial Highnesses were pleased to return from Gostilitsy to St. Petersburg."

[41] Journal of the Court Quartermasters, 1748: "July 8. In the third hour of the afternoon Her Imperial Majesty deigned to drive from Peterhof to Czarskoe Selo and Their Imperial Highnesses to Oranienbaum."

[42] Journal of the Court Quartermasters, 1748: "July 20. Their Imperial Highnesses arrived from Oranienbaum at Peterhof."

[43] Tchoglokov left four sons and three daughters.

[44] Countess Mavra Yegorovna Shuvalov was born Shepeliov.

[45] Margarete and Darya Glueck.

[46] Empress Catherine I, really Martha, the daughter of a Lithuanian peasant,

2 : DEDICATED TO BARON TCHERKASOV 163

called Skavronsky, had three brothers and two sisters. Two brothers, Carl and Fiodor, were elevated to Counts Skavronsky in 1724. Her sister Christina married the Lithuanian peasant, Simon Heinrich, who became Count Hendrikov. Carl's daughter is Countess Vorontsov; Christina's daughter is Madame Tchoglokov; both are therefore nieces of Empress Catherine I.

[47] Stehlin's Memoirs: "He often related that once as a lieutenant with a division of Holsteiners he had crashed through a Danish division and put them to flight. People generally assumed that he brought out these very improbable stories only as a joke. But because he told them so often, and especially to foreigners, he came to believe in them himself and no longer looked on them as a joke."

[48] Probably Wednesday, November 9, 1748.

[49] On November 13th, 1748, a ukase was issued: "Count Lestocq is to be arrested owing to weighty reasons for suspicion and guarded in his house separate from his wife." On November 17th, he was taken to the fortress.

[50] Lestocq's property was confiscated November 24, 1748, after he had been put to the torture on the 23rd. The judgment was given November 29 ("unsparing punishment with the knout, life-long banishment to Ochotsk in Siberia, confiscation of all movable and stationary goods"). But Lestocq remained until 1753 in the fortress at St. Petersburg and was then banished to Veliki Ustiug (Gubernia Vologda).

[51] Catherine Petrovna Vojnov.

PART THREE

CONTINUATION OF PART TWO

IN the middle of December [1] we left Petersburg in a heavy thaw and on very bad roads. On the 18th of December, the birthday of Her Imperial Majesty, we were in Tver, where we heard mass, and then journeyed further. The Empress was now ahead of us, although she had set forth after us. The Monarch was accustomed to travel very swiftly and usually the whole retinue remained behind. On the way I learned from the Chamberlain, Prince Alexander Troubetsky, who had taken a place in my sleigh, that Count Lestocq had tried to take his own life in the fortress by starvation and had eaten nothing for eleven days.[2] The Empress had then commanded him to take nourishment and had threatened if he did not obey to find a way of compelling him. To Prince Troubetsky and myself this treatment seemed very barbarous, especially towards a man to whom the Empress owed so much. Prince Troubetsky had learned this through his brother, Prince Nikita Yuryevich, who was attorney-general and might very well know the truth.

As soon as we arrived in Moscow, Princess Gagarin told me in confidence that her brother-in-law and my Chamberlain, Prince Alexander Golitsin, had received orders to go to Hamburg as Ambassador to lower Saxony. That meant a kind of banishment; Count Bestushev did not favor him and had put him down for the Empress as a confederate of Count Lestocq.

In Moscow the Grand Duke and I occupied the apartments which I had had with my mother in the year 1744. We could not have been more uncomfortably housed. Our dwelling consisted of a double suite of rooms; my apartment was on the right and on the left lay that of the Grand Duke. We could not move without disturbing each other.

The Grand Duke had at that time only two occupations: part of the time he scraped his violin and the rest of the time he trained dogs, the so-called Charlots, for hunting. I was obliged to listen from seven o'clock in the morning until late in the night either to the ear-splitting discords which he vigorously drew forth from his fiddle or to the barking and terrible howling of five or six dogs which he cudgeled horribly the whole day through. I must say that I was beside myself and suffered terribly from both kinds of music which tortured my ear-drums from early morning till late into the night. Excepting perhaps the dogs, no one was as unhappy as I was. Yet I read something; I had undertaken at the time to read the "History of Germany" by Peter Barre, Canon of St. Geneviève, in nine volumes quarto.[3] In the course of the winter and a part of the spring I read all nine through.

Immediately after our arrival in Moscow there came such a frost as I have never since experienced. One Sunday the Empress even excused us from going to mass on account of the cold. In order to reach the great chapel we had to drive around the palace in a carriage. The Empress had the habit of changing the furniture of the entire palace. She never left her apartment for a walk or a visit to the theater but something was changed in the meantime, if it was only that her bed was moved from one corner to the other or carried into another room (she seldom slept for two days successively in the same spot), or that one partition was replaced by a new one. Even the doors were always in different places. This time she had thought proper to change the ordinary chapel into living rooms and to house a part of her retinue in the ante-chambers, which had previously formed the connection between our apartments and her own.

During the first days of our sojourn in Moscow I was obliged

GRAND DUKE PETER FEODOROVICH

From a painting by Grooth

3 : CONTINUATION OF PART TWO

to keep to my room, because my forehead was full of pimples and I had a very bad color. I even had to summon Boerhaave, who with the help of talcum oil brought my countenance again in order.

While I was thus confined to my room at the beginning of the year 1749, I heard partly through my servant Yevreinov and partly through Madame Vladislav, who concealed it however from each other, that the Empress was very ill with acute indigestion. The Tchoglokovs said not a word to us about it and we did not dare to inquire after the health of the Empress. That would have been a crime; we should have been asked how we had heard that she was ill, and that again would have brought misfortune to the person who had told us or caused his banishment at least. I told the Grand Duke exactly what my people told me. We both decided to keep silent about it until the Tchoglokovs should speak of it, but they said not a word.

We heard that one day when the Empress was very bad Count Bestushev and General Apraxin had spent the night in the apartment of the Tchoglokovs or had slept there. The Grand Duke and I were disturbed to some extent by the illness of the Empress which they concealed from us; the Tchoglokovs scarcely looked across their shoulders at us. Without permission we did not dare to leave our rooms. We heard that Count Bestushev, General Apraxin, and others on whose loyalty we could hardly count, were constantly holding secret counsels behind locked doors and we did not know what to make of it. The Grand Duke especially, timid as he was, did not know which saint he should pray to. I told him to have courage and bade him to remain cheerful and quiet. I would try to keep myself advised through my people about the Empress's condition, and if she should succumb to the illness I would open the doors for him so that he could leave his rooms, in which he was at present, so to speak, imprisoned. If no other way was left, the windows of our ground floor apartments were so low that in case of necessity one could leap into the street. I told him also that Count Zachary Tchernishov, on whom I thought that I could count, and his regiment in the city, and several corporals of the body-guard whom I mentioned to him by name would not leave him in the lurch. All this quieted him so far that he could amuse himself again in his corner with his violin and his dogs.

After several days of serious danger, during which various things were whispered in every room of the palace, the Empress grew better and everything fell again into the beaten track. I was kept informed pretty accurately two or three times a day by my servant and by Madame Vladislav. The latter had numerous connections with the people of the Empress, in whose immediate circle she had relatives, acquaintances, and friends. Besides this she was closely associated with the clergymen and church singers, and they told her at the three services which she attended almost daily, all that they could learn and she reported it to me with the greatest accuracy.

During her convalescence, toward the end of the Carnival, the Empress ordered that the wedding of two of her ladies-in-waiting, who had long been betrothed, should be celebrated: that of Mademoiselle Skvortsov with guardsman Neronov and that of Princess Repnin with Monsieur Narishkin. The two weddings took place on the same day; at the banquet I sat on the right of one of the brides and on my right accidentally sat Madame Shuvalov, favorite of the Empress. It so happened, because she was very merry and always ready with a jest, that I made bold to ask her about the health of Her Majesty. She replied that she was better, and that on this day she had for the first time sat up in bed. I told her how greatly I had been disquieted by this illness. She received that very well and, being talkative, she reported the conversation to the Empress. The next day we sat at the same table in the same places. She said that she had spoken about our conversation of yesterday to Her Majesty, who had listened without the least displeasure; her recovery was making progress but she was still very weak.

The next day Madame Tchoglokov, snorting with rage, appeared in my room; and since I was with the Grand Duke in the chamber of Madame Vladislav adjoining, she took one leap into the room, turned to me and said that her Majesty was beside herself because I had not once inquired about her during the whole two weeks of her illness and had only spoken of her sickness to Madame Shuvalov when she was already on the way to recovery. Such neglect on the part of the Grand Duke as well as from me, not to inquire about the welfare of the Empress, was unpardonable. I answered Madame Tchoglokov that neither she nor her husband had allowed one word to escape them about the illness of the Empress. She replied: "And yet you spoke to Madame Shuvalov about it!" I said that she had given the occasion, and this was true. Madame Tchoglokov went away finally, after she had scolded some more and said all kinds of things, each of which was more disagreeable than the last.

When she went out the Grand Duke began to scold me because I had spoken to Madame Shuvalov about the sickness of the Empress, for without that it would have been assumed that we knew nothing about it. He went away and was sulky with me the whole day, to which he was inclined by nature; he did this for the merest trifles.

When I was alone with Madame Vladislav, who was more intelligent than the whole company, I burst into tears and said to her, "Just imagine, is it possible to do anything right for these people? In the first place, if I had asked Tchoglokov or his wife point-blank to inquire about the health of the Empress, their first question would certainly have been, how did I know that the Empress was ill; who had told me that. Should I then name you or somebody else? It would have been the surest means of calling down misfortune on the person I mentioned! Neither Tchoglokov nor his wife had hitherto said a mortal word to me about this sickness; this was the first time that Madame Tchoglokov had ever spoken of it. In the second place, how am I to understand that the Empress does not like me to show Madame Shuvalov my interest in her condition, and that she scolds me under this pretext?"

Madame Vladislav was much too sensible to regard my point of view as unreasonable, and said: "The Empress must be told that the Tchoglokovs have never spoken with you about her condition; it was their duty to inform you. The Empress will then understand in what embarrassment you stood, when you had to choose between the two possibilities,—to be scolded because you had asked or because you had kept silence."

She gave me to understand that she would lay it before the Empress, but carefully guarded against saying this openly because she did not wish to admit that she had direct communication with the Empress and served the monarch faithfully by secretly informing her of my most unimportant actions. On the other hand, she managed very cleverly to keep my confidence, which she did not wish to lose, and made it her special study to retain it. The only obstacle for all these bearers of information (who did it out of flattery) was the difficulty of seeing her Majesty frequently. But however cleverly the woman managed it I knew all her tricks and my servant Yevreinov, who feared and disliked her, took pains to inform me of all he could discover about her.

This time Madame Vladislav kept the promise she had given; she did not like the Tchoglokovs who thwarted her desire to dominate. So the Empress learned from her that the Tchoglokovs had concealed her sickness from us, and that when her Majesty afterwards charged them to tell us she did not think it right that we had not inquired about her, it did not occur to them to tell Her Majesty the truth about what had happened.

When the Sovereign was better and again showed herself in public, she came to me one day in court and said: "Why do you

3 : CONTINUATION OF PART TWO

look so sad?" I answered: "I fear that I have offended Your Majesty during your illness; I did not dare to make inquiries because neither Monsieur nor Madame Tchoglokov had ever spoken to me about it." She replied: "I know that; I know also that you were much troubled. We will not speak of it any further," and went away again.

I discovered at this time that Ivan Ivanovich Shuvalov, who had become chamber-page, was rising to the highest favor of the Empress. This discovery delighted me.

Meanwhile Madame Vladislav came to me one fine morning and said that she had been with Madame Tchoglokov and the latter had told her in the name of the Empress that within three days I should marry Catherine Petrovna, the Finnish maiden of whom I was so fond. I had striven with as much care as pains to conceal my liking for the latter.

This was a trick of Madame Vladislav, who in spite of her good nature, could never tolerate people if only once she had something against them.

I was much troubled by this but I made the best of it and married the girl on the appointed day. But since I saw that everyone who was suspected of having only just a little liking for me was taken away, I told Madame Vladislav that as long as matters stood this way I no longer wished to have my maids remain in the same room with me, which was formerly the custom. I preferred that they should remain in my dressing-room and not come to me unless they were summoned, because I wished to avoid bringing misfortune upon them. This new arrangement would prevent my becoming intimate with them. Madame Vladislav did not dare oppose such a definite command from me. For she had made it her task to win my affection and confidence completely and she carefully avoided anything that might in the least prejudice me against her. So she informed the maidens of my wish, and from that time on I remained in my bed-chamber with my book, a pleasure for which I had long waited. In this manner I got rid of all the spies who watched everything even to my slightest glance.

Perhaps Madame Vladislav hoped to take her place with me; meanwhile she would have liked to stick her nose into my books but she knew no French, as did no one else in my environment. My replies were always very laconic; I said quite briefly that once I had read a book I straightway forgot what there was in it.

After our departure from Petersburg, Andrei Tchernishov and his comrades were released from the place where they had been so long imprisoned. The former went to his post at Orenburg. He wrote to me on the journey and Catherine Petrovna sent me the letter by her husband. I answered him and sent him a few hundred rubles.

General Apraxin had bought a new house in Moscow. At that time the Empress thought that even the weather hung on him and Count Bestushev, and the Lestocq affair had strengthened both in their position. In order to demonstrate this clearly before a larger circle, Apraxin invited the Empress, the Grand Duke, and myself to dine at his new house. I have never in my life seen a more brilliant feast. Everything was of the rarest and most magnificent kind; after dinner he threw from the windows handfuls of money to the people who had crowded in front of the house. On this occasion I saw for the first time his eldest daughter, who later married Prince Kurakin; she was fourteen or fifteen years of age and unusually pretty. The younger, now the wife of Chamberlain Talyzin, was a child of six, thin as a skeleton and with a hectic look. One would never have believed that this child could become the colossus with the height and the terrible circumference whom we now know. At that time she suffered constantly from hemorrhages and bleeding at the nose. Towards evening General Apraxin had the blind Prince Michael Dolgorukov come to his house, an old man of nearly eighty years. He was the brother of the deceased Field Marshal of that name and had been a

Senator in the time of Peter the Great. Although he could neither read nor write, he had the reputation of possessing great intelligence and a character more substantial than that of his brother. The Empress received him with great respect; he then withdrew, led away by his two sons. The conqueror of the Crimea, the second son, was at that time only a Colonel.

The next day I heard that the third daughter of General Apraxin had died of small-pox in the night. It gave me a severe shock; he and the whole court knew that I had not had the small-pox. It was strange that he had exposed me to such danger by inviting me to his house. People were constantly coming and going between the sick-chamber and the room in which I remained the whole time. It looked as if I had been invited to the house that I might contract the sickness; I would not like to vouch for the contrary. The least that one can say was that attention and consideration for me did not go very far, when purely out of thoughtlessness and without necessity they exposed me to such a serious danger, and when no one had enough kindness or good-will or human sympathy to protect me against it. But Providence arranged it otherwise; the child died and I escaped from this great danger in the most fortunate manner conceivable. I confess that afterwards I often trembled at the thought.

In the last week of Lent we prepared for communion, Tchoglokov like all the rest. On Wednesday we went to confession and on Thursday to communion. Monsieur Tchoglokov said he was ill on that day and for the rest of the week. We knew well from what he was suffering. When he went to confession the Father Confessor, who was also the Father Confessor of the Empress, had forbidden him to take communion for one year on account of the affair with Mademoiselle Kosheliov. It was whispered that the Father had acted under orders from the Empress, who had been in a bad humor ever since her much discussed vexation with Monsieur Tchoglokov. He had grown thereby somewhat more gentle, yet the couple still possessed sufficient power to do harm. But they could not be helpful to anyone; indeed they had scarcely the desire for that.

Annunciation Day fell this year on Easter Sunday. The Empress had the habit, which I have continued, of rising in the night between Friday and Saturday for early mass and the burial of Our Lord. The Grand Duke as a rule pleaded sickness on this day; so I went alone at night to the Church.[4] When I returned home I thought it would not be worth while to undress and go to bed, since it was a high mass and the mass would be early. But I was deceived in my expectations; on this Saturday I sat on my chair fully dressed from four o'clock in the morning until three o'clock in the afternoon. I did not venture once to ask for a cup of tea, although since Thursday evening I had eaten nothing. Madame Vladislav was very strict in these religious matters, especially in all that pertained to the fasts. I would not have dared to hurt her feelings by asking even for a crust of bread. I slept on my chair and suffered silently.

At three o'clock I was called to mass; I could scarcely drag myself thither and learned that the long delay had been caused by the Empress's going to the bath between early mass and high mass. Madame Vladislav was quite enraged at what Her Majesty had done. How could anyone go to the bath on such a holy feast day as that of the Annunciation? I tell this to call attention to the little that was needed at the time to offend the feelings of our people, the greater part of whom in those days would have felt exactly like Madame Vladislav. She had a great deal of intelligence but was an extreme pietist and very strict in all the little matters. For this reason I have taken care to avoid each and everything to the smallest trifle which could offend the national peculiarity still dominating the masses at that time. I strove all the more to adapt myself, because I knew the old rule which teaches that the neglect of such trifles does more harm on the whole than more essential things. For there are more minds which allow them-

3 : CONTINUATION OF PART TWO

selves to be governed by little things than there are reasonable beings who despise them.[5]

The next day, Easter Sunday, we first attended early mass in the house chapel and later we were sent to high mass in the great cathedral which adjoins the summer house of the Golovin Palace. We thought that we would perish from the cold and returned quite frozen to the house. I remember that I was as blue as a plum when I reached my room again.

About this time Messieurs Pechlin, Bremse, and Bestushev were always at the Grand Duke about the enormous debts which weighed upon Holstein and the yearly deficit in his purse resulting from his outlay. He therefore decided to cut in half the salaries of all those in the service of this country. Thereupon a great outcry arose; nor was this at all to the taste of the three gentlemen above mentioned. Pechlin and Bremse lost in this way half their yearly incomes. But the worst part was that this provision gave the Grand Duke some means at hand to satisfy his creditors, and that was exactly what they did not wish. Count Bestushev wished to remove every occasion for strife between that branch of the house of Holstein which had been transplanted to Russia and that reigning in Denmark, and desired that the Grand Duke would cede Holstein to the King of Denmark. But the Grand Duke's attack of economy did not last long. They knew how to approach him on his weak side: he had one hundred dragoons recruited and the debts remained.

At the beginning of Spring the Empress took us with her to Perovo, a country seat of Count Razumovsky's, two or three versts from Golovin Park.[6] We fared quite well there; we often ate with the Empress. Twice a day we went into the great hall of the castle; there the whole court was assembled, for card-playing or promenading. The Empress drove with us to supper at the country place of Count Sheremetiev and to the mill of the Strogonovs. One day while the Empress and the Grand Duke were hunting with the head of the house, I suddenly had a violent attack of headache such as has never happened since. Madame Tchoglokov proposed that we take a walk; I agreed but the ailment constantly grew worse. I returned to my room and went to bed. Scarcely was I in bed when a violent attack of vomiting began. The headache and the nausea lasted through the night; Boerhaave was called and gave me every remedy possible until I finally went to sleep. The next morning I was bled. The rest of the day I was quite weak, but the illness had no further consequences.

Two or three days later the Empress had a new attack of acute indigestion, by which she had been laid so low the previous winter. She wished to be carried over to her palace. They took her in her carriage, which was driven at foot-pace and stood still every moment. We followed in ours. The whole train was very restless on account of this method of progress; we were almost two hours on the way from Perovo to the Golovin Palace. But the relapse remained no secret for us this time; at our request the Tchoglokovs escorted us daily to the waiting-room of the Empress, where we inquired about her condition. They did not dare to refuse us that. We were not permitted to enter the private apartments of Her Majesty; we remained in her reception room and when some one who had access to her apartments appeared, we asked for information which was given us, whereupon we withdrew.

When Her Majesty was better, she summoned us one day to Pokrovsky to dinner. There were many people there; among others the widow of the Grand Chancellor, Prince Dolgorukov, once the favorite of Peter II. At that time she still looked very well. It was not until several years later that she went to Kiev to become a nun.

The Grand Duke got drunk at this dinner, and after we left the table he began to pay court to the Princess. He would call her nothing but "the beautiful widow" and wooed her with great persistence. This relation lasted during the whole of this year's

3 : CONTINUATION OF PART TWO

sojourn in Moscow; but it did not go beyond soft looks and words, and she treated him just like a child. In fact she had children who were about the same age as the Grand Duke.

After dining in Pokrovsky we took a drive through the Preobrashensky forest. The Grand Duke was on horse-back, but so drunk that he swayed from one side of his horse to the other. There were a great many people in the forest; I sat in the carriage and blushed for him but the situation could not be changed.

At the beginning of May, Madame Shuvalov invited us and Her Majesty to supper. The evening was very joyous; we danced until late in the night and separated in general contentment. A little English dog belonging to the hostess made great friends with me on this evening. The next morning Madame Shuvalov sent me the dog, and this attention pleased me all the more because I was not accustomed to anything of the kind from anyone. I was often scolded and severely snubbed usually without a trace of justice. To expect attention or favors from anyone never came into my head.

Soon afterwards the Empress undertook a pilgrimage on foot to the Troitsa Monastery, and as she covered scarcely more than five versts a day and on many days did not progress at all, the journey lasted over a month. During this time they had us live in a place, situated on the way to Troitsa, which belonged to Monsieur Tchoglokov and was called Rajevo; it was lacking in every comfort.[7] Round about was a thick wood, the place lay in marshy ground and its only ornament was a slimy pond. Nevertheless it seemed an earthly paradise to Tchoglokov, and all because this wretched barrack was his property. For he was one of those men who think that all that belongs to them is wonderful. In spite of this weakness he was always envious of the prosperity of others; whatever made others fat made him lean. As long as we were shut up in that miserable Rajevo, hunting was our only amusement. Every day we rode out hunting. I rode at that time an English ladies' saddle, and when I galloped at full speed,

I received the admiration of the most ardent huntsmen. They put nothing in my way; I could ride as much as I liked, break my neck, too, if I wished; it lay in my own hands.

The only person from the great court who came to Rajevo almost every day was Count Cyril Razumovsky, the brother of the favorite. He amused us well and liked to be with us; but the truth was he took pleasure in conversing with me. Long afterwards, he confessed to me that I was then much closer to his heart than I had any idea of. He accompanied us often on the hunt. Tchoglokov and his wife saw no occasion to object to his visits. They were simple enough to imagine that Count Razumovsky liked their wonderful estate and they felt endlessly indebted to him for that. Because he was so jovial in his disposition, he was as a rule not taken very seriously.

When the Empress came near the Troitsa Monastery, she sent us orders to join her. From my constant riding in the forest I was as sun-burned as a satyr; I had been out of doors the livelong day. When the Empress saw me, she cried out at my sunburned countenance and that evening sent me a face-wash to make my skin soft again. I used it and my dark color in fact went away.

From the cloister we were sent back to Rajevo and continued there our hunting trips until St. Peter's, when we had to return to Troitsa again.[8] Our retinue was very small. The Empress had gone to the Voskresensky Cloister. On the afternoon of St. Peter's day, as it was the day of the saint whose name he bore, the Grand Duke wished to grant himself some kind of amusement. He arranged a ball; but since there were neither dancers nor music, he played the violin himself and my maids and his lackeys danced. This ball almost killed me with its tediousness; I took a book and sat down in a corner to read. He was drunk and did not bother about what I did; otherwise I should not have escaped without a scolding.

From the Cloister we returned to Rajevo [9] again and the hunts were resumed. On one of these occasions, an officer of the Butyrsky Regiment by the name of Asaf Baturin, whom no one knew, made the acquaintance of the German hunters in our retinue; he talked to them about his devotion to the Grand Duke and asked them to give him the opportunity for a conversation with him. The hunters, who were on a very confidential footing with His Imperial Highness and always surrounded him while hunting, reported this to him; and in fact the said officer appeared one day in the forest and introduced himself to the Grand Duke. He declared to him that he recognized no other master than himself, and that the Grand Duke could rely on him and the whole Regiment in which he was lieutenant. The Grand Duke was a little frightened at this unexpected introduction and answered, I believe, nothing of importance. He guarded himself against speaking to me or anyone else about this experience, as well as about the talk of his three huntsmen. His companions had not heard what the officer had said, or at least wished to act as if they had heard nothing. It was only darkly hinted that a man who was either crazy or drunk had spoken to the Grand Duke but no one had grasped the meaning of his talk. Baturin, however, interpreted the silence of the Grand Duke and his consent to the meeting on the occasion of the hunt as a formal agreement and began to contrive in the worst way imaginable a stupid plot to place the Grand Duke on the throne, to thrust the Empress in a convent, and murder all who should oppose his plans. I will leave the account of the discovery of this affair until Fall, for it was then that I first heard of it, and I will then tell how I heard of it, for up to that time I knew nothing whatever about all this.

At the beginning of August, Monsieur Tchoglokov quarreled with Count Bestushev in a way not to be reconciled and I believe the Grand Duke and I gave the first occasion for it. It happened thus. I have already told how, since the misfortune of Mademoiselle Kosheliov and the disfavor of the Empress, Tchoglokov had grown a little more endurable. The refusal of the sacrament in passion week had given renewed proof that the Empress was still angry with him. Also he could no longer rule his wife as completely as before; she was somewhat less obedient than formerly. All this made him dejected. On the other hand, it often happened that the Grand Duke in his cups met with Count Bestushev who was always tipsy. The Grand Duke complained to him about the attitude and manners of Tchoglokov, who was always brusk and disagreeable to him. Count Bestushev said, partly just to talk, partly because he was drunk—perhaps there was also a grain of flattery in it because he wished to be liked and win the Grand Duke's confidence: "Tchoglokov is a stupid churl, conceited and puffed up; but leave me alone, I will put his head on straight!"

The Grand Duke had told me this. I called his attention to the fact that if Tchoglokov knew this he would never forgive Count Bestushev and might well wonder why one whom he regarded as a friend should speak so badly of him. The Grand Duke now fancied he could bring Tchoglokov over to his side if he told him about the conversation with Bestushev. Then he, the Grand Duke, would be Tchoglokov's friend and would replace Bestushev with him; in a word, he would command him in the future if he revealed the falseness of the pretended friendship of Count Bestushev. So my good Grand Duke rejoiced in anticipation at the fine consequences which must follow the betrayal of the secret he possessed. He had nothing more pressing to do than to seek an opportunity to repeat to Tchoglokov the various conversations he had had with Count Bestushev which dealt with him. Tchoglokov was beside himself about it and offended in his self-love.

On one of the feast days Bestushev invited him to dinner as he was accustomed to do. Tchoglokov went but was on his high horse. After dinner, half intoxicated, Count Bestushev wished to talk with him but found him extremely haughty and reserved. He then grew angry in his turn, and their conversation became

3 : CONTINUATION OF PART TWO

terribly heated. Tchoglokov reproached Count Bestushev for the conversations he had carried on with the Grand Duke and for all the ill that he had said of him. Count Bestushev, on his side, upbraided Tchoglokov for his stupidity; for his thoughtless conduct in Vienna where, it was said, he had entertained the Empress and Queen by talking only of his wife and children; and for the affair with Mademoiselle Kosheliov, reminding Tchoglokov how much he was indebted to him for his position and for his protection since this last piece of scandal. Tchoglokov was, according to his nature, the last person who could bear to hear any truth whatever; he became furiously angry and regarded all this as an insult.

General Apraxin wished to reconcile them, but Tchoglokov only became the more stubborn. He fancied that he was necessary and they would run after him. He swore that he would never again set his foot across Count Bestushev's threshold, and kept his word and never went to visit him again. So after this Tchoglokov was the sworn enemy of Count Beshushev, who was never again able to pacify him.

At this time the strong influence of the Shuvalovs on the Empress began. Her intimate relations with Ivan Ivanovich Shuvalov gave the opportunity for it. Aside from this relation to their cousin, the Empress had always given her friendship and confidence to Messieurs Alexander and Peter Shuvalov, who had been close to her since her childhood. Madame Shuvalov had been educated from childhood with Her Majesty, who was of the same age. Her cheerful temperament was agreeable to the Empress, and at certain times she could not get along without her. Yet in her favor there were heights and depths; momentarily the barometer of the Shuvalovs was rising.

They did not esteem Count Bestushev, who was bound by common relationships to their opponent Count Razumovsky. They tried to alienate as many supporters of both Counts as possible, and as they knew that I did not number Count Bestushev among my friends, they showed me secretly all manner of favors, especially the new favorite, who anxiously concealed his pains however in order not to awaken the jealousy of the Empress, which was hard to avoid.

The Empress wished this summer to visit Sofyina, an imperial estate about one hundred versts from Moscow, whose situation was quite famous. The Shuvalovs arranged it that the Grand Duke and I should also take part in this pleasure trip, which really turned out to be none as I shall report. There was not one habitable house. The Empress ordered tents to be put up and the whole court had to camp in them. The day after our arrival the Empress and the Grand Duke went hunting; as the Empress never took me, although she knew that I liked very much to hunt, I remained in my tent, where I could read my book and let the time hang heavy on my hands.

The next day at the dinner hour, we went to the tent of the Empress and found the table covered. A few moments later she appeared and all those present knew by the twitching at the corners of her eyes that she was in a bad humor. When according to her custom, she had kissed the Grand Duke and myself, she began to talk about the dullness of yesterday's hunt, and as she spied the man entrusted with the management of the estate, she said to him in Russian: "If you were not a scoundrel, I should have found it more amusing here. You have apparently been bribed by the neighboring Lords and you do not hinder them from hunting on my grounds. There is not a single rabbit here and if there had been no hunting, there would certainly be a great many." The poor fellow began tremblingly to swear by the most sacred oaths he could think of in order to convince her that no one in the neighborhood had hunted there. But she continued to scold and to threaten.

Then she talked about the good old times when she used to hunt with Peter II and the great number of hares which they had killed every day. From this she went on to talk about the Princes

3 : CONTINUATION OF PART TWO

Dolgorukov, saying the worst possible things about the men who had been close to the Emperor; how they had tried to separate her from the monarch. They led her to recall the kindness and the friendship of the Emperor for her and the enmity which the Empress Anna had for her. She retailed for us her income of those days and said: "Although I had no more than thirty thousand rubles at the time with which to pay my entire household, I still had no debts." Here she threw a glance at me. "I had none because I feared God and did not want my soul to fare to the devil if I should die without having paid my debts." Here I received a second look, and the Empress continued: "It is true that at home I dressed very simply. Usually I wore a skirt of black *grisette* and a jacket of white taffeta; also in the country I wore no costly fabrics." At this point she cast a very angry look at me. I wore on this day a beautiful expensive jacket and was well aware that the Empress took it very ill. Following the example of everybody present I kept silent and listened respectfully without growing excited.

Her Majesty continued a long time in this vein, springing from one subject to the other, here and there giving someone a thrust, but nearly always returning to some prick or other which was intended for me.

When the conversation had lasted three-quarters of an hour, during which she did all the honors while the rest of us paid the cost, there came into the tent a man by the name of Aksakov, a kind of jester but not very funny, whom the Empress had taken into her court. He had a hedgehog in his hat. She asked him where he had been; he said he had been hunting and had caught a strange animal. She wished to know what it was and came near to see what he had in his hat. At that moment the hedgehog lifted its head. Her Majesty had a deadly fear of mice and she thought the head of the hedgehog looked like the head of a mouse. She uttered a terrible cry and ran with might and main to the tent which served as her bed-chamber. A moment later she sent orders to remove the table which had been prepared for dinner. All went away; we dined at home, and received orders in the afternoon to return to Moscow. When I was in my tent Madame Tchoglokov said to me: "You got your share; you understand that?" I said to her: "Yes"; but that I did not know why Her Majesty was angry with me. She said she also did not know. I can swear that to this day I do not know.

In the course of the summer we witnessed the arrival at court of the Princess of Courland,[10] daughter of the Duke Ernst Johann who had resided in Jaroslav since the Empress had recalled him from Siberia whither he had been banished by Princess Anna of Brunswick. The Princess of Courland was not loved either by her father or her mother; she had always had to endure bad treatment from them. When she finally grew tired of the life that she led, she turned to the wife of the local Vojevod by the name of Pushkin. The latter proposed to her that she enter the Greek Church and under cover of this change of religion, she would undertake to bring her at once to the court. The Princess, who was very clever, did not hesitate a moment; she answered on the contrary that she had long felt an inward impulse to do so. Madame Pushkin wrote to Madame Shuvalov about it; then with the consent of the Empress, she took the Princess away from her parents and conducted her to Moscow to the Empress who lodged her in the castle and was her god-mother when, a few weeks later, she entered the Greek Church.[11]

Towards the 5th of September, her name day, the Empress went to the Voskresensky Cloister; we had orders to follow her.[12] There she appointed Ivan Ivanovich as Chamberlain, and from this time on her favor was no secret, so that everybody whispered it as in a comedy. I was very much rejoiced over his elevation in rank, for I wished him all good fortune in those days as his family also knew.

On our return to Moscow, the Shuvalovs brought it about that the Empress should sup with us in Rajevo at the Tchoglokovs.

3 : CONTINUATION OF PART TWO

The evening was very gay and stimulating, we danced until late in the night and then returned to Moscow.[13]

The autumn of this year was especially beautiful. We stayed at Rajevo once more and the Empress sojourned in our immediate neighborhood at Tajninskoye. One Sunday she invited us to dine with her at Tajninskoye. At dinner Her Majesty sat at the head of a long table, which was set up in a tent, with the Grand Duke on her right and me on her left. Opposite the Grand Duke, next to me, sat Madame Shuvalov and next to the Grand Duke Marshal Buturlin. On his right the Father Confessor of Her Majesty had his place. The Marshal, who liked to drink to people's health, made both of his neighbors drunk; that is, the worthy father and the Grand Duke. In his intoxicated state the latter made the most horrible grimaces and cut the most ridiculous and unpleasant capers. I saw that it displeased the Empress and as I then sincerely sympathized with all that concerned my husband, the tears came to my eyes when he conducted himself so indiscreetly at table. Madame Shuvalov saw it and understood my feelings. She gave a signal to the Empress who rose hastily from the table.

In spite of his intoxication, the Grand Duke went hunting with Count Razumovsky and I went back to Rajevo. I had scarcely arrived there when I began to have a violent tooth-ache. I no longer knew to what saint I should pray and suffered terribly. Madame Tchoglokov's brother, Count Ivan Hendrikov, who was present, wished to cure me and I took his suggestion. He left the room and soon returned with a little paper roll and bade me lay it on the aching tooth. I did that but I had scarcely pressed it with my teeth as he advised me when the pain increased so terribly that I was obliged to go to bed. During the night I had a high fever and from time to time delirium.

Madame Tchoglokov was much disturbed by this incident which had occurred in her house and through the fault of her brother. She took hold of him and scolded him properly. She did not move from my bed-side during the night and seemed to be much disturbed. One might say that the longer she was with me, the more liking she had for me, but it was quite unnoticeable and unintentional. It did not happen immediately, but now and then definite signs of a change of attitude were to be seen in Madame Tchoglokov.

The next day, ill as I was, I was packed into a carriage and brought back to Moscow, where my tooth-ache lasted over fourteen days and then only gradually ceased.

During this illness Madame Vladislav made efforts to distract me and she succeeded in this manner. She was, so to speak, an animated archive; she knew the gossip of all the families of Russia from the time of Peter the Great, and even further back. She sat beside my bed and told stories without stopping. She knew also how to talk well and vividly. Through her I came to know the mutual relations of the various families, their kinships to the second and third degree, and a great fund of anecdotes which are often useful to him who knows how to draw the moral. Since I was in no condition to read on account of my suffering, there could have been nothing more instructive for me than Madame Vladislav's conversation, which taught me to know the world in which I lived. And so I found pleasure in it.

Now and then she told me stories of the day. Among other things I learned from her that there was much talk at the time about a marriage between the son of Count Bestushev and the daughter of a Princess Dolgorukov, born Argamakov, with whom Madame Vladislav was very well acquainted and who had very peculiar habits. She often got up in the night and went to the bed-side of her sleeping daughter in order to see, so she said, whether the girl, whom she idolized, might not be dead. Frequently she waked her daughter up to convince herself that her slumber was not unconsciousness. Beside this she was always anxious lest the maiden, who was rich, clever, pretty, amiable, might fail perhaps to get a husband, and she was therefore inclined to give her to the first that came along. At the moment there were three suitors; young Count Bestushev, who was even more eccentric than his mother (and that is saying a great deal) and as much given to drink as his father, none of whose virtues he possessed. The second to enter the lists was Count Skavronsky, a nephew of Empress Catherine I, whose ugliness was equalled by his stupidity. The third, finally, whom the Princess really married, was Prince George Gruzinsky. He was less ugly certainly than Count Skavronsky, but absolutely stupid withal, and this quality stood out all the more because he could speak no language at all except his mother tongue, which nobody in Russia understood except his Georgian countrymen. The poor Princess, who was so poorly provided with suitors, finally decided in favor of the last. I confess that, through Madame Vladislav, I helped to dissuade the mother from the union with Count Bestushev, whom she liked the most because he was the son of the Grand Chancellor who played an important rôle at the time.

Princess Maria Jakovlevna always recognized with gratitude that I had helped to dissuade her mother from the thought of giving her to Count Bestushev, who was a veritable monster in his character and vices. Although she was not happy, she would have been much less so with him. But if ever a woman deserved to be happy she was one. She was truly a rare being, with her great gentleness, her purity of morals, her kindness of heart. It would be harder to say what were the good qualities she lacked than to enumerate her virtues. Never was a woman so universally revered as she, and she had won a high personal esteem in the hearts of all who knew her or had only heard her spoken of. And she would have done so to a still greater degree, had she not died in the prime of life, on the 25th of December, the same day on which Empress Elisabeth died. I mourned for her sincerely, for this excellent woman always showed me in her life-time the most sincere friendship and affection; and had she lived to witness my accession to the throne, which she ardently desired, she would certainly have played an important rôle near me. She was a dependable, sensible, loyal, intuitive, and prudent friend. Never have I seen a woman who united more good qualities. If she had been a man, the world would have rung with her praises.

At this time, the Empress attached the two eldest daughters of Count Roman Voronsov to the Court. The elder, Maria Romanovna, who was thirteen or fourteen years old, became lady-in-waiting of the Empress, and the younger, who was somewhere between eleven and twelve years of age, came to me in the same capacity. The elder promised to be pretty; the younger had no trace of it. On the contrary, she was then very ugly. The pockmarks which she later acquired disfigured her in the way in which we now know her. Both sisters had a dark olive skin which did not make them beautiful. They later found a remedy in various artificial colors.

At the beginning of October I had a severe catarrhal fever and was obliged to keep to my bed for several days. I did not rise until Madame Tchoglokov informed me that the Empress had fixed the wedding of Alexander Alexandrovich Narishkin, the Chamberlain of the Grand Duke, with Anna Nikitichna Rumyantsov for the following day. I declared to Madame Tchoglokov that, on account of the fever that I had had and the weakness that still remained, I could not take part in the wedding. Madame Tchoglokov admitted that I might thereby bring on a relapse and went away. A few hours later she returned with a command from Her Majesty that I should go the next day to the wedding and should also adorn the bride, who would be brought to me for that purpose. I considered the order somewhat harsh, all the more as the Empress had visited me a few days before and had convinced herself of my high fever; my temperature was so high that they feared inflammatory fever. But since the arrangement seemed so very definite and Her Majesty could only have given it with full knowledge of the circumstances, I did not dare to make any reply although possibly my life was at stake. Madame

3 : CONTINUATION OF PART TWO

Vladislav thought the order very cruel and even barbarous, and even said as much to me.

So the next morning at daybreak, I dressed myself as well as I could, although I was very weak. They brought the bride to me and I adorned her. At least they excused me from going to church,[14] but instead of that I had to get into a carriage and drive from Annenhof to the house of the Narishkins on the other side of the Kremlin. My retinue consisted of three coaches and about twenty horsemen. It was very slippery out of doors because a sudden freeze had followed on a heavy rain. There was no time to shoe the horses for the icy weather. We went forward at a foot-pace, but in spite of this there was not one of our horses which did not fall several times in the course of the seven versts which at the least was what we had to lay behind us. To make our misfortune complete, we encountered between the Kazan Cathedral and the Kuriatnaya Gate the entire wedding procession of the sister of Ivan Ivanovich Shuvalov who was being driven to her marriage with Prince Nikolai Feodorovich Golitsin. The horses of the wedding train fell with every step that they took. In the end we took I believe two and one-half hours for the journey thither and just as much for our return. Neither before nor afterwards have I ever experienced anything like this trip, and this day could have well been called the day of somersaults. So far as I know no one came to harm.

I was the first to arrive at the house of the newly married pair; an hour later the rest of the wedding party arrived also. After the supper and ball, the Grand Duke and I were sent to escort the young couple to their apartment. For this purpose we had to pass through the corridors and go up and down several flights of stairs of this great house. Afterwards we withdrew.

This wedding produced just as little in the way of consequences as our own, and our similar situation helped to form the bond of friendship which has long existed between Madame Narishkin and myself. With me the state of things was changed nine years after my wedding day; but with her it is still the same after twenty-four years of married life.[15]

On the day after the ceremony we again visited the married couple. I had a little fever but it passed away and had no further consequences.

A few days later the Grand Duke entered my room suddenly wearing a very troubled look. I saw that he had something on his mind and that it tormented him; but since I had no idea what it was I did not notice it at once. Finally he tried himself to roll away the stone that oppressed his heart. He told me that his huntsmen, on whom he was so dependent, had been arrested and sent to Preobrashensky, where the Secret Chancellory had been since our sojourn in Moscow. That disturbed me but little; but he said it might have serious consequences for him. I then asked him how he happened to have this thought, and he confessed to me that these people had told him of the zeal on his behalf manifested by Baturin, the Lieutenant before mentioned; that the latter had spoken to him while hunting and had assured him of his own loyalty and that of the Butyrsky Regiment, and had declared that he owned him only as his master. Afterwards a good deal had passed between the huntsmen, the Grand Duke, and this officer. The Grand Duke knew that the latter had also been arrested.

I had the impression that the Grand Duke was making only half of a confession and was afraid to tell me all lest I should criticise him for his thoughtlessness. The uneasiness from which he suffered aroused my sympathy; I tried to comfort him, but the matter oppressed him greatly for two or three weeks longer. When he saw that no one spoke of it to him and the affair bore no consequences, he gradually forgot it.

A few years after my accession to the throne, the records of the affair fell into my hands. I found them among the papers of Empress Elisabeth; they had been laid before Her Majesty for

3 : CONTINUATION OF PART TWO

her decision. They were very voluminous and therefore Her Majesty, until her death, had no clear idea of what was in them. She certainly had not read them.

The whole business was perhaps one of the most serious of her entire reign, although it was so thoughtlessly and imprudently concocted. It was, to speak frankly, a conspiracy in all respects. This Baturin had persuaded about a hundred soldiers of his regiment to take the oath of allegiance to the Grand Duke, by insisting that he had received the consent of the latter to allow himself to be placed upon the throne. Under torture he had confessed his connections with the Grand Duke through the mediation of the huntsmen of the latter. A grenadier whom he had tried to enlist had denounced him. The huntsmen were convicted of having introduced him to the Grand Duke; but they had been only lightly questioned.

When I compare the proceedings with the state of terror in which I beheld the Grand Duke and with what I heard him say, I do not doubt that he knew all about it and that his huntsmen did not wish to charge him with it or did not dare to speak the real truth.

Although I doubt whether the Empress ever knew it at all, she certainly knew enough to lose completely the little confidence that she had in him. After this occurrence she refrained from kissing his hand when he came to kiss hers. And in the following years she let him feel her wrath though only indirectly, as I shall describe in the proper time and place.

Count Alexander Shuvalov had Baturin shut up in the fortress of Schluesselburg to await the Empress's decision, which never came. Later, in the year 1770, I sent him to Kamchatka on account of the stupid stuff he wrote and wished to have distributed by the soldiers who guarded him. From Kamchatka he escaped with Benyovsky and many others after murdering the Vojevod of Bolsheretsk and fled across the Pacific Ocean to Macao. I have not given up the hope that some of the wretched fellows will yet return to Europe. Benyovsky has already been there; every one of them deserves the halter at least.[16]

I must do justice to the truth and describe things as they were. After this time I observed that the wish to rule grew stronger in the Grand Duke's heart; it nearly killed him yet he did nothing to make himself worthy of it.

In November, 1749, I had my tooth-ache again. I had to keep my bed and the continuous suffering brought on a high fever. In my bed-room, which adjoined the apartments of the Grand Duke, I had no rest on account of his violin and his dogs. For he would not have sacrificed these amusements if he had known that they were killing me. I succeeded therefore in gaining Madame Tchoglokov's consent to having my bed moved into the third room out of reach of the noise that the Grand Duke constantly made in his apartment. The room that I selected was scarcely suited to anyone who suffered constantly from colds, for it had windows on three sides. I retired with my bed to the fourth wall near the stove, but still between two doors. After I had endured a great deal, I was able to go out again.

We left Moscow in December.[17] On the journey I had tooth-ache again. I was driving in the same sleigh with the Grand Duke; whatever the weather, he would not allow the sleigh to be covered. It was not without difficulty even that I gained his consent to have a little curtain of thin green taffeta hung up in front of me to protect me from the gusts of wind.

At the last station we received an order from the Empress to go to Czarskoe Selo. I arrived there in unbearable pain, which caused me to lose patience. I sent for Boerhaave and bade him to extract the tooth which gave me such misery. He wished to postpone the operation until the next day, but I insisted so that he finally gave in. Guyon, my surgeon, was called and all was prepared for the operation. I had to sit down on the ground, Boerhaave seated himself opposite on my right, Monsieur Tchoglokov

3 : CONTINUATION OF PART TWO

similarly on my left, and they held my hands. Guyon came from behind and seized the aching tooth with his instrument. As he turned it round, I had the feeling that he was breaking my jawbone. But he kept on pulling and brought out a piece of bone with the tooth. Never in my life have I suffered such agony as I did at this moment. It was so violent that after the tooth had been extracted, the tears gushed from my mouth and nose, like water poured from a tea-kettle, not drop by drop, but like a brook which flows without ceasing. I had besides to spit out blood, but I did not lose consciousness.

At this moment the Empress came into my room, from which every one had been banished. She could not restrain her tears when she saw me suffer so. They explained to her what it was about. When I could speak again, I said to Boerhaave that half of the tooth had remained in its place. Guyon wished to convince himself of it and to touch the place I showed him with his finger, but I would not allow him. I learned then from my own experience that the pain from which one suffers often engenders anger against him who causes it. Boerhaave, who evidently knew this, began to laugh, and begged me to allow him to examine the spot and he convinced himself by touching that one of the roots remained in the jaw while the tooth itself had taken with it a piece of jawbone as large as a silver ten sous piece. From the moment when the tooth was out, I felt relieved.

I slept well into the night and the next morning I could drive to the city. The Grand Duke however would not think of having his sleigh closed, although the weather was freezing. On reaching the city, I retired to my apartment and could not go out for four weeks, for my right jaw and the under side of my chin were blue and swollen, as if I had fallen and bruised myself in these places. And so I had come to the beginning of the year 1750.

After New Year, the Empress went to Czarskoe Selo,[18] and we remained in the city. Only a few of the members of the court household had arrived in Moscow.

At that time it was more difficult than now for the nobles to leave Moscow, the city which all of them so love, where sloth and indolence are the chief employments. They would gladly spend their whole lives there, driving about in a decrepit coach extravagantly gilded and drawn by six pairs of horses, a symbol of the false luxury which reigns there, concealing from the eyes of the masses the uncleanliness of the master, the complete disorder of his household and his way of life. It is not unusual to see a richly-gowned lady, in a wonderful carriage with six shabby horses in dirty harness, drive forth from a great court filled with heaps of dirt and trash and belonging to a wretched barrack made of rotten boards. Her unkempt lackeys in handsome livery disgrace her by their uncouth manners. In general men and women become soft in this great city. All that they see and do is sordidness, which would cause the most undoubted genius to pine and fade away.[19]

Since they only follow their whims and their humors, they evade all laws and execute them badly. The result is that they never learn to command or else they become tyrants. Nowhere in the inhabited world is the ground so favorable to despots as here. From earliest infancy the children grow accustomed to it, because they see with what cruelty their parents treat their servants. For is there a single house which has no pillory, chains, whips, and similar instruments to torture for the least offense those who belong by birth to this unhappy class, who can not break their fetters without committing a crime? Scarcely does one dare to say that they are just as good as we are, and if even I say that it means that I run the risk of being stoned for it. What did I not have to suffer from blind and harsh opinion when this question was handled in the commission on laws; and the noble mob, whose number was infinitely greater than I had ever thought because I judged too much by the people who surrounded me, began to suspect that these discussions might bring some improvement in the present situation of the peasants! Have we not all seen how

3 : CONTINUATION OF PART TWO

Count Alexander Sergeievich Strogonov, a gentle and at bottom a humane man, whose kindness of heart almost went too far,— how this man, I repeat, defended with fury and passion the institution of serfdom, which in his innermost heart he was obliged to condemn! In the long run it is not my affair whether he acted under the influence of others or as a coward; I only mention this example as one of those that astonished me the most. All that one can say is that if he sinned at least he did it with full consciousness. But how many were there who let themselves be guided by prejudice and false understanding of their interests! I believe there were not then twenty people who had reflected humanely on the subject and like real human beings. And in the year 1750 there were certainly still fewer, and I believe that very few people in Russia had ever entertained the thought that there could be any other condition for the servant class than that of serfdom.

But it is time for me to return to the current year, the beginning of which has led me to make this wide digression from my subject.

While Her Majesty sojourned in Czarskoe Selo and the city was still empty, we did not know at first, the Grand Duke and myself, how we should employ ourselves. We grew accustomed in the afternoon to visit the Tchglokovs who still occupied the same dwelling, of which I have already spoken. There we met assembled the small retinue which had accompanied us upon the journey and those members of the Empress's household who had not yet followed her to the country. We met there also the Princess of Courland.

We amused ourselves by playing tredille.

The Grand Duke played with the Princess of Courland and in the course of the game he took a liking to her. The greatest advantage that she had in his eyes was that she did not descend from Russian ancestors. For the Grand Duke already had a great partiality for foreigners and something like an aversion or the beginning of an aversion for everything that was Russian or belonged to Russia. This aversion became stronger later on; but at that time His Imperial Highness was still clever enough not to display such feelings, although he occasionally let fly little sparks which were significant enough.

Besides the advantage of being a foreigner, the Princess of Courland had another priceless value in the eyes of the Grand Duke; she liked to speak German and this set the Grand Duke all aflame. The real attractions of the Princess of Courland touched him less. One must do her justice and admit that she was clever; she had very beautiful eyes, but she was not pretty; only her hair, which was a lovely chestnut brown. She was small besides and not only poorly developed but actually hunch-backed. This fault however would not pass as such in the eyes of a Prince of the house of Holstein. For they have never allowed themselves to be repulsed by a physical deformity. For example, the late King of Sweden,[20] my uncle on my mother's side, never had a mistress that was not hunch-backed or one-eyed or crippled.

The Grand Duke did not conceal his attachment from me but he nevertheless insisted that it was merely a matter of friendship. I did him the favor to believe him; besides I knew that it would not go beyond languishing glances on account of the peculiarities of the said gentleman, which had remained always the same though five years had elapsed since we were married.[21]

The visits to the Tchoglokovs became a daily habit. They did not take it ill, because to some extent it elevated their *salon* and they liked to see a numerous company around them so they could spend the day at the card table. The Princess of Courland cultivated a faultless attitude towards me and she never for one moment forgot herself, although this relationship lasted for some time.

After a sojourn of several weeks in the country, the Empress returned to the city during the last weeks of carnival.[22] I devoted myself in those days more than ever to my toilette and to following the new fashions. Princess Gagarin encouraged me in this; she always had some kind of advice to give concerning my dress, and this naturally tended to raise her value in my eyes. At this time, dresses with zig-zag borders had come in. I had two of them made, one of white and one of pink satin, quite covered with flounces. When the Empress was again in the city I lost no time in putting on my white satin dress with these trimmings for the first court day. It was the first dress of the kind that Her Majesty had seen. I had adorned myself with many emerald ornaments and my hair was dressed in curls. Her Majesty did not like new fashions very much, and least of all such as were becoming to the youthful; before all she could never bear anything that was becoming to me. She regarded me very sharply this evening, and her eyebrows twitched oftener than usual, which was always a bad sign. In the gallery she took Madame Tchoglokov to one side and talked to her a long time. When she took leave of us she looked very much flushed.

We withdrew; I had scarcely had time to undress when Madame Tchoglokov entered and informed me that Her Majesty had thought my dress horrible and had sent word that I was never again to appear before her in that kind of dress or with that kind of coiffure. Besides Her Majesty was very indignant with me because after four years of marriage I still had no children;[23] the fault must lie with me; apparently I had a secret infirmity of which nothing was known. She would therefore send a midwife to examine me. The Grand Duke, who happened to be in my room, was a witness to this whole conversation. I replied, with regard to the dress, that I would punctually follow the commands of Her Majesty; and, with regard to the second point, that Her Majesty was in all things my sovereign and I was in her power, so I had nothing to offer in opposition to her will. This time the Grand Duke took my part. Perhaps he felt that the fault was not all on my side; or else he felt offended on his part. In short, he told Madame Tchoglokov quite openly his opinion about the matter of children and about the examination and their argument grew heated. They reproached each other with every possible wickedness; I wept in the meantime and let them talk. Madame Tchoglokov went away in high dudgeon, saying that she would report it all to Her Majesty. But it was not so easy to see her and even Madame Tchoglokov did not find an opportunity so very soon.

When Madame Vladislav saw I had been weeping, she wished to know the reason. I told her all that had happened and the disgrace that threatened me. Madame Vladislav thought the Empress's way of acting toward me was unjust and she added: "How can you be at fault for having no children when you are still a virgin?[24] The Empress must know that and Madame Tchoglokov is a simpleton to come here and talk such stuff. Her Majesty should hold her nephew responsible or else herself because she married him too early." Incidentally I heard much later that Count Lestocq had advised the Empress to marry the Grand Duke not earlier than at the age of twenty-one; but the Empress did not follow his advice.[25] Madame Vladislav comforted me and gave me to understand that she would see to it that the true statement of affairs, as she understood it, should come to the knowledge of the Empress. I do not know what she did, but she did not cease to murmur between her teeth that the pretty coiffure and the flounces had evidently spoiled Her Majesty's humor and I was certainly to be pitied with a husband whose disposition did not suit my own and, instead of an aunt, a mother-in-law with whom it was hard to get along and who was influenced besides by a mischief-making woman. By the mischief-making woman she meant Madame Tchoglokov, of whom she said the worst kind of things since her husband had been alienated from Count Bestushev, the friend and protector of Madame Vladislav's son-in-law.

My position was certainly not one to be laughed at. I stood completely isolated among all the people there; the reading of good books and the natural cheerfulness of my temperament helped me easily over the situation. Besides this, a presentiment of my future destiny always gave me courage to bear what I had to bear and to suffer the disagreeable things that were daily inflicted upon me from more than one source. Already I wept much less frequently when I was alone than in the earlier years. I had always taken great pains to conceal these tears with which I reproached myself as a weakness; I concealed them because I had always thought it base to arouse the sympathy of others and if any one had showed this feeling toward me, it would have driven me to desperation. I esteemed myself too highly to think myself deserving of such a lot.

During the carnival this year a stage was erected at the command of the Empress in a hall of the castle, on which the cadets played Russian tragedies from the pen of Monsieur Sumarakov.[26] Among the cadets was one who was conspicuous because of his acting as well as his good looks. The Empress seemed to take great interest in this troup and in the handsome Truvor, who played a part in the tragedy of "Sinav." She was never tired of seeing this tragedy performed, and was concerned about the costumes. We saw the handsome Truvor wear in turn all the colors that she liked and all the costumes which pleased her. She painted the actors herself, and we could see the whole company in costume coming from the private apartments of the Empress where they had dressed, and immediately afterwards they walked on the stage.

During the last week of the carnival we had to see nine tragedies. I must confess that Melpomene was a little too much for me; I yawned quite often; nevertheless I had them tell me the names of the players, who bored me to death. From the mouth of the Empress I learned that the beautiful Truvor was named Beketov. He awakened a great longing in the Princess Gagarin and she made his acquaintance. The opportunity came of itself, for under the pretext that it was dangerous to cross the river the Empress had the whole troup of cadets who were playing in her theater lodged in the rooms of the palace during Lent. These rooms lay on the route which the Princess took to come to me and in this way my lady began to flirt outrageously with this Monsieur Beketov and thus became a second time the rival of Her Imperial Majesty. She played a daring game, for she knew quite well that more than one waiting-maid who had only been suspected of turning her gaze upon one of those who for the moment had enjoyed the favor of the Empress had been driven forth in shame and disgrace. Mademoiselle Gagarin also knew that in spite of her ugliness the Empress did not like to see her adorned, and she was often scolded on account of her attire. The Empress also had a grudge against her because Monsieur Shuvalov, who had been elevated to the place of favorite, had previously entertained for her so serious a liking that he wished to marry her.

In the first weeks of Lent the Grand Duke and I began our devotions as a preparation for communion. I sent Madame Tchoglokov to Her Majesty to ask that I might be allowed to go to the bath in the house of the Tchoglokovs. I will mention here in passing that neither the Grand Duke nor I dared to leave the house, not even for a drive, without obtaining the Empress's permission; and we could not have ventured to offend this well-established custom without calling down upon us the wrath of Her Majesty. Another fixed custom, which I at least would not have neglected for fear of exposing myself to the reproach of impiety, was that of going to the bath during the week in which I prepared myself for communion.

On Tuesday towards evening Madame Tchoglokov came to my room and informed me in the presence of the Grand Duke that Her Majesty gave me permission to go to the bath; she then turned to the Grand Duke and said to him that he would do well to go also. He took the proposal badly and said he would not do it; he had never been there before, and the bath was a laughable ceremony to which he attached no importance. Madame Tchoglokov answered that it would please the Empress if he went; but he replied that it was not true and he would do nothing of the kind. Madame Tchoglokov grew excited and said she was astonished that he showed so little respect for the wishes of the Empress. The Grand Duke said that whether he went to the bath or not had nothing to do with the respect he owed the Empress; that he wondered how she, Madame Tchoglokov, made so bold as to say that kind of thing to him; and that if she were a man he would know how to answer her and would not listen twice to words of such a nature,—he meant the reproach of disrespect to Her Majesty.

Madame Tchoglokov, who did not put up with anything and thought that his last words contained a threat against her husband, flew into a terrible rage and asked the Grand Duke if he did not know that for such talk and disobedience toward the Empress she might simply shut him up in the fortress of St. Petersburg. I have said before that this fortress served as a prison for those who had been guilty of *lèse majesté,* and had been handed over to the Secret Chancellory which held its sittings there. The Grand Duke fired up at this and asked in his turn whether she said this on her own behalf or in the name of the Empress. Madame Tchoglokov replied that she was only pointing out the consequences which his thoughtless behavior might have, and if he wished it the Empress herself would repeat what she, Madame Tchoglokov, had just said. Her Majesty had already threatened him several times with the fortress, she certainly had her reasons for it, and he should remember what had happened to the son of Peter the Great on account of his disobedience.

The Grand Duke then moderated his tone and replied that he would never have believed that he, the Duke of Holstein and a sovereign Prince, who had been sent to Russia against his will, would be exposed there to such shameful treatment. If the Empress was not satisfied with him she only needed to release him to go back to his own country. He then sank into his own thoughts, strode up and down the room, and finally began to weep. He finally went away after he and Madame Tchoglokov had exchanged all the invectives which their bad humor could suggest. But it was nothing in comparison with what they had said before.

I remained a peaceful observer of this whole scene, and when they turned to me I tried as far as possible to pacify the parties, both of whom argued with great heat over a misunderstanding and, far from coming to an agreement, only confused the matter more and more.

When both of them had gone I began to reflect on Madame Tchoglokov's words and I said to myself: "Much of this she said of her own accord, but much comes from the Empress." I reached the conclusion that the threat of the fortress must have come from the monarch and saw in it a sign of her violent anger with the Grand Duke. The business with the huntsmen crossed my mind but vaguely because at the time I did not know exactly what all this was about. But now I know the story of Asaf Baturin and can connect the time of this investigation with the time when Madame Tchoglokov gave the above-mentioned hints. And when I add that it was after this conversation between Madame Tchoglokov and the Grand Duke that the Empress ceased to kiss his hand when he came to kiss that of the monarch, I conclude that those hints had some connection with the affair and were thrown out in order to make the Grand Duke see the imprudence of his behavior.

The next day Madame Tchoglokov came again to the Grand Duke and informed him that she had reported to the Empress the scene of the evening before and that he had positively refused to go to the bath, and Her Majesty had answered: "Very well, then, if he is so disobedient towards me, I will kiss his damned hand no more." Thereupon the Grand Duke replied: "That depends on herself. I will not go into the bath; I cannot stand the heat there." After this various attempts were made to induce him to go to the steam-bath; but they were all in vain and every time he stub-

3 : CONTINUATION OF PART TWO

bornly refused. At every such attempt he remembered this case of the bath, when he had been threatened with the fortress. He thought of no other reasons; they had brought no other to his knowledge, and he had no suspicion of anything. But if that was what they had intended, they certainly had gone about the business as awkwardly as possible.

On the 17th of March the Empress went to Gostilitsy, the country seat of Count Razumovsky, there to celebrate his name day; while we received orders to go with our court, and the Empress's ladies-in-waiting, at the head of whom was the Princess of Courland, to Czarskoe Selo.[27] This order was exactly to the taste of the Grand Duke. The remarkable thing about this journey was that nowhere did we find any snow; rather, we left the city in dust and returned the same way.

At Czarskoe Selo we tried as well as possible to amuse ourselves; during the day we promenaded or went hunting. The swing played an important rôle; while swinging, Mademoiselle Balk, a lady-in-waiting of the Empress, aroused the interest of Monsieur Sergei Saltikov, Chamberlain of the Grand Duke. He made her a proposal of marriage the next day, which she accepted, and they were married soon afterwards.[28]

In the evening, we played cards; this was followed by supper. One evening I had a bad headache; I had to leave the table and go to bed. The Grand Duke had on this evening paid court to the Princess of Courland more than was his usual custom, which Madame Vladislav had observed through some crack or key-hole. Incidentally, she possessed the praiseworthy habit of satisfying her curiosity in this way. When I went to my room to undress, she could not refrain from seeking the reason for my indisposition in my jealousy of the Princess. She began by saying all manner of ill about her, whereby His Imperial Highness also came in for several thrusts because of his bad taste and his relation to me, for which she had all manner of descriptive terms. Madame Vladislav's talk, although it was in my favor, made me weep. I could not endure the thought that I had aroused anybody's pity and she had let me see that she sympathized with my position.

I went to bed and fell asleep. The Grand Duke, very much intoxicated, came to bed at last; for in the first nine years of our marriage he never slept anywhere but in my bed. Later however he slept there but seldom; that is a peculiarity which in my opinion is not without importance in view of the state of things which I have already mentioned.[29]

As I lay in bed, he awakened me, although he knew that I was ill, and began to talk about the Princess of Courland, of her personal charm, her talents, and her gift for conversation.

My imagination had been aroused by Madame Vladislav's words, my head was not quite clear on account of the pain, and I was indignant at the lack of consideration shown by this intoxicated man who awakened me only to talk about unpleasant things. So I replied with a few words, in which my bad humor was not wholly repressed, and pretended to go to sleep again. Both of these things angered him. He gave me a couple of rude thrusts in the side with his elbow, turned his back on me and went to sleep.

This new treatment was very painful to me. I wept the whole night over it but was on my guard against saying a word about it to anyone. Whether the Grand Duke had forgotten it the next morning, or whether he was ashamed of it, in any case he said not a word about it and never afterwards did he mention the occurrence to me.

After we had remained a few days longer in Czarskoe Selo, we returned to the City. On Easter Saturday towards evening, the Grand Duke received some fresh Holstein oysters. During the first and the last week of Lent we were allowed to eat mushrooms only and during the other five weeks, we ate only fish. Consequently the Grand Duke, who always had a good appetite, was very much starved out. To be sure he received meat in secret with the help of his servant throughout the whole of Lent, but the portions were necessarily quite small because it could only be brought to him in someone's pocket as his people thereby ran a great risk. So he came leaping for joy into my room, where I was in bed and asleep, for I had not slept in the night between Friday and Saturday and had to be awake again from Saturday to Sunday. I was obliged to get up and eat the oysters with him. They were excellent; I ate twenty perhaps, then went to bed again and slept until it was time to dress for early Easter service.

While I was dressing, I felt the indigestion coming on; but as I had always despised that kind of pain I continued with my toilet and went to church. During the service the pain grew worse but I heard about half of the mass; but after the reading of the gospel I was obliged to leave the church. The Princess Gagarin followed me; Madame Tchoglokov lay in child-bed. When I reached my room, I found my ladies missing; they had all gone on this day with Madame Vladislav to take communion in the little chapel of the Empress. Princess Gagarin had to undress me. My illness grew worse; I had frequent and violent spasms. I sent for Boerhaave who however had gone to his church to communion service. Finally my pain passed into diarrhœa and this relieved me.

The Princess Gagarin, who was timid by nature, was quite alone with me and asked me every moment: "Do you wish me to fetch your Father Confessor?" In spite of the terrible pain which I suffered I could not help laughing at her anxiety. She said several times also: "I am dying of fear that you may pass away while I am alone with you." Finally my people came, also the physicians, and that put an end to the uneasiness of the Princess; she withdrew and turned me over to them. They gave me rhubarb and the illness passed away. Yet I was obliged to stay in bed the whole Easter holiday.

When my women had recovered a little, they told me that they had been witnesses of another scene. The Empress had left the great cathedral during mass several minutes before me. She often did that although she was very pious. As a rule she did not stand long in one spot during the service but walked about from one place to the other in the church. There was no chapel in which she did not have two or three places for herself.

On this day, then, she had left the great cathedral and gone directly to her little chapel. There she had showed such a bad humor that everyone trembled; the devotions of my ladies were very much disturbed thereby.

She had scolded all her young and old attendants, whose number was not small and reached upward to forty. The singers also and everybody up to the pope had got their share. Much was whispered on all sides about this ill-temperedness, and secretly it sifted through that this wrathful mood had its basis in the embarrassment of Her Majesty who found herself between three or four favorites, namely Count Razumovsky, Monsieur Shuvalov, a singer by the name of Katchenovsky, and Monsieur Beketov, whom she had just appointed adjutant to Count Razumovsky. One must admit that anyone else would have been embarrassed no less than Her Majesty. To handle four men rightly at the same time and prevent their temperaments from clashing with each other,— not everyone can do that!

At the beginning of spring they had us take up our residence in the little summer palace of Peter the Great.[30] We were glad of this because the apartment which we were to inhabit opened immediately on the garden. A wing had been added to the great wooden palace against the side of the church, and we were to occupy it. By this the Empress signified that she did not wish to have us as near her as formerly. We did not grieve for our old apartments in the Summer Palace, for they were very uncomfortable. They formed a double suite of rooms with two exits; the one leading to the stairs which everyone who came to us had to use; the other, opening into the state apartments of the Empress. Consequently everything we needed for private service in the apartment and all our people came through the former entrance. One day it happened that some strange Ambassador or other was

3 : CONTINUATION OF PART TWO

entering for an audience and the first thing that he saw was a night-stool which some one was just carrying out in order to empty it.

From the Summer Palace they sent us to Peterhof and lodged us in one of the wooden buildings which are at the end of the avenue of Monplaisir.[31] This was a ground floor with only one row of rooms with windows on both sides. This dwelling was quite pleasant.

I seated myself at one of my bed-room windows, on the right or the left according to where the sunshine did not fall, and read. My book at that time was the "Turkish Spy." [32] For several years past I had accustomed myself to have a book in my pocket as a remedy for boredom and whenever the time was favorable I sat down and read. That saved me many a tedious minute. This "Turkish Spy" made me almost melancholy. Perhaps the manner of life that they required us to lead contributed more to this than the book. However that may be, for a period of several months I was in such a mood at certain times that I had to weep and all looked dark to me. Besides I was at the time, or fancied that I was, very weak in my chest; I had continued to be quite thin. I soon understood that this desire to weep without sufficient reason was either weakness or a tendency to hypochondria. I ascribed this to the wretched life we had to lead for eight months of the year in the city and during a part of the summer, when we were in the Summer Palace or at Peterhof. Our way of life was about as follows:

I rose between eight and nine in the morning, took up a book and read until it was time to dress; no one except my women came into my room. At most I went to the Grand Duke or he came to me; but I did not feel comfortable in his apartments and when he came to me it was only one more cause for boredom. I preferred my book and while my hair was being dressed, I went on with my reading. At half past eleven o'clock I was dressed; I then went into my reception room, in which there were usually only two or three of my ladies and as many of the gentlemen in my service. Here it was no less tedious, for the Empress at that time took great pains to furnish the court with only the most stupid men, and if by chance she erred in her selection, the one-eyed person, who seemed like a king among these blind ones, was in every case banished. At twelve o'clock we dined with this company and Monsieur and Madame Tchoglokov. They took the greatest trouble to prevent the conversation from becoming amusing; it had to be as stupid as possible, for if it once in a while grew interesting they were always bored. In this they had the fullest support of the Grand Duke. She and he were soon at each other with some kind of rudeness or contentiousness, which made the whole company uncomfortable for the rest of the meal-time.

After dinner I went back to my room and my book until about six o'clock. This was the hour for promenading and refreshment, but one was necessarily surrounded by the insipid company above described. Princess Gagarin was the best of all; she possessed a great deal of intelligence but had for me one unpleasant trait. Whenever there was an opportunity she could not refrain from making me feel the tedium and disharmony by which I was surrounded. She wondered that I did not suffer from it more than I did. Princess Gagarin had a strong preference for the fine world, for luxury and city life. She hated the country which I preferred to every other residence.

Towards eight o'clock in the evening we had to be back to supper, which passed off as joyfully as did the dinner. After this I retired and about ten o'clock I went to bed, to begin the next day the same life over again. In Oranienbaum I had more freedom. For although I could just as little choose my company as when in the city or in Peterhof, I could at least go driving or walking whenever and as long as I wanted to.

Our stay in Peterhof this year lasted longer than we had wished. One day when I was sitting by my window and reading as usual, I saw Count Cyril Razumovsky and Prince Repnin passing by.

3 : CONTINUATION OF PART TWO

I called them to my window and talked with them. Madame Tchoglokov, whose windows opened on the same *allée*, saw this and came into my room like a fury to scold me because I had dared to speak with them through the window. She scolded them also because they had remained standing there. She then announced that she would report it to the Empress. Count Razumovsky told her outright that he did not understand what was wrong in passing along the garden walk; our conversation had been as innocent as possible and only those could find fault with it who liked to set up a secret chancellory wherever they might happen to be.

To reconcile Madame Tchoglokov they then went with her to play cards. I too went often to her apartments, especially when I hoped to find there a somewhat less tedious company and when I knew that Monsieur Tchoglokov was not there. Madame Tchoglokov was always well disposed when I came to her, and, provided that she could play cards, she did not observe me closely.

The Grand Duke had given me a little black dog, one of his *Charlots*. He was the funniest animal that I have ever seen. He was only six months old; but it was just the same to him whether he walked on his hind legs or used all four. Indeed he liked very much to use only two. Whether from disposition or from some other reason, he often walked sideways to the place he wished to go. The dog was really quite absurd; my whole household was fond of him. Incidentally he had no name. One of the servants who tended my stove won the dog's attachment especially, perhaps because he really liked him or only to create an impression. He did what he liked with the dog and my ladies finally called him "Ivanova sobaka," which means Ivan's dog; then, since that was too long, simply Ivan Ivanovich, because the said stove-tender, who gave him so much attention, was named Ivan Ushakov. We laughed at the name and for several days everyone wished to say Ivan Ivanovich as often as possible, and everyone played with the dog thus christened, who was really as funny as a monkey. We put caps on him, dressed him in mantles and skirts, and Ivan

Ivanovich was pleased with it all. My women decked him out and sewed the whole day making new articles of finery for their Ivan Ivanovich. As long as the dog did not leave my room these jokes had no consequences.

We left Peterhof to go to Oranienbaum.[33] This year the Grand Duke arranged that the wives of the gentlemen of our court should accompany us to Oranienbaum.

From Peterhof, then, we went to Oranienbaum. The live-long day, from morning until evening, we went hunting, I like all the rest. I remember that I was several times this year on horse-back for thirteen hours out of the twenty-four. I adored this exercise and was indefatigable. The amount that I took reduced considerably the hypochondria to which I was periodically inclined.

This year, if I remember rightly, I saw in Oranienbaum a total eclipse of the sun. At mid-day we saw the stars, it was so dark, and the moon which passed in front of the sun permitted no more than a ring of the star whose disk it covered to be seen.[34]

During this entire year I suffered continually from bad colds, so that I used up to twelve pocket handkerchiefs a day, although I did not change them until they were thoroughly wet. When I blew my nose, I could feel the moisture which came from my breast and the inside of my body in a never-ending quantity.

When it was autumn, we returned to the city [35] and remained this year to the end of October in the new apartments added to the Summer Palace. They were very inconvenient and divided as unfavorably as possible.

At the beginning of October I took a catarrhal fever, which left me with a lingering temperature that returned every evening. Boerhaave promptly called it tuberculosis. He lost no time in having them procure an ass whose fresh milk I had to drink in bed every morning at six o'clock and then sleep again for two or three hours. This did me good and freed me from the cold and fever. I continued the cure on into the winter and became well again.

3 : CONTINUATION OF PART TWO

During this indisposition the Grand Duke began to pay court to a little Greek maid of mine,[36] who was really very beautiful. This affair ran its course in Madame Vladislav's room next to mine, where the Grand Duke spent the whole day and a part of the night. Madame Vladislav watched them both closely. But the relation did not last long and did not go beyond tender glances; the maiden afterwards married General Melissino. This little romance of the Grand Duke's, however, did not disturb the other with the Princess of Courland.

The carnival was very gay this year. The cadets began to play their comedies again and Monsieur Beketov rose more and more in the favor of the Empress.

Madame Tchoglokov now found me in the Winter Palace very entertaining. She often sent to me in the afternoon and begged me to come to her. All sorts of people gathered there; now and then there were also people of the world. This amused me to some extent but not always. In general I was very gay this winter, so that I often made my whole household dance and skip. I could imitate all kinds of birds and animals, their voices as well as their posture and walk. This made Madame Tchoglokov laugh and even cheered her husband, but this was only seldom.

I must admit that I had grown quite exceptionally absurd and apish; but they were used to my peculiarities and began to scold me a little less. I alone would often fill the room with the noise that I made. Count Hendrikov, Madame Tchoglokov's brother, who had been absent for a year, insisted one day when he saw me romping thus that it made him dizzy to behold my capers. This delighted me and for a couple of days I told everyone about his expression.

There arrived this fall, as Ambassador from Denmark,[37] Count Lynar, brother of him whom Princess Anna of Brunswick had so much loved. He was charged with a commission to deal with the Grand Duke concerning the exchange of Holstein for the lands of Oldenburg and Delmenhorst. Count Bestushev, as Grand Chancellor of Russia, strongly wished for this exchange, in order

214 CATHERINE THE GREAT : MEMOIRS

to remove the obstacle to an alliance between Russia and Denmark, whose interests in more than one sense were exactly the same. Count Bestushev did not let himself be frightened by the passionate attachment of the Grand Duke for Holstein where he had been born. He opened the negotiations and almost succeeded in talking over the Grand Duke. I shall come back to this subject later.[38]

NOTES

[1] Journal of the Court Quartermasters, 1748: "In the first hour of the night between the 15th and the 16th of December, Her Imperial Majesty deigned to leave the Winter Palace and to set forth on the road to Moscow from St. Petersburg."

[2] From the 17th to the 23rd of November Lestocq refused to accept nourishment.

[3] Histoire générale d'Allemagne par le p. Jos. Barre, chanoine régulier de Sainte-Geneviève et chancelier de l'université de Paris. Paris, 1748, 11 vol. (10 tom.).

[4] Journal of the Court Quartermasters, 1749: "March 25. On Easter Saturday and Annunciation Day, a night mass was celebrated in the 4th hour of the morning in the Royal Chapel, in the presence of Her Imperial Majesty and Their Imperial Highnesses."

[5] Catherine to Madame Geoffrin, January 15th, 1766: "In my youth I also had attacks of bigotry; I was surrounded by bigots and hypocrites. A few years ago one had to be either one or the other to give one's self a little authority (but do not think that I belonged to the second group.)"

[6] Journal of the Court Quartermasters, 1749: "On the morning of May 22d Her Imperial Majesty and Their Imperial Highnesses deigned to drive to the village of Perovo for the mid-day meal."

[7] Journal of the Court Quartermasters, 1749: "On the 21st of June,, at 12 o'clock noon Her Imperial Majesty deigned to go again to the Sergievo Troitsa Lavra. On the same day Their Imperial Highnesses deigned to set forth on the journey from Moscow to Troitsa and took up their residence in Rajevo."

[8] Journal of the Court Quartermasters, 1749: "On June 29th, at eleven o'clock in the morning, Her Imperial Majesty and Their Imperial Highnesses deigned to enter their coaches and drive to the Troïtsa Monastery."

[9] Journal of the Court Quartermasters, 1749: "July 1st. Their Imperial Highnesses deigned to take supper at Rajevo."

[10] Princess Hedwig Elisabeth (Biron).

[11] August 26, 1749, with the name Catherine Ivanovna.

[12] Journal of the Court Quartermasters, 1749: "September 2. Her Imperial Majesty deigned to set forth from Moscow in the morning for the Voskresensky Cloister.—On the 3d, Their Imperial Highnesses deigned to arrive at the Voskresensky Cloister and to dine there in the newly erected palace.—

3 : CONTINUATION OF PART TWO 215

On the 5th, Her Imperial Majesty with Their Imperial Highnesses deigned to attend the mass in the great cathedral of the Voskresensky Cloister."

[13] Journal of the Court Quartermasters, 1749: "September 17. Her Imperial Majesty and Their Imperial Highnesses with a few distinguished persons of both sexes deigned to partake of a repast in the new building in the village of Tajninskoye. Their Imperial Highnesses condescended on the same day after the mid-day meal, to repair to the village of Rajevo to remain there until the 22nd and on this day to return to Moscow."

[14] Journal of the Court Quartermasters, 1749: "October 8. Her Imperial Majesty and His Imperial Highness deigned to be present at the wedding of Monsieur Narishkin, Chamberlain of His Imperial Highness."

[15] "To-day after twenty-four years of married life": Catherine must have written these lines in 1773.

[16] These lines were written before Catherine learned of Baturin's death, which took place in 1772 during the passage from Canton to the Isle de France (according to Benyovsky's Memoirs in Macao at an earlier date),—and also before her letter to Prince Viasemsky of October 2, 1773: "Seventeen of the men who were betrayed and led away by the rascal Benyovsky have returned here with my permission. I promised them pardon and it must be granted them, for they have already been sufficiently punished for their sins. It shows how the Russian loves his Russia, and their trust in me and my mercy has touched my heart."

[17] Journal of the Court Quartermasters, 1749: "December 14. Their Imperial Highnesses, the Grand Duke and the Grand Duchess, deigned to depart from Moscow for St. Petersburg at mid-day in the twelfth hour."

[18] Journal of the Court Quartermasters, 1750: "On the 18th of January Her Imperial Majesty deigned to leave Gostilitsy for Czarskoe Selo, and to remain there until the 25th."

[19] In the state archives is a page in Catherine's handwriting: "Reflections on Petersburg and Moscow": . . . "I do not like Moscow at all, but I have no partiality for Petersburg. I will allow myself to be guided only by the good of the state and frankly speak my mind. Moscow is the seat of idleness, and its unwieldy size is chiefly to blame for that. I make it a rule when I am there never to send for anyone because you can only learn the following day whether the person concerned can come or not. To pay a visit you must spend the day in your carriage and the whole day is lost. The nobles gathered there enjoy themselves and that is not surprising. But from earliest youth, they adopt the tone and attitude of idleness and luxury. They grow effeminate, spend their time in driving in a coach and six and see only sordid things, which is obliged to weaken the most outspoken genius. Besides there was never a people that had so many objects of fanaticism before their eyes; such as miracle-working saints at every step, churches, parsons, cloisters, bigots, vagabonds, thieves, useless servants in the houses,—and such houses, what dirt in the houses, which occupy a great deal of ground and which have miry bogs for court-yards. In general every person of importance in the city has not merely a house but a small country estate. . . ."

[20] King Adolf Friedrich (died 1771).

[21] The words "on account of the peculiarities" ... to "since we were married" are suppressed in the edition of the [Russian] Academy.

[22] Journal of the Court Quartermasters, 1750: "On the 17th of February Her Imperial Highness deigned to return from Czarskoe Selo to Petersburg."

[23] In the Instructions written by Bestushev for Madame Tchoglokov May 10, 1746, it is specified in Par. 2, among other things: "Since Her Royal Highness has been chosen as the high consort of Our dear nephew, His Royal Highness, the Grand Duke and Successor to the Throne, and has been elevated to her present dignity as Imperial Highness solely with the expectation and the hope that through her insight, understanding, and virtues, she would gain the sincere love of His Royal Highness and win his heart, that thereby the desired Heir of the Empire and offspring of Our Imperial House might grow, which however cannot be expected other than on the basis of mutual and sincere love and marital confidence; we cherish therefore the most gracious hope that Her Royal Highness, remembering how her own happiness and her welfare depend upon this, may consider well this important expectation and most diligently leave nothing possible undone on her part for its fulfillment.—You, however, We command most emphatically to impress upon Her Royal Highness, the Grand Duchess, most forcibly at every opportunity this desire so important to Us and the whole Fatherland."

[24] The words "when you are still a virgin" are suppressed in the edition of the [Russian] Academy.

[25] Stehlin's Memoirs: "1745. The Empress hastened to marry the Grand Duke. (The physicians advised her to postpone it at least one year.)"—"The Empress hastened the marriage of the Grand Duke against the advice of the Court Physicians."—The Austrian Resident von Hohenholz had written Feb. 29 (old style), 1744: "I have not hesitated to state my poor opinion to the effect that perhaps the Princess of Zerbst has not found in the person of the Grand Duke what she might have hoped, namely the fulfillment of the marriage as soon as possible, as the very incompetent personality of the Grand Duke may postpone the hope for this until the future. The intervals in this Empire are exposed to many accidents."

[26] Journal of the Court Quartermasters, 1750: "February 19. At the court of Her Imperial Majesty the rehearsal of a Russian tragedy took place in the new state apartments where a theater had been erected. It was played by cadets."

[27] Journal of the Court Quartermasters, 1750: "March 14. Her Imperial Majesty deigned to go from St. Petersburg to Gostilitsy and on the way to dine at Czarskoe Selo. Their Imperial Highnesses condescended on the same day to repair to Czarskoe Selo after the mid-day meal. On March 17th, that is the day of St. Alexis, a banquet took place in Gostilitsy. During the dinner and supper hour salutes were fired and Italian music was played in the apartments, opposite to which fireworks were set off."

[28] This marriage had already taken place on December 29, 1749.

[29] The words from "for in the first nine years" to "already mentioned" are suppressed in the edition of the [Russian] Academy.

[30] Journal of the Court Quartermasters, 1750: "On April 30th, after they had

3 : CONTINUATION OF PART TWO

dined, Their Imperial Highnesses deigned to go on foot through the garden to their apartments in the Summer Palace, which have been fitted up as a residence for Their Imperial Highnesses."

[31] Journal of the Court Quartermasters, 1750: "June 6. Their Imperial Highnesses deigned to leave Petersburg in the afternoon and to stop on the way at the house of Herr Wulf on the sea-shore, and they arrived at the 9th hour in the evening at Peterhof; and after their arrival they all deigned to repair to Monplaisir to the newly furnished wooden apartments, where they deigned to take up their residence with their retinue."

[32] L'Espion du Grand Seigneur et Ses relations secretes. Par le Sieur Jean-Paul Marana. Amsterdam, 1684. The impression *Privilege du Roy* of November 29th, 1683, which appears at the close of this book refers to "un livre intitulé L'Espion Turc."

[33] Journal of the Court Quartermasters, 1750: "June 7th. Their Imperial Highnesses deigned to repair to Oranienbaum this day."

[34] In the year 1750 there was an eclipse of the sun on January 9th (New Style); but in the year 1749, on July 14; in 1751, May 25th.

[35] Journal of the Court Quartermasters, 1750: "August 1st. Their Imperial Highnesses deigned to arrive from Oranienbaum in the 11th hour of the evening.—September 7th. Their Imperial Highnesses went to Oranienbaum on this day before the arrival of Her Imperial Majesty; and from Oranienbaum they deigned to return to St. Petersburg, arriving on the 27th in the 7th hour of the evening."

[36] Maria Dmitriyevna Kotserev.

[37] Count Rochus Friedrich zu Lynar arrived in Petersburg February 7, 1750.

[38] In the "Chronological Remarks" (Cf. p. 87, Note 143.) there are several notes not used in the foregoing fragment. "1750. Banishment of Yevreinov and the coffee service. Pretext for this. The materials of my mother. Strife about them. 1751. Begins very gayly. Masquerades and coquetry. Affair of Zachary Tchernishov. Sergei Saltikov, Count Bernis. Frau Arnim. Holstein affair. 1750. Little dog, called Ivan Ivanovich. Great scandal on account of this dog. 1751. Great scandal in Peterhof."

PART FOUR

WRITTEN BETWEEN 1756 AND 1758

ADDRESSED TO SIR CHARLES HANBURY WILLIAMS

I WAS born at Stettin in Pomerania on the 2nd of May (new style) 1729. My mother, who had married my father in the year 1727 at the age of fifteen years had almost died when she gave birth to me. Only with a struggle did she recover from a sick-bed lasting nineteen weeks.

At the age of two I was put into the hands of a French governess, the daughter of a Professor at Frankfort on the Oder, by the name of Cardel. At three and a half years I am told that I was able to read French. I have no recollection of it.

In the year 1733 my mother took me with her to Hamburg to visit her grandmother. I attended the opera with her; but when a battle was presented on the stage, I began to cry so loudly that I was taken out.[1]

I remember that my mother in the year 1734 was delivered of a second brother. This is the one who is still living; the elder, who was born in 1730, died at the age of thirteen years.[2]

In the year 1735 my parents visited their relatives and left us at home with our governess, the wife of an old officer. I wrote a letter to my parents every week and gave them news about ourselves, chiefly about my elder brother, who in playing had fallen against the table and broken his head in two places. He had been close to death. After this the younger took the chicken-pox. These letters were composed for me but I copied them.

In November my parents returned. I contracted a cough and a stiff neck, so that I almost became hunch-backed. For six months I was bed-ridden. When I was about to be dressed again, it was discovered that I was quite crooked. There was a woman who advised that no other remedy should be employed except to rub the protruding places with the spittle of a person who was fasting. My right shoulder, left side, and right hip were two fingers higher than the corresponding parts on the other side, so that the backbone formed a zig-zag line.

My father, who had great affection for me, inquired of everybody who could give him any counsel. I had to wear a stiff bodice day and night, and this together with the above-mentioned remedy brought me around again in less than a year, so that scarcely anything could be noticed.

In the year 1736 my mother visited the benefactress by whom she had been educated and portioned, the old dowager Duchess of Brunswick-Wolfenbuettel, born Princess of Holstein-Norburg. After the loss of Schleswig at the time of my grandfather's administration, the latter, who had a large family of children, willingly gave one of his daughters to this lady, who requested one of him as the rightful successor of the first wife of her husband, a sister of my grandfather.[3]

My mother, on whom the choice fell, was brought up by her as if she had been her own daughter.

I took part in the journey above mentioned. I was spoiled and petted, being so small. I was often told that I was clever, that I was already a big girl, so that I believed it myself. Like the others I stayed awake whole nights through at festivals and masked balls; I was present at everything, I chatted like a magpie and was extremely bold. As a proof of this the following episode will serve: When I was four years old, the late King of Prussia came to Stettin.[4] They told me I must kiss the hem of his coat. He asked for me and I was brought. I approached him and as I tried to seize his coat and he hindered me, I turned to my mother and said quite angrily, "His coat is too short, I can not reach it." He asked what I had said. I do not know who repeated it to him. but in any case he said: "The maiden is saucy,"[5] and afterwards he inquired for me whenever my father came to Berlin or he came to Stettin.

In the year 1737 I was with my mother for the first time in Berlin. The present queen, who happened to be there just then, wished to see me. I went to court, and was allowed to chatter and play; I supped with the Queen, then with the Crown Prince. We remained the whole winter in Berlin.

From this year on to 1743, I spent two months of every year in Brunswick, the winter in Berlin, and the rest of the time up to 1740 in Stettin, later in Zerbst.

I became gradually taller and the extreme ugliness with which I was endowed left me when, in the year 1739, I visited my uncle who was then Bishop of Luebeck. I saw the Grand Duke for the first time; he was really handsome, amiable, and well-mannered.[6] They told wonderful things about this eleven-year-old-boy, whose father had just died. My mother, who was then very beautiful, pleased him; he paid court to her. I scarcely noticed him; but I heard my uncles and aunts and all the household intimates drop a word here and there which made me believe that they intended us for each other. I felt no kind of resistance to it. I knew that he would be King of Sweden sooner or later, and although I was still a child the title of Queen flattered my ear. After that time my family teased me about him, and gradually I grew accustomed to the thought that I was intended for him.

Two or three years passed and these thoughts dropped into the background. My sojourn in Berlin caused very different ones to rise. Prince Heinrich of Prussia saw me often, liked me, and spoke about it to his sisters, the Duchess of Brunswick and the Queen of Sweden,[7] who was at that time still unmarried and who liked my mother very much. But the latter thought I was still a child. I was in fact thirteen years of age but taller and more developed than is usual at this age. I do not know how I gained my knowledge of their talks and was not angry about it. The sojourn in Berlin did not at all displease me. Matters stood just as I have related and I believe in the year 1744 they had developed still further.[8] My mother returned in the autumn from Hamburg, where she had taken leave of the King of Sweden, who had just been chosen Crown Prince and was departing for Sweden. She went by way of Brunswick and stopped at Zerbst for some time, intending to go on to Berlin and spend the winter there.

On the 6th of January, 1744,[9] we were sitting at the table at dinner when it was announced that a courier from Berlin had arrived for my mother; my father was also present. This was something unusual. She asked for her letters. I recognized Bruemmer's hand-writing. As I sat next to her when she opened her letters, a fleeting glance allowed me to recognize the words: "The Princess, Your eldest daughter." That was sufficient for me and I said to myself, "That concerns us!" It was by no means an unpleasant thought.

We rose from the table. My father, my mother, and my uncle, the elder brother of my father, locked themselves in. I gave no sign and they told me nothing.

Three days passed thus. There was an incessant coming and going! Within myself I knew the reason very well; but I thought it strange that my mother, who for the last six months, that is, since the journeys to Hamburg, had given me her confidence and discussed everything pretty openly with me, still said not a word to me about the matter.

On the evening of the third day I went to her room. When she saw me enter she said: "You seem to be very much excited; you are dying of curiosity." "Yes, indeed," I answered, "I know through my powers of divination what is written in your letters." "Aha, what is it then?" she asked. I was ashamed to confess that I thought it was concerned with my marriage and answered, "I will question my oracle." (A woman whom she knew dealt in matters of this kind: she could extract from the name of a man that of the sweetheart which he wished to know.) "We shall see," she said, "what you will be able to bring out."

The next day I brought her a slip of paper, on which I had written the following words: "The omens say that Peter III will be your husband." [10] She looked at me sharply and said: "You are a rogue, but you will learn nothing more about it." She rose and went to my father. She soon returned and told me it was certainly true that propositions of that kind were being made from here.[11] But all lay in the distant future; it would be too much of a risk. Neither she nor my father nor my uncle wished to hear anything about it. A refusal would have been sent without asking me at all if I had not guessed it. She added, "What do you think of it then?" I answered, "If it does not please you, it would ill become me to desire it." She responded, "It seems that you have nothing against it."

The thought of leaving her, and especially my father who loved me tenderly, struck me so painfully at this moment that I began to weep. My father entered, kissed me, and said he did not wish to force me to such an important step and my mother should take the journey under the pretext of thanking Her Majesty for the marks of favor which her family had received (namely: for the pension of 15,000 rubles which she had allowed my grandmother on the third day of her reign; for the royal dignity of my uncle; for the portrait of the Empress set with jewels and valued at 25,000 rubles which my mother had just received because the Empress had accepted the place of godmother to a daughter born to my mother one month after her accession to the throne). He added that in case I did not wish to accompany my mother, that depended on myself alone; if however I journeyed with her and returned home again I would always be welcome. He was aware of all the risks and wished by no means to expose himself to self-reproaches later because he had made me unhappy.

I burst into tears. Seldom in my life have I been so touched as I was at this moment; a thousand diverse feelings moved me, gratitude for my father's kindness, distress lest I should displease him, the habit of obeying him blindly, the tender love I had always had for him. The respect which he really deserved finally won the upper hand.

Never did anyone more deserve the highest possible esteem than did he; the strictest rectitude ever guided his footsteps. I can truly say I never in my life heard him say a word that was inconsistent with his character. I believe that a kindred feeling was the reason why he so loved the republican form of government and was its zealous advocate. Whether it was because of my respect for him or whether it can be otherwise explained,—in any case I too could not help having a partiality for it which seems almost incredible in view of my position and my ambition.

Ten days later I departed with my parents for Berlin.[12] It had been decided,—why I know not,—that I should not appear in public. But the King knew the secret of my mother's journey. I say secret for the matter had been decided here [13] by Count Bruemmer, a Swede and governor of the Grand Duke, Count Lestocq, and the Marquis de la Chétardie in order to thwart the designs of the Chancellor, who intended to marry the Grand Duke to a Saxon Princess, namely, the Princess of Bavaria.[14] Count Bruemmer, out of interest for the Holstein family, and Count Lestocq, out of hatred for Bestushev, had sent forth a rumor that they were suing for the hand of a French Princess. The Marquis de la Chétardie who saw how little was the prospect of success for a daughter of his master induced both of his friends to oppose the Saxon party and frankly declared himself to the Empress in favor of me. He had seen me less than six months before in Hamburg. Bruemmer received a secret command to write to my mother, and Baron Mardefeldt, the Prussian Ambassador, dispatched the courier at once to the King. Count Peter Tchernishov knew nothing about it until Koenigsberg lay behind us.

When we had been in Berlin a few days, the King was desirous of seeing me. He had me invited to dinner; my parents, however, did not take me with them. When he saw them arrive without me, he sent again for me and waited with the dinner until three o'clock. At last I arrived; he spoke with me, was agreeable, praised me, and sent a message that I should sup with him at the masquerade.[15]

That evening he had me sit beside him at the table, talked with me continuously, asked me about a thousand things, talked of the opera, of the comedy, of poetry, the dance, I know not what all. In short he spoke of a thousand things about which one can chat with a fourteen-year-old maiden. At first I was very timid with him, but I soon adapted myself, and at last we conversed in a very friendly manner, so that the whole company stared because His Majesty was conversing with a child. Finally someone, I know not who, passed behind us. The King called him and reached his arm out towards a dish of *confiture* which stood in front of me. I took it and handed it to him, whereupon he said: "Give it to that gentleman there!" He mentioned his name but I have forgotten it. He then turned to him and said: "Accept this gift from the hand of the Loves and Graces!" I blushed. We then arose from the table.

After a few days we took leave and departed from Berlin,[16] ostensibly for Stettin in Pomerania where my father was Governor. A few miles before we reached Stettin my mother parted from him.[17] The parting was as painful as one can imagine. It was the last time that I ever saw him.

Our journey was long, very tedious, and quite strenuous. My feet were so swollen, that they had to carry me to and from the carriage. We were six weeks on the way. My mother had assumed the name of Countess of Rheinbeck as she had been directed to do from here.[18]

When we arrived in Mitau,[19] the Lieutenant-General, at that time Colonel Voyeikov, presented himself. My mother was greatly astonished at his visit, put me out of sight, and bade him enter. He said that he had orders to inform Riga that a lady of rank would arrive and that he came to ask whether she had any commissions for him. The royal carriages and Chamberlain Narishkin had been there for eight days. She was certainly the lady who was expected. My mother replied that she knew nothing about it but was delighted to make his acquaintance.

He sent word to Riga, bade my mother to postpone her departure until the messenger arrived, dined and supped with us, and departed with us. He instructed my mother about all kinds of things which foreigners as a rule do not know. Among other things I remember that he told her, when she spoke of the boyars, that they no longer existed; it had formerly been an office which carried a certain rank, as for example at present the General *en chef*, etc., etc.

Half-way between Mitau and Riga, we encountered at mid-day Lord Marshal Semyon Narishkin,[20] at that time Chamberlain. I knew him already for I had seen him in Hamburg when he was returning from his post in England. He accompanied us to Riga, where we were received with great pomp. The garrison under arms, the Magistrate, the Vice-Governor Prince Vladimir Dolgorukov, and the whole city had crossed the Dwina to receive us. Thus we were conducted to our quarters, where we found the court officials, a Lieutenant of the Guard . . .[21] by the name of Ovtsyn, now a Chamberlain of mine, and an equerry.

We remained two days in Riga. At that time, Princess Anna of Brunswick resided there with her husband and her children under the supervision and control of General Vasili Saltikov, who came from Duenemuende, where they were staying, to greet us.

We left for Petersburg[22] in sleighs, which was something new to me, and arrived there four days later.[23] The court was in Moscow. We were welcomed by a salute of cannon; the whole city stood on the steps of the Winter Palace where we were to alight. Prince Repnin, General of Artillery, did the honors.

We dined and supped with the nobles of the city, for most of them had not yet followed the court to Moscow. On this occasion I made the acquaintance of Lord Marshal Bestushev, who after the unhappy affair with his first wife, which had just ended, went away as envoy, I know not whither.

The foreign Ambassadors called on us daily; the most zealous among them was Marquis de la Chétardie and Baron von Mardefeldt. The first advised my mother to set forth as soon as possible and gave her many other suggestions, most of which did not come to my knowledge.

After three days of rest, I set forth with my mother,[24] accompanied by four ladies-in-waiting of the Empress, who had remained in Petersburg to receive us. They were Mademoiselle Mengden, later married to Count Lestocq, Mademoiselle Saltikov, now married to Prince Gagarin, daughter of the General whom I had seen in Riga, Mademoiselle Karr, subsequently the wife of the head-groom Prince Peter Golitsin, and the daughter of Prince Repnin, who married Peter Narishkin, Lieutenant of the Guards.

We travelled day and night and reached there in fifty-two hours. The people said along the way, "There goes the bride of the Grand Duke!" At a distance of seven versts from the city, Sievers, the Groom and now Lord of the Bed-Chamber (whom I had known in Berlin whither he had brought the Order of St Andrew to the King), came to greet us in the name of the Empress. He seated himself in the sleigh which my mother and I occupied. After we had passed through the entire city, we alighted at the Golovin Palace,[25] where we were met by the Prince of Homburg and the whole court at the foot of the stairs.

When we had rested a moment, the Grand Duke appeared, and a moment later Count Lestocq came to inform us that the Empress awaited us. She received us at the door of her bed-chamber. More than all else her tallness astonished me. She talked a great deal with my mother and regarded me closely.[26]

During their conversation the Grand Duke devoted himself to me and was so well pleased with me that he did not sleep the whole night, and Bruemmer induced him to say that he would have no one else but me alone. He came to supper with us; I was astonished to find him so childish in all his talk, although on the next day he would complete his sixteenth year. Nevertheless he did not entirely displease me; he was handsome, and I had so often heard it said that he showed a great deal of promise, that I had long believed it.[27]

The next day, his birthday, February 10 (Old Style), there was such a crowd at court as I have never since beheld. The enormous Moscow Palace, which burnt down in 1753, by comparison with which the wooden one that you know can at best be called a grandson, was so crowded that one could only shove. At eleven o'clock the Empress had my mother called; she went alone as I was not yet ready with my toilette. Almost the whole court came forward to meet me and I alone was conducted by all these people, many of whom climbed upon the chairs in order to see me.

As I entered the bed-chamber, the Empress came towards me with the ribbon of the Order of St. Catherine which she hung upon me and then upon my mother. Thereupon we followed her to the Grand Duke, who thanked her for having bestowed the order upon me.[28] When we returned we stayed with all the ladies who were in the reception room.

They assigned to us as our attendants Monsieur Betsky and the late Prince Alexander Troubetsky; the former was Lord of the Bed-Chamber, the latter Groom of the Bed-Chamber to the Grand Duke; also Lord of the Bed-Chamber Narishkin, who accompanied us, remained. One of the ladies-in-waiting was in daily attendance and besides a Groom of the Empress.

Betsky, the Prince of Homburg, Bruemmer, and Lestocq assured me that I had pleased their sovereign as well as the nation. I presented always a cheerful countenance and was profuse in bows and compliments. Far from being proud, I went almost too far in the other direction in being over-friendly, so that Zachary Tchernishov, who was later assigned to my service, said that I greeted the Chancellor like a stove-tender. I did not say much, but they shouted so loudly that I was clever that people believed it before they had proofs of it.

You can judge how they hastened to conclusions by what I shall relate. On the tenth day after my arrival,[29] I became ill; before my illness they had twice summoned a council, consisting the first time of the lords of the empire, the second time of the lords and the bishop, in which it was decided, after a discussion of the prospective marriage from the point of view of religion, politics, and family relationship, to advise me to change my religion. They chose the Archimandrite Simeon Teodorsky, later Archbishop of Plescau, and charged him to instruct me. He had already begun his visits, as had Adadurov for the Russian language.

But the hopes of all those who wished me well were almost destroyed by this terrible illness. The Empress had set forth upon a pilgrimage to a celebrated cloister near Moscow, by the name of Troitsa,[30] when I was seized with a violent headache one day while undressing. My mother put me to bed. The fever I had became so bad that Boerhaave thought it must be the small-pox. First of all I lost consciousness; at the end of the fifth day they wished to bleed me but my mother would not permit it. Boerhaave sent a courier to Count Lestocq to inform him that if they did not bleed me I was lost. I had such severe pains in my right side, they thought every moment that I would die. In short I lingered between life and death for twenty-seven days. When they had elapsed and I had been bled sixteen times, the abcesses broke inside my body. Then I had a fever, the attacks of which lasted sixteen hours. Finally, as if by a miracle and because it was decreed that I should live, I recovered.[31]

All the lay people and the simple folk thought I was poisoned and complained loudly to the Saxon Ambassador Gersdorff. This went so far that I, who lay almost the whole time in delirium, was infected by the rumor.

During the crisis of my illness, only the physicians were allowed to enter my room. The Empress had even refused admission to my mother for three days, because she always wrangled with the physicians. There was a Portuguese, by the name of Sanchez, Boerhaave, and a surgeon, by the name of Werre, who never leaves the Grand Master of the Hunt. They also concealed from her the frequent bleedings which I underwent.

On April 21st, the day on which I was fifteen years old, I was able to stand on my feet and receive congratulations.[32] The Empress had me put on rouge on account of the striking paleness which I still retained.

I convalesced rather quickly by comparison with the illness which I had passed through.

Scarcely had I recovered, when the notorious catastrophe with the Marquis de la Chétardie took place. They found in his letter reports of imprudent talks he had had with my mother, at which the Empress grew so angry that my marriage almost came to naught on account of it. Since the affair was concealed from me because of my extreme youth, I do not know all the particulars. One morning Count Lestocq came to our apartment and said to my mother: "Get ready for your departure!" Afterwards the Empress came with papers in her hand; she, my mother, and Lestocq, locked themselves in, and after a conversation which lasted two whole hours, they separated apparently on friendly terms. All this took place in the Troitsa Monastery, whither the Empress had gone to fulfill a vow she made during my illness.

On the day before St. Peter's, I made my confession of faith and received communion in the public royal chapel in the presence of a vast crowd of people. I read in the Russian language, which I did not at all understand, quite fluently and with a faultless accent fifty quarter-pages, and recited afterwards from memory the symbol of faith. The Archbishop of Novgorod and the Abbess of a nunnery, who stood in the odor of sanctity, were my godparents.[33] I received the name which I now bear, solely for the reason that my former name was hated on account of the plots of the sister of Peter the Great, who had been called the same.

4 : ADDRESSED TO SIR CHARLES WILLIAMS

From the moment of my change of faith I was prayed for in all the churches.

In the evening we went incognito to the Kremlin, an old castle, which served the Czars as a residence.[34] I was lodged in a room so high that you could hardly see the people who went along the foot of the wall.

Early in the morning of the day afterwards, St. Peter's day, on which my betrothal was to take place, I received as a present from the Empress her portrait set with diamonds, and a moment afterwards that of the Grand Duke, equally valuable.

Immediately afterwards I was taken to the Empress, who, with the crown upon her head and wearing the imperial mantle, set forth under a canopy of massive silver borne by eight Major-Generals. The Grand Duke and I followed her, after us came my mother, the Princess of Homburg, and the other ladies according to their rank. Incidentally, from the moment of my change of faith it was arranged that I should have precedence over my mother, although I was not yet betrothed.[35]

We descended the famous stairway, known as the Krasnoe Kryltso, crossed the square and proceeded on foot to the cathedrals, while the regiments of the Guard formed a lane. The clergy received us as usual. The Empress took the Grand Duke and me by the hand and led us to a platform covered with velvet in the middle of the church. There the Archbishop Ambrosius of Novgorod betrothed us and the Empress exchanged the rings. The ring which I received from the Grand Duke was worth twelve thousand rubles, and the one, which he received from me, fourteen thousand.[36]

After the mass, the cannons fired a salute. At mid-day the Empress dined with the Grand Duke and me on the throne in the room which is called the "Granovitaya Palata." My mother had demanded to be present at the dinner, whereupon they told her she could only have a place among the other ladies, but she demanded to be seated on the throne only one step lower. When

Lord Tyrawley heard that he declared that, as the representative of a crowned head, he would also take his place there. So a table was set for her in the place from which the Princesses of the Czar's family used to look on during ceremonial occasions; that is a little room high up behind a glass wall. She ate there, so to speak, incognito, for the Princess of Homburg and several other ladies took part.

In the evening a ball took place at the foot of the throne, on a carpet on which, of the ladies, only the Empress, my mother, myself, and the Princess of Hessen danced; of the gentlemen, only the Grand Duke, the Ambassadors of England, Holstein, Denmark, and the Prince of Hessen. The rest of the company danced on the right. We were almost smothered with the heat and the crowds. The chamber is so constructed that a great pillar supports the arch in the middle and takes up almost a quarter of the room.

After the ball we returned to the Annenhof Palace, behind the German Sloboda which we occupied.

Some time later the peace with Sweden was celebrated with a public festival. Immediately afterwards we departed for Kiev.

From my betrothal, up to our departure, not a day passed on which I did not receive presents from the Empress, of which the least was worth from ten to fifteen thousand rubles,—jewels, money, fabrics, and so forth, everything that can be imagined. She also manifested the tenderest love for me. They wished in some way to take advantage of this. My mother had won the Troubetskys by her very intimate friendship with the Princess of Hessen; she induced the Procurator-General, when the ukase was issued concerning my appointment as Grand Duchess with the title of "Imperial Highness," to inquire, as if to avoid an error, whether they should not have me take the oath of allegiance and add the title "Successor to the throne." But he was sent away with a flat refusal, which nevertheless did not prevent the declaration from being published with a burst of trumpets.[37]

In the middle of July [38] we left Moscow for Ukrainia. On the way

4 : ADDRESSED TO SIR CHARLES WILLIAMS

my mother, who had been deprived of Chamberlain Betsky and was very much troubled about it, began to confide in me a great deal again. Her relations with me had grown somewhat cooler because of Countess Rumyantsov with whom I had grown friendly since my illness, during which she had been assigned to me, so to speak, as my companion. My mother looked on her as a spy who was the cause of her troubles and did not like her.

On the occasion of the peace festival a sort of court had been formed for me: it consisted of three Chamberlains, Prince Alexander Golitsin, Count Hendrikov, Count Yefomivsky, and three grooms, namely: Alexander Villebois, Count Zachary Tchernishov, and Count Andrei Bestushev-Ryumin. My mother wanted me to frown upon Countess Rumyantsov because of her behavior, but since I looked on her as my future stewardess I thought I ought to please the Empress and was very little inclined to make of her an enemy. I was especially strengthened in this opinion by the governor of the Grand Duke, Count Bruemmer, who loved me tenderly and whose advice I valued highly. Add to this that my ideal of heroic virtue, which I was mad about at the time, did not make me very hospitable to feelings so wholly opposite to mine.

Count Bruemmer and Countess Rumyantsov had, as my mother knew, a strong dislike for Count Zachary Tchernishov, whose character as we now know it was then already developed. In order to annoy them, she paid him especial attention. He was foolish and puffed up and ascribed what he had not expected to quite different reasons, boasted about it and by a thousand follies induced people to believe what I swear was not the truth.

In Kiev I saw Count Flemming again, whom I had known in Pomerania. He had been sent by the King of Poland to congratulate the Empress on her arrival at the boundary. We stayed there twelve days [39] and then returned from this pilgrimage in short daylight journeys.

When we were again in Moscow,[40] my mother found still more reason to be displeased. On all sides she was maligned to the

Empress. I was, however, not injuriously affected by all these discords; I passed for a child and was too much on my guard to give displeasure. On the contrary I did my best to win those among whom I was to spend my life. My respect and gratitude to the Empress were extraordinarily great; she was like a divinity in my eyes in whom there could be no fault. She used to say she loved me almost more than the Grand Duke. It rejoiced her to hear me well spoken of; but I was quite timid with her. The Grand Duke loved me passionately and everything taken together helped to make me hope for a happy future.

Under these circumstances, we departed from Moscow.[41] Halfway on our journey, the Grand Duke felt unwell and twenty-four hours later small-pox declared itself. I was just then in his room. Boerhaave who was present noticed it first and advised my mother to take me from the room and before all to conceal from me the reason. They decided to have me go away the same night and dispatched a courier to the Empress. When I was told that I must depart I suspected what it was about and was very much affected by it. On the way we met the Empress, who came from Petersburg to go to the Grand Duke in the village where he was; it was called Chotilovo.

In Petersburg I led a very retired life. I used the six weeks during which I was alone with my mother for the study of Russian, which I had already begun to understand and to speak. I wrote to the Empress several times in this language which gave her great joy.

After my arrival in Petersburg they assigned my mother and me to different rooms, I believe because her apartments were never free from visitors, particularly foreign ambassadors, yet we ate together. She noticed this change with dissatisfaction, which was not however taken into consideration. She was treated with more coldness and contempt from day to day.

Preparations were made for my wedding, which was to take place early in June, 1745.

4 : ADDRESSED TO SIR CHARLES WILLIAMS 237

When the Empress and the Grand Duke returned to Petersburg and I saw him, I received such a shock as surely no one ever had. He had just gone through the small-pox and his face was completely disfigured and extremely swollen; indeed, if I had not known that it was he I should not have recognized him. My blood congealed at the sight of him and had he been a little more sensitive he would have rejoiced but little at the impression that he made on me. He supped every evening with me and the nearer the time of my marriage came the more I wished that I might follow my mother.

My court was now completely formed. Countess Rumyantsov performed the office of a Stewardess without having the title. As ladies-in-waiting, I was given the two Princesses Gagarin, of whom the elder is dead, the younger married to Prince Alexander Golitsin; further a Mademoiselle Kosheliov who in consequence of an unprofitable adventure was later banished from my court. Then all my servants and women were Russian, except only one whom I had brought with me.[42]

Among the maidens there was one [43] whose cheerful disposition pleased me so that I was more friendly with her than with the others. Yet this friendship could not go far because of ten words that we spoke scarcely one was understood. But however innocent this sympathy was, for to call it an attachment would have been too much, my mother took offense at it. She spoke with me about it; and although I did not believe that anyone would think ill of me because I treated my Russian servants well, I nevertheless assured her that I would restrain my friendship for the young maiden. She was only one year older than I; judge whether that could be very dangerous.

My wedding was postponed until the 21st of August (Old Style), 1745, and then celebrated with all possible splendor. The festivities lasted ten days and the court resumed the fashionable splendor which Empress Anna had given it.

Two weeks later, they let my mother know that she could go

whenever she liked. She answered that she had urgently wished it for a long time. She had only waited for the fulfillment of my marriage; now however she did not wish to remain a single moment. The Empress sent her 70,000 rubles; since, however, she had made so many debts I took the rest of them upon myself and laid thereby the foundation for my own debts. After my wedding I saw her less frequently and she assumed a more friendly attitude towards me. But on the way to Czarskoe Selo I did not sufficiently scold someone who had failed in respect for her, and this put her again in a bad humor with me.

Finally she thought it necessary for my best interest to banish the maiden whom I liked so well. Two days before her departure, she asked to speak to the Empress. The latter told me two days later that my mother had begged her to remove the little seventeen-year-old thing because it was dangerous to allow me favorites. To this hour I do not know what that signified. For at that time I had never had a thought of evil; on the contrary if I had died I should have gone straight to Paradise; I was so innocent in heart and mind.

On the day of the departure of my mother,[44] to whom I had given escort, they removed this very dangerous person. She would have had to beg her bread, if I had not supported her surreptitiously and later married her. Now that she is a widow, I have given her the means to buy a little country place on which she lives.

For fear of distressing me too deeply, my mother went away without taking leave of me.

On the same evening I returned with the Grand Duke to the city. I asked for the maiden; the others answered, with sad faces, that she had gone to visit her mother who had fallen ill. The next day someone whispered to me how matters really stood; but for fear of making the person concerned unhappy, I kept silent. We then went to the Winter Palace, where the Empress told me of her conversation with my mother.

A few days later Countess Rumyantsov received orders to return to her husband. After my marriage I had been given the mother-in-law of Sievers [45] who immediately from the very start forbade my servants to speak softly to me. I had given no sort of occasion for behavior of this kind; I was astounded and kept silent. When I sat in my room, she came with two old dwarfs, who had been assigned to me, and they watched through the keyhole whatever I did. If I only changed my position, everything was set in motion to see what was going on. I observed all this activity and let them be. When they see what I am doing, I thought, and then find nothing to say against it, they will soon give it up.

I wrote frequently to my mother. Bruemmer and Lestocq reported to me the Empress said I wrote to the King of Prussia and kept him informed of current events here through my mother. I can swear that the King of Prussia never saw my handwriting except as the signature beneath official letters which were set down in the College of Foreign Affairs.[46] The two gentlemen mentioned ascribed all this talk and the bad treatment to the Chancellor, whose ill humor grew from day to day. They advised me to speak to the Empress about it, but my timidity and the justice of my cause held me back from following their advice. Incidentally the influence of these two was sinking every day.

Scarcely a day passed on which I was not scolded or annoyed. Once I rose too late or dressed too slowly; another time, I did not take enough pains with the Grand Duke; but if I visited him too often, it was said I did it, not on his account, but because of those who came to him. I pined away and grew thin. If they saw me sad, they said, "She is satisfied with nothing"; if I was merry, they suspected some kind of secret tricks.

If all these reproaches and criticisms had come directly from the Empress or had been delivered by people in her confidence, it would not have hurt me so much. But usually they had the coarsest things said to me by lackeys or maids. It went so far that they made the Grand Duke believe that I was in love with Bruemmer, whom he began to hate. They also tried to make a crime out of my liking for the King of Sweden, from whom they had alienated the Grand Duke on account of his administration. The chief instigator of these scenes was my uncle,[47] the Bishop of Luebeck, whom they expressly sent for to play this unworthy rôle. When the Empress saw that the Grand Duke did not on this account stand on a worse footing with me, or that his ill humor simply remained ill humor, she talked against me herself and he was influenced to such a degree that he induced me to give up the friendship of Count Bruemmer. He spoke to me about it very roughly, and repeated his conversation with his aunt. That provoked me so that I told him very positively that no consideration in the world would force me to neglect my obligations to a friend whom I valued. No plots or vexations would move me to forget the sense of honor which I thought that I possessed. The Grand Duke and everybody bothered me but I became all the more steadfast.

At the beginning of May, 1746, Count Bruemmer was taken away from the Grand Duke and his place was filled by Prince Repnin, General of Artillery.[48] Although I felt very sensibly the loss of a man who loved me like a daughter, the honorableness and the unselfishness of Prince Repnin carried me through this to some degree. He was affectionate with me, strove to improve my relations with the Grand Duke, and quite openly took my part. The principles of this honest man, who was incidentally but little of a courtier, brought him small happiness. In the first three weeks he won the hatred of all who were not of his opinion as well as the mistrust of the Empress. This caused the latter to assign Madame Tchoglokov to me with the title "Stewardess"; [49] (for she was just as much dissatisfied with Madame Kruse, the mother-in-law of Sievers, my first waiting-woman, who got drunk almost daily and did not justify the confidence that had been placed in her; besides this she had attacks of good-will towards me from time to time). Had they known a more malicious creature, she would certainly not have received the post. She installed herself in my apartment by announcing that if I wished to write to my mother or father I should send a message to the College of Foreign Affairs, for it was not proper that the Grand Duchess herself should write. She added also that it was probably too troublesome for me to go daily to the Empress's dressing-room, for which I had permission. If I had any necessity to address the Empress, I could transact my business through herself. These speeches astonished me greatly and I answered nothing further than that I could only obey since she spoke in the name of the Empress.

In the morning of the next day, on which they were going to have me bled, I rose very early. Madame Kruse informed me that the Empress had already inquired twice whether I had risen. A moment later she entered my room herself and ordered me with an angry look to follow her. She paused in a room in which no one could see or hear us (incidentally, in the two years that I had been in the country this was the first time that she had spoken confidentially with me or at least without witnesses). She began to scold me roundly and asked whether the rules of conduct that I followed proceeded from my mother. I was betraying her to the King of Prussia; my villainy and treachery were known to her; she knew all! I was to blame that my marriage was still lacking in fulfillment (in a particular where the woman cannot be the cause). It was not her fault if I did not love the Grand Duke, for she had not married me against my will. In short, she said a thousand horrid things, of which I have forgotten the half.

I saw the moment coming when she would beat me; fortunately the Grand Duke entered and in his presence the conversation took a different turn and nothing could be noticed. I do not know what might have come of it; she really looked like a living fury. Several times I tried to justify myself. But as soon as she saw me open my mouth, she cried: "Be silent. I know that you can answer nothing." I have reflected since and I believe now that the whole scene was intended to frighten me or hold me in terror; for otherwise it was wholly incomprehensible.

When the Empress had gone the Grand Duke, who found me bathed in tears, asked me what had happened.

I was in despair such as never before and told him briefly what had been said to me during the half hour. Madame Kruse observed that I suppressed the story about the attendants and since she knew very well that it must be told, she went after him to tell him when he had gone away. He came back very angry; I believe this was intended to set us at variance. But he was no longer angry when I told him the whole story.

The following had, namely, taken place. The Grand Duke had a waiting man whom Madame Kruse liked very well because he often brought her wine and got drunk with her. He used to pump her afterwards and draw from her all that she did and made notes about that and everything that the Empress might have in her head. He then shared this with me, and since, in order to avoid suspicion, this could only happen in the Grand Duke's room, I often talked with him when I went there. Madame Kruse had encountered us three or four times in conversation; she became jealous and figured out the story for herself which I have told you here.

I was so terribly desperate, that this in combination with the heroic feelings peculiar to me made me resolve to kill myself. A life so full of excitement and so much injustice on all sides with no prospect of improvement brought me to the thought that death was to be preferred to such an existence. So I lay down on the sofa and after a half-hour of the deepest affliction, I fetched a large knife that lay on the table and tried with the greatest determination to thrust it in my heart. Just then, one of my maidens entered, I know not why, and found me in this pretty situation. The knife, which was neither very sharp nor very pointed, went through my stays with difficulty. She threw herself upon it; I was almost unconscious and was terrified when I saw her, for I had not noticed her. She was a stupid girl (she is now the wife of a Colonel by the name of Kaschkin, who is in command of the Tobolsk Regiment).[50] She tried to dissuade me from my preposterous idea and offered all the grounds for comfort that occurred to her. Gradually I came to regret my fine deed and made her swear an oath not to speak of it. She kept it faithfully.[51]

The evil conduct of Madame Tchoglokov remained always the same. She forbade everyone to speak with me. And indeed not only the ladies and gentlemen of my household; on court days when I showed myself she said to everyone: "If you say more than 'yes' or 'no' to her, I shall tell the Empress that you are plotting with her, for everyone knows about her intrigues," so that they all avoided me or stood back when I approached. I acted as if I knew nothing about her tricks and went my way, spoke to everyone, was exceedingly amiable and strove to win everybody, even Madame Tchoglokov herself.

In the summer following my wedding, we journeyed to Reval.[52] There the Empress noticed that I was visibly pining away and inquired for the reason. The little one,[53] who after two years of disfavor, had been taken up again, spoke in my behalf at the request of Countess Rumyantsov and Prince Repnin. She told the whole truth about the bad treatment that I had to bear and added several personal complaints which she had to bring against Madame Tchoglokov, as also against the Grand Duke, who liked the latter fairly well. This brought reproaches to the Grand Duke; among other things he had to listen to was that if he behaved badly they would put him on a ship and send him back to Holstein. I would be kept and the Empress could then choose whom she liked to occupy his place.

I received some kind of present and thought that everything would now take a turn for the better; but it only had the result of arousing Madame Tchoglokov still more against me. She thought that the disfavor which she had to put up with was the result of my complaints, which was in part the case. She waited until the storm had passed and managed with such skill that after our return from these journeys I was worse scolded and more ill-treated than I had ever been before. Every month, someone was driven forth and if there was ever a man or a woman whom I looked on with a friendly eye, the person was surely banished.

At the beginning of the year 1747, troops were sent to the aid of the Empress and Queen; that the command had to be occupied was used as a pretext to remove Prince Repnin, who was my friend and too much devoted to me to be tolerated.

The husband of Madame Tchoglokov, Chamberlain and Knight of the Danebrog-Order and the White Eagle, had just returned from Vienna where he had gone to congratulate the Emperor on his accession to the throne.[54] and where he had committed as many follies as he had performed official acts. He was assigned to the Grand Duke. His first act was to forbid everyone to enter the Grand Duke's room without first obtaining permission from him. Since he was however the most impolite and uncouth person that could be imagined, nobody willingly exposed himself to a refusal from him.

In this way we were deprived of all society, I since the last year and a half, the Grand Duke after the official entrance of this man. He now devoted himself to music and I occupied myself with reading. I bore all this patiently, without humiliation or complaint; the Grand Duke however was full of impatience, of quarrels, and threats. This made him bitter and depraved. He was driven to seeing his servants only and having them around him; so he adopted their talk, their habits, and their manners.

In May, 1748, the Grand Master of the Hunt invited us to Gostilitsy, his country seat. Bretlach, who had been there as Ambassador of the Emperor, was just going away. The Empress saw him leave with regret; and since he had taken official leave she used the pretext of showing him the estate in order to see him again. So he came thither.

In order to vary our style of dressing, we had to attire ourselves somewhat like shepherdesses: pink skirts, white dresses, and English hats formed our adornment, which in my opinion was extremely ludicrous.

4 : ADDRESSED TO SIR CHARLES WILLIAMS

We walked so long that it was six o'clock in the morning when we returned to our dwelling.[55] At eight o'clock, when I had scarcely fallen asleep, Monsieur Tchoglovok suddenly entered my room. I awoke and started up, and he said: "Get up as quickly as possible. The foundations of the house are falling in." The Grand Duke, who was fast asleep, sprang out of bed and fled. I rose without hurry, because I did not realize the danger, dressed myself and waked Madame Kruse who slept in the adjoining room. In short, we delayed so long that at the moment when we finally wished to go out, the house fell in. I fell upon the floor; two stoves in the very tiny so-called salon leaned in such a way that Madame Kruse and I were covered by them; but aside from the great shock, we suffered no harm. A petty officer of the Guard, by the name of Levashov, who had been sent to urge me to hasten, carried me out. The steps broke through beneath him; everything fell, everything broke, but fortunately nothing struck us, and more than five or six people passed me from one to the other as well as they could. I was bled; at first I felt no other troublesome consequences.

For the rest there were sixteen people killed and four fatally wounded, among them the Princess Gagarin, who married Matiushko.[56] At that time she was my lady-in-waiting.

The next summer the following adventurous business almost released us from these inconvenient people. If the Chancellor had not retained them, this time it would have been the end of the couple he had chosen. Mademoiselle Kosheliov had become the intimate friend of Madame Tchoglokov; she never left her room. She was very blonde and young, but pretty stupid though still not as stupid as those with whom she had to do; for them she made both rain and sunshine. I had liked her very much before her new friendship, but gradually left off. Monsieur Tchoglokov was tired of his ever-pregnant wife and was pleased with this Mademoiselle. The friendship went so far that he gave her a child. In the fifth month of her pregnancy everyone noticed it; I was one of the first to suspect the matter. One of my maids had told Madame Kruse that she had surprised them as they lay together. At first the Empress would not believe the story, but finally she had it investigated, and the Mademoiselle was sent back to her parents; Monsieur Tchoglokov, however, was threatened with banishment to Siberia and separation from his wife.

After such a scandal he could not be decently left in our household. They tried to find a substitute for him. The place was offered to the Hetman [57] who was Chamberlain at the time and very close to us,—it was just the time when his brother stood in the highest favor,—but he declined outright. Then they wanted to appoint General Apraxin, but they were afraid of him. They considered it a long time back and forth but in the end found no one for the place.

In the year 1748 we went to Moscow.[58] A year passed and Tchoglokov's affair was forgotten. The last and only punishment that he received was that his father confessor was ordered to forbid him the communion for two years. His reputation, however, had suffered under the affair. A short time afterwards the Grand Duke had occasion to make severe complaints against him. Also the influence of his friends was declining. He thought he made a lucky stroke when he finally broke with the Chancellor, who had supported him and raised him to his position. So he fell between two stools. . . . Incidentally he showed a rather friendly attitude towards me, and as it pleased me to have him quarreling with the Chancellor, whose activities I had to thank for many a trouble and sorrow which Tchoglokov had inflicted on me, I repeated to him the remarks that the Chancellor had once made to me when he was not so ill-disposed toward me as usual. Tchoglokov, swollen with vanity and conceit, never afterwards made it up with him. He allowed us, the Grand Duke and me, more and more freedom daily and took pains to please us. But now, whether from habit or disposition, he was sensitive to every trifle, and often the Grand Duke and I stood opposite to him and his wife as if on knives.

4 : ADDRESSED TO SIR CHARLES WILLIAMS

We came back here in the year 1750.[59] Tchoglokov suddenly fell in love with me, or perhaps he only acted as if it were so. I laughed at him and likewise my whole court, who could speak to me with less constraint since he had improved. The Grand Duke knew of the matter.

During the summer there was more strife and we decided to give the last blow to Tchoglokov by telling the Empress of his infatuation. But this man's lucky star ordained that she should only laugh at it and say that if we ourselves complained about it, it could not be so serious.

His wife and he were only united when it was a matter of doing someone harm and they were the scorn and laughing-stock of the whole court. People pitied us and tried to win our favor by wishing them ill.

A year passed thus. Then the couple had the idea of approaching the matter from another side, in order to raise his sinking influence again. They made a great outcry because after six years of marriage I still had no children. But it was generally known that the fault was not mine; all knew that I was still a virgin.

Those who did not know the plan of the Tchoglokovs (among them the mother-in-law of the Pugovishnikov,[60] who had been assigned to me two years before in the place of Madame Kruse, whose influence had been damaged by her drunkenness and who had won my liking to a certain extent) and who did not esteem them, were astonished when they saw them doing everything humanly possible to attract us and were indignant when we responded to their advances, although we had grounds to complain of them and be on our guard against them. Many of them, fearing to be regarded as secret enemies of the Tchoglokovs, took offense at it.[61]

There were the most diverse interpretations. Some insisted that the plan of the Tchoglokovs was to become favorites, consequently with designs on me. Others thought it happened at the instigation of the younger Saltikov, and that Tchoglokov intrigued on his behalf by allowing the Grand Duke to have his own way in order to throw sand in his eyes. In reality, Tchoglokov, in spite of his liking for me, acted without self-interest (for he knew very well and without any self-deception my dislike for him) and solely with the intention of securing for his fatherland a successsor to the throne.

Saltikov, who was for seven years the rival of another and for a period of six months found a better reception than formerly, induced Tchoglokov to undertake that on which he had based his plan: either to compel the Grand Duke to resort to medical aid or to find some other way. Madame Tchoglokov, who regarded her husband's feelings as by no means so pure, favored Saltikov's feelings; thus in order to work against her husband, she strove for the same object but with the intention of vexing him.

At last the boundless innocence of the Grand Duke compelled them to seek somewhere a mate for him. The choice fell upon the widow of a painter by the name of Grooth.

When all was in train, they thought that the service which in their opinion they had done deserved to be recognized. Exactly the opposite occurred. The Shuvalovs, their enemies, raised such an outcry because of their claims that they thought they would be banished, and declared that all had been done at the instigation and in favor of Saltikov, who required the utmost influence of his mother, who lay dying, to save him from banishment. But it is true, and I can swear it, that until his death the late Tchoglokov knew nothing of Saltikov's rôle at the moment; if he had had any suspicion of it, the latter would have been lost. Moved by jealousy of her husband, then by friendship for Saltikov, and finally, when she had reason to complain of him, by honesty, Madame Tchoglokov favored his suit and employed all possible arts of persuasion to seduce me. This, combined with the good looks and talents of him for whom she spoke, would have encountered less resistance with anybody else than with myself. It is really true that I was distinguished by good judgment and exemplary innocence.[62]

At the end of the year, we went to Moscow.[63] I became pregnant and had a miscarriage in July, 1753.[64] All was quiet until November when the palace burned down.[65] After the fire we lived in private houses. Tchoglokov had to go frequently to the great court and to remain there longer than usual. Perhaps this innovation had bewitched him or something had been put into his head from another quarter; at all events he suddenly had the idea of falling in love with the Empress. This he first confided to Monsieur Saltikov, then to me. He met with an excellent reception and all went well, but his extreme ardor wrecked everything. The Shuvalovs became suspicious; the frequent masquerades which took place twice a week contributed to this. Someone cast tender glances at him all too openly! They twisted the matter about until they regarded the whole thing as an intrigue of Monsieur Saltikov's and mine. This was not true; but I can not deny that we urged him on when we saw that all went well. Finally she suggested his departure and called him publicly at dinner a blockhead and a traitor, which he took so to heart that he fell ill with the jaundice.

Kondoïdi, wholly loyal to the Shuvalovs, was called, and since he had known for a long time that this man was their enemy, he thought he might do them a service by murdering him. At all events the physicians who were called in his last days declared that he had been treated like a man whom one desires to kill. Four days after his death his wife was told that she could remain in Moscow and they assigned to us Ivan Ivanovich Shuvalov.[66] I believe that Saltikov would have been banished at the time if I had not been pregnant and they had not feared to give me pain by such an affliction.

In May, 1754, I arrived in Petersburg after a twenty-nine days' journey.[67] On the 20th of September I was delivered. There was inexpressible rejoicing over it. Three weeks later Saltikov was sent to Sweden with this message. This distressed me very much, for I was thus exposed to the talk of the whole world. In December orders were sent to him to go to Hamburg, but I made such energetic efforts with the Chancellor that he returned hither before the courier reached Stockholm. After a wearisome noise, many complaints, and much talk, we decided that for his own good he should go away. Less from liking than from determination I held fast to what I had begun, and strove tirelessly, by overcoming every difficulty and straining every nerve in the battle with every kind of obstacle, to accomplish his return. I succeeded also against all expectations. Yet I had promised myself no happiness from his return; the difficult character of this gentlemen stood in the way of that.[68]

When in December I . . . But why should I repeat all this, which you already know? In case you find that much has been omitted here, then ascribe it to the speed with which I am scribbling. For example, the reasons for my coldness toward the only survivor of the party which brought me here, the Vice-Chancellor, and my intimate friendship with the Chancellor. I will at least speak briefly of these here.

Count Lestocq was imprisoned, in November, 1748. The sorrow I felt at the loss of an intimate friend oppressed me greatly, and notwithstanding all that was told us about his plots against us, I can not believe it, for I have never seen anything actionable. I believed that the Vice-Chancellor would later behave like Lestocq; but he was far removed from that. During the intrigues of the Shuvalovs against Tchoglokov and his wife, he sided with them; although he knew that that was indirectly opposed to me. He was one of the strongest opponents of the Tchoglokovs and then of Saltikov's also. Because I saw through his conduct and knew that he would not use his growing influence in my favor, and that he would rather avoid everything that could awaken the appearance of still liking me as formerly, I came to the conclusion that I would adapt myself to his way of acting. Besides this, I had doubts; and my native judgment, the more I developed it, led me to believe that the interests of Russia are very different from those

4 : ADDRESSED TO SIR CHARLES WILLIAMS

of France; at least the state of doubt in which I found myself did not combine with the sincere intentions that I had.

I knew that the Chancellor had always wanted to have me for a friend, and that the stubbornness and steadfastness which I showed on behalf of his enemies was the only circumstance which embittered him and forced him in a way to do me harm. The first proposals that I made to him were received by him with open arms. We decided to forget the entire past; he paid me most honestly with the friendship of all the friends whom he gave to me and offered to support me with his advice. Well and amiably treated and respected by him and his friends, I thought myself sufficiently avenged for the coldness of those who had neglected me. And as I believe that I have now taken hold of the proper handle, I think that death alone can wrest it from me. I believe that in my present course lies the true interest of Russia and that I may hope for great fame for myself in the future. I have skilful and steadfast friends and have no reason to doubt their loyalty.

I have likewise forgotten to relate why Countess Rumyantsov was banished from my household. My mother had spoken against her in her last conversation with the Empress; the Chancellor, whose power was on the increase, did not esteem her; and Madame Kruse, finding that she was in her way, contributed the influence of her sister and her son-in-law towards her removal.

You will perhaps think it necessary to answer me with the question, why did I never, if I thought myself so badly treated, speak with the Empress directly to justify myself against the myriad scandals, lies, and so forth and so forth. You must know then that thousands upon thousands of times, I have begged the Empress to be allowed to speak with her alone but she would never consent to it.[69] Her dislike of me increased from year to year, although my aim has always been to do her pleasure in everything. The Grand Duke is my witness that I have done all I could to persuade him to conduct himself likewise. My respect, my submis-

252 CATHERINE THE GREAT : MEMOIRS

sion towards all her wishes has been carried to the uttermost extreme to which a human being can carry it. It is true that since November, 1754,[70] I have changed my attitude. It has become more regal. They have grown more considerate of me and I have more peace than formerly.

NOTES

[1] Cf. p. 4.
[2] Cf. p. 72, Note 9.
[3] Catherine's maternal grandfather, Duke Christian August of Schleswig-Holstein-Gottorp, had twelve children; he left four daughters and four sons behind him. His sister Sophie Amalie was however the second wife of Duke August Wilhelm of Brunswick-Wolfenbuettel, whose third wife was Elisabeth Sophie Marie, daughter of Duke Rudolf Friedrich of Holstein-Norburg (widow of Prince Adolf August of Holstein-Ploen).
[4] According to Part I (p. 5) this scene took place in Brunswick.
[5] The words "The maiden is saucy" are German in the MS.
[6] Cf. p. 18.
[7] Duchess Philippine Charlotte and Princess Luise Ulrica of Prussia.
[8] Cf. p. 74, Note 23.
[9] Part I: "On the 1st of January, 1744. . . ." p. 29.
[10] "Augure de tout que Pierre III sera ton époux." Cf. p. 30.
[11] That is, from St. Petersburg.
[12] January 10, 1744.
[13] In St. Petersburg.
[14] Maria Anna. Cf. p. 32.
[15] Cf. however p. 33.
[16] January 16, 1744.
[17] In Schwedt, January 17, 1744.
[18] In the postscript of Bruemmer's letter of December 17, 1743 (see p. 78, Note 73), we read: "If it is agreeable to Your Highness, you might travel to Riga under the name of Countess of Rheinbeck. There you will disclose yourself and receive the escort appointed for you."—This name, which Catherine still remembered when writing these lines, was later forgotten (see p. 34). For this we may conclude that she did not have Part IV at hand, though it was written earlier than Part I.
[19] February 5, 1744.
[20] Semyon Narishkin was Lord Marshal until 1756. Part IV then was not written before 1756.
[21] Illegible in the manuscript, apparently: "of the Semyonovsky Regiment."
[22] January 29 (Feb. 9), 1744.
[23] February 3/14, 1744. Cf. p. 80, Note 90.
[24] February 6/17, 1744.
[25] Part I: "On the 9th of February, 1744, we arrived at the Annenhof-palace." See p. 39.

4 : ADDRESSED TO SIR CHARLES WILLIAMS

26 Cf. p. 80, Note 94.
27 Cf. p. 82, Note 105.
28 Cf. p. 81, Note 97.
29 March 6th, Cf. p. 41, f.
30 The remark that "Troitsa" is a famous cloister is one of the indications that this piece was not written for a Russian.
31 Cf. p. 81, Note 102.
32 Cf. p. 82, Note 106.
33 Cf. p. 84, Note 114.
34 This explanation, dispensable for every Russian, proves that the piece was written for a stranger.
35 Cf. p. 84, Note 117 and p. 120, Note 85.
36 Cf. p. 84, Note 117.
37 Cf. p. 50.
38 July 26, 1744.
39 From August 29 to September 8, 1744.
40 December 15, 1744.
41 December 15, 1744.
42 Fraeulein Schenk.
43 Maria Petrovna Shukov.
44 September 28, 1745.
45 Madame Kruse.
46 Catherine wrote such a letter when King Frederick congratulated her on her appointment as a Russian Grand Duchess. "Sire: I perceive too clearly the share which Your Majesty had in the high position which I have just achieved to forget the gratitude which I owe you for it. Accept my thanks, Sire, and be assured that I shall not regard my position as glorious for me until I have had the opportunity to convince you of my gratitude and devotion, with which I have the honor to remain, Sire, Your Majesty's very devoted and obedient Cousin and Servant, Catherine. Moscow, July 21 (August 1), 1744."
47 Prince Friedrich August.
48 Cf. p. 159, Note 12, and p. 161, Note 16.
49 May 26, 1746.
50 Mademoiselle Skorochodov, married since 1748.
51 Cf. p. 104 however.
52 The court arrived in Reval July 9, 1746.
53 Countess Mavra Yegorovna Shuvalov.
54 Cf. p. 161, Note 20.
55 May 25, 1748.
56 This marriage was consummated November 6, 1754. Cf. p. 254, Note 70.
57 Count Cyril Gregorievich Razumovsky.
58 December 16, 1748.
59 The departure from Moscow took place December 14, 1749.
60 Madame Vladislav.
61 The following from "There were . . ." to "exemplary innocence" (p. 248) are suppressed in the edition of the [Russian] Academy.
62 The passage from "There were" . . . (see p. 247) to here was suppressed in the [Russian] edition.

[63] The Grand Duke and the Grand Duchess arrived in Moscow December 20, 1752.
[64] June 30, 1753.
[65] November 1, 1753.
[66] The following from "I believe" to "affliction" is suppressed in the edition of the [Russian] Academy.
[67] This almost tallies. They left Moscow May 10, 1754, and arrived in Petersburg June 7.
[68] The passage beginning "Three weeks later" to here is suppressed in the edition of the [Russian] Academy.
[69] This conversation came to pass after Bestushev's imprisonment (1758). So this piece was probably written before 1758.
[70] So this piece was written after 1754. Cf. p. 253, Note 56.

PART FIVE

WRITTEN DURING PETER'S REIGN

IN THE EARLY PART OF 1762

I WAS born May 2, 1729 (New Style), at Stettin in Pomerania, where my father, Prince Christian August of Zerbst was at that time Commandant for the King of Prussia and chief of a regiment of infantry. In October, 1727,[1] he had married Princess Johanna Elisabeth of Schleswig-Holstein. I was their first child and my mother almost died when I was born.

I was educated by two French emigrants in turn,—sisters by the name of Cardel. I learned French and at the age of three I could already read and speak this language.

My mother made frequent journeys to visit her numerous relatives, and she usually took me with her. People liked me very much. I remember that at the age of seven years I was conscious of being very ugly but very clever.

As a child I learned history, geography, reading and writing in German and French, a little drawing, a little music, dancing and needlework of all kinds. I was instructed in the Lutheran religion; I was terribly inclined to ask questions, was very headstrong and very persuasive. I had a kind heart and was very sensitive to impressions: I wept very easily and was unusually impressionable. I did not love dolls, but every kind of bodily exercise. No lad was bolder than I and I was proud of it; and when I was afraid I often concealed it, so ashamed was I of it. I was rather secretive. . . .[2]

Chancellor Bestushev was arrested in the year 1757 on a Saturday, the 14th or 15th of February.[3] Early the next day I was informed of it. This frightened me greatly, because I heard that an Italian merchant, my jeweler,[4] was also arrested, as well as my teacher, the Master of the Heralds, Adadurov. As both of them were especially close to me, I had cause to fear that I might be involved in the matter; all the more as Count Bestushev, since his influence with the Empress had declined, had urgently courted the favor of the Grand Duke and especially of myself. He had gone so far as to work out a project, according to which I, in common with my husband, should take over the crown and the government in the event of the death of the Empress (whose health had been quite shaken for several years). I had seen this plan and had corrected it with my own hand. Although it was in my hands, I could not be sure that the rough draft might not be among the papers of the Count, as well as several letters from me. All this would have signified just as many crimes for me. I kept silent and waited the development of events.

On Sunday the marriage of young Count Buturlin with Countess Vorontsov was celebrated at court. I went thither and asked Prince Troubetsky and the wife of Field Marshal Buturlin (who together with Count Alexander Shuvalov had been appointed as commissioners to investigate the conduct and crime of Count Bestushev) whether the Count, Bernardi, and Adadurov were not sure to go unscathed nor have any harm done to them. I have made a vow to God to pardon all those who offend me; I know that the whole matter was put in train against me, and that by the Marquis de l'Hôpital. They promised me to do their best.

The next day I sent a servant of the Grand Duke's, a Frenchman by the name of Bressan, who knew how to force his way in everywhere, to bear the same message to the Procurator General Glebov, a tool of Count Peter Shuvalov's. This had its effect. The next day but one there was already talk of sending Count Shuvalov to his estates and the order was set down which was published two years later.[5]

Since it meant a great deal to the Empress and Count Alexander Shuvalov to follow up the matter, I did not neglect meanwhile to

5 : WRITTEN DURING PETER'S REIGN 259

inform myself of the details of the process, which was very difficult, as we were so to speak locked up and could not, dared not speak to anyone. Besides everyone avoided me because it was assumed that I was involved in the affair.

I set about the matter in the following way. Herr Stambke, the Grand Duke's minister for Holstein affairs, which my husband had entrusted to me at the time, was allowed to visit me, and Count Bestushev, whose tool he was, had found the means of delivering to him the questions presented and his answers. Adadurov did the same through Bressan, who had bribed some of the people who guarded him. Through my servant I had the same thing done with Bernardi; when my name was mentioned, the petty officer made no difficulties about giving him as many letters as he wished and brought the answers, so that all went pretty well. Stambke's servant, however, betrayed his master; and the unfortunate result was that Stambke was dismissed. With the help of the guards the connections were soon restored again and all the answers arranged.

In April of the same year they took from me an old woman whom I liked very much [6] and that under the pretext that she knew all the relations of Count Bestushev to me. The real reason, however, was that, when she was assigned to me, the woman told all that I did to the late Empress Elisabeth,[7] but ceased to do this when I had won her attachment for myself by presents and good treatment. I have always been successful with all the spies by whom I was surrounded; and as a result of this system and many others of this kind it came about that at the time of the Emperor's death I had debts amounting to 600,000 rubles (while I received for my expenses 30,000 rubles).

When this woman was taken away from me I naturally thought that they were angry with me. I had Count Alexander Shuvalov called, who exercised the office of governor over us, and asked him for the reason of this abduction. (I can in truth say this, for when I was hearing mass one Friday, at which the woman was also present, she was told that the Count was asking for her. When she entered his room, he packed her in a carriage and sent her to his house, which he did not occupy because he had rooms in the palace, and for a period of four years she went from one prison to the other, until the death of the Empress.) He told me that she was involved in the affair of Count Bestushev. I replied: "In vain do you try to deceive me; I know that this woman's loyalty to me has caused her downfall. But mark you well, however badly you treat her, she can tell you nothing, especially about me. For I have always concealed my acts from her; my domestics are neither my confidantes nor my advisers. As far as I am concerned, you may take them all, and you will still learn nothing. I know very well that all this is directed against me. You will have to give an account before God for inflicting so much evil on the innocent."

He went stiffly away. But I wept very much, for the bad treatment on the part of the Empress and the Grand Duke grew worse from day to day.

NOTES

[1] November 8, 1727 (see p. 73, Note 19).
[2] The narrative breaks off here.
[3] Saturday, February 14, 1758.
[4] Bernardi.
[5] Manifesto of April 5, 1759.
[6] Madame Vladislav.
[7] "The late Empress Elisabeth"—so this was written after December 25, 1761.

PART SIX

WRITTEN AFTER PETER'S DEATH

IN THE LATTER PART OF 1762

THE death of the Empress Elisabeth plunged all Russians into deep mourning, especially all good patriots, because they saw in her successor a ruler of violent character and narrow intellect, who hated and despised the Russians, did not know his country, was incompetent to do hard work, avaricious and wasteful, and gave himself up wholly to his desires and to those who slavishly flattered him.[1]

After he was master, he left his business to two or three favorites and gave himself up to every kind of extravagance. First he took from the clergy their possessions in land,[2] and introduced a thousand useless innovations, for the most part in the army. He despised the laws, and to put it briefly, justice was for him who offered the most. Dissatisfaction spread everywhere and the poor opinion they had of him made them finally misinterpret the little good that he did. His more or less considered plans were: to start a war with Denmark on account of Schleswig, to change the religion, to divorce his wife and marry his mistress,[3] and to ally himself with the king of Prussia, whom he called his master and to whom he insisted he had sworn the oath of allegiance. He wished to surrender to him a part of his troops. Scarcely any of his plans did he keep secret.

After the death of the Empress, his aunt, various proposals were made secretly to Empress Catherine. But she never wished to listen to them, hoping always that time and circumstances would somehow alter her unhappy situation, all the more as she knew for certain that they could not attack her position or her person without great danger. The nation was completely devoted to her and saw in her their only hope. Various groups had been formed to put a stop to the suffering of their Fatherland. Each of these groups separately turned to her; the one knew nothing of the other.

She listened to them and did not take from them all hope, but always bade them wait, because she believed that things would not come to the worst and because she believed that every change of that kind was a misfortune. She regarded her duties and her reputation as a strong barrier against ambition. Even the danger that she ran was a new luster whose worth she recognized. Peter III was a permanent patch on a very beautiful face.

Catherine's attitude toward the nation has always been irreproachable. She has never wanted, wished, or desired anything but the success of this nation, and her whole life will be employed for the sole purpose of furthering the welfare and happiness of the Russian people.[4]

Having reached the opinion, however, that things were growing worse, Catherine let the different groups know that the time had come for them to combine and consider ways and means. An insult which her husband offered her in public gave an excellent excuse.[5] So it was agreed that after his return from [6] the country he should be arrested in his apartment and declared incompetent to reign. His mind was really no longer just right and certainly he did not have in the whole kingdom a worse enemy than himself.[7] Not all were of the same opinion. Some wished that it should happen in favor of his son; others, in favor of his wife.

Three days before the arrival of the time set, Lieutenant Passek, one of the principals in the plot, was arrested in consequence of the imprudent talk of a soldier.[8] Three brothers Orlov, the eldest of whom was a captain of artillery,[9] began to act at once. The Hetman [10] and the Privy Counsellor Panin thought it was too early. But the former sent of their own accord to the second brother with a coach to Peterhof to fetch the Empress.

6 : WRITTEN AFTER PETER'S DEATH

Alexei Orlov appeared at six o'clock in the morning on June 28 (Old Style), and awakened her from her sleep. When she heard that Passek was arrested and that for the sake of her own safety there was no more time to lose, she arose and drove to the city. She was received on her arrival by the elder Orlov and Prince Bariatinsky and conducted to the barracks of the Izmailovsky Regiment, where on her arrival only twelve men were present and a petty officer and everything seemed quiet. The soldiers knew all about it but remained in their rooms; but when they came they hailed her as Autocrat and Empress.

The joy of the soldiers and the people was indescribable. She was conducted from here to the Semyonovsky Regiment; the people came to meet her dancing and shouting for joy. Thus escorted, she repaired to the Kazan Cathedral, where the Horse Guard made their appearance in transports of joy. The grenadiers of the Preobrashensky Regiment also came. The people asked pardon because they were the last to arrive; their officers had wished to hold them back, otherwise they would certainly have been the first. After them came the artillery and Villebois, Master of Ordnance. Amid the shouts of numberless people the Empress reached the Winter Palace, where the Synod, the Senate, and all the high dignitaries were assembled. The manifesto and the oath were drawn up and everyone recognized her as sovereign.

The Empress called a kind of council which consisted of the Hetman, Privy Counsellor Panin, Prince Volkonsky, the Chief Master of Ordnance, and several others; it was decided, with four regiments of the Guard, a regiment of cuirassiers, and four regiments of infantry, to go to Peterhof and secure the person of Peter III. In this Council Prince Volkonsky said it was a pity there were no light troops. He had scarcely had time to pronounce the words, when an officer asked to speak with him and announced that a regiment of hussars had just arrived in the outskirts.

While the council was still sitting, Count Vorontsov, the Chancellor, came as envoy from the deposed Emperor to reproach the

Empress for her flight and ask her for her reasons. She told him to enter, and when he had very earnestly presented the purpose of his mission, she told him she would let him know her answer. He went, and in another room he was generally advised to take the new oath of allegiance. He said that to relieve his conscience he would like to write a letter and make a report on the success of his mission; then he would take the oath. This was permitted him.

After him came Prince Troubetsky and Field Marshal Shuvalov. They had been sent to hold back the first two regiments of which they were the chiefs and to kill the Empress. They cast themselves at her feet and informed her of their mission. Thereupon they went away to take the oath.

When all this had been dispatched, the Grand Duke and several divisions which were to guard the city were left in the care of the senate.[11] The Empress, however, in the uniform of the guards [12] (she had had herself appointed a Colonel of the Guards) departed on horseback at the head of the regiments. They marched the whole night and towards morning arrived at a small monastery two versts from Peterhof. Hither the Vice-Chancellor, Prince Golitsin, brought a letter from the deposed Emperor to the Empress. A little later General Izmailov came with a similar commission.

The following circumstance gave the occasion for this. On the 28th, the Emperor was to come from Oranienbaum where he was staying to Peterhof for dinner.[13] When he learned that the Empress had driven away from there he was disturbed and sent several persons to the city. Since however all the streets leading thither were guarded at the order of the Empress, none of them came back. He knew that there were two regiments about thirty versts from the city and had sent for them to come to his defense. But these regiments had attached themselves to the Empress.

Thereupon the elderly Field Marshal, Muennich, General Izmailov, and several others advised him to take a dozen persons and either go to the army or cast himself at Kronstadt. The women, of whom

6 : WRITTEN AFTER PETER'S DEATH

there were not fewer than thirty in his retinue, advised him against it on account of the alleged danger. He listened to them and sent to Kronstadt General Devier, who was disarmed when he arrived by Admiral Talyzin who had been sent by the Empress. The Emperor had no news of it.

After he had lingered in his indecision until evening, he finally decided, with the ladies and the rest of his court, to board a galley and two yachts and go to Kronstadt. When he arrived there,[14] he demanded to be admitted but an officer on the guard [15] on the bastion at the entrance to the harbor turned him back and threatened, although he really had no power at all, to fire upon the galley of the monarch. When the latter heard this, he ordered his people to return and disembarked at Oranienbaum, where he went to bed.

The following day he wrote the two letters above mentioned. In the first he requested that he might be allowed to return to Holstein with his mistress and his favorites; in the second he offered to renounce the throne and begged only for his life. He had about 1,500 armed men, Holstein troops, more than a hundred cannon, and several Russian divisions with him. The Empress sent General Izmailov back [16] with a letter, in which she demanded this resignation. Peter III quietly wrote this document [17] and then came with General Izmailov, his mistress, and his favorite Gudovich to Peterhof. To protect him from being torn to pieces by the soldiers, he was given a reliable guard with four officers under the command of Alexei Orlov.

While preparations were being made for his departure to Ropsha, a very pleasant but quite unfortified country palace, the soldiers began to grumble. They said that for three hours they had not seen the Empress. Prince Troubetsky was frankly trying to make peace between the monarch and her husband. It must be made clear to her that she must resist; she would certainly be betrayed and hurl herself and all those with her to destruction. When Catherine heard of this talk she went to Prince Troubetsky and bade him enter his carriage and drive to the city, while she would make the round of the troops on foot.

As soon as the soldiers saw her, the shouts of joy and jubilation began again; Peter III was sent to his destination.[18]

With the arrival of nightfall the Empress was advised to return to the city, because for two days she had not slept and had scarcely eaten anything.[19] But the troops begged her not to leave them, and she agreed with pleasure when she saw their great enthusiasm for her. Half-way there, they rested for three hours, and towards 10 o'clock in the morning of June 30th (Old Style), 1762, the Empress, at the head of the troops and the artillery and amid the indescribable jubilation of the multitude, rode into Petersburg. A more beautiful sight can not be imagined. Her court went ahead and the troops had oak-leaves in their hats and caps. They had stamped under their feet all the new articles of clothing they had received from Peter III.

Thus she arrived in triumph at the Summer Palace, where all the people of rank and importance were assembled to wait for her. The Grand Duke came to meet her in the middle of the court. When the Empress caught sight of him, she dismounted and kissed him.

The applause was endless. They went to church, where a Te Deum was sung to the thunder of cannon. The exultation of the people went on the whole day but no kind of disorder occurred.

The Empress had gone to bed and had scarcely fallen asleep, when Lieutenant Passek came to awaken her and bade her to get up. For the fatigue, the long wakefulness, and the wine had helped to make hotter heads than usual, and loyalty to her had aroused in the Izmailovsky Regiment fears for her safety. Without a moment's delay the people had set forth to defend her. When they were told that there was nothing to fear and that she was asleep, they declared that in this matter they could and would only believe their own eyes.

So the Empress arose at two o'clock in the morning, and came out

6 : WRITTEN AFTER PETER'S DEATH

to them. When the soldiers saw her they raised a shout of joy. But in a serious tone she bade them go to bed and allow her to sleep. They should have confidence in her officers, and she urged them strongly to obey them. This they promised, while they begged her pardon and reproached each other because they had been persuaded to waken her in this way. They went home quite peacefully, often looking back to see her as long as it was possible. (Incidentally, in Petersburg there is scarcely any night in summer.)

For the two following days the jubilee held on the entire day, but there were no excesses and no disorders. This is certainly remarkable with such great excitement.

Several weeks later anxiety about the person of the Empress arose again among the troops; on several evenings they assembled to defend her or to see her. Then she signed an order forbidding them to assemble again. She assured them that she would herself provide for her security and had no enemies. Concerning this order they said to one another: "It must indeed be true, for she will not become her own enemy by believing herself safe if she is not." Since that time the greatest peace reigns everywhere.[20]

ANECDOTES CONCERNING THIS EVENT

When Lieutenant Passek was arrested, the soldiers who were guarding him opened the doors and windows to allow him to escape. "For," said they, "you suffer for a good cause." Although he had to be prepared for torture and could not foresee what would happen if all the conspirators agreed to strike the blow in this event, he still retained the steadfastness to remain under arrest in order not to spoil things. For the whole regiment had been alarmed and they might perhaps have closed the city in order to find him.

When Admiral Talyzin was sent to Kronstadt we all thought him a lost man. For it was inconceivable that the Emperor had not thought of this harbor and fortress. It was not more than a mile by water from Oranienbaum, while it was four miles from the city, and he was not dispatched until towards mid-day.

When he really came, he found General Devier with 2,000 men, who had been stationed in the harbor. The latter asked him what he wanted there. He replied: "I have come to hasten the departure of the fleet."—"And what are they saying and doing in the city?"—"Nothing," said he.—"Where are you going now?"—"I am going to take a rest; I am dying of the heat." He was allowed to go through. He entered a house which he left by the back door, proceeded to Commandant Nummers and said to him: "Hark you! In the city the news is quite different from here; everyone has taken the oath of allegiance to the Empress. I advise you to do the same. I have 4,000 sailors here, you have only 2,000 men. Here are my orders; make your decision." The latter answered that he would do what the former wished. "Very well," said he; "go and disarm General Devier." He did this; he called Devier aside and took his dagger; then all took the oath of allegiance.

When the Empress left Peterhof, she lost more than an hour in going through the gardens. Consequently she missed the carriage and was recognized on the road by some passers-by. She had with her only a maid who would not leave her and her servant who was looking for the carriage.[21]

While she was marching to Peterhof with the troops, the people thought that Peter III might come by water. Several thousand of them assembled on the shore of the Vassili Ostrov where the Neva joins the sea and armed with sticks and stones firmly determined to sink every boat that should come from the sea.

When the Empress had returned in triumph to the city and had retired to her apartment, Captain Orlov[22] fell at her feet and said: "I behold you as Autocrat and Empress; my Fatherland is freed from its fetters; it will be happy under your government. I have done my duty; I have served you, my country and myself. I have only one favor to ask of you; permit me to retire to my estates. I was born an honest man; court life might corrupt me. I am young; your favor will expose me to hatred. I have means; I shall be happy in retirement, covered with fame because I have given you to my Fatherland."

The Empress replied that it would injure his work if he permitted her to seem ungrateful to the man to whom she believed herself most of all indebted. The common people would not believe in his magnanimity but would think that she had in some way given him grounds for dissatisfaction or had not sufficiently rewarded him. She was obliged to some extent to exercise her authority to induce him to stay. He was moved to tears by the red ribbon of the Order of St. Alexander and the Chamberlain's key which she bestowed upon him and which carries with it the rank of Major General.

The wrath of the soldiers against Peter III was quite violent; here is a slight instance. After the oath of allegiance, while the council was being held, the troops were drawn up around the wooden Winter Palace. They had been permitted to resume their former uniforms, and it occurred to one of the officers to tear off his golden shoulder-piece and throw it to the people, because he thought they would make it into money. They seized it greedily, caught a dog, and hung it around his neck. And the dog thus decorated was driven forth with a great roar. They stamped with their feet on everything which came from this monarch.

The Empress appointed Alexei Orlov, Prince Bariatinsky, and three other officers to go with Peter III to Ropsha. They selected a hundred men from the regiments of the Guard. They had orders to make life as pleasant as possible for the monarch and to provide everything he wished for his entertainment. It was the intention to send him from there to Schluesselburg and as circumstances developed to allow him in time to depart for Holstein with his favorites. So little was his character considered dangerous.

When the Monarch learned that the Empress had left Peterhof, he betook himself thither, looked for her everywhere, even under the bed; he questioned all his people who had remained there but could come to no decision. All those surrounding him suggested different plans of action, of which he chose the weakest. He walked up and down in the garden and demanded that dinner be served.

When the grenadiers of the first regiment of the guards met the Empress near the Kazan Cathedral, the people wished to place themselves next to the Empress's carriage. But the grenadiers of the Izmailovsky regiment said to them with bitter reproaches that they were the last to come and refused to give way to them. This was a dangerous moment; for if the former had insisted on their purpose, the bayonets would have sprung into action. But they did not do this at all; they said it was the fault of their officers who had held them back, and quietly fell into line in front of the coach of the Empress.

When after her return from Peterhof the Empress dismounted from her horse in front of the Summer Palace, the crowd was so great that she had to be carried by arms, which was a beautiful sight. It seemed as if she had been forced to do what had been done. This was indeed the case; for if she had refused she would have run the risk of sharing the fate of Peter III. There was therefore no choice.

The Regiment Voronesh was, on the morning of June 28, in Krasnoe Selo, 27 versts from Petersburg. The German officer who had been dispatched by Peter III to induce the regiment to march

6 : WRITTEN AFTER PETER'S DEATH

to Peterhof, arrived shortly before the Empress. The regiment was about to start on its way without knowing what it was about when Colonel Olsufiev arrived with an officer of the Guard to administer the oath for Catherine. The Commander of the Regiment hesitated. A grenadier uttered some words that displeased the German officer; he drew his dagger and wished to give the soldier a blow with it. Thereupon the soldier began to shout that they would go to Petersburg and join the Empress. They set out and as the monarch left the city she met them. Since the people were fatigued, she wished to leave them in the city, but they marched on with her for 23 versts and were then ordered to halt at the country place of Myza Strelna, because the Colonel was not wholly trusted. The same night when everyone returned to the city the regiment returned also. Thus they had marched, in twenty-four hours, a distance of 73 versts, which are ten and one-half German miles.[23]

After leaving the city on the evening of the 28th, the first halt was made ten versts from the city at a hostelry by the name of Krasny Kabatshok. Here everything made the impression of a real campaign. The soldiers lay on the highroad, the officers and a number of city people who had come along out of curiosity, and everyone who could find room in the house had entered. There had never been a day so rich in adventure; everyone had had his own and wished to tell of it. Everyone was highly pleased and no one had the slightest hesitation. One would have thought that everything was already decided, although in truth no one could foresee the end of this great catastrophe. It was not even known where Peter III was. We were obliged to assume that he had hurled himself at Kronstadt, but no one thought of it.

In the meantime Catherine was not as peaceful as she seemed; she laughed and jested with the others, called across the entire room to this one and that one, and if she had moments of abstraction, she attributed it to the exertions of the day. They tried to induce her to lie down; she threw herself on the bed for a moment but could not close her eyes. But she kept quiet in order not to disturb Princess Dashkov who lay by her side. When she accidentally turned her head, she saw that the great blue eyes of the latter were open and gazing at her. Thereupon they both burst into a loud laugh, because each had thought that the other was asleep and respected her sleep. They then went back to the others, and soon afterwards they broke camp.

Princess Dashkov was concerned in this event in the following manner. She was the younger sister of the mistress of Peter III, nineteen years old and prettier than her sister, who was very ugly. If their outward appearance was dissimilar, their souls were still more different. The younger had much intelligence and understanding; she was industrious, well read, had a strong liking for Catherine and was loyal to her with heart, mind, and soul. Since she did not conceal this liking and since she believed that the happiness of her Fatherland depended on this monarch, she expressed herself everywhere in accordance with these feelings, which did her endless harm with her sister and Peter III.

In consequence of this point of view, which she did not conceal, many officers who could not speak to Catherine herself turned to Princess Dashkov to assure the Empress of their devotion. But this happened long after the offers of the Orlovs. It was rather the conversation and schemes of the latter which had led these officers, who did not know about the direct way taken by the Orlovs, to turn to the Empress through the mediation of Princess Dashkov, whom they thought closer to her. Catherine never mentioned the Orlovs to the Princess, in order not to expose their names. The great zeal and the youth of the Princess caused her to fear that, in the throng of her acquaintances, there might be some one who would inadvertently betray the matter.

Finally the Empress advised the Orlovs to make the acquaintance of the Princess in order that they might be in a better position to communicate with the above-mentioned officers and to see what

CATHERINE THE GREAT
From a painting by Ericsen

use they might derive from it. For however well-intentioned these officers were, they were, according to Princess Dashkov's own admission, less firmly decided than were the Orlovs, who found the means of carrying out their plans.

As for the rest, not all the courage which Princess Dashkov really showed to such a high degree, would have decided anything. She had more flatterers than confidence, and the character of her family always caused a certain mistrust.

Finally the Princess demanded, or rather through her mediation Lieutenant Passek demanded on one side and the Orlovs on the other, that Catherine should give them something in writing with which they could convince her friends of her consent. Through the Princess she sent a note which was confined to the following expressions: "Let the will of God be done, and that of Lieutenant Passek; I am in agreement with all that is useful for the Fatherland." To the Orlovs she wrote: "Regard what is said to you by him who shows you this note as if I myself said it to you, I am in agreement with everything which can save the Fatherland, together with which you will save me and your selves." Both papers she signed with her name. It is easy to understand that these notes were torn after they had served their purpose.

After the death of Empress Elisabeth, the daughter of Biron, Duke of Courland, who was the wife of Baron Tcherkassov and who, in spite of her deformity, had once been loved by Peter III, induced the Emperor to recall her father from Yaroslav whither the late Empress had banished him. Many things helped to increase the natural dislike which the Emperor felt for Prince Carl of Saxony after his sojourn in Petersburg. He was so jealous of him that it sufficed merely to mention his name to put him in a rage.

He had promised the daughter to restore to the father his dukedom and he thought kindly of this until the arrival of Prince

George of Holstein, who with his followers caused him to change his mind and to demand from Biron and his sons the abdication of Courland in favor of himself, the Prince of Holstein.

The Birons turned with their complaints to the Empress, who could do nothing more than assure them that she knew the justice of their cause and that it did not rest with her to help them. On the day of her accession to the throne, the Birons were to sign the abdication.

When events now took another turn, Biron was freed and the Empress had no grounds for throwing him back into prison. His daughter had always been loyal to him and his rights had been found just a thousand times. Russia had no occasion to keep this family at the expense of the country. It was therefore decided to give Courland back to them; also it did not displease Catherine to create a Duke in the first days of her reign.

On the day of the peace celebration Chamberlain Stroganov received orders not to leave his house because he had manifested sympathy for the Empress, who had been publicly insulted by the Emperor.[24] This scandal had made a great impression on everybody's feelings, which were already enlisted on the Empress's behalf and excited over the bad behavior, the violent temperament, and the hatred of Peter the Third for the Russian people which he did not even strive to conceal. This ferment continued, spread, and increased up to June 27.

The plans of Peter III were no longer a secret. They consisted in this: to send the regiments of the Guard away and bring his Holstein troops into the city; to incarcerate the Empress (already orders had once been given for her arrest and had then been withdrawn);[25] to marry his mistress, Countess Vorontsov; to change the religion; and a thousand other innovations just as thoughtless.

On the evening of the 27th a Captain of the Preobrashensky Regi-

6 : WRITTEN AFTER PETER'S DEATH

ment by the name of Passek was arrested. The whole regiment was aroused over the event because they knew that he was devoted to the Empress and was arrested on her account. The other friendly spirits, at whose head were the three brothers Orlov, one of whom was a Captain of Artillery, at once understood the danger which threatened the Empress if this state of things continued. They employed a part of the night to inform the Hetman, Prince Volkonsky, and Privy Counsellor Panin. Toward morning Captain Alexei Orlov went to Peterhof to inform the Empress of the danger that threatened her and bring her to the city. For they were all firmly convinced that it would be sufficient for her only to show herself to win the hearts of all.

At six o'clock in the morning the above-mentioned officer entered her room, and bade her rise and save the Fatherland in saving herself. After a few explanations, the Empress arose, and, accompanied by three officers, and a servant,[26] all Russians, entered the carriage fetched for the purpose. Thus attended, she arrived at the barracks of the Izmailovsky Regiment, where everything seemed to be perfectly quiet; for only twelve men were there, as well as a petty officer and a drummer, who at once beat the alarm. Within three minutes the officers and soldiers assembled around the Empress, and led forward a priest [27] by the arm, that he might administer for them the oath of allegiance to the Empress; then she was bidden to step into a carriage.

She got in with the Hetman and drove to the Semyonovsky Regiment, where she was received with indescribable shouts of joy. From here she proceeded onward to the Kazan Cathedral where the Horse Guard came to meet her in a frenzy of joy.

The people took up the cry; all were bathed in tears and thanked Heaven for their salvation.

From there she went to the Winter Palace, where the Senate and the Synod had already assembled. Here she had the manifesto inscribed and the oath was administered. Later a council was held

278   CATHERINE THE GREAT : MEMOIRS

in which it was decided to march to Peterhof. The Empress donned the uniform of the Guards and left the city at the head of 14,000 men.

Chamberlain Passek often said of Peter III that this monarch had no worse enemy than himself, because he neglected nothing that could do him harm.

The equerry Narishkin, a favorite of the monarch, said in his time: "It is a reign of folly; all our time is spent in eating, drinking and madness."

It often happened during his reign that the monarch went to see the guard changed, and that he beat the soldiers or onlookers, or carried on absurdly with his negro or his favorites, and that frequently in the presence of an innumerable crowd of people.

NOTES

[1] In her book "Antidote" (1770) Catherine writes: "Unfortunately this Prince had stupid people around him who instilled hatred in him against the nation, and he did not even conceal his sentiment. Hatred however is no way to win love. By his scant foresight and his behavior he lost the respect and confidence of public opinion; his incapacity did the rest. The people realized that the downfall of the Empire must be the consequence of a reign in which reason and justice would not be on the side of the monarch and the word Fatherland would be a crime. Every state in such a situation is near a revolution. This came June 28 (Old Style), 1762, and never did an event fall out more fortunately than did this one which rescued an Empire that was close to destruction."

[2] Ukase of March 21, 1762.

[3] Countess Elisabeth Vorontsov.

[4] This promise indicates that Catherine probably wrote this piece at the very beginning of her reign.

[5] June 9, 1762, at the banquet to celebrate the Peace with Prussia, Peter drank to the imperial family. Catherine pledged him seated. Thereupon the Emperor sent Gudovich with an abusive message, and then to make sure shouted loudly across the table: "dura" (silly woman).

[6] Peter had gone to Oranienbaum June 12, 1762, Catherine to Peterhof June 17. Catherine had seen her husband for the last time, probably on June 19 when she attended a theatrical performance at Oranienbaum.

[7] During March and April of 1789 Catherine read a book by Abbé Denina, *Essai sur la vie et la règne de Frédéric II, roi de Prusse* (*Berlin, 1788*), and made with her own hand a great number of notes on the margin. This note

6 : WRITTEN AFTER PETER'S DEATH

appears on p. 223: "Peter III had no greater enemy than himself; all his actions bordered on insanity. Besides this, whatever aroused the sympathy of other people moved him to anger. He took pleasure in beating animals and men, and was not only insensible to their tears and cries but they enraged him, and when he was in this state he quarreled with everyone that came near him. His favorites were very unfortunate on this account, they did not dare to speak with each other without arousing his distrust. When this was awakened, he beat them soundly before everyone. The Grand Master of the Horse Narishkin, Lieutenant-General Melgunov, Privy Counsellor Volkov were cudgelled at Oranienbaum in the presence of the diplomatic corps and about a hundred spectators, men and women, at a festival which the Emperor gave. The English Ambassador Keith went on this occasion to Countess Bruce and said to her: "Do you know, the Emperor is quite mad." . . . By ascending the throne, Empress Catherine saved the empire, herself, and her son from the hands of a madman who was almost raving."

[8] June 27, 1762.

[9] This refers to Gregory, who was however, the second of the five brothers (born 1734); the eldest was Ivan (born 1733).

[10] Count Cyril Razumovsky.

[11] Ukase written by her own hand June 28, 1762, at 10 o'clock in the evening: "Messieurs and Senators: I now go with the army to secure and safeguard the throne and leave, in the fullest confidence, the Fatherland, the people, and my son, in your protection as my highest governing authority. Catherine."

[12] The uniform which Catherine wore belonged to Alexander Feodorovich Talyzin, husband of Maria Stepanovna Apraxin frequently referred to.

[13] Peter came to Peterhof June 28, 1762, at two o'clock in the afternoon.

[14] Towards 1 o'clock at night.

[15] Michael Gabrilovich Koshukov.

[16] On the margin of the manuscript this note is added: "When the latter came to the Empress, he threw himself at her feet and said: 'Do you regard me as an honorable man?' She said: 'Yes.' 'Very well,' he replied; 'depend upon it, I am yours. If you will trust me I will save my Fatherland much bloodshed. It is a pleasure to be in the company of people of intelligence. I give you my word, if you will release me, I will bring Peter here, I quite alone.' And this he carried out."

[17] In her detailed manifesto of July 6, 1762, Catherine gives the wording of Peter's abdication: "In the short period of my reign as autocrat of the Russian Empire I have realized its hardships and burdens, to which my powers are not equal, so that neither as autocrat nor in any other way can I rule the Russian Empire. Thus I perceived that inward changes were leading to the destruction of its safety and would necessarily bring lasting disgrace to me. I have therefore taken counsel with myself and herewith solemnly declare without hatred and without compulsion, not merely to the Russian Empire but to all the world, that I renounce the sovereignty of the Russian Empire for my whole life. As long as I live I will never reign over the Russian Empire as autocrat nor in any other way, and I will never myself nor with anyone's help strive for it. I swear this sincerely and without hypocrisy before God

and the whole world. This entire abdication I have written and signed with my own hand. The 29th day of June, in the year 1762. Peter."

[18] On June 29, 1762, towards 8 o'clock in the evening, Peter arrived at Ropsha, where on July 6 he perished.

[19] Catherine to Poniatovsky, July 2, 1762: "I have not slept for three nights, nor eaten but twice in four days."

[20] Catherine to Poniatovsky, August 9, 1762: "If anyone tells you there is fresh unrest among the troops, you must know that this is only exaggerated affection for me, which begins to be burdensome to me. The soldiers are dying of fear that something might happen to me. I can not leave my apartments without loud applause." To the same November 11, 1762: "My position is such that I have to observe the greatest caution. The least soldier of the Guard thinks when he sees me: 'That is the work of my hands.' "

[21] Catherine had with her Mademoiselle Sharogorodsky, the Groom Bibikov, and a servant, Shkurin.

[22] Gregory Orlov.

[23] This explanation clearly shows that Catherine wrote the piece for foreign readers.

[24] June 9, 1762; Cf. p. 278, Note 5.

[25] Cf. p. 311.

[26] Cf. Note 21 above.

[27] The Chaplain of the Regiment Father Alexei (Michailov).

PART SEVEN

WRITTEN AFTER 1794

AN EXPLANATION

– 283 –

Count Alexander Andreievich Bezborodko has written a brief account of the politics, wars, and domestic government of Empress Catherine II, Autocrat of all the Russias, as well as the most important events of her reign.[1] He begins as follows: "In the year 1762. Accession to the throne of all the Russias by Her Imperial Majesty."—Explanation:[2]

IN the year 1761, during the illness of Her Majesty, Empress Elisabeth Petrovna of blessed memory, I learned from the mouth of Nikita Ivanovich Panin, that the Shuvalovs, Peter Ivanovich, Alexander Ivanovich, and Ivan Ivanovich, were in great anxiety, owing to the impending death of Her Imperial Majesty, about their future destiny. In consequence of their fears, the people around her produced the utmost variety of plans. They all feared the successor of the Empress; he possessed the love and respect of nobody. The Empress herself was not sure to whom she should transmit the throne. It was known that she was inclined to exclude the incompetent successor, who had given her so much vexation, and choose instead of him his seven-year-old son, giving me the regency. But the idea of my being regent did not please the Shuvalovs.

Owing to these considerations, the Shuvalovs were reconciled with Peter III through the mediation of Melgunov, and the Empress died without other orders. But this did not end the excitement in the public mind, the beginning of which may be discovered in the bad administration of the Shuvalovs and the illegal affair of Bestushev, that is, as far back as 1759.

Immediately after the death of Empress Elisabeth Petrovna,

Prince Michael Ivanovich Dashkov, at that time Captain of the Guard, sent this message to me: "Give the order, and we will place you on the throne!" I sent him this reply: "For God's sake, do nothing foolish. All will happen as providence wills. But your undertaking is premature and untimely." In the home of Prince Dashkov at that time were gathered, as his intimate and confidential friends, all those who later on took part in my elevation to the throne, as, for instance, the three Orlovs, five Captains of the Izmailovsky Regiment, and others. He was married to a sister of Elisabeth Romanovna Vorontsov, the mistress of Peter III. Princess Dashkov had been especially devoted to me from her childhood. But an extremely dangerous person existed in the brother of the Princess, Semyon Romanovich Vorontsov, whom Elisabeth Romanovna and with her Peter III quite particularly loved. The most dangerous of all was the father of the Vorontsovs, Roman Larionovich, on account of his querulous and untrustworthy nature. Incidentally he had no fondness for Princess Dashkov.

Empress Elisabeth Petrovna died at Christmastide exactly, on December 25, 1761, at three o'clock in the afternoon.[3] I remained beside the body. Peter III left the room, went to the Conference, and sent Melgunov to tell me that I should remain beside the body until I heard from him. I said to Melgunov: "You see that I am here, and I will obey the order." I concluded from the message that the ruling party was afraid of my influence. They were still occupied with the washing of the body of the Empress, when I was told that Procurator General Shakovsky had been dismissed at his request, and that the Chief Procurator of the Senate, Alexander Ivanovich Glebov, had been named Procurator-General. This meant, then, that a man who was considered one of the most upright of the time had been discharged and in his place a well-known good-for-naught, whom Peter Shuvalov had protected from criminal prosecution, had been made Procurator-General.

They had scarcely dressed the body of Empress Elisabeth Petrovna and laid it in the canopied bedstead when the Lord Marshal brought me word that a supper would take place in the gallery (that is, three rooms away from the body) and it was decreed that bright clothing should be worn at the feast. I ordered my festival garment to be brought to my son's apartment which was next to that of the Empress. I dressed there and returned again to the deceased, where I had been ordered to remain and await commands. Here the windows were already opened and the gospel was being read.

Somewhat later the Emperor sent me a request to come into the church. When I arrived there I found all assembled to take the oath, after which instead of the Requiem a Te Deum was sung. Then the Metropolitan of Novgorod, Setchenov, turned to the Emperor with an address. The latter was beside himself with joy, and he did not try in the least to conceal it; he behaved quite disgracefully. He made all manner of faces and talked in silly phrases which corresponded neither to his dignity nor to the circumstances. He acted more like a ridiculous harlequin than anything else, yet demanded all respect.

After leaving the church I went to my room, where I wept bitterly, as much for the departed Empress, who had shown me many favors and had taken quite a liking to me in the past two years, as for the present state of things.

When all had been prepared, it was announced to me, and I went to supper. The table had been set in the electoral gallery for 150 persons, and the gallery was full of spectators. Many who had found no place, ran hither and thither around the board, among them Ivan Ivanovich Shuvalov and Melgunov. From a pick-thank of the Shuvalovs he had become their protector. On the cheeks of Ivan Ivanovich Shuvalov the signs of desperation were evident, for the skin had been scratched by all five fingers. Nevertheless he jested, standing behind the chair of Peter III, and laughed with him.

I sat beside the new Emperor; at my side Prince Nikita Yuryevich Troubetsky, who talked across the entire table of nothing else but his great joy because the Emperor had begun his reign. A number of ladies also supped with us; many of them like myself had red and swollen eyes and many, between whom otherwise no friendship existed, had become reconciled. The supper lasted about an hour and a half.

When I was again in my apartments, I began to undress to go to bed. Someone then brought me word that the ladies should don their festival garments on the morrow and that a great dinner would take place in the same gallery; the places at table would be assigned by lot. I then went to bed.

But slumber refused to come, although I had spent two nights without sleep in the apartments of the Empress. I could not go to sleep and began to reflect about the past, the present, and the future. And I came to this conclusion: if in the first hour of the reign they dismiss an honorable man and do not hesitate to promote a scamp to fill his place, what is indeed to be expected? I said to myself: "They are afraid of your influence, keep away from everything. You know with whom you have to deal. They will not act according to your ideas and principles, so there is neither honor nor fame to be earned here; let them do what they wish."

I took this as the rule for my behavior, and during the whole six months of Peter III's reign, took part in nothing, with the solitary exception of the funeral of the departed Empress. The mourning commission had been ordered to put themselves in connection with me for this purpose and I carried out everything with the greatest zeal and earned applause from every side. In this I let myself be advised by the more elderly ladies, Countess Maria Andreievna Rumyantsov, Countess Anna Karlovna Vorontsov, Madame Agrafena Leontyevna Apraxin, and others who happened to be within reach, and made myself very popular thereby.

On the morning of the following day I put on a festival robe and went to mass, then to make my obeisance before the body, and from there to the table, according to lots. Almost everyone pres-

7 : AN EXPLANATION

ent had tear-stained eyes and there were few indifferent faces. Fatigue was visible in all of them. After dinner I retired to my apartments.

While we were dining, they had dissected the body of the departed Empress. Toward evening I learned that couriers had been dispatched to Biron, Muennich, Lestocq, and the Lopuchins to recall them to Petersburg, and that Gudovich was on the way to Berlin with the news of the Emperor's succession. I said of this: "All goes very quickly."

On the third day I put on a black dress and went to the body, where a requiem was sung. The Emperor was not there, nor was anyone else; only those who were in attendance on the dead and my retinue.

From there I went to my son. Then I visited Count Alexei Gregoreievich Rezumovsky in his apartments in the palace, where he lay ill of sincere grief for the departed Empress. He wished to fall at my feet, but I would not permit it and embraced him. We fell into each other's arms and cried heartily together, scarcely able to speak a word. I left him then and returned to my apartments.

When I reached my room again, I heard that the Emperor had given orders that the room which was separated from mine by an ante-chamber and was occupied by Alexander Ivanovich Shuvalov should be prepared for him, and that Elisabeth Romanovna Vorontsov was to dwell in his room next to mine.

On this day the Emperor went into society towards evening to attend a Christmas celebration.

When the apartments of Alexander Ivanovich Shuvalov were ready two days later, the Emperor moved into them and Elisabeth Vorontsov into his. But my reception rooms were draped in black and the Emperor received in them his guests. Mornings and evenings he paid visits to all the important people, who prepared great banquets for him. I kept away from these feasts on account of a violent cough.

On the evening before the day on which the body of the late Empress was to be taken from the room in which she died and placed in state upon the bier, the Emperor dined with Count Sheremetiev. On this occasion Elisabeth Vorontsov became jealous and made a scene; I do not know who was the cause. They came home in a violent dispute.

The next day after dinner, at five o'clock, she sent me a letter in which she begged me for Heaven's sake to come to her; it was necessary that she should speak with me but she could not come to me because she lay ill in bed. I went to her and found her dissolved in tears. When she saw me she could not speak for a long time. I sat down beside her bed and asked her what was wrong. She seized my hands, kissed them and pressed them and wet them with her tears. I asked her what it was that afflicted her so much. She replied: "I pray you speak softly." I inquired, "And for what reason?" She answered: "In the next room is my sister, Anna Michailovna Stroganov, with Ivan Ivanovich Shuvalov." (This is, she had helped them to a *rendezvous* while she talked with me.) [4]

I laughed; her tears ceased to flow, and she began to beg me to go to the Emperor and ask him in her name to allow her to return to her father. She did not wish to remain any longer in the palace. And she abused his circle and himself. To the astonishment of everyone, she had done this on the day before at the house of Sheremetiev, and the Emperor had in consequence commanded that her father be arrested. But they had pacified him with petitions.

I said to her that she should not choose anyone else for this task, for that would probably be unpleasant for him. But she tried to convince me that it must be so; she could only ask through my mediation, for all the others were heartless rascals and she put her entire hope in me. To make an end of my visit to her, I promised her to go to him and place her petition before him.

When I returned to my apartments, I made inquiry whether he

7 : AN EXPLANATION

was at home and whether one could go to him. They told me that he was resting. When he awakened at seven o'clock, I was informed and went to the Emperor. I found him in his dressing-gown; he was walking up and down the room and still very sleepy. I began to present my petition: "If you are surprised at my visit, you will be still more astonished when you hear why I have come." I told him everything, word for word: how Elisabeth Romanova Vorontsov had written to me and what she had said, and how I had declined the commission and her reasons for trusting no one except me.

He listened to me in a surprised and reflective manner and allowed me to repeat what had been said. In the meantime Melgunov and Leo Alexandrovich Narishkin came into the room. Angered at Elisabeth Vorontsov, he told them on what mission I had come.

This lasted for about an hour. Finally I asked him: "What answer do you order me to give her, or will you send some one else?" At this Melgunov and Narishkin advised him to say that he would send her his answer. So I withdrew and let Elisabeth Vorontsov know that the answer would be sent to her.

Later she sent to me again to say that she had been dismissed, and that she was dressing while she waited for the carriage in order to leave the palace and go to her father. She asked only for permission to visit me and say farewell. I said: "She may come." In the meantime a great running to and fro began in my antechamber in front of my dressing-room; first Melgunov, then Narishkin, went to her and returned again. This lasted until eleven o'clock. Then came the Emperor himself; he tarried with her and returned again to his apartments. But she sent me a note, saying that she would not come to me because she had been commanded to remain in the palace.

I went to bed and slept. On the evening of the next day, Peter III came to me with Melgunov and Leo Narishkin. They scolded and abused Elisabeth Vorontsov with a vengeance and apparently desired that I should join in with them. But I only listened in silence. The Emperor then told me that she had not wished to wear my portrait when he had appointed her as maid-of-honor, but had demanded his. He thought that this would make me angry; but when he saw that I only laughed at it and was not angry at all, he left the room.

Thereupon Melgunov and Narishkin reproached me, saying that I had lost a fine opportunity to drive her out of the house. I answered them: "I am still more surpised at you, that you did not carry out your wish yesterday."

After the day on which the late Empress died, there was a double guard in the palace; that is, a full guard for the body and a second one for the Emperor. But a severe frost reigned at this time. The guard room was small and narrow, so that all of the people could not enter and many of the soldiers were obliged to remain out of doors. This circumstance aroused dissatisfaction among them and the public, and increased the discontent that already existed. Every day brought new stories from the palace. Now this one was arrested, now the other; with the women, whom he daily invited to supper in large numbers, he quarreled at his own table and that of others; he ordered a dagger to be taken from a husband or else engaged in a dispute about trifles with some one in the service and had him locked up in the guard room. He seldom rose from the table otherwise than stupidly drunk. Many new favorites began to appear, among others the Captain of the Preobrashensky Regiment, Prince Ivan Feodorovich Golitsin, whom he suddenly decorated with the Order of St. Anna, although up to that day scarcely anyone had known him. At this time the Emperor brought into the Cabinet as Secretary Dmitri Vasilievich Volkov, formerly the Secretary of the Conference. Nikita Ivanovich Panin was of the opinion, as he told me, that he would make short work of Melgunov and the Shuvalovs. People thought at the time that he had unusual intelligence; but later it was seen that, although quick and eloquent, he was extremely frivolous. Because he wrote well,

7 : AN EXPLANATION

he wrote a great deal and did very little; but he liked to drink and amuse himself.

Two weeks after the death of the late Empress, Count Ivan Ivanovich Shuvalov died.[5] A few days before his death, he and his elder brother, Alexander Ivanovich Shuvalov, had been appointed Field Marshals by the Emperor.

And there were still other new appointments. The Emperor suddenly named four Chiefs for the four Regiments of the Guard: they were, for the Preobrashensky Regiment, Field Marshal Prince Nikita Yuryevich Troubetsky; for the Semyonovsky Regiment, Field Marshal Count Alexander Ivanovich Shuvalov; for the Izmailovsky Regiment, Field Marshal Count Cyril Gregorievich Razumovsky. For the Horse Guards, he wished to appoint Count Alexei Gregorievich Razumovsky, but he asked for leave on this account and Prince George of Holstein became Chief. These new Chiefs were opposed in every way to their appointment and tried to prevent it, but they did not succeed. For the Regiments of the Guard this was a severe, unbearable blow.

Although pompous burials and showy processions had been forbidden by a ukase of the departed Empress, the Messieurs Shuvalov obtained permission from the former Emperor to bury Count Peter Ivanovich with ostentatious ceremony. The Emperor himself promised to take part in the obsequies.

On the appointed day they waited long for the Emperor, but he only arrived toward noon on the mourning day. But the people had been waiting since morning to see the ceremony. It was a very cold day. Because the people were impatient, there was all kind of talk. Some remembered the tobacco monopoly of Shuvalov and said they were bringing him so late because he was strewn with tobacco. Others said that he was strewn with salt and recalled that he was the originator of the salt tax. Others insisted that he had been laid in seal-blubber, because he had the monopoly of seal-blubber and codfish. Then they remembered the codfish had not been obtainable this winter for money and began to insult and abuse him in every way.

At last they bore the body from his house on the Moika to the Nevsky Cloister. General Korff, at that time the Chief of Police, rode in front of the great procession and he told me that he heard on this day every conceivable term of insult and abuse against the dead. Finally he lost his patience and gave orders to arrest several of the shouters and lock them up. But the people took their part and wished to free them; in view of this, he ordered that they be released, and thereby he prevented a fray and, as he said, preserved the peace.

Three weeks after the death of the Empress, I went to the body for the Requiem. On my way through the ante-chamber, I met Prince Michael Ivanovich Dashkov, who was quite beside himself and weeping for joy. He hastened to meet me and said: "The Emperor deserves to have a golden statue raised to him; he has freed the whole class of nobles, and has now gone to the Senate to announce it publicly."[6] I asked him: "Were you serfs then, and could you be bought up to this day? Wherein consists this freedom?"

It developed that it consisted in this: that each should choose of his own free will whether he would take service or not. This had previously been the case also, for one only needed to ask for a discharge. But from ancient times the custom had remained that the members of the nobility, as holders of feudal and hereditary lands, should all serve except the very old and feeble and the very young and were listed as standing in the service of the state. Peter I began to enlist recruits instead of the nobles, but the nobles remained in the service. For this reason they imagined that they were not free.

Roman Vorontsov and the Procurator-General thought they were doing something great when they recommended to the Emperor that he grant freedom to the nobles; but in reality they asked for

7 : AN EXPLANATION

nothing more than that each should have the right to serve or not to serve.

When I returned from the Requiem, I saw standing at the rear entrance a state coach with the crown; the Emperor was driving in it to the Senate. But this procession aroused discontent among the people. They asked, "How does he dare to drive out with the crown? He has not been crowned and not anointed. Too early has he bethought himself to drive out with the crown." The entire nobility was highly delighted with the right to serve or not to serve. They all forgot completely that their ancestors had earned through their services to the state the honors and the possessions which they now enjoyed.

Ten days before the burial of the Empress, the body was laid in the coffin and this was carried into the hall of mourning amid all the regalia. Twice a day the people were admitted, as had been done from the day of her death. The Empress lay in her coffin in a cloth-of-silver robe with lace sleeves; on her head she had a great Imperial crown of gold with this inscription on the lower band: "Elisabeth Petrovna, Most Pious Autocrat, Monarch and Empress, born December 18, 1709, ascended the throne November 25, 1741, died December 25, 1761." The coffin was placed upon an elevation under a canopy of gold cloth with ermine hangings which reached to the ground; behind the coffin in the hangings was the golden shield of the Empire.

On January 25, 1762, the body of the Empress in the coffin was carried with great pomp and fitting marks of honor from the palace across the river to the Cathedral of St. Peter and St. Paul in the fortress. The Emperor himself, and I behind him, then the Skavronskys, behind them the Narishkins, then all the others according to their rank followed the coffin on foot from the palace to the Church.

On this day, the Emperor was in a particularly good humor, and during the funeral ceremony he allowed himself the following jest:

he lingered from time to time behind the mourning carriage and allowed it to advance about thirty sashen,[7] and then tried hastily to catch up with it. The elder Chamberlains, who carried the train of his black robe of state, especially Lord Marshal Count Sheremetiev, who had the end of the mantle, could not keep step with him and were obliged to let the mantle go. As the wind blew it out, Peter III was still more delighted, and repeated the joke several times. And so it happened that I and all who followed him remained far back behind the coffin. Finally a message had to be sent up to the front and the whole mourning procession halted until those who were behind could catch up again.

This undignified behavior was talked about a great deal, not to the Emperor's advantage, and there were all kinds of stories about his foolish actions on many occasions.

After the burial of the late Empress, they began to prepare her apartments in the palace for the Emperor.

NOTES

[1] Catherine to Grimm, July 5, 1779: "Monsieur Bezorodko has had the idea of founding a record of the facts, the noteworthy and public occurrences of the last seventeen years. He brought it to me on the day on which began the eighteenth year of Our reign." To the same, July 21, 1781: "On June 28th of this year, Monsieur Bezborodko again brought me my report brought up to the present day. He is to complete it yearly by adding the events of the current year."

[2] The "Explanation" [in Russian] to Bezborodko's draft (as well as the second Russian fragment Part VIII) was not written before 1794, for the paper in both cases bears the imprint: 1794.

[3] Catherine writes in her book "Antidote" (1770): "At the moment when Empress Elisabeth breathed her last, Peter III and his consort were standing by the death-bed. . . . When the three physicians who were in the room had declared that the Empress was dead, the doors of the ante-chamber were opened: the members of the Senate, the high dignitaries of the state, and the entire court came in. There was no one who did not give definite signs of grief; everybody sobbed. The Emperor withdrew; the Empress had agreed with him that she would remain in the room with the deceased until he went into the chapel. . . . The Empress gave such definite orders that within less than two hours the whole city could enter the apartment in which the body of the Empress was laid out. Then the Emperor sent her a request to come into the chapel. . . . There she heard the prayer and was merely

7 : AN EXPLANATION

a spectator while those present took the oath of allegiance to the Emperor."
[4] The words in parenthesis are French in the manuscript.
[5] January 4, 1762.
[6] The Manifesto of February 18, 1762 (announced January 18), freed the nobility from the obligation to serve the state.
[7] Thirty sashen: 70 English yards.

PART EIGHT

WRITTEN AFTER 1794

*A DOCUMENT
FROM HER LAST YEARS*[1]

WHEN I ascended the throne in 1762, two-thirds of the land army in Prussia had received no pay. In the state treasury the imperial ukases concerning the payment of seventeen million rubles had not been carried out.
Since the time of Czar Alexei Michailovich the coin in circulation amounted to one hundred million, of which it was reckoned that forty million flowed from the Empire and was given away *in natura* because at that time the circulation of bills was but little known or but little used.
Almost all branches of business were given over to private persons as monopolies.
The taxes of the whole Empire had been farmed out for two millions.
The sixty million rubles which remained in the Empire were of twelve different weights: silver coins of the standard 82 to 63, copper coins from forty rubles to the pood [2] to thirty-two rubles to the pood.
Empress Elisabeth Petrovna of blessed memory tried during the Seven Years' War to float a loan of two million rubles in Holland, but no one was inclined to take up this loan. For Russia there was neither credit nor trust.
In the interior of the Empire the peasants in the factories and on the church lands were openly rebellious against the authorities and in certain places those on the estates were beginning to join them.
The directing Senate had at that time one department. This heard cases on appeal not by means of abstracts but with all particulars. A process about a meadow of the town of Mosalsk, at the time

of my accession, occupied the first six weeks of the Senate sessions with the reading of the records.

Although the Senate sent ukases and orders to the gubernias, the ordinances of the Senate were so badly carried out that the expression: "They are waiting for the third ukase" had almost come to be a proverb, because the first and the second were never complied with.

The whole Empire was divided into the following gubernias: Moscow, Nizhni-Novgorod, Kazan, Astrachan, Siberia, Belgorod, Novgorod, Archangel St. Petersburg, Livonia, Viborg, and Kiev. Little Russia, that is, Tchernigov and Novgorod Seversky, was managed by the Hetman. Each gubernia was divided into provinces, and each province had its district cities, in which the Vojevods and their chancellories were located. They received no salary but were permitted to draw their incomes from their occupations, although bribes were strictly forbidden.

The Senate appointed the Vojevods but did not know the number of cities in the Empire. When I asked for a list of the cities, they confessed their ignorance. Likewise the Senate had never since its installation owned a map of the whole Empire. When I was in the Senate I sent five rubles to the Academy of Sciences on the other side of the river and bought the atlas published by Cyrillov which I at once presented to the directing Senate.

In case anyone would like to know what was expected of the Vojevods in the provinces and cities, let him read the manifesto which stands at the head of my prescription for the administration of the gubernias.[3] In it can be seen the picture which caused the changes to be adopted.

After my accession the Senate gave me a list of the state revenues, from which it appeared that they amounted to about sixteen million. After two years I had Prince Viasemsky and Privy Counsellor Melgunov, then President of the College of the Exchequer, prepare an estimate of the revenues. They kept accounts for several years and corresponded up to seven times with every

CATHERINE THE GREAT
Painted by Ericsen for Baron Dimsdale

8 : DOCUMENT FROM HER LAST YEARS

Vojevod. They finally placed the amount at twenty-eight million, twelve million more than that fixed by the Senate.

At my coronation I had three secretaries. Each of them had three hundred petitions, altogether nine hundred. I strove as far as possible to satisfy the petitioners and received petitions myself. But that soon ceased, for on a holiday when I was going to mass with the whole court the petitioners cut off my progress and knelt around me in a semi-circle with their papers. The elder Senators came to me and said that this disorder was the result of my indulgence and patience and, besides, the law forbade the handing of petitions directly to the monarch. I agreed to renew the law against the handing of petitions to the monarch, because I saw that this really led to a nuisance.[4] Many told me at that time that all Moscow did nothing else but write letters to me about things which had long since been decided or else in course of time would vanish of themselves. But it gave evidence of great dissatisfaction with the methods of the reign just past.

At the beginning of the reign of Empress Elisabeth Petrovna the order had gone forth that everything was to be managed according to the ukases of her father, Peter the Great.

During her reign Field Marshal General Prince Vasili Vladimirovich Dolgorukov was President of the War College. In accordance with her wish he strove to bring the army back to its former condition, which led to great confusion in the so-called Muennich organization.

Field Marshal Muennich had been President of the War College during the reign of Empress Anna.

After Prince Dolgorukov the principal member of the War College was the General in Chief, Stephan Feodorovich Apraxin. He was a hospitable gentleman; he loved horses but seldom rode on account of his height and great corpulence and the weight of his colossal body. He overlooked every lack of discipline in the soldiers; neither he nor his subordinates, who fished in troubled waters, cared for any form of organization. In his time, there were four or five colonels who were distinguished for the fine condition of their regiments, namely: Peter Alexeievich Rumyantsov, Count Zachary Gregorievich Tchernishov, Peter Ivanovich Panin, Michail Ivonovich Leontyev, Prince Vasili Michailovich Dolgorukov, and in the Cavalry Michael Nikitich Volkonsky. As a reward for this, Apraxin sent the best regiments to work at Rogerwyk.

At the beginning of the Seven Years' War it became really necessary to introduce a better organization in the army, and although much was improved there was just as much left to be improved. But in spite of all the disorganization, we conquered all Prussia, went to Berlin, took Kolberg, and won three battles as important as those of Grossjaegerndorf, Palzig, and Frankfurt.

The Generals, who came to Moscow for my coronation, recommended that a War Commission should be appointed and that it should treat the state of the whole army. I declared myself in agreement with the plan. To form this, all the best Generals were called, a plan of organization for the army was drawn up and ratified by me, and the money for the army was separated from the rest of the revenues. The two-thirds that was lacking was for this first time and immediately after my accession taken from the cabinet fund and assigned to the army.

At my order three tables or catalogues were then made. The first, quite general, listed all those persons who were in the service of the state, from the Field Marshal down to the lowest grade or rank. The second, the Generals serving in the army and all the other staff and higher officers. The third, those persons who were employed in the state's service but were not active.

Then followed the establishment of a salary for the provincial and municipal chancellories and the Vojevods throughout the Empire.

In the year 1763 the Senate was divided into six departments, two in Moscow and four in St. Petersburg. It was also ordered that the processes should be heard by means of extracts, and not the whole material.

Some time after my return to the city, in June, 1763, I went to the Senate. On the order of the day was the new revision, for the end of the twenty years' interval was at hand. I was requested to issue orders for the appointment of examiners for the whole empire and of innumerable military detachments, and it was estimated that the revision would not cost less than 800,000 rubles. In their conversation with each other, the Senators mentioned the countless investigations which the revision would bring in its train and the flight of numerous eligible persons to Poland and abroad,—the disadvantage which the empire would have from every revision. Still they all regarded the revision as a necessity. I listened for a long time to everything they said, and only allowed myself to ask a few questions for information. The gentlemen of the Senate finally grew tired of talking and were speechless. Then I asked: "Why all this summoning of troops and these burdensome costs for the state treasury? Can it not be done otherwise?" Thereupon they answered: "It has formerly been done so." I replied: "But it seems better to me thus: Announce throughout the empire that every place shall send to its Chancellory a list of all the people there, the Chancellories shall send them to the gubernias, and the gubernias to the Senate!"

About four Senators arose and explained to me that those who failed to register would be numberless. I said to them: "Set a penalty upon such failures." They replied that in spite of the severe punishments that had formerly been threatened, a number of these failures occurred. Whereupon I said: "Grant exemption from punishment to all those not registered until now and command the different places to inscribe them in their present lists." Prince Jakob Petrovich Shakovsky now became excited and said: "But that will be an offense to justice, and the guilty will be treated exactly like the innocent. I have always listed carefully and no one was left out. But those who have had the advantage of omissions will now stand just as well as I." The Procurator-General at that time was Alexander Ivanovich Glebov. From his table he heard this conversation and saw Prince Shakovsky's excitement; he sprang up from his chair, came to me, and asked me to tell him just how I wished to have the revision made. That was very easy for me. He ordered that this should all be written down and took over the elaboration of the plan which he also carried out. And to this day the revisions are conducted thus in each district, without circumstance and expense, and there are no omissions and nothing is heard about it.

Before the revision and soon after my coronation was celebrated,[5] the mint was ordered to change all the silver money then in circulation and in the future to coin it with the standard of 72, but copper money with that of 16 to the pood. This order was issued for the following reason: because in every country it is the same what the standard of the money in circulation is, provided that (1) the standard always remains the same, (2) the standard is less easily adapted to export and counterfeit, and because (3) more rubles of the standard 72 than other standards and more copper coins at 16 rubles to the pood were given out by the mint.

Incidentally, there were only a million gold coins in circulation in the whole empire, and this coin had been brought into conformity with the rest at 28,000 rubles to the pood.

Immediately after my coronation a commission was established, known as the ecclesiastical, on which many Bishops, Senators, and lay persons sat. This Commission made a study of the estimates for the pontifical households and the monasteries and settled the amount for their support. But the villages belonging to the monasteries were placed under the administration of the College of Agriculture, especially appointed for this purpose. The rebellion of the peasants in these villages came to an end at once.

The rebellion of the peasants in the factories was suppressed by the Major-Generals Prince Alexander Alexeievich Viasemsky and Alexander Ilyich Bibikov, who were sent to these places and investigated the complaints against the manufacturers. Yet in many cases they had to resort to the use of weapons; it even went

8 : DOCUMENT FROM HER LAST YEARS

as far as cannon shots and the uprising did not cease until the Goroblagodatsky Works were restored to the crown to pay off a debt of Peter Ivanovich Shuvalov's amounting to two million. For the same reason the works of the Vorontsovs, the Tchernishovs, the Yagushinskys, and others were again transferred to the crown for management. The whole evil sprang from the arbitrary division by the Senate of these works and the peasants belonging to them during the last years of the reign of Empress Elisabeth Petrovna. The open-handedness of the Senate went so far that it distributed the three million which formed the capital of the copper bank almost entirely among the manufacturers, who increased the work of the peasants but paid them irregularly or not at all and squandered the money received from the crown on their residences. These troubles only ceased in the year 1779 in consequence of my manifesto concerning the peasants in the factories.[6] Since that time nothing has been heard from them.

At the beginning of my reign all monopolies were abolished and all branches of business were allowed their free development. The taxes were entirely taken over by the crown and a commission was appointed which made rules to govern business and then fixed a tariff. All this was ratified by me. Every two years the tariff was gone over according to the accepted rules. That has been continued until this day and business has not vanished but increases yearly and the revenues of the Petersburg tax office alone amount to more than three million.

When the Petersburg tax office had been under the management of the crown for several years, the directing Senate suddenly sent a reprimand, because it brought in too little. The matter came before me and I asked whether it brought in less money than at the time when it was farmed out by the Senate, or more. It yielded half a million more. I then sent word to the Senate that as long as the tax office brought in more than formerly, the Senate had no occasion to reproach it.

During the first three years of my reign, I discovered from the petitions handed me, from the acts of the Senate and of the various Colleges, from the dealings of the Senators and from conversations with many other persons that there were no fixed and uniform rules on any subject. The laws, too, which had been made at different times and in accordance with the conceptions of that time, seemed to be very contradictory. It was desired and requested that the laws should be put into a better form. From this I decided in my own mind that the general attitude and the civil law could only be improved by the adoption of useful rules, which would have to be written and ratified by me, for all the inhabitants of the Empire and for all circumstances.

And to this end I began to read [7] and then to write the Instruction for the law-making Commission.

I read and wrote two years and said not a word for a year and a half, but followed my own judgment and feelings, with a sincere striving for the service, the honor, and the happiness of the empire, and with the desire to bring about in all respects the highest welfare of people and of things, of all in general and each individual in particular. When in my opinion I had pretty well arrived at my goal, I began to show parts of the subjects I had worked out to different persons, laying before each that which would be of interest to him, among others Prince Orlov and Count Nikita Panin. The latter said to me: "Those are principles to cast down walls." [8] Prince Orlov thought very highly of my work and often wished to show it to this person or that; but I never showed more than one or two pages at a time. At last I composed the manifesto [9] concerning the calling of delegates from the whole empire, in order to learn more about the conditions of each district. The delegates then assembled in Moscow in the year 1767.[10] I summoned several persons of quite different ways of thinking to the Kolomensky Palace, where I was living at the time, in order to have them listen to the finished Instruction for the Commission on Laws. At every section there was a difference of opinion. I permitted them to cross out and efface whatever they liked. They

CATHERINE THE GREAT
From a painting by Roslin

8 : DOCUMENT FROM HER LAST YEARS

crossed out more than a half of what I had written, and the Instruction remained as it was printed.[11] I ordered that it should be taken for what it is, that is, as rules on which to base an opinion but not as a law. They were therefore not to be taken over into the acts as laws; but it was permitted to base an opinion on it.

The Commission on Laws assembled and brought me light and knowledge from the whole empire, with which we had to deal and which we had to care for. They collected all parts of the law and went through them according to material, and they would have accomplished more had the Turkish wars not broken out. Then the delegates were dismissed and the soldiers went away to the army.[12] The Instruction for the Commission on Laws brought more uniformity into the rules and considerations that had formerly been present. Many now began to judge the colors according to the colors themselves and ceased to talk about them like the blind. At least they learned to know the will of the law-maker and began to act in accordance with it.

NOTES

[1] In Russian.
[2] One pood equals 36.11 English pounds.
[3] Manifesto of November 7, 1775.
[4] Ukase of December 2, 1762.
[5] Catherine had herself crowned September 22, 1762, in Moscow.
[6] Manifesto of May 21, 1779.
[7] In the first place, Montesquiu's Spirit of Laws; further Beccaria, Deo delitti e delle pene, 1764, French by Morellet (Traité des délits at des peines, 1765); Voltaire, Essai sur l'histoire générale et sur les moeurs et l'esprit des nations, 1756; Bielefeld, Institutions politiques, 1760.
[8] These words in the manuscript are French.
[9] Manifesto of December 14, 1766.
[10] The sessions of the Commission were opened on July 30, 1767, interrupted in December, 1767, and reopened in St. Petersburg in February, 1768.
[11] The Instruction, written in French, was first printed in Russian by Kozitsky, and was distributed among the delegates in August. The first translation was the German edition: "Instruction of Her Imperial Majesty for the Commission instituted for the Preparation of a Plan for a new Book of Laws." Moscow, 1767. (Russian and German.)
[12] Ukase of December 18, 1768.

APPENDIX AND INDEX

CATHERINE II TO COUNT PONIATOVSKY

August 2 (Old Style), 1762

I AM sending Count Keyserling at once to Poland to make you King after the death of the present King.[1] In case he should have no success for you I desire that Prince Adam shall be King.[2]

The minds of all are still excited. I beg you not to come here and add still more to this excitement.

My accession to the throne had been under preparation for six months. Peter III had lost still more of the little understanding that he once possessed. He tried to thrust his head through the wall. He wished to cashier the Guard and for this reason he sent them into the field; he had replaced them by his Holstein troops, who were to remain in the city. He wished to change the faith, marry L. V. (Elisabeth Vorontsov) and lock me up in prison. On the day of the peace celebration he insulted me in public at dinner and in the evening he gave an order to arrest me. My uncle, Prince George, induced him to withdraw this order.[3]

After this day, I lent my ear to the proposals which had been made to me since the death of the Empress. The plan was to arrest him in his room and lock him up, like Princess Anna and her children. He went to Oranienbaum. We were sure of a large number of the principal people in the regiments of the Guards. The threads of the plot lay in the hands of the brothers Orlov. Osten remembered how he had seen the eldest always running after me and committing a thousand follies. His passion for me was generally known, and he has done everything from this standpoint.[4] They are people of the utmost resolution and much beloved by most of the soldiers, for they have served in the Guards. I am under the greatest obligation toward them; all Petersburg is a witness to it.

The minds of the guard had been prepared and at last there were thirty to forty officers in the secret and about 10,000 soldiers. For three weeks there was no betrayer because there were four separate groups, whose leaders were united for the execution of the plan. The real secret was in the hands of the three brothers. Panin wished that the enterprise should be in favor of my son; but they would never agree to that.

I was in Peterhof. Peter III lived and got drunk at Oranienbaum. We had agreed in case of a betrayal not to await his return, but to assemble the Guard and proclaim myself as ruler. Zealousness on my behalf accomplished for me what a betrayal would have done.

On the 27th a rumor that I had been arrested spread among the troops. The soldiers became excited; one of our officers quieted them. Then a soldier came to a captain by the name of Passek, the leader of the groups, and told him that I was certainly lost. He assured him that he had news of me. The soldier, still disturbed on my account, went to another officer and told him the same. The latter had not been initiated in the secret and was startled when he heard that an officer had let this soldier go and had not arrested him. He went to the Major and the latter then ordered the arrest of Passek. The whole regiment was now in action. During the night the report was sent to Oranienbaum. There was great distress among my confederates. They decided before all else to send the second of the Orlov brothers to fetch me to the city; the other two went everywhere spreading the news that I would soon arrive. The Hetman, Volkonsky, and Panin had been initiated in the secret.

At six o'clock on the morning of the 28th, I lay quietly sleeping.

"it gives me pleasure to be with people of spirit. The Emperor offers to abdicate the throne. After his wholly voluntary abdication I will bring him here. Thus without difficulty I will save my Fatherland from civil war." So I gave him this commission and he went to carry it out. Peter III abdicated in Oranienbaum in complete freedom, surrounded by 1590 Holsteiners, and came with Elisabeth Vorontsov, Gudovich, and Izmailov to Peterhof, where I gave him six officers and several soldiers as a guard.

Since it was already about mid-day of the 29th, St. Peter's day, it was time to eat. While food was being prepared for the many people the soldiers imagined that Peter III had been brought by Field Marshal Prince Troubetsky and that he was striving to make peace between us. They said to all who came to them, among others the Hetman, the Orlovs, and several others, they had not seen me for three hours and they were perishing of fear that the old rascal Troubetsky might betray me, "in that he might make a false peace between you and your husband and hurl us all to destruction; but we will tear him to pieces." These were their expressions. I went to Troubetsky and said to him: "I beg you to get into your carriage while I make the round of the troops on foot." I told him what was happening. Quite terrified he drove to the city and I was received with unheard-of jubilation.

Then I sent the deposed Emperor, under the command of Alexei Orlov with four officers and a division of peaceful chosen people, to a remote and very pleasant place called Ropsha, 25 versts from Petersburg, while decent and suitable quarters were fitted up in Schluesselburg, and so had time to provide relays of horses for him.

But the good God arranged it otherwise! The anxiety had caused him to have a diarrhœa, which lasted for three days and still continued on the fourth. On this day he drank immoderately, for he had everything he wanted except his freedom. (He had incidentally asked for his mistress, his dog, his negro, and his violin; but in order to avoid a scandal and prevent increasing the excitement of his guards I had only sent him the last three.) He was attacked by a hæmorrhoidal colic and fever phantasies. For two days he was in this condition; this was followed by great weakness and in spite of all that medical aid could do he breathed his last,[6] after he had asked for a Lutheran pastor.

I feared the officers might have poisoned him. Therefore I had the body dissected; but it was completely proved that not the least trace of poison existed. His stomach was quite healthy, but an inflammation of the intestines and a fit of apoplexy had carried him off. His heart was unusually small and quite shrunken.

After his departure from Peterhof, I was advised to go straightway to the city. I foresaw that the troops would be disturbed at this. I sent forth a rumor to this effect under the pretext of wishing to know at what hour they would be ready to start after these three fatiguing days. They said: "Towards ten o'clock in the evening; but you must come with us." So I started with them, and half-way there I withdrew into the country house of Kurakin, where wholly dressed I threw myself upon a bed. An officer took off my boots. I slept two hours and a half and then we resumed our march. From Catherinenhof onward I rode again at the head of the Preobrashensky Regiment. A regiment of hussars went ahead; then came my escort from the Horse Guard; then immediately in front of me my court. Following were the regiments of the guard according to their rank and three field regiments.

Amid a never-ending jubilation I entered the city and went to the Summer Palace where the court, the Synod, my son, and all those who were entitled to appear at court were awaiting me. I went to mass; then the Te Deum was sung. Afterwards I received congratulations. Then, having scarcely eaten or drunk or slept from Friday morning at six o'clock until Sunday evening, I went to bed and fell asleep.

At midnight, when I had scarcely fallen asleep, Captain Passek entered my room and waked me with the words: "Our people are terribly drunk; a hussar in that condition has just been running about and crying out: 'To arms! 30,000 Prussians are coming and wish to take our Mother.' Thereupon they seized their weapons and are now coming here to inquire about your welfare. They say they have not seen you for the last three hours and they will go home peacefully if they see that you are well. They will not listen to their leaders nor the Orlovs." So I was again on foot, and in order not to alarm needlessly my watch-guard, which consisted of one batallion, I went to them and told them why I was going out at this hour. Accompanied by two officers I entered my carriage and went to them. I told them that I was well and that they should go to sleep and also allow me to rest. I had only just lain down after not having slept for three nights and I wished that in the future they would hearken to their officers. They replied that the alarm had gone out among them on account of these accursed Prussians and they were all ready to die for me. I said: "Fine. I thank you; but now go to sleep." Thereupon they wished me goodnight and good health and went away like lambs, frequently turning back as they went to look after my carriage.

The next day they asked to be excused and regretted that they had awakened me. They said: "If all of us should see you all the time, we should injure your health and disturb you in the business of the state."

I should have to write a whole book to describe the attitude of each of the leaders.

The Orlovs shone by reason of their skill in controlling public sentiment, by their foresight and boldness in great and small particulars, by their presence of mind and the authority which they had won by their attitude. They had a great deal of sound common sense and nobility of spirit. They are enthusiastic patriots and very honest people, passionately loyal to myself and friends such as no brothers have ever been. There are five of them but only three were here.

Captain Passek distinguished himself by the steadfastness which he showed in remaining under arrest twelve hours although the soldiers had opened the doors and windows for him. For he did not wish to give the alarm in his regiment before my arrival. Yet every moment he had to expect that he might be conducted to Oranienbaum to undergo a painful examination. This order came but only after my arrival.

Princess Dashkov, the younger sister of Elisabeth Vorontsov, wishes indeed to take all the honors because she was acquainted with a few of the leaders. But on account of her family connections and her age, which was only nineteen, she did not stand in good repute; she inspired confidence in no one. To be sure she always insisted that everything had come to me through her. But all of the conspirators had been in touch with me for six months before she even knew their names. It is true that she is very clever, but besides her great vanity she has a muddle-headed character and our leaders did not like her. Only thoughtless people put her in possession of what they knew and this consisted only of small details. I. I. Shuvalov, the basest and most infamous human being that could be imagined, has nevertheless, it seems, written to Voltaire that a nineteen-year-old woman has changed the government of this country. Please teach this great author better! We had to conceal from the Princess the ways by which the others communicated with me, five months before she knew the least thing and during the last four weeks she was told as little as possible.

Praise is due to the strength of character of Prince Bariatinsky, who concealed the secret from a beloved brother, adjutant of the former Emperor, because he would have been not a dangerous but an unnecessary confidant.

In the Horse Guard a twenty-two-year-old officer by the name of Chitrovo and a petty officer of seventeen,[7] by the name of Potiomkin, carried on the affair with ingenuity, courage, and zeal.

APPENDIX

There you have approximately our story. The whole thing, I confess to you, happened under my own direction, and at the close I even poured water on the fire because the departure for the country presented the execution of the plan and all had been ready for the past two weeks. When the former Emperor heard of the uprising in the city, the young women who formed his retinue prevented him from following the advice of the old Field Marshal Muennich, who recommended that he throw himself at Kronstadt or go to the army with a small escort. When he betook himself to Kronstadt in a small galley, the city was, owing to the swift action of Admiral Talyzin, already in our hands. On his arrival, he had disarmed General Devier who was already there in the name of the Emperor. A harbor officer,[8] of his own impulse, stopped the unfortunate Emperor with the threat that he would fire upon his galley. The good God finally brought everything to its appointed end, and all this is a miracle rather than a foreseen and prearranged affair, for the coincidence of so many fortunate circumstances can not occur without the will of God.

I have received your letter. A regular correspondence would be exposed to a thousand disadvantages, and I have to take twenty thousand precautions and have no time to read dangerous love letters.

I am under a great compulsion. . . . I can not tell it all to you, but it is true.

I will do everything for you and your family, be assured of that!

I must observe a thousand proprieties and take a thousand things into consideration; and withal I feel the whole burden of the business of government.

Consider well that everything had its origin in hatred of the foreigners; Peter III himself is regarded as such.

Adieu! There are some very strange lots in the world.

THREE LETTERS OF PETER III.

I.[9]

[1762]

Madame:

I beg Your Majesty to rest assured on my account and have the goodness to give orders that the guards be removed from the second room; because the room in which I am is so small that I can scarcely move about in it, and because you know that I always run about in the room and shall get swollen legs from it. Then I beg you further to order that the officers shall not remain in the same room when I have necessities; that is impossible for me. Finally I beg Your Majesty not to treat me like a great criminal; I am not aware that I have ever offended you. I commend myself to your generous consideration and beg you at least to let me go to Germany with the persons I have named. God will certainly reward you and I am

Your very devoted servant,
Peter.

P. S. Your Majesty can rest assured that I will not think or do anything against yourself or your reign.

II.

[1762]

Your Majesty:

If you do not wish to murder a human being outright and one who is already unhappy enough, have pity on me and grant me my only comfort, which is Elisabeth Romanovna. You will thereby do one of the most merciful deeds of your reign. As for the rest, if Your Majesty would visit me for a moment my highest wishes would be fulfilled.

Your very devoted servant,
Peter.

APPENDIX

III.

[1762]

Your Majesty:

I beseech you to allow me, as I have fulfilled your will in all respects, to go abroad with those for whom I formerly begged Your Majesty, and I rely upon your generosity not to leave me without nourishment.

Faithful servant,
Peter.

THREE LETTERS OF ALEXEI ORLOV

I.[10]

July 2, 1762.

Little mother, gracious Empress, health we wish you for uncounted years. As this letter leaves us, we and the whole command are well, but our monster has become very ill with an attack of colic which has unexpectedly befallen him. And I fear that he might at last die to-night, and fear still more than he might recover. I fear the first, because he chatters pure nonsense and that is no joke, and the other because he is really dangerous for us all in that he often talks as if he had his former position.

Following your imperial orders, I have paid the money to the soldiers for half a year; also the petty officers, with the exception of the guard-master Potiomkin who is serving without pay. Many of the soldiers spoke with tears of your gracious favor; they had never deserved so much of you, to be rewarded after so short a time. Herewith I am sending you a list of the whole command that is at present here; but a thousand rubles were lacking, Little Mother, and I have added them in ducats. There was much laughter here among the grenadiers on account of the ducats when they received them from me; many inquired because they had never before seen any, and gave them back because they thought they were worth nothing. Tchertkov, who was dispatched to Your Majesty, has not yet returned and therefore I have been delayed with my report. This however I am writing on Tuesday, at the middle of the 9th hour.

Till death, your faithful servant,
Alexei Orlov.

II.

(*July* 1762)

Our little Mother, gracious Empress, I know not how I shall begin for I fear the anger of Your Majesty, lest you should deign to believe dreadful things about us and whether we were not the cause of the death of your rascal and also all Russia and our law; but now the lackey Maslov who was given him for service has fallen ill, and he himself is so sick that I do not believe that he will live till evening, and he is already almost unconscious, of which the whole command here is aware and is praying to God that we may be rid of him as soon as possible; and this Maslov and the officer who was dispatched to you can inform Your Majesty in what condition he now is, if you deign to doubt me. This wrote,

Your faithful servant,
_____11

III.

(*July* 6, 1762)

Little Mother, merciful Empress! How shall I tell you, how describe, what has happened? You will not believe your faithful servant but before God I will speak the truth. Little Mother! I am ready to die, but I do not know myself how the mischief came about. We are lost if you do not have mercy on us. Little Mother, he tarries no longer on this earth. But no one would have believed it, and how could we have thought of laying hands upon the Emperor! But, Empress, the misfortune has happened! He fell into a quarrel at table with Prince Feodor;[12] we could not separate them and already he was no more. We ourselves could not remember what we had done, but we are all guilty to the very last one and deserving of death. Have mercy upon me, if only for my brother's sake! I have made my confession, and there is nothing to investigate. Pardon, or else command quickly that an end be made! I do not wish to see the light; we have angered you and hurled our souls to eternal destruction.[13]

CATHERINE II TO POTIOMKIN

(1774)[14]

When Maria Tchoglokov saw that after nine years matters were just the same after the marriage as they had been before, while she was often scolded by the late Empress because she took no pains to change them, she concluded that there was no other way than to propose to both parties that they should choose according to their own desire some one of those whom they had in mind. On the one hand, they chose the widow Grooth, who is now married to Lieutenant-General Miller of the Cavalry, and on the other Sergei Saltikov, who was selected more on account of his obvious liking and at the persuasion of his mother who regarded this as a great need and necessity. After two years had elapsed they sent S. S. away as an ambassador, for he acted without discretion and Maria Tchoglokov could no longer keep him at the great court. After the passage of one year and much sorrow, the present King of Poland came, who was not at all regarded. But good people made it necessary, by the merest hints, to notice that he was in the world, that he had strikingly beautiful eyes, and that they were more often turned in one direction than in any other, although he was so short-sighted that he could not see beyond his nose. He was amiable and was loved from 1755 to 1761. After he had been away three years, that is, after 1758, and since Prince

Gregory Gregorievich [15] was taking so much trouble, to whom again good people called attention, my way of thinking changed! He might have stayed forever, if he had not grown tired! I learned this on the very day of his departure from Czarskoe Selo for the Congress [16] and simply drew from this the conclusion that with this knowledge I could have no more confidence. This thought cruelly tormented me and forced me from desperation to make a choice at random.[17] During this time, yes up to this month, I have grieved more than I can say and never more than when other people were satisfied. Every act of tenderness caused my tears to flow and I believe I have never wept so much since I was born as in this year and a half. In the beginning I thought I would get used to it, but the longer it lasted the worse it became, for the other party began to pout for months at a time and I must confess that I was never more contented than when he was angry and left me in peace. But his tenderness forced me to weep.

Then came a certain hero. By his merits and his never-failing tenderness, this hero was so wonderful that as soon as his arrival was reported, people began to say that he should settle here. They did not know that we had summoned him privately by a note,[18] with the secret intention, however, not to act quite blindly after his arrival but to find out whether the inclination was present of which Bruce had told me had long been suspected by many; that is, the kind that I desired him to have.

Now, Sir Hero, can I hope after this confession to receive forgiveness for my sins? You will deign to see that there were not fifteen but only one-third of that.[19] The first, against my will, and the fourth taken out of desperation, can not at all be set down to frivolity. Of the other three only think rightly. God is my judge that I did not take them out of looseness, to which I have no inclination. If fate had given me in youth a husband whom I could have loved, I should have remained always true to him. The trouble is that my heart would not willingly remain one hour without love. It is said that we strive by this to cover up our human vices, as if this had its foundation in kindness of heart. But it can happen that such a condition of the heart is more a vice than it is a virtue. But I write this to you needlessly, for according to this you will love or will not wish to go away to the army for fear I might forget you. But really I do not think that I could commit such a blunder; if you wish to fetter me to yourself eternally, then show me as much friendship as love, and above all love and speak the truth!

CATHERINE II TO SENAC DE MEILHAN

(May 7, 1791) [20]

Wednesday morning.

. . . Here you have a rough portrait of me. I have never believed that I possessed the creative spirit; I have known many people in whom I perceived, without envy and jealousy, considerably more intellect than I have. It has always been easy to lead me, for to be able to do that it was only necessary to have better and more worthy ideas than my own. Then I was as docile as a lamb. The reason lay in this: that I was ever firmly resolved to make only those things happen which served the state's welfare. I have had the good fortune to discover principles that were good and true; it is therefore written that I have had great success. I have also had misfortunes, but this was the consequence of mistakes in which I had no share, perhaps also because my instructions were not exactly carried out. In spite of my natural pliancy, I could be stubborn or steadfast, as you will, if that seemed necessary to me. I have never done violence to anyone's opinions but I have also in a given case had my own view. I do not love argument because I have always found that in the end each remains of the same opinion. Besides I have never been skilful in raising my voice. I have never borne a grudge, because providence has placed me in such a position that I could not be resentful towards individuals and because, in order to be just, I could not look upon the circumstances as equal. In general I love justice; yet I am of the opinion that there is no absolute justice and that reasonableness alone corresponds to human weakness. But in all cases I have preferred humanity and indulgence toward human nature to the rules of what seemed to me a falsely understood severity. To this my own heart, which I regard as mild and good, has led me. When the old preached to me of strictness, I confessed with tears my weakness, and many of them also with tears in their eyes came over to my opinion. I am disposed by nature to be cheerful and ingenuous, but I have lived too long in the world not to know that there are bitter natures which do not love cheerfulness and not everyone's character can endure truth and candor.

EPITAPH

(1788) [21]

Here lies
Catherine the Second
born in Stettin April 21/May 2, 1729.

In the year 1744 she went to Russia to marry Peter III.
At the age of fourteen she made the threefold resolution, to please her Consort, Elisabeth, and the Nation.
She neglected nothing in order to succeed in this.
Eighteen years of tediousness and solitude caused her to read many books.
When she had ascended the throne of Russia, she wished to do good and tried to bring happiness, freedom, and prosperity to her subjects.
She forgave easily and hated no one.
She was good-natured and easy-going; she had a cheerful temperament, republican sentiments, and a kind heart.
She had friends.
Work was easy for her; she loved sociability and the arts.

APPENDIX

LAST WILL AND TESTAMENT

(1792) [22]

In case I should die in Czarskoe Selo, then lay me in the graveyard of the Sofia.

In case—in the city of St. Peter's—in the Nevsky-Cloister in the cathedral or the burial church.

In case—in Pella, then bring me along the water-ways to the Nevsky-Cloister.

In case—in Moscow—in the Donskoy Monastery in the new city graveyard.

In case—in Peterhof—in the Sergei-Cloister.

In case—in some other place—to a graveyard near by.

The coffin shall be borne by Horse Guards and no one else.

My body shall be laid out in a white dress, with a golden crown upon my head, on which my name shall stand.

Mourning shall be worn for half the year but no longer; the less is the better.

After the first six weeks, all popular amusements shall be permitted again.

After the burial, betrothals shall be again allowed, weddings, and music.

My library including all manuscripts and all papers I bequeath to my beloved grandson, Alexander Pavlovich; likewise my jewels, and I bless him with my soul and with my heart. For the purpose of a better fulfillment, a copy of this shall be deposited in a safe place, and is already deposited, so that sooner or later shame and disgrace shall overtake him who does not fulfill my will.

It is my intention to place Constantine on the throne of the Grecian Oriental Empire.

For the welfare of the Russian and Greek Empires I advise that the Prince of Wuerttemberg be removed from the concerns and the counsels of these Empires, and that he should have as little to do with them as possible; likewise the two half-Germans should be removed from the counsels.

NOTES

[1] Poniatovsky became King of Poland at Catherine's instigation in the year 1764 under the name of Stanislas II August, but was obliged to renounce the throne again in 1795.

[2] Prince Adam Czartoriski.

[3] In her copy of Denin's 'Essai fur la Vie et le règne de Frédéric II' (Cf. p. 278, Note 7) Catherine wrote (1789) on the margin of p. 223: "He had ordered Prince Bariatinsky (who was later Ambassador to France) to arrest the Empress in her room. Bariatinsky was startled at this command and did not hasten to carry it out. In the waiting room he met Prince George of Holstein, Uncle of the Emperor, and told him of the order which he had received. The latter went to the Emperor and requested him to withdraw the order; he threw himself at his feet and with much trouble induced him to do so."

[4] Poniatovsky remarks in his memoirs: "I was soon replaced by Orlov. This was concealed from me for a few months, but the letters became gradually cooler." On April 11, 1762, Catherine had borne a son (Count Alexei Gregorievich Bobrinsky) whose father was Gregory Orlov. Cf. p. 279, Note 9.

[5] The Chaplain of the Regiment Father Alexei (Michailov).

[6] Manifesto of July 7, 1762: "On the seventh day after we had ascended the throne of all the Russias, we received the information that the former Emperor, Peter III, along with one of the hæmorrhoidal attacks to which he was subject, had fallen ill with a severe colic. Therefore mindful of our Christian duty and the sacred commandment, which makes it incumbent upon us to care for the life of our neighbor, we commanded that they should send to him immediately everything that was needed to ward off the dangerous consequences of this attack and to give immediate medical aid. But to our deepest sorrow and distress, yesterday evening we received the further information that by the will of the most high God he had passed away."

[7] Potiomokin was already born in 1736.

[8] Michael Gavrilovich Koshukov.

[9] The first two letters are written in French, the third in Russian. The originals are in the State Archives.

[10] The three letters are written in Russian; the originals of the first two are in the State Archives.

[11] The signature is torn off.

[12] Prince Feodor Sergeievich Bariatinsky.

[13] This letter was published in 1881 with the following "Remark by Count F. W. Rostopshin": "Copied on November 11, 1796, five days after the death of Empress Catherine. Her cabinet was sealed by Count Samoilov and Adjutant General Rostopshin. Three days after the death of the Em-

APPENDIX 329

press, Grand Duke Alexander Pavlovich and Count Bezborodko were commissioned to look through all her papers. On the very first day they found this letter of Alexei Orlov and brought it to Emperor Paul. After he had read it and had given it back to Count Bezborodko, I had it in my hands for a quarter of an hour. It was the well-known handwriting of Count Orlov. The paper was a gray dirty sheet. The style indicates the state of mind of this villain; it clearly shows that the murderers feared the wrath of the Empress and places in the right light the slander which reflected on the life and memory of this great Empress. The next day Count Bezborodko told me that Emperor Paul had again demanded the letter of Count Orlov. He read it in his presence and threw it in the fire; in this way he himself destroyed the proof of great Catherine's innocence. Later he regretted it exceedingly."

[14] After a copy preserved in the private Imperial Library, Russian.
[15] Gregory Orlov.
[16] The Congress of Fokshani.
[17] Alexander Vasiltchikov.
[18] Potiomkin was in St. Petersburg in January, 1774.
[19] A letter of Potiomkin to Catherine reads: "Do not wonder that I am disturbed about our love. Besides your countless benefits to me, you have enclosed me in your heart. I wish to stand there higher than all the others!" In the margin beside this Catherine wrote these words: "You are that, surely and steadfastly, and will always be."
[20] Catherine's correspondence with Sénac de Meilhan is in the State Archives.
[21] This epitaph, written in French by her own hand, was mentioned twice by Catherine in letters to Grimm in the year 1788. The original in the State Archives was first put in print in 1863.
[22] The original in Russian is in the State Archives. Chrapovitsky, Catherine's secretary, intimates in his Journal under date of April 28, 1792, that he had seen the Last Will and Testament in Catherine's bed-chamber.

INDEX

Adadurov, 48, 231, 258, 259
Adolf Friedrich, Prince of Holstein-Gottorp, 16, 18, 22, 23, 25, 29, 60, 215, 223, 224
Aksakov, 185
Alexander (I) Pavlovich, Grand Duke of Russia, 72, 329
Alexei Michailovich, Czar, 299
Ambrosius, Archbishop of Novgorod, 232, 233
Anna Ivanovna, Empress of Russia, 113, 116, 160, 185, 201, 237
Anna Leopoldovna, 35, 37, 83, 100, 160, 213, 228
Anna Petrovna, Duchess of Holstein, 16, 76
Annenhof Palace, 39, 80, 134, 252
Ivan Antonovich (Ivan VI), 35, 36, 160
Anton Ulrich, Duke of Brunswick, 35, 160, 228
Apraxin, Stephan Feodorovich, 156, 169, 174, 175, 246, 301

Balk, Mlle., 63, 95
Bariatinsky, Prince Feodor, 313, 318, 323
Baturin's Conspiracy, 181, 192-194, 215
Beketov, 201, 202, 208, 213
Bentinck, Countess of, 23-25
Benyovsky, 194, 215
Bergholz, 51, 52, 98, 99, 159, 160
Bernardi, 258, 259, 260
Bestushev-Ryumin, 32, 33, 42, 44, 47, 48, 103, 108, 109, 116, 119, 121, 122, 125, 152, 155, 161, 167, 169, 174, 177, 188, 200, 216, 226, 251, 257-260
Betsky, 43, 44, 62, 230, 235
Bezborodko, Count Alexander, 283, 294, 329
Bibikov, Alexander, 304
Bibikov, Vasili, 280
Bielcke, Frau von, 76, 77, 158, 161
Biron, Duke of Courland, 113, 186, 276
Bobrinsky, Count Alexei, 328

INDEX

Holstein, administration of, 177

Instruction for a Commission on Laws, 306, 307
Izmailov, General, 266, 267, 314, 315

Jever, 22-25, 77
Johann August, Prince of Anhalt-Zerbst, 22, 77
Johanna Elisabeth, Princess of Anhalt-Zerbst, 3-6, 9-14, 17-19, 21-23, 29, 30, 32-34, 42-44, 46, 50, 54, 55, 60, 64, 65, 68, 78, 79-87, 93, 158, 224, 226, 227, 237, 238, 241, 251, 258
Johanna Elisabeth of Holstein-Gottorp, see Johanna Elisabeth of Anhalt-Zerbst
Johann Ludwig, Prince of Anhalt-Zerbst, 22, 43, 224

Karl Peter Ulrich, Duke of Holstein, see Peter III
Kayserling, Count, 311
Khayn, Frl. von, 17, 19, 20, 34, 51, 52, 59, 64, 158
Kiev, 53, 54
Kolomensky, 306
Kondoidi, 249
Korff, General, 292
Kosheliov, Mlle., 55, 133, 134, 140, 147-150, 237, 245, 246

Krasny Kabatshok, 273
Kremlin, 50, 233
Kronstadt, 266, 267, 269, 270, 273, 314
Kruse, Mme., 70, 92, 98, 101, 103-106, 112, 119, 122, 123, 126, 127, 240-242, 245, 251
Kurakin, Prince Boris, 174

Laurent, 4, 71, 75
Lestocq, Count, 32, 39, 42-46, 51, 57, 64, 130, 132, 136, 155, 156, 163, 167, 226, 229, 232, 239, 250
Levashov, 245
Lynar, Count Rochus zu, 213, 217

Mardefeldt, 79, 226, 229
Marianna, Princess of Bevern, 11, 74
Maria Theresa, 11
Maslov, 322
Melgunov, 285, 289, 290, 300
Mellin, Countess von, 77
Mengden, Julia, 35
Menshikov, Prince, 35, 36, 146
Mitau, 34
Monopolies, 29, 299
Monplaisir, 209, 217
Moscow, 196, 215
Muennich, 266, 301, 319

Narishkin, Semyon, 35-37, 44, 228, 252

INDEX

Narishkin, Leo, 278, 279, 289, 290
Nummers, Commandant, 270

Oranienbaum, 267, 312
Orlov, Alexei, 265, 267, 277, 313, 315, 321, 322, 323
Orlov, Gregory, 270, 271, 279, 280, 306, 324, 328, 329

Peter III,
    character, 92, 101, 111, 120, 121, 124, 127, 129, 130, 137, 153, 168, 178, 179, 182, 198, 230, 263, 278, 285, 294
    attacked by small-pox, 59, 60, 237
    relations with Empress Elisabeth, 202-207
    relations with Catherine the Great, 18, 44, 45, 63-66, 68-70, 92, 104, 105, 120, 146, 194, 195, 199, 200, 205, 206, 223
    letters to Catherine the Great, 320, 321
    reign, 263, 276-279, 311
    abdication, 267, 315
    imprisonment, 267, 268, 271
    death, 315, 316, 328
Panin, Nikita, 264, 283, 290, 306, 312
Paul (I) Petrovich, 266, 268, 314, 316, 329
Passek, Captain, 264, 265, 268, 269, 275, 278, 312, 316, 318
Peterhof, 270, 272
Poniatovsky, 280, 328

Potiomkin, 236, 318, 321, 329
Prascovia Feodorovna, 160

Quedlinburg, Abbess of, 14

Rajevo, 179
Repnin, Prince Vasili, 36, 100, 106, 108, 111, 113, 116, 119, 210, 211, 228, 240, 244
Razumovsky, Count Alexei, 41, 42, 52, 69, 93, 101, 107, 110, 114, 136, 138, 141-143, 160, 177, 183, 187, 208, 244
Razumovsky, Count Cyril, 180, 210, 246, 253, 264, 265, 277
Rheinbeck, Countess of (Princess of Anhalt-Zerbst), 227, 252
Riga, 35, 36
Ropsha, 271, 280, 315
Rostopshin, Count F. W., 328
Rumyantsov, Countess, 43, 44, 56, 57, 59, 64, 68, 70, 92, 235, 237, 238, 239, 243, 251

Sacromoso, Chevalier de, 144-146
Saltikov, Peter, 151, 152
Saltikov, Sergei, 113, 151, 205, 217, 248-250, 323
Saltikov, Vasili Feodorovich, 35, 229
Schenk, Frl, 63, 66, 237, 253
Schluesselburg, 272
Schriever, 38, 78, 106

A NOTE ON THE TYPE IN
WHICH THIS BOOK IS SET

This book is composed (on the Linotype), in Scotch. There is a divergence of opinion regarding the exact origin of this face, some authorities holding that it was first cut by Alexander Wilson & Son, of Glasgow, in 1837; others trace it back to a modernized Caslon old style brought out by Mrs. Henry Caslon in 1796 to meet the demand for modern faces brought about by the popularity of the Bodoni types. Whatever its origin, it is certain that the face was widely used in Scotland, where it was called Modern Roman, and since its introduction into America it has been known as Scotch. The essential characteristics of the Scotch face are its sturdy capitals, its full rounded lower case, the graceful fillet of its serifs and the general effect of crispness.

MANUFACTURED BY MONTAUK BOOKBINDING CORPORATION